Shades of Pleasure:

Five Stories of Domination and Submission

TAWNY TAYLOR

CONTENTS

What He Wants

TAWNY TAYLOR

Chapter 1

"I'm sorry, but I just locked the house up." I said to the handsome man who'd just come strolling up my mother's front walk. Selling the house had been an absolute nightmare. Not just because the building brought so many memories to the surface, but also because it wasn't in the best of shape. It was a great house in a wonderful neighborhood. If only I could get just one person to see past all the ugly linoleum, godawful paneling, and circa 70's shag carpet.

Twisting to look over my shoulder, I shot the man-- who happened to be well dressed and gorgeous--a quick smile. "But if you give me a minute, I'll make a quick phone call and then let you in."

"I'd appreciate that. Thanks." His voice was a low, rich rumble. For some reason, it resonated through my body, and the feeling of familiarity sparked inside me. Did I know this man?

Once I had the lock engaged, I click-clacked out to my car, my pinched toes probably blistered, and flounced into the driver's seat. I dug my phone out of my purse, and studied the strange man who didn't seem to be a stranger as I called my best friend Jill to let her know I'd be a little late meeting her for lunch.

Was the man another real estate agent, looking to list the house? Could be. His clothes were impeccable.

A brief conversation--primarily ample apologies--and I had an extra forty-five minutes to not only figure out where I'd met the man before but also how to convince him to buy the house instead of sell it for me. I was getting seriously strapped, paying the utilities and property taxes on the place, in addition to my condo. Because of this silly need to cling to my childhood, I'd put off selling the place as long as I could. It was time to make something happen and move on.

Determined I'd found the buyer for my mom's place, I pasted on my best smile, fluffed my hair and headed back up to the front porch. As I unlocked the door, I said, "This house is a wonderful investment. It's in a great location, on a dead end street. The neighborhood is excellent, a great place to raise a family."

"Hmmm." The man walked inside. He moved with a rare fluidity for a male. I watched him as he wandered through the rooms on the first floor. Living room. Dining room. Kitchen (that was in dire need of a full gut job). The longer I studied him, the more I felt I knew him. Trying to concentrate on the house, I pointed out the beautiful, original hardwood floors, the baseboards and window and door trims, the lovely hand carved handrail.

His wandering took us upstairs. He stopped outside of my mom's bedroom and stared. It was then that I knew who he was.

"Uncle" Shane.

He wasn't legally my uncle, no. That was just what I'd called him. I hadn't seen him in...ten years, maybe. Since I was about twelve. Uncle Shane had been the subject of my first crush. Of course, he hadn't known that at the time.

"I can't believe she's gone," he said.

"Uncle Shane?"

He scrutinized me closely, his intense gaze making me uneasy. "Of course. I don't know why I didn't see it before. Bristol?"

"Yes, that's me." I extended a hand. "It's been a long time. A very long time. Good to see you again."

His hand enveloped mine. He shook it, stopped, but didn't release it. His gaze was focused on my face. Sharp and intense. Assessing. "It's good to see you again, too. Your mother was a good friend. I'm sorry I lost touch with her...and with you. I haven't been in town for many years."

"I'm sure she understood."

"Yes, I'm sure I did. That was how Katherine was. Always understanding. Generous. Giving."

I couldn't help saying, "Too generous sometimes. She nearly went bankrupt. And this house...it's mortgaged for more than it's worth. And you can see how well she kept it up. Mom always told me it didn't matter, that the house was falling down around her. All that mattered was how many people she touched in her life."

His smile nearly took my breath away. For a man I guessed was within a handful of years of my mother's age, he was strikingly handsome and fit. Ten years had done nothing to change that. His hair was very dark, almost black. Not curly. But not straight either. His features, as they had been then, were well balanced and masculine. Not pretty, but not too rugged either. And his body, from what I could tell, was also still in great shape. Shoulders broad. Waist narrow. His black jacket fit him perfectly, as if it had been sewn just for him. Same with the pants. The white shirt was a stark contrast against the jacket and the honey brown color of his skin. The only thing a decade had done was add a sprinkling of silver hairs glinting at his temples, just enough to make him look sexy and distinguished.

"Katherine Deatrich was a one-of-a-kind woman." He turned, facing me. "Why are you selling the house?"

"I can't afford the mortgage payments or the upkeep,

and it's too big. I live alone...unless you count my cat."

"I see." He reached up, caught a curl that had flopped over my face and tucked it behind my ear. For some reason, the intimate touch sent me careening back into that old place, back into the childhood crush. Our gazes tangled, and my heart did a little hop in my chest. "I can't get over how much you've changed."

"Kids do that," I said, holding my breath.

"They do. How old are you?"

"Twenty-one."

He shook his head. "Damn. Where's the time gone?"

Still feeling a little wobbly, I shrugged. "I couldn't say." I motioned to the bedroom. "Erm, the master bath is a nice size."

"Oh, yes. The house." He glanced around, almost as if he'd forgotten where he was. "I'll take it. What are you asking?"

My insides did a flip flop. Could it be I'd just sold the house? Or was he just playing with me? "Three forty-nine, nine. That's the balance of the mortgage. I'm not making a penny from the sale."

"No agent?"

"No, I didn't want to have to pay another five to ten percent out of pocket. The closing costs alone are going to kill me."

"I'll have my attorney draw up the papers and schedule the closing with the title company."

This couldn't have gone any better. It was honestly too good to be true, which made me a little nervous. Thankfully, my best friend was an attorney. She'd offered to handle the closing for me pro bono. "I already have someone."

"Fine." He reached in his inside jacket pocket, pulled out a card. "I'll be expecting a call then."

"Do you need time to secure financing?" I asked. My fingertips brushed his as I took the card from him.

"No, I'll be paying cash."

Cash. I couldn't imagine paying three hundred fifty thousand dollars cash for anything. "Wonderful! We'll be seeing each other soon, then."

"Soon." He took my hand again, and little buzzing electrical charges seemed to zap between us. I couldn't believe it. After all this time, ten years, there was still something there. I wondered if he felt it too. "Goodbye, Bristol. It was a nice surprise, running into you today."

* * * * *

Three weeks later, I slid a cashier's check into my purse.

Jill congratulated me with a sparkly-faced grin. "How are you feeling, now that the house is officially gone?"

"Relieved." An understatement.

"Excellent. Want to go celebrate?" she asked, smoothing a few stray away amber hued hairs that had slipped out of her slick bun. "I have a few loose ends to wrap up, but I can be ready to go in about an hour."

"Sure. Okay. I guess..." I said, following her from the building. "I could go run a few errands while I wait."

"Cool. See you soon." She tossed her briefcase into her sparkly new Subaru, and climbed in. I threw her a wave before unlocking the door to my trusty old Toyota. As I was pulling it open, a car pulled up behind mine and parked. Out of habit, I glanced at it.

The door opened and a man stepped out.

A man I recognized.

Oh God, please tell me he isn't having buyer's remorse already.

I smiled, though it probably wasn't one of my brightest.

"I was hoping I'd catch you," he said as he strolled toward me.

"Is there a problem?"

"No, no. Nothing like that." He leaned against my car's trunk, and immediately I regretted not having washed the car in weeks. Those impeccable black pants weren't going to look so impeccable in a minute. "I was wondering if you'd like to go to dinner?"

11

"When?"

"Tonight? Now?"

"Oh, I..." *Have plans. But what the hell?* "I think that'll be okay. But I need to make a call first."

"Sure. You can do that while we're driving." He reached around me, pushing my car door closed. My nerves buzzed at his nearness. Wow, was there some serious chemistry there.

I hit the button on my key fob, locking the doors and followed him to his car. Nice car. Black. Sleek. BMW. And it smelled really nice inside. Like leather and expensive cologne and man. He got the engine purring while I buckled in. And within moments, we were backing out of the parking spot.

"I hope you enjoy the house," I said as I fished in my purse for my phone. "It really is a wonderful old building. With some TLC, it could be spectacular."

"I have big plans for the place." He smiled as he steered the car through the parking lot. "I hope you'll come see it when the renovations are finished." At the driveway, he hit his turn signal, waiting for a break in traffic.

"I'd love to. I'm just glad the house has gone to someone who could see its full potential."

"That's one thing I've always been good at--seeing the full potential of things...and people." He turned his attention to me. "But in your case, I vastly underestimated you. I knew you'd grow up to be a beautiful woman. But I had no idea you'd be so stunning."

My cheeks warmed. "Thank you."

"You're welcome." Turning his focus back on the road, Shane hit the gas and we zoomed out onto the clogged street.

"You know--this is embarrassing, and I don't know why I'm telling you, but what the hell?--I had a crush on you when I was a kid."

His grin was charming and genuine. "Really?"

"Really."

"But I was an *old* man."

"Older but not old. And charming. And nice. And you talked to me like I was an adult."

We pulled up to a light, and he glanced at me. "You were always mature for your age."

"Being the only child of my mother, it would be impossible for me to be otherwise."

He chuckled. The light turned green, and once again, we were humming along, zigging and zagging through traffic. "I could see that. The truth was, I respected you."

"Respected?" A twelve year old? That surprised me.

"And now that we've reconnected, I respect you even more." He turned the car into a parking lot. Maggiano's. I'd eaten there before. "Is this okay?"

"Absolutely."

He parked and we headed inside. We shared a plate of spinach dip and drank wine and exchanged compliments. He told me about the wife he'd lost while he'd been living in Spain (Spain!), and the children he'd never had. The joys of his life and regrets. And I told him about losing Mom, finishing school, and the bumpy start to my career. The chemistry kept building and building with each minute we spent together. By the time our stomachs were full and our wine glasses empty, I was hoping I'd get a kiss, a real one with hands grasping and tongues twining.

Shane Trant was a hundred times more the man than my juvenile mind could have comprehended. He was intelligent, successful, charming. And he emanated a certain male power, charisma, confidence. I was mesmerized. And a little nervous, too.

At the end of the meal, he paid the bill then led me back to the car, placing a hand on the small of my back. That touch was so distracting I almost went the wrong way when we stepped outside. In fact, I started walking around the wrong side of the building, and he grabbed my shoulders to stop me and turned me back around, facing him.

My gaze jerked up, to his face.

He was looking down at me, eyes glimmering.

"The dinner was delicious, thank you," I said, staring at his mouth. Could it be any more perfect? *Kiss me, please. Kiss me now.*

He licked his lips. His head tipped. A muscle on his jaw clenched. "You are something else."

"Tell me more. I never tire of compliments."

His laughter seemed to vibrate through my whole body. One of his hands cupped my cheek. I flattened my hand on his and held my breath. The moment was magical, and I wanted it to last a lifetime. Erotic energy was arcing through the still night air, leaping from his big, hard body to mine, zinging along my nerves, igniting little blazes everywhere.

But then he said, "I think I'd better take you back to your car now."

You could kiss me first. "I'm in no hurry to go home."

"Hmmmm." The hand that was holding my cheek wandered south a little, fingers curling around my neck. It was a strange way to hold me, a strange place. But it excited me, thrilled me. "You don't know me. Maybe it's better you keep it that way."

"What do you mean? Of course I know you. I've known you for years."

"But not really."

I didn't understand. Was he hiding something? Was he not the man I thought? What I saw was a sexy man, a widower, an old friend, and a successful businessman who had turned his father's one-man operation into a multi-billion dollar corporation. I also saw a man who could make my blood simmer with just a look. "What do you mean by that? Are you dangerous?"

"You might say that." His hold on my neck tightened a tiny bit. It was just enough for me to notice, make me shiver a little, but not enough to make me really scared.

"Dangerous, how?"

"Just dangerous..." Moving fast, he grabbed both my arms and jerked them around my back. My heart jumped. I gasped. "Like this," he said, tipping his head lower, whispering. "Dangerous, like needing things you might not be ready for."

"What kind of things?"

He gathered my wrists into one fist and walked me backward until my body was smashed between him and the side of the restaurant. It felt so good, being trapped like this, powerless and waiting breathlessly for his next move. I didn't have to wait long. His mouth slammed against mine. His lips smoothed over mine, and his tongue shoved into my mouth. He tasted so good, like man and wine. He felt so good, hard and hot. He smelled so good too, of need and woodsy cologne.

I surrendered willingly. His kiss was a possession. Hard and demanding and feral. Intoxicating. Wild rushes of erotic need slammed through me with every flick of his tongue, and I moaned into our joined mouths. I ached. I wanted more. I needed more.

When he broke the kiss, I whimpered. He didn't back away. His body was crushed against mine, and I was so glad about that. My pelvis rolled forward and back in time to the pounding heat throbbing in my center.

"Dammit." He jerked back, stared at me.

"What's wrong?"

"You're Katherine's daughter."

"So what? I'm an adult."

"But--"

"But, what?" I didn't understand what his problem was. Clearly, he was feeling guilty because he was Mom's old friend. But that wasn't a problem for me. "Like I said, I'm an adult."

"Yes, so I can see." As if to illustrate, his gaze shifted south, landing at roughly boob level.

"So, treat me like one."

His eyes narrowed for a brief moment. Then he took my hand in his. "Okay." He hurried me back to his car, circled around the rear to open my door. Once I was in my seat, he went around to the driver's side, folded his large frame into his seat and within seconds we were roaring down the road. "But I have an idea you'll change your mind about this."

Chapter 2

What the hell is this?

I was stunned.

I was speechless.

I was in complete shock.

I had been wrong, when I'd thought I knew Shane Trant. How wrong I had been.

We were at his house, which was completely gorgeous. It was one of those high priced condos in town. He had the top two floors of an industrial building turned luxury condominiums. Huge and gorgeous, furnished with stuff that looked expensive and probably cost a crap ton of money. Recently, I'd started watching home design shows on TV. I'd developed something of an eye for quality. Shane's house was like a showroom, full of priceless antiques, mixed with sleek, high-priced contemporary furniture. An interesting combination.

Something like the man, himself, now that I thought about it.

That had come as no surprise. I'd expected he would have a nice home.

The problem was one particular room. This one.

It was, for lack of better words, a torture chamber.

Dotting the landscape were pieces of creepy looking furniture with big metal rings and heavy chains bolted to it. And in one corner stood a human-sized metal cage. And there were rings bolted to the floor and ceiling. What were those for? I shuddered as I imagined a woman chained up, begging to be freed.

His bulky body was leaning against the doorframe, blocking my exit. "So, now you see why I told you I couldn't…I wouldn't take things to the next level?" he asked. "You're a beautiful, intelligent woman. And I want you. But I'm not the man for you. Because this is what you get."

"I didn't know." I was hugging myself, arms wrapped protectively around my torso.

"You know now." He motioned for me to leave the torture chamber.

I just couldn't believe it. This…awful place…belonged to Uncle Shane. Handsome, mysterious, sexy Shane Trant. My mother's oldest and dearest friend.

Wow. Just…wow.

Dammit. Why? You're such a sexy, intelligent, fascinating man. Why do you need this?

"Can I get you something to drink before I take you home?" as he stepped to the side to let me pass.

The shock, maybe the gaping, had given me a bad case of cotton mouth. "That would be nice, thanks." I followed him to the open living-slash-kitchen space. He went to the refrigerator, no doubt top of the line. My gaze wandered around, taking in the expensive furnishings, gorgeous chandelier hanging over the dining table, artwork. By the time it had made its way back to Shane, he was looking at me expectantly. He'd asked me a question.

"What was that?" I asked, my face warming. "I'm sorry."

"What can I get you to drink?"

Something with a lot of alcohol. "I'll take water. Thanks."

"I have some of this flavored water. How's that?" He

pulled a white and pink bottle from the refrigerator. I recognized the label immediately.

"Perfect. My favorite."

"Mine too." He filled a tall glass with ice then poured some of the faint pink-colored water to the top.

I scurried over, accepted the glass with a smile and a thanks, and guzzled half of it in one long gulp.

"Thirsty?" he asked, his voice bouncing with laughter.

"A little." I drained my glass, and he reached for it.

"More?"

"No thanks." I suppressed a belch. Mistake, chugging that water. But I was nervous and uncomfortable. I couldn't stop myself.

At least it had been water. If it had been something stronger, I might have found myself chained to something in that torture chamber.

A little quiver shot through me.

He polished off his water and set the glass on the counter. "I guess we'll head out now."

"Okay." Somewhat relieved, somewhat not, I followed him to the door leading out to the elevator. He stepped aside, letting me exit first. As I was brushing close, I turned to face him. I couldn't stop myself. My heart jerked in my chest, and before I could stop it, the word, "Why?" slipped out of my mouth.

"Why, what? Why, that?" He jerked his head toward the dungeon.

"Yes, why?"

"It's difficult to explain. It's an expression of who I am, essentially."

"You're...what? Sadistic?"

"No. I don't get any pleasure from causing others pain. I have a need to control, to dominate. It's difficult for some people to understand the difference."

I thought about my mother, how she controlled me, my life, my every move. She was a wonderful woman, just like Shane had said. But she was also extremely controlling.

"Actually, I can see it. I was raised by a woman who probably had the same drive."

"She did."

A chill swept up my spine.

I didn't want to ask how he knew that, or what he might be implying by that statement. I knew for a fact that there'd been no torture dungeon in our house. But I suppose she could have gone somewhere else to exercise those demons, out of my sight.

Another shiver swept through my body.

Standing close enough to touch, close enough to smell, he said, "I'm sorry if I said something you weren't ready to hear."

"It's okay." I forced a smile, hoping it would ease his guilt. For some reason I looked deeply into his eyes. I don't know what I saw there, shadows, sadness, loneliness, maybe. Regret, perhaps. Something dark. "I still think you're one of the most amazing men I've ever met."

"And I think you're one of the most amazing women." He set his hand on my shoulder, and another buzz of electricity zapped through my body. "That will never change."

I felt myself leaning toward him, as if some kind of force was drawing me in. And the electricity was getting stronger with every inch I moved closer. I wanted him to kiss me. Despite the torture chamber. Despite the voice in my head, screaming, *he's not for you! Get out of here now!*

"Bristol."

"What?" I was so close now. Near enough to feel the heat radiating off his big, lean body. His mouth was still too far away, though. Much too far. No, too close. Much too close.

I leaned in, drawn to him by that invisible current. Pulling me.

Something like a low growl rumbled from him. "If you don't leave now, you're going to learn firsthand what happens in that room."

I heard him. But part of me didn't care. The other part, the one that did, wasn't being very vocal at the moment. "I'm not afraid of you," I said. The minute the words came out, I regretted them. The way my heart was racing, that had to be a lie. I was afraid. Afraid of that room and what he might do to me in it.

But also afraid that he might shove me out the door and say goodbye and not speak to me for another ten years.

Stay? Go? What did I want?

He cupped my cheek, ran his thumb over my lower lip. "Sure, maybe you aren't afraid. But can you trust me?"

"I...don't know."

His head tipped, moved down, closing the distance between our mouths. "That's not good enough. But dammit, I want you."

At the sound of torment in his voice, I threw my arms around his neck and crushed my body against his.

He growled, hooked an arm around my waist and whirled around so I was flat against the wall and his body was holding me there.

Oh. My. God.

His mouth descended upon mine, his tongue shoved its way in, and within seconds, I was writhing against him while he kissed me into a coma.

I felt him scoop me up into his arms. He was carrying me, walking, while our tongues mated and battled. I was losing the war, ready to surrender to him, to the fierce heat boiling in my veins, to the blinding need he'd sparked in my body. He broke the kiss, stared down at me with eyes full of male hunger. "I'm sorry, Bristol. I can't let you go now. I can't."

We kissed again, and again, as he carried me into the dungeon. At some point he set me on my feet, but I was too shaky to stand, and I wasn't about to let him stop kissing me. I hung onto his neck, arms wrapped tightly, and lost myself in his aggressive, demanding, plundering kiss.

I'd been kissed plenty of times, but never like that.

Never like the man couldn't get enough.

Never like he was staking a claim.

Never like he was conquering me.

When the kiss ended--not my choice--I clung to him and fought to catch my breath.

"Wow," I murmured. My gaze started at his mouth but quickly moved to the closest piece of torture furniture. I felt myself backing up.

"You've never been in a dungeon, correct?" he asked, hands sliding down my sides.

"Never."

He blocked my exit with his hulking body, held me at the hips. "If I do something you don't like, say, Red."

"Red?" I echoed, trying to wiggle my way free. I wasn't ready for this. That kiss. It was the kiss's fault I was in here. I didn't belong here, no.

He cut me off completely, cornering me against another wall, his body a giant obstacle I couldn't push past. He caged my head between his hands, arms stretched out. His eyes were dark, hard. "You may beg me to stop, but I won't. You may plead with me and cry, but I won't stop. But if you say red, I will cease immediately."

"Red," I muttered.

His fingertip trailed down the side of my face, down my jaw, my throat to the center of my breastbone. I sucked in a deep breath and fought to regain my composure. But he was so big and so sexy and so intimidating, I couldn't speak. "I promise I won't be too hard on you this first time." He closed his hands around my waist, forcing me deeper into the room.

Ohmygod, what was happening? "On second thought--"

He kissed me again. His tongue shoved its way into my mouth. It was a hard kiss, a feral one. I was swept up in pulsing waves of sensual heat, barely realizing I was being half-carried, half-shoved as we traveled through his torture dungeon. My head was going blank. I tried to repeat the word red in my head. Would I remember it? What if things got too intense?

Red, red, red.

When the kiss had finally ended, I found myself standing next to the table in the center of the room. He reached under it, pulling out a step stool. The table wasn't very tall, maybe typical counter height. He patted the table top. "Let's get you up here."

Red, red, red.

Why couldn't I speak? Why couldn't I move?

He picked me up and plopped me down. My legs dangled over the edge.

Red, red, red.

He eased my knees apart and stepped closer, and I realized, when his hips wedged between my thighs that the table was the perfect height for him to have sex standing up. A flood of warmth pulsed to my core. He caught my wrists, pinning them behind my back and gathering them into one hand. Now there was a hard lump grinding against my crotch and I couldn't use my hands.

Mmmmm. I liked it.

I didn't want to like it.

I didn't want to be in this scary place.

I licked my lips, and his gaze locked on my mouth. "What do you want?" I whispered.

The corners of his lips curled. "You'll soon find out." With his free hand, he cupped my breast. The air whooshed out of my lungs, and my spine arched. That only pushed my boob into his hand harder. His lips parted slightly, and I stared at them, wishing I could taste them again.

"Kiss me," I whispered.

"In this room, I'm the one who gives the commands." He squeezed, and my head spun. "We need these clothes off." He released my hands. "Undress."

With clumsy fingers, I started to undo the buttons of my blouse. But I stopped after only two. What was I doing?

His brows furrowed.

I said, with my heart beating so hard it physically hurt, "I...think I should go home."

He fisted my wrists, pulled them out away from my body. "You don't want to leave. You know how I know that?"

I was dizzy. I was scared. And, ohmygod, my body was on fire. I shook my head.

"I can smell your need." He dipped down a little, inhaling deeply. "And does it smell good. You're wet."

My inner muscles clenched, and I felt the slickness of my damp panties. He was right. But that didn't mean I was ready for this. "I...I..." Holding both my wrists in one hand, he eased back slightly, which allowed him to wedge a hand between our bodies. His fingertip grazed the sodden crotch of my panties, and my face heated.

"Wet." He curled that finger, working it inside at the leg band. My sex heated even more. When that first touch came, I whimpered. He eased his hand out, lifted it to his mouth and slipped his index finger between his lips. "Sweet. Delicious. I must have more." Still holding my wrists behind my back, he unfastened my blouse buttons, and I watched his expression as more and more of my skin was exposed. The hard male hunger in his eyes grew and grew. By the time the garment had slid over my shoulders, I was squirming and my whole body was burning.

Hot and cold.

Tight. Very tight all over.

And breathless.

And scared.

And aroused. Incredibly aroused.

I was crazy. Had to be.

I want to leave. I should leave. Right now. Say the word. Say it!

Chapter 3

Unaware of my inner conflict, Shane reached around my side and unzipped my skirt. With his bulk trapped between my legs, there was no way he'd get it off. Or my panties. That made me feel a little less panicked. He turned his attention to my breasts.

"This has to go." He hooked a finger under the little bow sewn between the cups of my bra. Then, he glided a flattened hand up my stomach, over my ribcage, and around my back. With a snap, my bra was unhooked. As the straps flopped down over my shoulders, the cups fell away, and my breasts bounced free. Embarrassed, I yanked on my hands. I wanted to catch the cups, hold them in place to cover myself. "Beautiful." That free hand was on the move again. This time, it weighed each breast. Then it kneaded the soft flesh. I watched, torn, confused, overwhelmed. My body craved this man's touch like none before. This was so new to me, this almost unbearable need. I was hot, shivering, tight all over. My panties were sodden. My head was spinning. My mouth was dry. "Good. Now let's get rid of the rest." Without releasing my wrists, he moved back enough to let me press my legs together. As he tugged my skirt over my hips, a thought would shot through my mind.

I need to leave. Right now.

As he pulled my panties down, I thought, *This is wrong. Dangerous.*

And as I was finally left sitting on that table completely nude, I thought, *If you don't stop this now, you're going to get hurt.*

But then he touched my face, looked at me with those dark, hungry eyes, and my heart started pounding harder, and my insides burned more, and I couldn't think about anything but having him inside me, filling me, stroking away the ache between my legs.

Before I realized it, he had me lying on my back, legs spread, wrists bound in leather cuffs and chained to the table so my hands were useless, tied over my head.

I was trapped, not completely powerless, but almost. I couldn't catch my breath. I wanted to be set free. And yet I didn't. It was all happening so fast.

My insides clenched as he fingered my slick folds, both in anticipation and fear. I'd seen internet porn, pictures of girls with smudged makeup, their mouths stuffed with gags, their bodies bound and clamped and paddled. Those images scared me, disturbed me. Did I really want to know if those things hurt as badly as the pictures led me to believe? I had a feeling if I didn't put a stop to things now, I was going to find out soon.

Red, red, red.

That finger, the one teasing, tormenting me, delved deeper, finding my entry and piercing it roughly. I bucked, blood surging through my body.

"You are so damn tight." He added a second finger, and I cried out. My insides clenched around the invading digits, warmth gushing, easing his entry as they slid deeper, teasing the opening of my womb before gliding out. He pushed them in again, out, knuckles scraping against that place inside that made me quiver with need. I could feel the first tremors of an orgasm quake through my body, but

I fought it, wanting this sweet torment to last much, much longer.

He groaned as I clenched my inner muscles again. "I have to have you."

I heard the ziiip of his zipper, the slough of fabric. The crinkle of a condom wrapper. My fingers curled into fists. My legs shook as I waited. I'd had so few partners. And it had been such a long time since I'd enjoyed a climax that wasn't produced from a battery operated device. I wanted this, God help me, I did. Wanted it more than I should.

Within seconds, I felt him, pushing his way past my sodden tissues, entering me slowly, inch by glorious inch. I stretched to accommodate his girth. He was big, very thick. Almost too big for me. It burned, but it wasn't entirely bad.

He pushed my thighs wider apart, hands on the backs, pushing them out and up toward my shoulders so my spine was curled, hips lifted. The friction of his forward thrust nearly sent me over the brink. The added torture of his finger flicking lightly over my clit finished the job. A white hot blaze swept through my body, igniting every nerve, from the tip of my toes to the top of my head. I convulsed around him so hard it almost hurt. I cried out his name as he surged forward and back, thrusting hard into me, driving toward his own release.

My orgasm had barely faded when I felt his member swell as he climaxed. My body still vibrating from the effects of the first one, I tumbled into another orgasm. I jerked and writhed and screamed as he pounded mercilessly into me, driving every drop of come from his body.

And then, he bent over me and laid his head on my chest. His semi-flaccid member remained buried deep inside me. Little twitches and tingles accompanied the warm afterglow of that mind-blowing experience. I'd never come like that.

"You are exquisite," he said a few minutes later. He

straightened, but only after giving me a sweet kiss on the chin. He grasped the base of his cock, holding the used condom in place and pulled out. My first instinct was to clamp my legs closed and look away.

Yes, that had been the most intense sex of my life. But I was confused. I wanted to leave. Now.

I needed to think.

I just had kinky sex with Uncle Shane.

"You'll come back next weekend." After he put his clothes all in order, he released me.

"I'll…I have to check my schedule." I wasted no time reclaiming my clothing and getting myself zipped and buttoned back in. I had to get out of there. I was confused, hordes of emotions washing over me. Regret. Curiosity. Guilt. Anticipation.

"Will you stay a little longer?" he asked, moving toward me as I scurried for the door. He caught my wrist, stopping me. "You're in such a hurry all of a sudden. Are you okay?"

"I'm fine." I blinked at him, catching a worried look in his eyes. "I'm fine," I repeated. "Really. It's just a lot to absorb all at once."

He cupped my cheek with my free hand. "I understand. You call me when you're ready."

"Will do."

He let me go.

Out I went. I rode the elevator alone, climbed into his car and buckled myself in while he locked up and rode the elevator down to the parking lot. Safe in his car, I watched him as he ambled over to the vehicle. He was such a handsome man. And his body, that body was absolutely incredible. And to top it all off, he knew exactly how to touch me, to kiss me, to hold me. On so many levels, we seemed to click. With the exception of one.

"What plans do you have for next weekend?" he asked as he steered the zoomy car out into traffic.

"I'm not sure."

"I see."

I made an attempt at small talk as he drove me home. I really did. But I failed. Thus, much of the drive was in silence. I let him kiss me goodbye in the car. Thankfully, it was just a small peck. Friendly but not overly intimate. Then I locked myself into my condo and had a good, long cry.

* * * * *

Three weeks later, that night with Shane still haunted me. He'd called me a few days later and left a message. He'd told me to return his call if I had an interest in seeing him again. I hadn't called him back. Not because I didn't want to see him again. I did. But because I didn't want to want him so much.

Since that night all I'd dreamed about was him and his dungeon. I woke up every morning, body tight, blood simmering. Thoughts of him popped into my head all day long, at the oddest moments. I'd hear a man's voice, and my heart would start galloping in my chest like a runaway race horse. I'd catch the scent of a man's cologne, and my blood would start simmering. I'd spy a dark haired man in a crowd and my knees would turn soft.

Shane Trant had become an obsession. There was no way I could face him. Not yet. Not for a long time.

So I went about my life, doing the best I could to pretend everything was normal. I went to work. I went to the gym. I went grocery shopping and paid my bills and tried to tell myself I was happy.

By the time the fourth week had passed, I had almost convinced myself that I was going to put Shane and that night behind me. I was in Antonio's, grabbing some vegetable lasagna to take home for a late dinner. I heard his voice, and every nerve in my body ignited.

"Bristol," he said, behind me.

I slowly swiveled, doing what I could to mentally brace myself as I turned. Still, the sight of his handsome face made my heart jerk in my chest. "Hello, Shane."

His lips were curled into a ghost of a smile. "It's good to see you again."

"Yes. How are the renovations going?" I asked, feeling myself leaning back, away from him. A little quiver of need shot through me as my gaze focused on his mouth. That mouth had done wicked, decadent things to me. And I knew, if I was brave enough to ask, it could do a lot more wickeder things to me.

He stepped closer, allowing a customer standing behind him to get through the crowded space. Now he was standing close enough to touch. Close enough to smell his cologne, to feel his head. He extended an arm, placing a hand on the bar behind me. "I'm just getting things started, thanks. And how's life without two mortgages?"

I inhaled deeply. "Wonderful."

"Miss, there you are." The bartender handed me a plastic bag, and I thanked her before turning back to Shane.

Holding the bag, I shifted my weight. Wow, was he close. I needed to leave. I could feel my willpower failing. What would happen if I asked him if I could go home with him right now? Would he take me back to that dark dungeon of his? Would he make me forget why it was such a bad idea? "Well, I guess I'd better get going."

"Sure. Wouldn't want your...?" He lifted a brow.

"Vegetarian lasagna," I said.

"Vegetarian lasagna to get cold."

"No, I wouldn't." I took a step away, two. I'd almost made it to the door before turning back. When I did, I discovered he was watching me. My face burned. I opened my mouth, but no words came out. I didn't know what to say. How could I explain everything to him? How?

That ghost of a smile warmed slightly. Then he turned away from me to talk to the bartender.

I left, scurrying outside, click-clacked across the dark parking lot. Just as I was remoting open my car's door lock, I heard him again. He'd followed me outside.

I opened the door and dropped my dinner onto the driver's seat. By the time I'd done that, he was behind me. I could sense his nearness with every nerve in my body. I turned, opened my mouth again to say something.

He cupped my cheeks and smashed his mouth down over mine.

Instantly my body ignited, and all the wanting I'd been trying to suppress surged to the surface, overwhelming my system like a tidal wave. Before I knew it, he had me pinned between his hard body and my car and his tongue was plunging into my mouth, filling it with his decadent flavor.

I was outside, where a passerby might see me, but I didn't care. All that mattered was how it felt to have his hands on me again, his heat radiating over my skin. My insides were twisting and turning, muscles coiling into tight knots.

Hands cupped under my ass, he lifted me, and I locked my legs around his waist and arms around his neck, and held on. My skirt was up over my hips, but it didn't matter. He wasn't going to let me go again, not now, not ever. No. I was his. He was mine. We'd figure everything else out later.

His hands left my butt, and I heard the ziiip of a zipper. Ohmygod, was he going to…?

He had my back pinned against the slightly angled face of the driver's side window. We were standing between my car and a minivan. It was dark.

But still I knew, even with the haze of need enveloping me almost completely, that someone could catch us at any moment.

His fingers hooked the crotch of my panties. There was a sharp yank, and the sodden material gave way. Cool air caressed my heated flesh, making me shiver.

"You aren't going to hide from me again," he said as he plunged his thick cock into me.

"No, sir," I promised, tipping my hips to meet his

thrust. "Never again."

He slid deep. Full at last. Oh God, it felt so good, so right. Even here. Yes, here.

"I'll never hide again," I promised. I meant it too, every word.

"You should be punished." He withdrew, to the tip then rammed deep again.

"Yes." A surge of carnal heat rushed through me. I was going to come already. I could feel it, tingles of a powerful climax buzzing and zapping through my body. "I'm sorry, sir. Punish me. Punish me hard."

He did. He took me without mercy, pounding into my tight tissues with all his might. I surrendered to his possession and let myself be carried away by a powerful orgasm, screaming his name as the first spasm wracked my body. I trembled and quaked, gasping for breath as his torment continued. He showed me no mercy, pushing me over the edge again, making me come a second time before finally reaching his own climax. He slammed his mouth over mine as he jerked his cock out of me. His low growl of satisfaction vibrated in my mouth, my head, my throat. Trembling all over, I clung to him and fought to catch my breath. I'd never done anything like this. I'd never even dreamed of doing anything like this.

Sex in public?

Ohmygod. I'd just had sex in public.

While I huffed and puffed, he tucked himself back in his pants and zipped up. Then, holding me tenderly, he eased me to my feet and smoothed my skirt down. His gaze locked on mine.

"I'm sorry," I said, tears gathering in my eyes. I dragged my thumbs under my lashes then crossed my arms over my chest. "I was scared."

"Bristol." Holding my hips, he pulled me into his arms. He kissed to top of my head and encased me in a warm embrace. "I want to protect you, if you'll let me." He cupped his hand under my chin, lifting it. "What were you scared of? Me?"

"No, not you. I was scared of how you made me feel, how powerful my wanting for you is."

He caressed my cheek, thumbing away a tear that had dribbled down the side. "Baby, my wanting for you has been driving me mad for four weeks. I haven't eaten. I can't sleep. I can't think. I haven't even started the renovations on the house yet because I can't concentrate on anything but you. I've wondered where you were, what you were doing, why you wouldn't call me. You see what you've done to me? You've tormented me, haunted me. And I'm thankful. You've given me a reason to live again, to think about tomorrow. To plan for next week, next month."

I'd never heard such beautiful words before. I was speechless.

"Tell me you're mine, Bristol. I need to hear you say it."

I looped my arms around his neck and rose up on tiptoes. He dipped his head down, lower, lower until our mouths were a breath apart. Then, I whispered, "I'm yours, Shane. I've been yours from the start, after that first magical kiss." And then, I sealed my promise with a kiss. It was as magical as the first one. Not because it was a possession. No, it was a surrender. It was an unspoken vow. He was my master, and I was his slave. For how long? I couldn't say. Yesterday, today, and tomorrow. Maybe longer. Maybe not. But now I understood. I didn't need to be afraid. Shane would never hurt me. I could trust him like I'd never trusted another man. In the dungeon, he would be my lover, my protector, my strength, my courage. But only if I turned myself over to him, mind and body.

When the kiss ended, he smiled. "Now, you deserve a reward." His hand slid around to my back, cupping my bottom, and a shiver of desire quaked through me. I leaned into him, feeling his hard, hot need pressing against my stomach.

"Here? Again?" I asked, a secret thrill setting my heart racing.

"No, eat first. You're going to need your strength. I have big plans for you tonight. *Big* plans."

My body ignited as he angled past me, opened my car door and pulled my bag of vegetable lasagna out. "Yes, sir." We walked hand in hand to his car. And minutes later, we were zooming through quiet streets toward his home, toward his dungeon.

My new playroom.

The End

At His Mercy

TAWNY TAYLOR

Chapter 1

"Let me guess, after last weekend's date with a bug-eyed, tentacled alien, you can't stop fantasizing about octopi?"

Elena Caine snapped to, realizing she'd been blindly staring down at a pan of...was that squid? Eww!

"Huh?" She hurried down the Asian buffet, past steaming pans of fried rice, sweet and sour shrimp, and moo goo gai pan, following her best friend Ashley to a table in the corner of the restaurant. "No. Trust me, tentacles do nothing for me," she joked. "But horns? Yum." The contents of her jacket pocket bounced against her hip as she dodged a toddler in a high chair, reminding her why today had been the worst day of her life.

She'd always thought politicians, judges, lawyers—those kinds of people—were the only ones who got blackmailed. People who were bad. Or had money. Or power.

But your run of the mill office manager? With no money, no power? Not hardly.

So why was she being blackmailed?

"Earth to Elena. Are you with me? What is with you?" Ashley waved a hand in front of Elena's nose. "I haven't seen you this dazed since that party in college. Are you high?" At Elena's fervent shake of the head, Ashley asked, "Sick? Or did you OD on allergy medicine again?"

"Well…" Elena wanted to tell Ashley about the letter in her pocket. It was so tempting, but the jerk who'd sent it had warned her not to tell anyone. Not a single person. If she did, he claimed she'd be the immediate recipient of a pink slip. And a free ride downtown…in a police cruiser.

Considering who she was dealing with, she believed him.

The way she saw it, she had no choice but to play along with his twisted scheme. The jerk had done his homework, known she couldn't afford to lose her job or risk going to jail. She certainly couldn't go to the authorities, not when the bit of information he held over her head was so…sensitive.

He had her by the so-called balls.

Yep, worst day of her life.

"Whooo hoooo? Gone on another trip, or are you still here with me?" Ashley, queen of exaggeration, waved her fork in the air.

Elena knocked Ashley's hand away. "I'm here. Just really tired. It's been a hellacious week at work, and I'm ready to go home and go to bed." She lifted her diet cola and took several swallows, trying to avoid eye contact with her best friend.

She knew that look. Ashley was going to pry.

Ashley shoved her plate away and dropped her wadded up napkin on the table. Her gaze was razor sharp and probing. "I'm worried about you."

"Don't be." Elena faked a smile.

"You're pale. I don't think you're just tired. What else is going on? Why won't you tell me? Don't you trust me? Is it your boss again? PMS? Your little brother?"

The questions came fast and furious, like balls being spat from a pitching machine gone haywire, and Elena fielded them like a world-class ballplayer. Quickly and efficiently, expending as little effort as possible. One word answers. That was all Ashley got.

Finally, Ashley gave up and went back to chattering about the new guy in the cubicle two down from hers. The one with the great butt and new 'Vette.

Pretending to listen, Elena picked at her dinner—what had made her decide the Chou Dofu was a good idea today? A little while later, Ashley heaved the sigh of the weary friend who felt neglected and did the little shooing motion she used on stray dogs and pigeons. "Go home and sleep. I'll call you tomorrow."

"Okay. 'Night." Elena shrugged into her coat, dug her keys out of the bottom of her purse, gave her friend a quick hug and hurried out to her car, one hand in her pocket, her fingers curled around that damn letter.

It was dark outside already—she hated fall! The restaurant's parking lot was murky and slushy, thanks to an early snow. It wasn't even Thanksgiving yet and already they'd had their first heavy snowfall of the year. Winter was bearing down on Michigan like a frigid white demon. She slipped and slid to the back where she'd parked. Unlocked her door, flung her purse onto the passenger seat, climbed in and cranked the engine. It started with a sputter and cough, threatening to stall. Like its owner, her ancient Volkswagen hated the cold.

Elena hit the gas and flipped on the heater, shivering and cursing her temperamental vehicle for making her freeze her butt off while it warmed up.

As she pulled the letter from her pocket to reread it for the bazillionth time, the passenger side door swung open. Assuming it was Ashley coming to keep her company— aka harass her some more—while she waited, she stuffed the letter back into her pocket and pulled her purse off the seat, depositing it on floor. But the body that slid into the seat was not Ashley's. It wasn't even female.

Oh God. "Kyler? Hi." Could it be a coincidence that the extremely attractive man on receiving end of her blackmailing jerk's devious plan had just plopped into her

39

front seat? In a dark restaurant parking lot? Probably not but she could always hope.

Then again, they'd shared quite a few looks in the office the past few weeks. Whether she was hallucinating or hopeful, she sensed there was some chemistry between them. Maybe he had been in the restaurant and she hadn't noticed, and he'd been dying to talk to her about…something…and he'd seen his opportunity…

Okay, so she was really reaching. The expression on his face wasn't exactly screaming *Hey baby*. Nope. More like, *You bitch*.

"What are you doing here?" she asked.

His smile wasn't even close to genuine. "I thought this would be the perfect place for a chat."

She was chilled before but now she felt like a human icicle. Maybe this was his way of asking a girl out? If that was the case, his brand of seduction bordered on creepy.

"Well, I'm really flattered you wanted some private time, went to all the trouble of tracking me down in a dark parking lot." *Yikes!* "But I'm not feeling very well and now's not a good time, so couldn't we continue—"

He planted one hand on the steering wheel, the other on the headrest of her seat, basically caging her in with his arms. "Now. Is. The. Per-fect. Time." He enunciated every single syllable.

"Okayyyy. So what do you want to talk about?" she asked, shooting for a casual tone as she ground the back of her head into the headrest.

Strangely, as she sat there, concentrating on regularly inhaling and exhaling, she couldn't help but be aware of how good looking Kyler Pierce, VP of Sales and Marketing, was. There was good reason why every single female in the company, married or not, lusted after the man, at least a little. But she would never have expected him to make her so incredibly hot when he was more or less holding her hostage.

A part of her thrilled at the thorough once-over he was giving her right now. He had the most amazing eyes and smelled sooooo good. And his mouth. Perfect lips.

He inched a smidge closer. "I know what Matt's up to."

Her stomach dropped to her toes. Crap! Now what? Beg forgiveness and hope he could somehow dig her out of this mess? But that would require her telling him everything.

Oh God! She couldn't!

"I don't know what you mean. Up to? Isn't Matt always 'up to' something? I wouldn't think that would be worthy of wandering around in a dark parking lot—"

"It most definitely is." He inched back a bit. Not enough in her opinion, but a little. She was grateful. "What's he got on you?"

"Me? Nothing." Her face flamed, totally giving away her guilt.

"Then why are you going along with it?"

"With what?" She was an absolutely terrible actress. The worst. But sadly, she couldn't give up the act.

Anger flared in his deep blue eyes, the shade of a night sky. He slammed his fists against her seat, one next to her shoulder, the other down closer to her waist, and she froze. The breath she'd just managed to suck in blasted up her throat.

She'd known Matt was playing uber-dirty, that the eventual outcome would mean the worst for Kyler—the loss of his job. A position that probably paid a lot. But did that give the man any right to bodily threaten her?

No. But she still had no idea what she could—or would—do about it.

She wanted to cry. She was trapped between these two power-hungry, manipulative jerks, out to ruin each other. And it was so unfair! She was just the office manager. The girl who filed their paperwork and answered their phones. She shouldn't be ducking punches and evading blackmail threats.

If only she had a way out of this!

She felt her eyes filling with hot tears. Her nose burned. She blinked, focusing her gaze on the radio's display, the glowing numbers blurring as the tears built up. She dragged a hand across her eyes and waited for him to say something. She wasn't going to speak. She couldn't.

"Fuck," he grumbled.

She'd agree with that sentiment.

Kyler inched back a little more. "Don't cry. I can't stand it when women cry."

"Believe me, I'm trying not to." Still staring at the radio, she sniffled, wiping some of the annoying wetness from her eyes again.

"That fucking bastard."

She'd agree with that sentiment too.

He turned, slumping back against the passenger seat, and she inhaled her first full breath in ages.

What now? The silent but vulnerable thing seemed to be working for her. Kind of. No sense switching gears now.

"His plan won't work without you." Kyler seemed to be thinking aloud. Thus, she didn't comment, just let him continue following his train of thought. "So, if you aren't there to help him, he's SOL."

Sounded like a good plan to her, but what exactly did that mean? If she didn't show up to work on Monday morning, as planned, and plant the evidence he was supposed to deliver to her this weekend, Matt Becker was taking the proof he had about her to Human Resources…and the entire board of directors…

And the police.

* * * * *

Kyler wanted to punch something—no, someone. That fucking shithead, Matt Becker, that's who he wanted to beat.

Using the office girl. The adorable, sweet and very proficient office girl. Manipulating her. Not only was it

42

illegal but it was low. Showed exactly what kind of guy Becker was.

Competitive, Kyler could respect. Coldhearted criminal, he could not.

Sad thing was, if a friend hadn't tipped him off, Becker's scheme would've worked, and he would've found himself without a job within a couple of weeks, regardless of the ten years of hard work he'd put in with this company. A flawless record and sixty percent growth in sales since he became VP wouldn't save him. He'd lived and breathed that fucking place to get it to where it was. Becker was not taking that away from him.

He sensed Elena was being forced to go along with Becker's plan, but she wasn't talking. Why? If he were in her shoes, he'd have spilled. VP of Marketing and Sales trumped Becker's Regional Sales Manager. She should be grateful and relieved that he'd found out, telling him everything and letting him clean up whatever mess Becker had already started making.

Instead she was sitting there crying. Not that she was blubbering and bawling. No, she was sniffling daintily, little chin quivering, and swiping at tears seeping from a set of pretty brown eyes that were wide and innocent and wary.

Crying women made him melt, dammit. Especially this one.

Becker had something bad on this girl. Bad enough that she didn't trust him enough to say what it was. What the hell could it be? The little office manager was so quiet, with a demure demeanor, soft voice that made him warm, and a sweet face that seemed so guileless. Lately, he couldn't seem to stop looking at her.

Then again, knowing Becker, maybe whatever he was holding over her head was completely made up. Just like the shit Becker was trying to pull on him—planting bogus evidence that he was stealing money from the company.

"Do you have any vacation time coming?" he finally

asked, deciding on a plan of attack. First thing he had to do was remove Becker's primary tool against him—Elena. Then he'd worry about whatever problem Becker had created for the office manager.

"Yes, a few days, but I can't take time off now."

"Because Becker's blackmailed you into helping him? And if you don't show up on Monday, the shit's going to hit the fan?"

Silence. Then a soft, "Yes."

"Want to tell me what he's using to blackmail you?"

"No."

"Okay." He sighed. Dammit, he wished she'd trust him, but he could understand why she didn't. Standing in her shoes, he and Becker probably looked like a couple of battling, territorial bullies, one no better than the other. "I can't let you go to work on Monday."

Her gaze dropped to her hands. He watched her toy with the button on her coat. "If I don't show, I'll be out a job by Monday afternoon."

Shit. "I can get the vacation time pushed through Human Resources," he offered. "You can tell them it's a family emergency."

She shook her head. "That's not going to help."

"Or you could call in sick."

"Again, not going to help."

Desperate to get something out of the pretty office manager, a hint, anything, he leaned forward, took her hand in his. She still refused to look at him. Dammit, why was she hiding? What was she hiding? "What is Becker holding over your head? Please, I don't just want to think about myself here. I want to help you too."

"I can't tell you. I can't tell anyone," she said to her clasped hands.

He wanted to scream. "Then how can I help you?"

Silence. The tense quiet dragged on for several agonizing seconds. "I guess you can't."

He sighed. "All right." Fuck it! He couldn't worry

about something he didn't know about. "I didn't want to do this, but…" He unfastened her seatbelt, grabbed the vehicle's key, and gave it a twist to cut off the engine.

Elena's reaction was delayed by several seconds. She'd clearly been caught off guard. But once she realized what he was about to do, she fought like a little banshee, clawing at the hand holding her keys, swinging at him with the other, cussing him, throwing her body across his lap as she made a desperate lunge for the keys.

He opened the passenger door, practically rolling out of the car, her keys still in his hand. He half expected her to tumble out of the car and run away, but she didn't. Instead, as he'd hoped, she scrambled from the vehicle, running around the front to meet him on his side.

Which happened to be adjacent to his own car. He'd planned this well.

He stuffed her keys into his pocket, and opened his car's driver-side door. "You're just going to have to trust me, I guess."

She crossed her arms over her chest and thrust her chin into the air. "Just because you have my keys doesn't mean I can't show up to work on Monday," she said, her little face red, her lush mouth drawn into a tight line, hair—which was always neatly pinned into an up-do—disheveled. Sexy, glossy waves tumbled from the loosened bun, falling over her shoulders and down her back. The wind picked up a tendril and sent it sailing across her face.

He realized, painfully, that he was getting hard with her looking like that. And suddenly he had the craziest idea.

He'd blackmail the sexy and mysterious little office manager too.

Elena was pissed. And scared. And ready to start crying all over again.

Oh hell. The tears were flowing and she wasn't going to even try to stop them anymore. Maybe she could guilt-trip Kyler into giving back her keys.

It was freezing outside, but she didn't feel the cold. She was so freaking furious her insides were an inferno. How dare Kyler take her keys and leave her here to freeze! What did he think he was going to accomplish by doing that? Keep her home Monday? Not a chance.

There were other means of transportation to be found. She could call Ashley and ask her to come back and pick her up tonight. And then…she'd be forced to come up with some feasible explanation for why she didn't have her keys and why it had taken her so long to realize they were missing.

And then there was the issue of getting over to see her brother tomorrow. He was in the hospital again. She had several errands to run. She couldn't ask Ashley to ferry her around all weekend.

This was so unfair! The battle between these two assholes shouldn't involve her. She shouldn't be facing these kinds of complications. Jerks! Bastards! Conniving, lowlife scumbags!

She stomped her foot then, giving Kyler's shiny black Jaguar a glare, decided it was in need of a little facelift. Of course, she'd give Kyler a warning first. Let him decide.

Plastering what she hoped was an evil you're-so-going-to-be-sorry-for-this grin on her face, she knocked on his window. "Give me my keys, or I'll make your car look like it just went through a hail storm…with hailstones the size and shape of my foot."

He didn't look threatened.

The window silently slid down. "Just get in the car. We need to talk." His breath made little white puffs in the air.

"Hell no! Why would I go anywhere with you?"

"Because it's better than freezing."

"Believe me," she growled through gritted teeth, "I'm not cold."

"You will be." Looking way too chipper, and much too handsome, he patted the seat. "Get in. Let's talk. I promise we can sort this whole thing out."

46

Sort it out. Hah. He had no idea. There was no sorting anything out. At least not for her.

He, on the other hand, could avoid trouble pretty easily, by taking whatever proof he had about Matt Becker's plans to the Powers That Be.

She supposed, if he wanted to be a jerk, he could easily implicate her in the scheme too. That was, if he had no proof that she was being blackmailed into helping the Regional Sales Manager.

Shit, what was she worried about? She'd be gone no matter what. And even if she was somehow able to avoid going to jail, she wouldn't be able to afford the atrocious premiums to keep her health insurance, and bills for her brother's treatment would mount to the freaking sky in no time.

Because of her secret, she couldn't file bankruptcy.

Welcome to the world of around-the-clock bill collectors, judgments, garnisheed wages.

She so didn't want to go there again. Desperately. Which was why she was in this position in the first place. But it seemed there was no avoiding it now.

The chill in the air had finally seeped inside her body, not so much cooling the fury churning within her, but adding another layer of sensation on top. She suddenly felt weary, tired of being the strong one, the one with all the answers. For once, she wanted someone else to take over, tell her everything was going to be okay, like she did for her brother. To shoulder all the pressures.

It was hell being a surrogate mother to a teenager with a debilitating, long-term illness that made health insurance more vital than a paycheck. But that was what she was, and nothing was going to change it.

"Get in. I'm not the selfish bastard Becker is, but I can't let you do this to me."

She knew that was probably true, that Kyler wasn't as selfish as Becker. But that didn't mean she was ready to hop in his car and go for a joyride. He would only start

47

asking questions again. And that would lead to nothing good.

She sighed and tried to gather her windblown hair out of her face. She smoothed the unruly locks back, tucked them behind her ears. "Look, if you truly wanted to help me, you'd give me back my keys and find another way to beat Becker at his game. Why not just take whatever proof you have against him to the higher-ups? Wouldn't that do it?"

He shook his head. "It would, if I had proof. All I had was a tip. Nothing substantial enough to counter the evidence you're going to plant."

Shoot! Then he had been fishing earlier. For details. Proof. How much did he know? "If you know about the evidence I'm supposed to plant, couldn't you just play interference? Remove it before anyone else finds it?"

He shook his head. "Not unless you tell me exactly where that evidence will be."

She considered telling him. Very seriously, for about ten seconds, then dismissed the idea. If she put the papers where she was supposed to, and then Matt saw Kyler immediately take them out, he'd know she'd spilled. "I can't. Matt'll figure it out."

He sighed again. That had to be at least five times now. "Whatever he's got on you, it must be bad."

She didn't respond. Even in the courts, a girl was permitted to plead the Fifth.

"But you see," he said, his expression turning wicked, "I've got something on you too. I could turn the tables on you, blackmail you too."

"You're bluffing. If you had anything on me, you'd have me fired so I couldn't plant the evidence, and therefore protect your precious little job." She held her breath, hoping that was the case. It made sense.

He tipped his head, narrowed his eyes. "So you're willing to take the chance I'm lying? Quite the gambler, aren't you?"

"Hey, you're the one trying to force my hand."

"No, you are, by holding your cards so close to your chest."

Great, now they had resorted to talking in poker clichés. She wasn't even a card player. She sighed. "I just want to go home. And Monday, I want to go to work, and keep my job."

More silence.

Dammit, could they just come to some kind of agreement here? She was tired, cold, worn out, emotionally drained.

"How about a wager?" he offered. "I win, you do what I say. You win, I'll find another way to stop Becker, or face the music if you two succeed."

"What kind of wager? I don't know any card games."

He thought for a moment. "Flip of a coin?"

At least that would be quick. She could be on her way home in less than a minute. Or she could be in even more trouble, depending upon the way the coin landed. "Just one flip?"

"How about two out of three?"

Just freaking great. Practically her whole life was about to be determined by the toss of a quarter. But she supposed the odds were better to go this route than just totally give up.

He patted the seat. "Better come in here where you can watch me, make sure I don't cheat."

Conniver.

"You'd better not cheat. Because that's just too low for words."

"I promise, I always play fair."

She didn't believe that bit of bullshit, but her hands were numb. She slipped and slid around the front end of his car, sat in the passenger seat. Ohhhh, the vehicle was toasty-warm inside, and smelled good, like the man who owned it. But she promptly reminded herself that this was not a date, but a serious bet they had going on. And losing would mean major problems for her and her brother.

"Ready?"

She nodded.

He held a quarter between his forefinger and thumb, twisting his wrist to show her both sides. "See? No trick coin."

"Okay. I got it. Just flip."

He placed the coin on his thumb. "Call it in the air. The ceiling's low, so I can't flip it high. You'll have to be quick."

Up went the coin and she blurted, "Heads!" as it landed on his palm. He flipped it over, onto the back of his hand.

He lifted the hand covering it. Her heart stopped.

"Heads it is. One point for you."

She inhaled. Exhaled. Whew! It was a small victory, but it put her one step closer to walking away from him, guilt free.

"Ready?" he asked.

She nodded again, deciding she'd stick with the same side for all three tosses. "Heads!" she called immediately after he flipped it the second time.

This time, when he uncovered the back of his hand, however, the coin was laying tails-up.

Shit. Now they were tied one-to-one.

Immediately she started questioning her strategy. Go with heads again? Or change to tails?

"Last one. Call it in the air." He flipped.

She called, "Tails!"

He caught the coin and flipped it onto the back of his hand. "Heads. I win."

Shit! No! "I meant to say heads. Can I have a do-over?"

"Nope. We had a deal. You lost. Consider yourself double-blackmailed." He dropped the quarter into her hand, put the car into reverse and pulled out of the parking spot. "Let's go home. I'm tired. And I have a feeling the next few days are going to be hell."

She dropped the coin into her purse, mumbling, "You can say that again."

Chapter 2

What an interesting turn of events.

Tonight, when he'd gone out in search of Elena—the supposed accomplice in a shady plan to get him fired— Kyler had expected to have a friendly chat with the scheming little office manager, gather whatever evidence he could, and then head to work on Monday armed to have her and Becker fired on the spot.

None of that had happened. They'd talked, but he'd quickly realized she was as much—if not more so—a victim as he.

He'd also discovered a couple of other things. First, for some reason this woman stirred a very strong protective instinct in him. And second, which he assumed was related to the first, he wasn't just a little attracted to her, like he had previously thought. He was wildly attracted to her.

He wasn't sure what it was about her. The huge, sad eyes, which made her look sweet and vulnerable. Or maybe that lovely heart-shaped face with that luscious mouth. Or perhaps it was her body—soft and feminine and delicate.

He'd been sporting a painful erection since he'd trapped her between his arms in her car, and their faces had been inches apart. Even now he was in pain. His cock was rock hard, his balls tight. The craziest images were zinging through his head—Elena lying over his lap, her rear end red from the spanking he was giving her.

Shit, he needed a cold shower.

He shifted in the seat. Just a few more blocks and they'd be home. He'd set her up in the guestroom, let her get some sleep. And then tomorrow they'd sit down for a serious talk about the whole blackmail thing.

And then...who knew?

There'd been more than one reason why he'd decided to bring the sexy little office manager back to his place for the weekend. The most obvious—this whole blackmail bullshit.

But also because of the chemistry. There was no doubt any more. He hadn't imagined the signs of arousal he'd read in Elena tonight. The way she'd looked at him. She was as attracted to him as he was to her.

Maybe this game of blackmail was exactly what she'd been looking for.

* * * * *

His house was freaking gorgeous.

Okay, so she supposed it shouldn't have surprised her. Not when the vice president drove a car that probably cost double her yearly salary—and she wasn't paid peanuts—and dressed like a bazillion dollars every day. Head to toe, he was always dressed to kill. Every scuff buffed out of his shoes. Fingernails neat and trimmed. Hair immaculate, but not overdone to the point where he looked fake or gay. Clothes fitting him so perfectly, every piece looked like it had been made just for him.

He was simply one well-dressed, well-groomed, well-built man. And his house belonged in the pages of some decorating magazine.

They stepped into a massive foyer with soaring ceilings. Much like the exterior, the house's interior was contemporary but not cold. Sleek and cool with hard lines and gleaming surfaces. Black tile floor with not a single piece of lint or a smudge to mar its mirror-like surface. A staircase with brushed silver-toned hand railings, winding up to a second story.

Beyond the foyer was a greatroom that opened to a state-of-the art kitchen, and living area boasting comfortable-looking but stylish furniture.

"Can I get you anything to eat or drink before we head up to bed?"

A little ripple of...something pleasant...worked through her body. It was the *we* associated with the word *bed* that did it to her. Her face was suddenly really warm. So were a few other parts of her anatomy.

"Maybe something to drink? Something cold?"

"Sure." He shrugged out of his jacket then helped her out of hers. Set them both on a nearby chair then reached for a glass from an open shelf.

She stared at his butt, partly because it was there and partly because it looked so good in those black pants. This guy did not have the typical guy flat-ass. His was rounded just enough to be sexy. She guessed the source of the shape was one hundred percent muscle. She'd spent enough time in a gym to know.

How she lusted after a guy with great glutes.

And shoulders. Of course, Kyler's were wide and thickly muscled. She could see the way the muscles bulged as he moved, even through the crisp white button-down shirt he wore.

He dispensed some ice into the glass then asked, "Any preference? Soft drink? Iced tea? Bottled water?"

Just for kicks, she blurted, "Perrier?" Not because she actually knew what was so special about that particular brand, but just because she hoped it made her sound a little refined. She was most definitely feeling a smidge outclassed. Not a feeling she was unaccustomed to, but for some reason, it was unusually uncomfortable tonight.

She didn't want to think why that might be.

"No problem." He opened the fridge, twisted open one of those recognizable bottles and poured some into the glass. "There you are."

"Thanks." Their fingers brushed as she took the glass from him, and a little buzz of energy licked up her arm. Their gazes met, and for a moment she wanted to forget all about the whole blackmailing thing and just pretend they were on a date, doing guy-and-girl kinds of things.

Tearing her gaze from his, she turned to admire the living room as she took her first sip of the French bottled water she'd never bothered to buy before. It was good, but not great. Did the job okay, which was really all she cared about at the moment. Her mouth was so dry she could barely speak. She swallowed several more mouthfuls. Yeah, not bad at all, but hardly worth the ridiculous price.

"How about a snack?" At the refrigerator again, he pulled some small plastic containers out and set them on the shiny black granite counter.

"I'm still pretty full from dinner." That was a lie. She'd barely touched her food. But she was too jittery to eat right now. Not to mention, she'd long ago made a rule against eating anything that could not be easily identified.

Orange pasty stuff. White creamy stuff. That was most definitely not identifiable. So, instead of digging in, she leaned back against the counter, sipped her water, and watched Kyler work.

"Would you like to sit?" He motioned to the row of bar stools lining the raised side of the kitchen island.

"Sure." She walked around the front of the island and sat, watched him collect a plate, knife, box of crackers.

The guy seemed to get better looking with every second that ticked by. How was that possible?

He sat beside her, and she was instantly aware of how close he was. The air between their bodies felt warmer than the rest of the room. And sort of zip-zappy, like little currents of electricity were jolting between their bodies.

He pulled out a cracker, smeared some of the orange

stuff on it and, smiling over his shoulder, offered it to her. "Are you sure you aren't hungry?"

She was, but her insides were kind of jumbled up, and she was a smidge afraid of putting something foreign—and potentially dangerous—into her stomach. There was no way she was going to tell him that though. So she just said, "I'm sure. Thanks anyway."

"Okay." He popped the cracker into his mouth, chewed. Washed it down with a sip of wine.

An uncomfortable silence hung between them, and despite the sensual awareness warming her skin and making her all tingly, a question hung from the tip of her tongue. A question that would totally put a dampener on the date-like vibe of the moment.

How would she ever sleep? In a strange house, with the stress of a job loss—and maybe jail, gah!—looming over her head.

She needed a little of that wine. Not a lot. She wasn't a big drinker, had the occasional glass on special nights, holidays, that kind of thing. She hadn't gotten loaded since college. Tempting as it was to do so tonight, there was no way she'd do something so idiotic.

"Mind if I upgrade to something a little harder?" She lifted her glass, motioning toward his.

"Sure. What can I get you?" He popped another loaded cracker into his mouth. A tiny smudge of orange clung to his upper lip, and she couldn't help staring at it.

"How about some of whatever you're drinking?"

"Coming right up." He got her a fresh wineglass, grabbed the bottle sitting on the counter next to the wine cooler, and sat back in his seat. He poured her a full glass then handed it to her. "There you go."

"Thanks." Her gaze still locked on that bit of orange on his lip, she took a cautious taste. Ooh, yum. She took several more swallows then pointed at her own mouth. "Um, you've got something there."

"Where?" He wiped the wrong spot, like people always

did. And she was forced to lean closer and actually touch his face with her finger. "There."

A big jolt of electricity charged up her arm, almost feeling as though she'd just touched a live wire. She froze, unable to pull her hand away, unable to move at all. He leaned closer, and she realized he was looking at her mouth.

Oh God, was he going to kiss her?

"I…uh…have always admired your shoes," she jabbered, so nervous she didn't even know what she was saying. Her brain was stuck, like an old fashioned record, playing the same thought over and over.

He's going to kiss me. He's going to kiss me. Ohmygod, ohmygod, ohmygod!

Then their mouths were touching. Just barely. And she quit breathing, which was not good. She closed her eyes, frozen in place, waiting, dizzy.

He cupped her face in his hands and gently brushed his mouth back and forth over hers. It was the softest, most sensual kiss she'd ever experienced.

"Oh God," she heard herself say.

He answered with a rumbling, sexy chuckle that made her warmer yet.

Her heart started banging hard against her breastbone and she took a little frantic gasp of air.

She felt as if she was melting inside, her bones softening, the rest of her turning into slick heat. A tingly warmth gathered between her legs.

"You want this, don't you?" he asked against her mouth.

She did, most definitely. In fact, crazy or not, she wanted a whole lot more than a teasing, sultry kiss. But all she could say was, "Ahhh…"

She slid her hands up the smooth material of his shirt until she felt the stiff collar. By the time she had her fingers wrapped around his silk tie, she was more than a little desperate for the kiss to deepen. Enough to take matters into her own hands. She climbed to her feet, so that she could wedge her body between his legs, and pressed against him. Her nipples were sensitive, hard little peaks, roughened against the lace cup of her bra.

And still, he kept that kiss soft and fleeting, the worst kind of torture. She looped her arms around his neck, angling her mouth, "You're so mean," she murmured.

"And you like that too, don't you."

She did. In a way. And in another, she most definitely did not. She pulled on his neck, trying to force him to possess her more fully with his mouth. But instead, he skimmed his lips over her cheekbone then kissed a tingly path from her ear to her collarbone.

He gently pulled her arms from his neck, pushing them down then forcing them behind her back. He used one fist as a handcuff, holding them together. With the other one, he supported the back of her neck.

Oh…she was going to need a whole lot more support than that, very soon. Goosebumps tickled the skin of her neck and back, her chest and stomach. Her bones were melting, her muscles twitching.

She could hardly believe this was happening. Kyler Pierce, the guy all the women in the office lusted after but no one got—including Nikki the office babe—was nibbling her neck right now. Hers!

So much for the theory that he was gay.

For the first time today, she was actually kind of glad she'd been blackmailed by Matt Becker. Look where it had led her. Into the arms of an absolute hunk. Gorgeous. Successful. Sexy.

"Time for bed," Kyler mumbled, tearing his lips from Elena's neck. Damn, but if he didn't put some distance between the sweet-tasting little lady and his hot self right now, he'd do something he'd seriously regret.

Business first. He had to deal with the Becker thing before he let himself explore the sizzling chemistry between them. It was only fair.

He jerked her against him one last time. Dammit, she fit against him so perfectly.

She looked bewildered when he finally released her. "Uh, okay." She caught the back of the stool, steadied herself.

He licked his lower lip, tasting her. Raked his fingers through his hair. His balls were heavy and tight, like lead. Her hair was mussed, her cheeks flushed, lips swollen, and he could still see those two beautiful, hard nipples poking through the fabric of her top. A woman ripe and ready for a good, long fuck.

But not tonight.

Wondering if a guy could die from blue balls, he downed the rest of his wine and led her up the stairs to the guest bedroom. After making sure she had everything she'd need for the night, he left, heading straight for the shower.

It was a poor substitute, but he'd have to settle for his hand and a bar of soap to relieve the pressure. But someday—maybe—he'd have the real thing. With the first woman who'd intrigued him in a long, long time.

* * * * *

Elena didn't sleep. It wasn't because she was physically uncomfortable. How could she be in this bed? The mattress was like a freaking cloud, it was so soft. And the bedroom was absolutely beautiful.

But the constant stream of thoughts running through her mind just wouldn't stop. She lay there all night, trying to figure out what Kyler was thinking, how she'd keep her job, why he'd stopped kissing her when it was so obvious she'd wanted things to go much, much farther.

She could taste him on her lips for hours afterward, smell his skin on her fingers. She'd always thought he was an attractive man. But now that she'd been this close, now that he'd looked at her like that—like he wanted her so bad it hurt—she found him absolutely irresistible.

It was hard to remember that he might end up causing her to lose her job and the insurance she so desperately needed. She didn't want to think about that right now. Not when she felt such an overwhelming connection with him. It was at least ten times more powerful than any she'd felt for a guy before.

Their timing just plain sucked.

Then again, she wondered, would she have ever realized how she felt about Kyler—or how he felt about her—if Matt hadn't shoved them both into this corner?

By sunrise, she was exhausted and ten times more confused than she'd been the night before. She ached to tell Kyler everything, including what Matt was holding over her head, and why she was so desperate to hold onto her job. But there were some secrets she simply couldn't tell anyone, especially people from work.

Only Ashley knew, and that was because they'd been friends for so long.

She showered and donned the fluffy white robe Kyler had given her last night. There was a knock at the door, just as she'd exited the attached bathroom. A towel wrapped around her long hair, she padded barefoot across the world's softest carpet to open the door.

Kyler.

Her heart did a weird little hop in her chest. "Hi."

"Good morning." His gaze swept down her body then back up. "Do you need a little longer?"

"Just a few minutes. Sorry, I didn't realize we were on a schedule. I never sleep in this late."

"It's okay." He smiled and her heart did another lurch in her chest. It was the oddest sensation. Strange and yet kind of good too. "Whenever you're ready, come on down for breakfast."

"Will do. Thanks." She wanted to say more, but she didn't. She just waited for him to turn away and then shut the door.

Anxious to get downstairs, she rushed to dress,

throwing on yesterday's clothes—sans the used underwear—and hurried downstairs. She found him in the kitchen, looking all domestic, stirring something in a huge frying pan on the stove.

Whatever it was, it smelled amazing.

Talk about amazing, he was wearing a pair of sweats and a snug tank top that provided her very first view of bare arms and shoulders.

Droooool!

"What are you cooking there?" she asked, her gaze focused on his narrow waist. She could imagine herself smoothing her hands around his sides, and tucking herself against his back. Instead, she stopped at the raised counter and slipped into a bar stool.

"It's my own creation. Egg beaters, vegi sausage, and cheese, onions and peppers. Would you like to try some? Or can I make you something else?"

Elena's mouth was watering, and she realized just how starving she was. It seemed her jittery nerves weren't going to stand in the way of eating this morning. "If that concoction tastes as great as it smells, you may need to make another batch. I might eat it all."

He chuckled. What a great sound it was. She could listen to him do that for hours.

He served up two plates, poured a couple of glasses of orange juice, set the newspaper between their plates and joined her at the bar. Such a gentleman, he didn't take a bite until she did.

Was this guy for real?

She stared at the Homes section of the paper as she ate, forced herself to pretend he wasn't there, just to get something solid in her stomach. She had a feeling she was going to need it.

Kyler seemed to respect her need for a little bit of quiet. He sat silent beside her, eating, reading the financial section. Just as she took her last bite, he folded the paper and cleared his throat. "Now that we're both rested—and full—I want to talk to you about Becker."

She pushed her empty plate forward and set her elbows on the hard countertop. She flattened her hands on the cool surface. "Yeah."

If only she were there for a different reason, like on a date. This sucked.

"I want to ask you again to tell me what Becker's holding over your head."

Staring at the black stone, the flecks of brown and gold, she shook her head. "It doesn't matter." A cordless phone sat within reach. She picked it up, weighed it in her hand, flipped it over and stared at the glowing keypad.

She heard him sigh heavily.

He gently took the phone from her and set it on the counter. "I'm trying to find a way to handle this situation so that neither of us gets hurt in the process. But if you don't tell me, I can't guarantee to do that."

How she wished he could handle Becker without her getting in the middle.

She glanced up at him, noticed how serious his expression was. How focused he seemed to be. "That's nice of you, but like I said last night, there's nothing you can do. I'm screwed."

He pushed his fingers through his hair. "I've been thinking about this all night."

"Me too."

Their gazes met, and she swore sparks were flying through the air.

Insanity. To be reacting this way when she was facing such a totally devastating threat to everything she cared about. It took her a few seconds to summon the strength to untangle her gaze from his, but she did. Went back to staring down at the countertop. And her thoughts took a swerve back in the right direction—toward the important stuff.

If only there was a simple answer. But if life had taught her anything, it had taught her that simple answers usually led to lots of complications in the future.

There was a loooong stretch of uncomfortable silence. Finally, Kyler said, "Okay, this is the deal. You're going to…" He sighed. "Dammit."

She looked at him. He was obviously struggling with this, and for that she felt sorry for him. Here he was, trying to deal with an asshole, while doing his best to keep her out of things. He was a nice guy. A nice guy who didn't deserve the shit he'd been dished.

Life was so unfair sometimes.

She'd lost the bet. He'd won. Fairly and squarely. But that didn't stop her from wanting him to tell her to just leave, go to work, do what she'd planned, and he'd deal with the fallout when the time came.

The insane part of her didn't want to go anywhere.

He sighed for the bazillionth time. "You're going to stay here, and I'm going to handle whatever happens."

She wanted to believe he could do just that—take care of everything. Make all her problems go away. Just like she wanted to believe he wouldn't totally freak if she told him exactly what dirt Becker had on her.

Maybe he'd believe it was a lie? Made up?

No, probably not.

She should just come clean. After all, he was bound to learn the truth soon enough. All the board members and vice presidents would know by lunchtime Monday. Wouldn't it be better to tell him now? Prepare him?

Oh God, she felt sick. She swiveled the stool, facing him. Took several deep breaths. Then a few more. "Okay. I'll tell you."

"Okay. Good." He didn't smile. He just sat there, looking at her expectantly, patiently waiting for her to untie the knot from her tongue.

God, this was hard. Where to start? She couldn't look at him as she spoke. "This goes back a few years. My parents died. It was one of those freakish things that never should've happened but did."

"I'm sorry."

She believed him. "Thanks." Still not sure she could do this, actually confess to a crime that might land her in jail for years, she took a few more deep breaths. "This is hard to talk about. I haven't told anyone, since what I did was against the law. But, well... I didn't have any choice. My brother and I were sent to live with an older cousin and well...she...something happened to her too...and I knew my brother would end up getting sent—"

The phone rang, interrupting the explanation she was trying so hard to get out. She was both glad and annoyed.

Kyler glanced at the caller ID screen on the phone's back. "Shit. I need to take this. Hang on."

He hit the button. "Hey. Give me a second," he said to the caller. To Elena, he said, "I'll be back in a minute." Then he left the room.

Oh. My. God. What am I thinking?

She had just about told Kyler her darkest secret, a man she was not only really attracted to but also a vice president at her work. Had she lost her mind? She wasn't telling him another word. She'd nearly made one of the biggest mistakes of her life.

Saved by the phone.

She needed to get out of there, before she did something she'd really regret.

She hurried upstairs to her room, found her purse, dug out her cell phone, and flipped it open. Two bars. She hoped she had enough battery power to talk her prying best friend into driving over here to pick her up. Quickly, she scrolled down to Ashley's phone number and hit send.

But just as Ashley answered, there was a loud knock at the door, and then it swung open and Kyler barged into the room, looking like a bull seeing red.

Shit. What now?

She snapped her phone shut and dropped it into her purse.

"Who're you calling? Becker?" He snatched her purse

out of her hands, and she shrieked, caught completely off guard, petrified. He threw it out into the hall and slammed the door, blocking the exit with his bulk. "We need to talk."

She just glared at him. Thank God she hadn't gone any further with him last night. Or told him anything this morning. He was acting like a total jerk all of a sudden.

God, she was such a total idiot!

He crossed his arms over his chest and stared right back at her. "I just had an interesting conversation about you."

Shit, maybe someone besides Matt knew her secret. But how?

"I was such an idiot. I didn't want to believe it at first. But then, all the evidence was pretty damning." He paused for a moment then started walking a wide circle around her. "You're quite the package. Hot body. Gorgeous face. It makes sense." He stopped directly in front of her, pinched her chin between his forefinger and thumb, lifting it until she made eye contact with him. "Too bad every word that comes out of your mouth is a lie. You almost had me." He actually snarled that last sentence.

"A lie? I—uh…" She had no idea what he was talking about. But that didn't stop her from feeling really crappy.

He released her chin and took a single step back from her. "Anyway, your little secret's out."

It was? Oh God! Now what? "I tried to explain, earlier—"

"Just don't," he interrupted. "I've heard all I can stomach right now. It's making me sick. I thought you were different, that you'd just found yourself dragged into someone else's shit…but I know better now." His eyes narrowed to cold, piercing slits. "I'll have the situation wrapped up by Monday afternoon…"

Did that mean she could go home? Right now, that sounded really, really good. She'd need to pull her brother out of the hospital if she could. Pack some things.

"But I'm holding you to your word. I know I can't trust you now. I let you loose, and you and Becker will have my career flushed down the toilet by the end of the day, weekend or not. No, since you lost the bet, you're going to pay the price." She could literally feel the heat of his enraged glare on her skin. It burned like a branding iron. "You're here with me. My slave. For the next three days. You won't speak until I tell you to. Eat. Nothing. I. Own. You. If you try to leave, I'll have you arrested."

Oh, this was just great. It was obvious Kyler was seriously pissed. Whether he knew that secret, or something else—whatever that might be—he had decided he was going to make her pay.

Revenge was one dish she'd never enjoyed, not serving…and especially not swallowing.

Chapter 3

Kyler had never felt so out of control of his emotions before. He was so enraged right now he wanted to pound something to dust.

He needed to get out of there now, before he did something he'd regret. Without speaking another word, he left the room, slamming the door behind him. He went down to his gym, cranked on the heavy metal music, and worked off his anger with a hard run on the treadmill and supersets for his chest and shoulders. By the time he was done, he was sweaty, sore and a little bit calmer.

Maybe he should send the scheming bitch home and deal with this situation a different way. For some reason, she pushed his buttons, made him feel things he didn't want to.

Dammit, he'd actually thought he knew her. What a fucking fool he'd been.

The information had come from the one person he knew he could trust. It couldn't be a lie. Stacy had no reason to make things up, especially something like this. She'd been his friend for years, long before he'd brought her onboard at work. They'd never been lovers. She couldn't be jealous in that respect, and she'd worked herself up in the company, to a position higher than Elena's. Again, no reason for her to be jealous there either.

It had to be true—Elena wasn't being manipulated into this thing with Becker like he'd thought. Elena was Becker's lover, and was expecting a promotion once Becker, the obvious choice for VP of sales, received his promotion.

Such bullshit, all of it.

He wanted to make both of them pay, but for some reason, more of his anger was directed at Elena. No doubt because she'd stung his pride. He thought he was a good judge of character. Becker, he'd always suspected was a shit. But Elena…she was quite the little actress.

Now, if only he could tell his dick she wasn't worth shit.

His cock still got hard when he saw her. His blood warmed. How could he be so fucking attracted to a woman he detested?

Yes, he should probably send her home and let his old man's private detective do his job. But he knew Becker would find a way to get his fake proof to the brass before the end of the weekend, and who knew whether the detective Kyler had just called would get anything to counter it in time? Nope, dammit, Elena couldn't leave. Not until his detective had something or she'd told him where the fake documents were. If he was going to save his ass, he needed something concrete to take to the board. He had to strike before Becker.

There was no way in hell those two scheming fucks were going to screw up his life. He knew exactly how to make Elena talk. He'd use the same tool against her as she'd used against him.

Sex.

* * * * *

Elena made it as far as Kyler's front door but she didn't have the guts to walk out. At this point, she had no idea what he knew and what he didn't. She also had no inkling of what proof he might have against her or whether he'd meant it when he'd said he'd have her arrested if she left. At the moment, she supposed the devil she knew was a better risk than the demon she didn't.

She went back up to her room and shut the door, flopped on the bed, closed her eyes and tried to think her way through this mess. Things were going from bad to worse somehow. Was it a coincidence?

Think, Elena, think.

This wasn't the first time she'd had to think her way out of an impossible corner. Many years ago, she'd found herself with her back up against a wall, forced to choose between two impossible options.

That decision had impacted so many things, including this whole crap with Matt and Kyler. And still, she knew if she'd been given a second chance, she wouldn't have been able to make any other choice.

It had been for her brother.

Worry for him made her insides hurt. When she didn't show up today, he'd be upset. That might not be a big deal for most kids. But for Eddy, a small disappointment could cause major problems. He was so fragile. Delicate.

She glanced at the clock. Kyler had been gone for over an hour. What kind of hell could he be planning for her? She didn't want to imagine.

If only he'd tell her what he'd learned, let her try to explain. Or not. Depending upon what it was, she supposed an explanation might make things worse.

The door swung open and he walked into the room. His skin was glistening with sweat, his face flushed, and the ends of his hair were spiked, wet.

"Glad to see you didn't leave." His words were clipped, his voice frigid.

"I wanted to," she confessed, sensing he needed to see a little honesty from her. Whatever had made him so upset, she guessed, had to be somehow directly tied to him, his pride. It was his emotional reaction that made her think so. The "I was such a fool" statement.

He nodded.

"Will you tell me why you're so angry?"

He looked away.

Her nerves crawling, she watched his throat work as he swallowed. Nothing.

"You won't give me a chance to explain?"

"I don't know if I can believe anything you say."

Where did that leave her? This man, whose eyes were cold as icicles, held her job in the palm of his hand. Her job, the medical insurance that paid for her brother's treatment. Her entire future. She couldn't get any more desperate than that. "What will it take to prove to you that I can be believed? I stayed. Right? You didn't lock me in. You won the bet, and I didn't leave, even though I wanted to."

"Yeah, well, that could also be because you didn't want your pretty little ass hauled to jail."

"I'm not sure that would be any worse," she said, frankly. "I mean, you're throwing these threats around, acting one way one second, totally different the next. It's confusing. Scary."

Her eyes were burning, darn it. Her nose. *Don't cry. He'll think you're trying to manipulate him.*

She blinked several times.

His eyes narrowed, his gaze becoming even chillier. Sub-arctic. "There you go with the waterworks again. I see now. Whenever you get backed into a corner, you throw the switch, the tears start to flow, and you're off the hook." He crowded her, grabbed her chin, and glared into her eyes. "It doesn't work with me anymore. I know the truth about you now. I know you're fucking Matt Becker, and you're itching for a promotion—from the whore of a sales manager to the whore of a vice president."

She felt sick. Was that really what he believed? "No, I'm not sleeping with Matt. You're wrong."

"Funny." He dragged his thumb over her lower lip. He

walked her backward, until her back hit the wall. He thrust his arms forward, caging her head between them. "But if you'd just come to me, I'd have fucked you. You could've had your vice president. In fact..." He dropped his head and kissed her roughly. His tongue thrust into her mouth, in complete domination.

Instantly, her body was on fire. Yes, this was what she'd wanted last night. Pulses of liquid heat pounded down her torso to the juncture of her thighs. Despite her confusion, she kissed him back, letting the searing heat of the kiss burn away everything.

Insanity! This was complete craziness. But she couldn't help reacting to his kisses. She'd been waiting, ready. She moaned, stroking his tongue with hers. Exploring the sweet depth of his mouth.

He bent his elbows, crushing his hard body against hers. Wedged a knee between her trembling thighs.

Crazy!

She moaned, rocking her hips back and forth, desperate to rub away the ache building between her legs.

He suckled her tongue and she slid her hands up his stomach, whimpering.

Her head was swimming. Her body melting. Her brain short-circuiting. She was falling, sliding down the wall, unable to remain standing another second. Her pussy rested on his knee, a support. Oh, the sensation. The glory of that hard leg against her soft, swollen tissues.

Insanity!

He caught her up into his arms and carried her to the bed, laid her on it and then climbed over her. More of those amazing nuclear-reactor-hot kisses. He gave her more, and she accepted him, eagerly. His hands started at the sides of her face but—much to her joy—didn't remain there for long. Down her neck they traveled, to her shoulders, lower. He cupped her breasts and she arched her back, pushing her breasts into his hands.

I need to stop this. Right now. Stop. Now.

She tried to turn her head, but he caught her face in his hands again, kissing her until she couldn't move, didn't want to move. Wanted nothing less than his hands on her naked body, his cock buried deep inside her wet pussy.

She'd be sorry for this later, no doubt about it. But for the first time in years, she just wanted to forget about shoulds and should-nots and let go, follow her impulses instead of her head.

When Kyler lifted his weight off her body, she slid her hands inside his shirt. Soft skin over flexing, shifting concrete. She found a hard little nipple, teased it with her index finger, and received a low groan as a reward.

He broke the kiss and gazed down at her through heavy-lidded eyes full of raw lust. They weren't cold anymore, nope. Instead of the arctic blue of a frozen sea they were the steamy blue of a gas flame.

She felt her face warming, her chest. His tongue darted out, slicking his full lower lip, and she stared, transfixed.

This man had the world's most stunning features. Eyes that instantly made a girl melt. Sharp cheekbones that cast deep shadows on his face. A masculine jaw stubbled with the hint of a beard. And that mouth, oh that mouth. He tasted better than anything.

She ached for another kiss, another touch—soft and gentle or hard and possessive. Either way, both ways. Didn't matter.

"Goddamnit," he muttered. "What the fuck are we doing?"

"I—I don't know." She reached up inside his shirt again, found that nipple, flicked her fingertip over the pebbled peak. His lips parted and his gaze heated up another hundred degrees or so. "But I want you to know, it's not because you're vice president. I just want you."

He squeezed her head between his hands, his gaze sharp as razors. "You say the right things...What the hell do I believe?"

She held his penetrating gaze, knowing if she glanced

away, she'd lose any chance of gaining his trust. "Believe your heart, Kyler."

He crushed her body under his and kissed her to oblivion.

Follow his heart. Yeah, that's what she said. That's what they all said—women who were looking to manipulate him. Just like his ex-fiancée. Some women knew how to work a man, knew how to use his weaknesses to get what they wanted. He'd made it really easy for Elena too.

Dammit, looks were so fucking deceiving. And here he thought he'd learned. He'd lived by the trust-none-of-them rule for over two years and things had been going so great.

Follow his heart. Hah.

I know what you're up to, you little schemer.

"Kyler? What's wrong?"

But dammit, he was so fucking hard right now. He could barely see straight. He'd bet she was wet, her slick passage ready for him. Why should he stop himself? If Elena was willing to give it up, why should he deny himself? He could fuck her, and then he'd leave her sit in this room until Tuesday. If that was what she wanted to do to herself—let men fuck her to get ahead—then that was what she'd get from him.

Still straddling Elena, on his knees, he yanked his shirt off then rolled off the bed and pulled off his pants and underwear. She was still wearing that clingy knit top and those black pants. He wanted to see her fully unclothed but lacked the patience. Instead, after she unbuttoned and unzipped the fly, he just yanked her slacks down her smooth, slender legs and tossed them on the floor. No underpants. Even better.

"Kyler!"

He didn't meet her gaze as he wedged his hips between her legs. Rolled on a rubber. He didn't kiss her again, just fingered her slick heat, prepared to drive his cock deep inside her. He replaced his fingers with the tip of his rod.

She shoved at his chest. "Kyler. Stop! Why are you acting like this?"

Dammit.

Fuck.

What the hell was he doing?

He couldn't go through with this. That would make him no better than that piece of shit, Becker. Disgusted with himself, with Becker, and with Elena, he jerked upright and tugged off the rubber.

"You bastard." She had no right to look that way at him now, like he was a heartless beast. She'd begged him, not the other way around.

"What's wrong?" he echoed. "Wasn't this what you expected?"

She didn't speak, just dragged her legs back together and pulled the coverlet over herself.

"I guess that's a no." He tossed the rubber in the trashcan then grabbed his pants and shirt. He stepped into his sweats, didn't bother with the underwear or the tank. He sat on the edge of the bed.

Elena's eyes were frigid, her gaze distant, her expression completely blank. For about three seconds, he was actually sorry for treating her like the whore she was determined to be. Then she swung her little fist at him, her target, his nose.

He dodged the blow and pushed to his feet. "A little hint. If you're going to use sex to get what you want, you've got to learn to look at it like a pro. It's just a fuck. A cock and a pussy."

He left, shutting the door behind him, closing himself off from Elena...and the guilt eating at his gut.

* * * * *

Elena wasn't sure what was worse—the shame she felt after that...whatever it was. The knowledge that she was fucked in an altogether different way. Or the fact that she was totally devastated by Kyler's absolutely frigid treatment.

He'd treated her like she was a worthless piece of crap. Why? He'd said she was using sex to get what she wanted. That was the farthest thing from the truth.

Maybe it was simply impossible for the two of them to communicate. It seemed he was always misreading her, mistrusting her, misunderstanding her. What had set him off this time?

Oh, who cared? She didn't need this shit. She just needed to go home, do some packing, and try to figure out how she'd start over again.

She was exhausted already. She inched open the door, finding her purse out in the hallway, empty, the contents strewn all over the floor. Eyes blurry with tears, she gathered her cosmetics, wallet, receipts and hair brush, stuffed them back in her purse. Then she hurried down the hall, making a beeline for the staircase. As she skipped down the steps, she kept looking, listening for Kyler, expecting him to pop out from somewhere and make good on his threat. She made it as far as the foot of the staircase before she stopped.

It sure would be nice if she could find her car keys. Was it worth a shot? She heard a sound from the general direction of the greatroom. Oh, hell, she was already eyeball deep in trouble. What worse could happen? She rushed back upstairs. There were seven doors, all closed. One of them, she knew, led to her room.

She started at the one closest to the stairs. Opened it. Peeked inside. Gasped. Shut it.

Not the room she was looking for, nope.

She opened the door again. Wow. She'd never seen a room like this before, well, not in person. A bondage room. Dungeon.

She'd always wondered what it would be like playing in a room like this. Playing. What a word.

The truth was, she'd been curious about BDSM for quite some time. She'd done a lot of reading, soul searching. She'd even mentioned it to Ashley.

Maybe Ashley was right, her fascination with domination and submission was because she'd been forced to grow up too early, had the weight of her younger brother's care dumped on her slender shoulders before she'd been truly ready to handle it. She didn't know. All she knew was that this world, of submission and trust and control, was calling to her. She sensed it would fill a deep need.

If only she'd been able to find the right man to explore these things with. Ironic, that Kyler was into this stuff. After today, he was the last man she'd trust with her vulnerabilities.

She glanced over her shoulder, checking the hall before moving deeper into the room. Touching the furniture would make it more real, more possible. She headed for the sex swing first. How'd the thing work? It was little more than a collection of metal poles and straps, now that she was closer. The seat was just a narrow band. Same with the back.

She headed for another piece, a pair of benches angling away from each other, a wooden cross was affixed to the wall at the point where they met. She sat on the benches, legs spread so that a thigh rested on each one, supporting her weight. Nothing sat directly beneath her bottom. She closed her eyes, indulging in a quick fantasy. If she was naked and with a dark and mysterious Dom…

The door swung open and, desperate to not be caught sitting on Kyler's bondage gear with her legs spread—especially after his last comment—she flopped forward, landing on her hands and knees.

Of course he'd found her here. It was just her luck.

"Now that's an interesting position," he said from the doorway. His voice was sharp, his gaze piercing, smoldering.

Oh God, she was mortified.

Trying to save face, she scooped up her purse and

scrambled to her feet. She wanted to give him some excuse for being in this room, but what could she possibly say that wouldn't make her look even worse? Already, he believed she was a whore, the kind of woman who fucked her way into a promotion. Nothing she'd said had convinced him otherwise. In fact, it seemed the last words she'd spoken had made things a lot worse.

So, rather than offer him up some more ammunition to use against her, she jerked her gaze from his and hurried past him, back to her room. Once inside, she collapsed on the bed.

What now?

She really, really wanted to find her keys before she headed out. Was it practical for her to leave without them? Never mind her car, her house was locked too. She'd have to break in to get inside.

She dug in her purse for her phone, flipped it open. Down to one bar now. Shoot! Did it have enough juice to call Ashley? Maybe she shouldn't use up the last few nanoseconds of her cell's battery life now, when she might be able to use a landline to call instead.

The cordless phone had been downstairs, in the kitchen. She wondered if Kyler had another phone upstairs. Most people had more than one phone jack, especially in a house this size.

She checked her room, found no phone. She listened at the door. It sounded like Kyler had gone back downstairs. Good. She'd go hunting again. Most people had a phone in the master bedroom.

She inched open the door, peered up and down the hall. No Kyler. Good. She tiptoed down the hall to the next door, opened it. Another bedroom. But it looked like another guest room.

What did one person need with a bazillion bedrooms, anyway? This house was ridiculously big for a single guy. He practically had enough beds to sleep in a different one each night.

She closed that door and headed to the next one. Another guest bedroom. Then a bathroom. Finally, at the end of the hall, she found the master bedroom. And oh, what a master bedroom it was.

The guestrooms were all very nice. Kyler's room made them look like rooms at a cheapskate motel. It was decorated nothing like the rest of the house. Instead of the contemporary style of the main living areas and guest bedrooms, it was much more elegant, sophisticated, yet traditional. A bed the size of a football field sat in the center of one wall, framed by floor-to-ceiling windows draped in gorgeous curtains. Three walls were painted a soft silvery-blue. The fourth, the one with the bed and windows, was a deep, cool brown, with the exception of directly behind the headboard. That section of wall boasted three large white panels, framed in ornate trim. The bed itself was a masterpiece. The black headboard had a sexy, slightly French-ish, curved shape and was hand-painted with swirling ivy and flowers. In another room, it might've looked feminine, but not in this one.

A noise downstairs reminded her of why she'd better hurry. She ran across the thickly carpeted floor to the first of two nightstands situated on either side of the bed. She checked the surface for a phone then ran around the bed and checked the other one.

No phone?

She did a quick three-sixty then headed for what she hoped might be a walk-in closet on the other side of the room. Nope. Bathroom. And no laundry basket. She tried the door next to it. Score!

She stepped into one of those closet rooms, the kind that had cedar walls and fancy built-in furniture with shoe racks and drawers. On one shelf, she found a basket, and her keys. No phone.

Well, one out of two wasn't bad. She could still use her cell, call Ashley, schedule a time for them to meet, and then head back to the restaurant to get her car.

On the way, she'd tell Ashley everything. No sense keeping it from her anymore. Ashley might be tempted to do something foolish to set things right, but now that Elena had pretty much accepted the fact that her job was history, there wasn't much damage an enraged out-of-control best friend could do.

She jammed her keys in her pocket and hurried down the hall, back to her room. She called Ashley, told her she desperately needed her help, told her the address—thank God Kyler had left a pile of mail in his closet. They planned on meeting in exactly one hour.

Elena didn't want Kyler to know she'd left, at least not right away. She told Ashley she'd meet her down the street, and warned her not to come to the house no matter what. Her phone chirped a warning just as they were wrapping up the brief conversation, and died just before she ended the conversation.

She stuffed her useless phone in her purse and rushed back down the stairs. She made it as far as the front door when Kyler came sauntering from a room just to the left of the door.

He looked her up and down. "Where are you going?"

She thought about lying. Then she thought about telling the truth. It was too late for the lies to do any good anymore. "I'm leaving. But don't worry, I won't bother going to work on Monday." She brushed past him, her gaze locked on the door's handle.

He caught her shoulders and jerked her around. "No, no. We had a deal."

He was not going to hold her to that stupid bet, was he? This whole blackmail thing was so over with. It wasn't a game anymore, and she wasn't deluding herself either. She wasn't his guest. They weren't on a date. And he didn't give a rat's ass about her.

Her heart was banging against her breastbone so hard it hurt. And she could literally see her hands shaking. "I think we both now the game's over." She spun back around, wrapped her fingers around the handle. "You win."

Once again, she was hauled back around. She growled as she tried to fight free of Kyler's iron-handed grip.

"You're not leaving." He dragged her toward the room he'd just exited, an office with an enormous desk, bookcases, couch, a pair of chairs and a sleek fireplace.

"Holding me here against my will is false imprisonment."

"So, are you going to the police?" He rough-handed her toward the couch. "Sit down." His face was the shade of a tomato as he glared down at her.

God, this dominating, controlling jerk thing was pissing her off. She crossed her arms and stared straight ahead, at the empty fireplace. "I'd rather stand, thank you. Actually, I'd rather leave but you're being a bastard."

"Fine. Stand then." He rounded the desk and eased into the chair behind it. "I'm going to ask you one simple question, and I expect you to answer it truthfully."

"Yeah, so, what's in it for me?"

"That depends," he said, coolly, resting his elbows on his desk. "I think you've got a whole lot more at stake than I do. Are you a gambler?"

At least five seconds ticked past, each one measured by the grandfather clock standing in the room's corner. "Fine, what's the question?"

"I just want to know one thing…who the hell are you? I have a picture of Elena Caine, and you're not her."

Chapter 4

Well, fuck. The cat was out of the bag now. How had he discovered her lie? And more importantly, she wondered how many other people knew.

Petrified, she dropped onto her butt on the couch and searched his face. Was he ready to call the police? She wished he was genuinely interested in knowing the answer to the question he'd asked—for more personal reasons. Wished he was back to being the concerned guy she'd met the first night. But that guy was long gone.

"I tried to tell you earlier," she confessed. "In the kitchen. Remember when I told you about the cousin my brother and I had been sent to live with?"

His brows furrowed, he nodded, steepled his fingers under his chin. "Yeah."

"Well, Elena Caine is—was—her name. How'd you find out?"

"My father has a private detective on the payroll."

"Your father needs a private detective on his payroll?"

"Long story. We don't have much time. I'd rather hear yours." His voice had softened a little, which was a surprise. She'd pretty much expected him to keep playing the heartless bastard he'd become since this morning.

"Mine's pretty long too, but I can give you the abbreviated version. I was born Amy Harris. Our cousin, Elena Caine, died shortly after my brother and I had been sent to live with her—and no, I did not kill her. And well…my best friend got rid of her body somewhere—I didn't tell her to—and I took over Elena Caine's identity."

He looked bewildered. She could understand his reaction. "Why would you do that?"

She stared blindly at the floor, unable to meet his gaze. "Seems pretty crazy, doesn't it? Right out of a movie script or crime television show. In fact, my friend got the idea from a TV program and convinced me it was the only way. I did it for one reason—my brother." She glanced up, afraid of what she'd see.

He encouraged her to continue with a nod. His expression was totally blank, devoid of all emotion. She had no clue what he was feeling.

"Eddy's…sick. He has been in and out of the hospital for much of his life. The only constant in his life has been me. I was afraid that if he were put into foster care he'd either be abused, misunderstood, neglected or die."

"What's wrong with him?"

"He's severely bipolar. But at the time of my cousin's death, we still didn't have a diagnosis. I was pretty much taking care of him around the clock. Later, I was given legal power of attorney, or rather Elena Caine was. I was forever trapped in my lie. There was no going back. And so I've carried around this secret for years. Until Matt found out somehow. He threatened to have me fired. Without insurance, my brother's treatment will stop."

"Maybe Becker stumbled upon the same photograph my father's detective found." Kyler's gaze dropped to his desk. His expression turned grim. He leaned back in his chair. Finally, he lifted his eyes. "Why didn't you tell me?"

"Because what I did is against the law, and frankly I didn't feel I could trust you. I don't just go to jail if my lie is discovered. I could live with that. It's what it would do to my brother…"

He bit his lower lip. "Yeah."

The most agonizing silence followed. She felt sick to her stomach, wondering, waiting. What would Kyler do with the truth?

He finally lifted his head and stood. She watched him walk across the room, stop in front of her. He scrubbed his face with his hands, then shoved his hands into his pocket. "Your car's outside. I had it towed here. Go home, Elena. I'll figure this out on my own."

* * * * *

Kyler hit the button, ending the call. Sure enough, at least some of Elena's story had been confirmed. Tom and Sue Harris had tragically died in a car accident, leaving their two children parentless. In addition, Edward—Eddy—Harris was a patient at the Longfellow Center in downtown Ann Arbor.

Elena had told him the truth, at least about those things.

Before he ended the call with the detective, he gave him one more assignment, "Check out Stacy Russell for me. Dig deep. Either she's dirty or she's being fed some shitty information from somewhere. I want to know which one it is."

* * * * *

Elena must have sat in her car for at least an hour, staring at Kyler's house. He'd given her her walking papers, told her she could leave. He'd take care of everything.

She should be home now, preparing. Checking in on her brother. And looking to see how much cash she had in her stash, getting ready to pack up and leave town in a hurry.

But she wasn't. She couldn't. Why?

First, because she wanted to know who had told Kyler she was sleeping with Matt Becker. That was so far from the truth. Just the thought of that man touching her made her gag.

As she sat there, trying to work up the nerve to leave, a million thoughts kept running through her head. Should she go to work on Monday and plant the evidence? Or should she just pack up and leave town? What exactly was Kyler thinking?

Finally, she decided to go back up to the house and ask him. There were too many things hanging in the air for her to know how to plan. She cut off her car's engine and hurried back up to the front door. Rang the bell. And waited.

Kyler looked so shocked to see her, she swore she could've knocked him over with a feather.

"I can't leave yet," she explained, coolly.

"I'm…surprised. Ummm, come in." He raked his fingers through his hair again as he stepped aside to let her in. "I've been thinking this past hour. And, well, earlier. When you…I had no right… Shit, I'm sorry. Not that I'm making an excuse, because there are none. No matter what, I have no right to treat you the way I did. But I'd heard one thing from you and something different from another person, and I was having one hell of a time knowing who to believe."

She could understand that. She nodded. "Who told you I was sleeping with Matt?"

"It doesn't matter who said what or who you're sleeping with. That's none of my business."

Wasn't his business? That was true, but she still felt like he'd punched her in the gut when he said it.

His gaze dropped to the floor. He shook his head. "I'm so fucked in the head." When he finally lifted his head again, his jaw was set. His expression was so dark, she didn't know what to think. Suddenly, he turned around and headed toward his office.

She stood in the foyer for a few minutes, not sure whether she should follow him or just forget it and head back out to her car. Finally, she decided to try to get the answers she'd come back for. She stopped at his office door and, leaning on the doorframe, peered in. "What are you going to do about Matt blackmailing me? I just need to know, so I can make plans."

He was sitting at his desk, his face buried in his hands. "I'm still trying to figure that out."

"Maybe I should just go away. Leave town. Start over somewhere."

He tipped his head up, looking at her. "Where will you go? What will you do?"

She shrugged. "I don't know yet. But I might not have a choice. Once Matt takes the proof he has about my cousin, I'll be fired. I wouldn't put it past him to take the information to the police too, like he threatened. He'd do that."

Silence.

"Not if I give him what he wants first."

"What do you mean?" She followed Kyler with her eyes as he stood, ran his hands down the front of his creased trousers.

"I could quit. It's a fucking shame. I didn't want to leave my job. It's the first thing I've accomplished without my father's help, and it's taken me over ten years to get where I am. But keeping my pride isn't worth the price you'd have to pay."

Did she just hear right? Kyler was willing to give up his job—the one that clearly meant more than she had ever guessed—for her?

She sat there, stunned, as he called Matt and told him he'd won, the VP position was as good as his, but only if he brought the evidence he had against her…all of it…to his house by six o'clock tonight.

No one had ever done anything that selfless for her. "Thank you," she said. It seemed so inadequate but she didn't know what else to say. She didn't have the means to pay him back.

He nodded, toyed with the cordless phone. "I want to

make another phone call. But I won't, if you tell me not to."

"Who're you going to call?"

"My father. I haven't asked him for any help in years, but I'd like to see what we can do for you. To keep something like this from coming up again."

Kyler had already gone above and beyond, no doubt trying to make up for his earlier mistreatment. Life had taught her that there was a price to pay for any favors done for her, at least favors that weren't owed. She never liked to owe anyone.

She shook her head. "I don't know about that. I'd rather you didn't."

"Okay."

She was relieved when he didn't push it, try to change her mind. She actually felt the air moving in and out of her lungs freely again. How long had she been holding her breath?

He walked to her, stopped within reaching distance but didn't touch her. Not a reassuring pat or a squeeze of the hand. Nothing. "Now go home. Get some rest. I'll call you after I've had my little talk with Becker. I'll let you know how it went."

This time, despite the heaviness in her chest, she had no problems getting into her car and driving home.

* * * * *

Kyler slid into the booth opposite Becker. "This is cozy." Settling into his seat, he eyed the place, an Italian restaurant with a dark atmosphere and tables covered in floor-length burgundy tablecloths. "I half expected you to stiff me."

"I thought about it. But I what the hell? You were singing a song I liked. I wanted to hear the rest."

The man was shit. It turned Kyler's stomach having to be even this close to Matt Becker. And God help the company if this kind of asshole was going to be VP. The missing money, which Becker had almost pinned on him, was the half of it.

"So, I'd like to know, how are you going to cover your ass, Becker?"

Becker waved a hand at the waiter and ordered his dinner and an expensive bottle of wine, speaking perfect Italian. "I'll manage."

Interesting. Becker wasn't exactly what he'd call cultured. Nor was he Italian. There was more to the slimeball than Kyler knew. Much more.

The waiter turned to Kyler.

Kyler shook his head. "*Niente, grazie.*" He didn't exactly have a stomach for *trenette alle vongole* or *fegato alla veneziana* tonight. "If I resign on Monday, you'll forget everything you know about the office manager."

After a long moment and several swallows of wine, Becker smiled. "I could be...convinced..."

The bastard was looking for more? Fuck that.

Disgusted, Kyler stood. Leaning over the asshole, he whispered, "Two can play this game, you fucking piece of shit. You want to make an innocent woman's life hell by dragging all her skeletons out of her closet, then I can do the same. Your closet isn't exactly uninhabited, is it?"

Something flashed in Becker's eyes. Fear, perhaps?

If things didn't go his way tonight, he'd get in touch with the detective again, see if he could dig up more details about this guy. He was hiding something.

Dammit, if he'd had more time, this conversation might have gone very differently. In fact, it might not have gone at all. Instead, he might have been talking to the police right now, giving a statement.

Eyes narrowed, Becker set down his wine glass. "How about you sit down and we talk about this?"

"Last chance." Kyler sat, crossed his arms over his chest. "Give me the proof I came for, tell me you're going to forget you've ever heard or read anything about the office manager, or I'll take what I have and go to the police."

"If you had anything, you wouldn't be talking to me right now. Giving up your job."

Kyler shrugged. "Maybe I was tired of playing the sales and marketing game?"

"I don't buy that. So, the question I want answered is why would you give up your job for the secretary? She's nobody."

No, that was just it. She wasn't nobody. Not to him. But admitting that would only make things harder for her. "Yeah, she is nobody. Like I said, I'm not giving up anything for her. What do you care, anyway? By Monday, I'll have my resignation handed in to the Board of Directors and by Tuesday, they'll be interviewing new applicants for my job. We both know who's on the top of their short list for the position. So, what'll it be? Vice president? Or state's ward?"

Becker thought about what he'd said, reached into his jacket and pulled out a manila envelope. "How do I know you won't take this and forget about our deal?"

"Because I'm not the double-crossing shit that you are. I actually keep my promises." He swept up the envelope, crammed it into his pocket and left the restaurant as fast as he could.

That was one conversation that left him feeling sick. It would be a long time before he'd be able to enjoy another Italian meal without his stomach lurching into his throat. A damn long time.

When he returned home, he called Elena. She didn't answer, so he left a short message, saying that things had gone well, and he hoped she had a good week at work.

Even though the situation had more or less been handled, he spent the next few days pacing his house, feeling caged-in and twitchy, restless. What was that bastard Becker trying to hide? The detective was still working on some things.

Stacy called to check on him a few times. He didn't answer, just let the voicemail pick up. She left a couple of messages, saying she was worried about him, hoped he was doing okay and letting him know that she'd heard through the rumor mill that he'd quit and Becker had been named VP. Would he please call her?

He didn't.

Instead, he spent his nights tossing and turning, thinking about a certain pretty little office manager. And he spent his days sitting in front of his computer, staring at his resumé and trying to decide what to do about a job.

It would be a piece of cake calling his old man and taking a job at Pierce Holdings. But Kyler knew he'd never be satisfied if he did that. For one thing, he hated investing.

No, he needed to find another job on his own. Something he could feel proud of. If he had to, he'd start at the bottom, roll up his sleeves, and sweat his way to the top, just like he had before. Yes, that was exactly what he'd do. In fact, maybe he'd go apply with his former employer's biggest competitor, AVR Manufacturing. Wouldn't it be convenient if they had an opening in their sales department? Hell, he might even like a job in Quality Control. He wasn't above getting his hands dirty.

Finally, he had a plan in place, a sense of purpose.

He printed out a handful of copies of his resumé and hit the pavement. Only after he had found himself a new job did he let himself think about Elena again. It had been almost a month since he'd last seen her. Instead of easing up over time, his feelings for her had only intensified. He wanted to know how her brother was doing. How Becker was treating her at work. If she had anyone to shovel the snow off her car after the first big snowstorm of the season. And if she would have anyone to spend Thanksgiving with. Somehow, he had to make things right. If she'd let him.

God only knew he didn't deserve a second chance, but that was exactly what he wanted—the opportunity to start over.

It took him another week to convince himself to ask her.

Despite the fact that it was only twenty degrees outside, his hands were damp with sweat as he drove to her place, a cute little bungalow in a quiet suburban neighborhood. Her car sat in the driveway. He hurried up the un-shoveled front walk and rang the doorbell. A blistering north wind whipped through his hair.

Finally, the door opened.

Kyler dragged in a long, deep breath. He knew he wouldn't stop thinking about this woman, no matter how long it was before he saw her again. This was it. His chance. He would kick his own ass if he fucked it up...again.

* * * * *

"W-well, hello Kyler," Elena stammered, so stunned to see him, she could have been blown over if he sneezed. What was he doing here?

Standing on her front porch, he looked at her long and hard for a few minutes, and she felt her face flaming again, like it had the night he'd blackmailed her. "I've been thinking about what happened between us." He tipped his head, his expression guarded. "I want to start over again. I'd like to get to know you better."

"I—I..." Oh, God! Was he asking her on a date? He was, wasn't he? She leaned against the door for support. It had been over a month since she'd left his house. Every night, she'd lain in bed, wondering how he was, what he was doing, if he ever thought about her. And every morning—as insane as it was—she secretly hoped she'd see him again. They lived on opposite sides of town. An accidental meeting was about as likely as being struck by lightning or winning the lottery, but in some ways she'd always been a hopeless romantic. She'd looked for him everywhere—gas station, party store, delicatessen.

Even this hopeless romantic hadn't imagined he would come to her house and ask her out.

"Oh hell." He shook his head and backed away from the door. "This was a bad idea." He started to turn around.

Stop him! "N-no." She lurched forward and grabbed the first piece of his anatomy that came into reach, his elbow. Awkwardly, she gave it a tug. "Sorry. I was just caught by surprise. I mean, it's been a long time, and I didn't hear from you. I thought…"

"Let me take you out tomorrow. On a real date."

"Tomorrow? Sunday?"

"Sure. I feel like such a shit for how I treated you. That's not me."

She hesitated, not sure if she wanted to believe what was happening. This was what she'd hoped for. But could she really trust him? "Okay, sure. One date. But that's all I'm agreeing to for now."

For just the briefest of moments, that thick veneer he'd been wearing since she'd opened the door cracked and a flurry of emotions played over his features. "Hang on to your hat, sweetheart. Tomorrow, you're in for the night of your life. I'm taking you on the date of your dreams." He left her with a twinkle in his eye and a promise that she wouldn't be sorry for giving him another chance. "By the way, what size dress do you wear?" he asked, just before strolling back to his car.

She couldn't wait to see what he had planned.

* * * * *

Kyler put his car into park, cut off the engine and fisted his keys. He'd known that sooner or later he'd have to have a heart-to-heart with Stacy. He'd avoided it for too long. After all, he didn't really have a solid reason for giving her the silent treatment. Sure, she'd given him some false information, back during that thing with Becker. But despite paying the detective good money, he had never discovered anything proving it was intentional. If anything, he figured she'd been used by Becker. Who knew what that bastard had been thinking?

The bottom line was they'd been friends for too long

to hold a misjudgment against her. She might have believed the wrong person's lies, but she had been, after all, trying to protect him. He headed up her front walk to her porch steps, eyeballing the car in the driveway, which, coincidentally, looked a lot like the Lincoln his former employer had leased for him.

Could be Becker's. Or it could belong to someone else. It wasn't as if all black Lincoln Town cars ever built were leased by TK Technologies.

He knocked.

She answered the door wearing a robe, her Domme platforms, some heavy makeup, and a blush. "Oh, Kyler. Hi." She didn't invite him in. In fact, she shuffled out and pulled the door shut behind her.

"Hey, I'm sorry if I've come at a bad time. I owe you an apology for not returning your calls."

She glanced over her shoulder before giving him a flat smile. "It's okay. I was just worried. You know how I can be."

He'd never seen Stacy act this nervous before. It wasn't like he didn't know she had a social life. Hell, they'd gone on double dates together. And occasionally played in the same dungeons. She was a Domme, he a Dom. Their social circles tended to overlap. "Sure, I know how you can be. I'll get going. We'll talk later." He started down the steps

"How are you? Have you found another job?" she called after him.

He turned again, catching her tugging on her robe to cover what looked like a strip of black leather. It didn't take a genius to figure out she was playing in her dungeon with someone. And for some reason, she didn't want him to know who that someone was.

The question was why? He'd never been a jealous friend. They'd never kept secrets from each other. There was never any reason to.

He forced a smile he didn't feel. "I sure did. Thanks.

And thanks for looking out for me, you know, with that Becker thing."

Something flashed in her eyes, but he couldn't read what that something was. "I'm relieved to hear you landed on your feet. And you're welcome. I couldn't sit by and watch Matt scheme against you and not say something. It just stinks that you ended up losing your job instead of him."

"I didn't lose my job. I quit."

"That's right. You quit." She nodded, pushing the door open and backing inside. "I'll call you later, okay? Maybe we can have lunch next week."

"Sure. Lunch." He walked to his car, checking the Town Car's license plate number as he passed. Yep, it was his former leased car, which should have been turned over to the new VP of Sales and Marketing upon his promotion.

Matt Becker.

Kyler got in his own car and drove around the blocks a few times. After about fifteen minutes, he turned back down her street.

The Lincoln was gone.

What the hell was Becker doing at Stacy's house?

* * * * *

Oh my God. The dress. It was gorgeous. Black, long, elegant and slinky, it skimmed over Elena's curves just right. Not too tight. Not too loose. The straps—if they could be called that—were chains of sparkling clear stones. Backless, the dress boasted several more chains of glittering jewels. They draped across her skin, tickling her as she moved.

She felt beautiful wearing this dress.

And there was more. Three boxes—two jewelry boxes and a shoebox—had also been delivered today. Inside the two jewelry boxes she found a gorgeous choker made of white gold and more clear stones and a pair of dangly earrings to match. And in the shoebox she found a pair of genuine Manolo Blahnik shoes. She'd never even seen a pair of Manolos in person, only on television.

Was this a dream?

Elena did some last minute fine tuning of her hair and makeup, brushed her teeth, swished some mouthwash in her mouth until her tongue was burning, and then slipped her feet into the shoes. They were a little higher than she was used to. At least that was the excuse she told herself as she wobbled down the hall and answered the door.

Kyler stood on her front porch, holding a bouquet of roses. And oh my God, did he look hot in that crisp black suit. He beamed the instant their gazes connected.

This was like a scene out of a movie or something. So unbelievably romantic, over the top.

"You look amazing." He took her hand as he stepped through the front door.

She was blushing like crazy. Her cheeks were about to melt. Or at least, her makeup was going to melt and slide off her face. Wouldn't that be attractive? "You do too."

"Ready for a great adventure?" He handed her the flowers.

They were the most beautiful, aromatic roses she'd ever seen. She inhaled their scent. "Adventure?" A little zip-zappy thrill charged through her body as she wobbled back to the kitchen for a vase. "Sure."

This was way too good to be true. When was she going to wake up?

As she filled the cut crystal vase and arranged the flowers, Kyler wandered from the kitchen. She found him standing next to the door, holding yet another large gift box. "Another present? Oh God, Kyler. I don't know if I can accept it."

Okay, so maybe it was over-compensation on his part—the dress, jewelry, shoes, flowers, and now yet another gift—but she would be lying if she said she wasn't appreciating the effort he was making. No man had ever treated her this way.

"This is vintage. I hope you like it." He lifted the box's lid, pulling out a full-length white fur coat. It was gorgeous. Soft. Luxurious. Real.

"Oh my God. Kyler?" she said as he helped her into it.

"I didn't want you to be cold." He led her outside to a waiting limo. The vehicle's inside was dark and cozy. She sat down and Kyler sat next to her. He stretched an arm out, resting it behind her shoulders, and she found herself leaning toward him, wanting to be closer. During the ride, they talked about insignificant things, typical first date stuff. Their education, hobbies, friends.

About a half-hour later, the car stopped in front of a gorgeous old building of some kind. Elena leaned forward to read the sign as the driver opened the door. Maplewood Country Club. Looked very elegant and exclusive.

They were led through a gorgeous lobby to a cozy room that housed a few tables, a fireplace, and nobody but them. The table in front of the fireplace was set for two. Kyler helped Elena into a chair and then sat next to her.

"Pinch me, will you?" she asked, lifting a glass of water. "This is unbelievable."

Kyler's eyes glittered as he looked around. "You like? I've been a member here since I was old enough to crawl. Never reserved a room like this before. This place has a very nice dining room for the members, but I wanted tonight to be special. Just you and me."

"Again, just pinch me."

"I might. Later." His smile turned wicked.

"Is that a promise?" With him like this, so charming and attentive and romantic, it was easy to forget about all the crap he'd done to her. Ninety-nine percent of her believed this was the real Kyler—the genuinely nice man with eyes that twinkled with laughter and a smile that made her heart skip beats. But there was that one percent that wouldn't allow her to believe this was real, that he honest-to-God liked her, wanted to get closer.

They enjoyed some easy conversation during the meal,

and lots of glances across the table. By dessert, she was not only totally stuffed but also much more at ease.

His expression turned just a little serious as he pushed the empty dessert plate away and stretched his arms. "Now that we've eaten, I want to talk to you about some serious issues."

Oh boy, was this the end of the fantasy? She tried to look cheerful, but her stomach took a dive. So did her mood. And yet, a small part of her was relieved. Hopefully, they'd finally talk about that day at his house. Finally, she'd have some answers. "Sure."

"First, about that day, why I snapped…"

"Hey, we were both confused and stressed. You apologized already. And I see you're trying to make up for it."

His expression darkened. "Nothing will make up for the way I treated you. There's no excuse. But I want to at least tell you what happened."

"Okay." Her insides felt like they were being stretched uber tight. It was hard to breathe, and her head felt a little swimmy, but she concentrated on taking slow, deep breaths and listened.

"You know Stacy Beautfort? From work?"

"Sure." She knew Stacy, although not very well. Stacy was secretary to the company's CFO, while Elena was the office manager for the sales department. They worked in the same five-story building but on different floors.

"She was the one who called me that day and told me about you and Becker. Some of what she said was true, and some wasn't."

"You believed her?"

"Sure. She is—correction, was—an old friend of mine, and I didn't think she had any reason to lie to me." He sighed, dragged his fingers through his hair. "I kept wanting to believe you. But she was calling, telling me something so different. It didn't help that you weren't willing to tell me the truth, although I completely understand why you couldn't. Keeping your mouth closed only made you look guiltier."

"Sure, I can see that." At least now she understood why his respect for her seemed to yo-yo up and down. And she was willing to admit if an old friend of hers had told her those kinds of things, she'd be reacting first, checking the facts second. "But you said 'was'. Does that mean you're not friends with Stacy anymore?"

"I don't know yet if she lied to me or if she was just passing on false information unintentionally. Until I do know, I'm keeping my distance. It's just better that way."

"Then I'm sorry that you've maybe lost a friend over this. It's all very sad, and I never felt it was worth it."

"So we're clear on that now, right?"

"Yes. I'd say you acted as any human being would. Emotions were running high. You were confused and angry, maybe trusting someone who was trying to manipulate you."

"You're being so understanding about it all."

"I still have my job, and my insurance, thanks to you. Maybe it's a little easier being understanding because of that." She hesitated. "Will you tell me now what happened after I left that day? Between you and Matt?"

"We had a little talk. I guarantee he's not going to whisper a word about your situation."

"Okay. That's all you're going to tell me?"

"Yeah."

"Fine. What about you? We've spent all this time together tonight and you haven't said a word about a new job. Did you find one?"

"I'm fine." He looked fine. In fact, he looked better than fine, but that didn't stop the sudden pang of regret from stabbing her in the gut and making her feel a little sick. He'd given up a great job for her. Even if he told her he'd found something ten times better, she'd still feel somewhat guilty. "I didn't have to go back to working for my father's company."

"You don't like working for your father?"

"It's not bad work. It's just that, since graduating from grad school, I told myself I wasn't going to ask for his help anymore. And I haven't, for years. I'm my own man. Make my own decisions and pay the prices for my own mistakes."

"I understand." She studied his face for a moment. That adorable chin and emotion-riddled eyes. The thick wave of hair that always tumbled over his brow. For just the briefest of moments, she could see the vulnerable young man Kyler had once been, the one who had set out to prove to his father that he had finally grown up and was ready to stand on his own two feet. "That means a lot to you."

"Yeah," he said casually. She knew better than to buy the easygoing tone of his voice. The truth was in his eyes.

There was this long moment of silence. Finally, she broke it. "I wish I could say I'm sorry for what Becker did, but I hate to admit this—don't take it the wrong way—I'm kind of grateful. In a very small way."

His eyes widened with surprise. "What do you mean?"

"If he hadn't tried to blackmail me, would you ever have taken the chance with me?" When he opened his mouth to speak, she added, "Honestly?"

His jaw snapped shut. He stared at her for one, two, three excruciatingly long seconds. Then he shook his head. "Probably not."

"Can I ask why not? Does that question make me sound as pathetic and desperate as I think it does?"

"Sure you can, and no it doesn't. There were several reasons why, but mainly I wouldn't because you worked for me."

"And I don't work for you anymore."

"Exactly." His smile wasn't exactly beaming, but at least his expression brightened slightly. "Which brings me to the second thing I wanted to talk to you about—the dungeon."

"Oh that." She giggled nervously, the memory of him catching her on her knees flashing through her mind. "I'm sorry for snooping. I was...um, looking for my keys so I could go home."

"It's okay. I'm actually not bothered that you found out. It's not something I would want to broadcast to the world, but I want you to know. If you hadn't discovered it on your own, we'd be having this conversation anyway."

Was that significant? Did he sit every woman down on the first date and tell her he had bondage gear in his house? "Okay."

"Forgive me if I ask you some silly questions, but I need to get a feel for what you do and don't know. Do you understand what that room is used for?"

"Well..." She imagined herself bound in that swing, Kyler standing between her spread legs. Her face grew so hot, she wondered if steam might be coming off it. "I'm guessing you participate in some kind of bondage play." She hoped he wasn't into the scary, hardcore stuff. Needles, blood, severe pain. She couldn't imagine him doing those kinds of things, not with what she knew of him. But she supposed anything was possible. They'd spent very little time together.

"That's correct. I'm a member of a very private and exclusive group. We come together once a week."

She nodded, glanced down to toy with the corner of her napkin. This was a very uncomfortable conversation. Not so much because she was shocked or horrified, but more because she was so unsure of what exactly Kyler was getting at.

Did he want to take her to the dungeon? Do things to her in there?

A part of her thrilled at that thought. The rest of her was extremely nervous.

He captured the hand that was picking at her napkin. His palm rested on the top of her hand. His fingers twined with hers. "What are you thinking, Elena?"

She looked at his face, in his eyes. "Believe me, I'm not judging you, Kyler. Not at all."

"But?"

"But this thing with you has been a bizarre rollercoaster ride, from the moment you got in my car back at the restaurant. And the bondage, submitting…I'll admit, I've been curious about domination and submission for a long time. I've even considered going to a play party. But it's very new to me, and it's going to take a lot of trust for me to feel comfortable. I guess I'm not the kind to blindly trust someone, especially if I've been hurt by him before."

He nodded. His gaze delved deep into her eyes. "I know. I'm very sorry. I guess there's no going back and starting over, is there? As much as I want to."

"I want that too. But it's a little hard to forget."

"I understand." This time it was Kyler who dropped his gaze first. He stared down at their hands, hers still beneath his, his tapered fingers splayed between hers. He rolled his wrist and fingered his watch with his other hand. "It's getting late. You have to work tomorrow. Do you want me to take you home now?"

"No. Not at all."

His gaze leapt to her face again, and she saw something there. Something she couldn't quite read. "Are you certain?"

She smiled. Nodded. "I-I want to see where this is going. I've always been attracted to you. Since the first time I saw you at work. There's a connection, a strong one. I'm scared. You hurt me. I can't tell you how much. But I can't just walk away from you."

"The feelings were mutual, believe me." He cupped her cheek and brushed his thumb over her lip. "I'm…scared too. You're the most beautiful woman I've ever seen. I waited a long time, watched you. I don't want to fuck up again. I don't ever want to hurt you." And then he blinked, and that…whatever it was…she'd seen in his eyes was gone, and a strength and sense of purpose that commanded her attention shone in its place. "You are a very special woman."

His words echoed in her head. He'd called her special, and that's exactly how she felt. Not because he'd bought her presents or rented a room at this country club. But because he'd let down his guard for those few precious seconds.

Yes, a man *could* be powerful and dominant, and yet still be vulnerable at times. He'd just shown her it was possible.

"I...um, wow. Thank you." Her face was going to ignite. The air between them was so superheated, she could practically hear it crackle, like burning paper. She just hoped he'd have the patience for her. No, she hoped it was fair asking him to be patient. Needing to change the subject, she asked, "Has it been a long time since you've been involved in a relationship?"

"A couple of years."

"Why so long?"

"I wasn't ready. I was in a bad place. For a long time. If I'd let myself get involved with any woman, I would've hurt her."

"So that's why..." That statement answered so many questions for her. Such as why he seemed to be such a loner. Why the rumors about him had started. And why he'd seemed so distant and unapproachable until now.

He released her face. His eyes, however, held her there as effectively as any physical restraint would. She felt herself wanting to surrender to this man, or more specifically to the feelings she had for him. She wanted to know everything about him, his darkest secrets. She ached to belong to him. To know that he wanted her, no others.

Oh God, it had been such a long time since she'd let herself feel anything for a man. It was terrifying in one way, thrilling in another.

"I need to ask," Kyler said, slowly. "Are you absolutely sure you feel the need to submit to a man? Sexually? Are you ready to explore this side of yourself?"

Chapter 5

Kyler's question hadn't shocked Elena. But that still didn't keep her from feeling a skittery unease.

Her tongue felt heavy. She couldn't speak for at least a handful of heartbeats. "I-I've read a little about it, and I've done a lot of thinking. But honestly, I don't know much at all, so I can't be sure I truly understand what it's all about. A lot of the stuff I've seen on the internet is either confusing or downright intimidating. Scary."

He nodded, pulling his chair next to hers, until they were wedged closely to each other. He leaned in, and she could literally feel the heat radiating from his body. She felt herself drawing nearer, pulled into the heat. "I think a lot of people feel that way when they first start exploring the lifestyle." He studied her carefully for a moment then rested a hand on top of hers. His fingers twined between hers. "Despite all the confusion, it's worth stepping out and taking some reasonable risks. I've been a Dom for a long time, and I usually can sense these things in people, especially women."

"What do you see in me?" she whispered, her breath wedged in her throat.

He tilted his head and inched closer still, until their

mouths were nearly touching. His breath warmed her lips, a gentle caress. "A natural submissive. A woman who craves complete surrender to a powerful, dominant man. A woman who wants to trust and love her man with everything she is."

He was right about that last bit for sure.

She let her eyelids fall closed and relished the sensual tension winding through her body. He was so close, and he smelled so good, and this moment, oh God, this moment was so amazing.

Would he kiss her already?

She lifted her heavy eyelids and met his smoldering gaze. She could read so many things in those eyes of his. On the very surface she saw raw, almost savage desire. No man had ever looked at her like that before. It was positively thrilling.

And below the surface, she saw something even more compelling. As their conversation meandered from one subject to another, over the next two hours, she saw the very beginnings of true caring. There, in those sparkles, when he talked about her. When he asked her questions about herself, her fears, her dreams.

This man was looking for a long-term relationship.

God help her, so was she.

He was looking for a woman who wished to join him in his lifestyle, a woman who would willingly surrender all control and power to him. To love and be loved.

She wanted to be that woman.

Finally, as her fears eased and her need to answer the urgent call thrumming through her body overtook her, she asked the question she hadn't been ready to speak at the beginning of the evening, "Will you show me how, Kyler? How to submit?"

"Yes, if that is truly what you want."

"It is. I think. I mean, I want to try."

He kissed her then. Hard and long. His tongue swept into her mouth to dominate hers. His arms wrapped around her, pulling her into a crushing embrace. She surrendered to him, welcoming him to take everything from her, to strip her bare of every defense, to topple the walls she'd erected around her heart, to claim her body.

As their kiss continued, the tension in her body swelled, until she was hot and tight and ready. She sighed into their joined mouths, begged, "Please, Kyler."

He broke the kiss, stood, took her hand and led her from the country club. They got into the car and he sat, pulled her toward him. His hands slid up her thighs as she leaned forward, taking the hem of her dress with them. The car rolled smoothly down the driveway.

Hands on her waist, he guided her onto his lap, facing him, legs straddling his hips. Her bent knees rested on the seat. The rigid bulge in his pants rubbed against her wet pussy. She rocked her hips back and forth, desperate to rub away the pounding ache between her legs.

He kissed her neck and shoulders. Caressed a breast through the thin, satiny cloth of her dress. The other reached around her back, fingers splayed against the small of her back, just above her buttocks.

The man was the worst kind of tease. He taunted her nipple, nipped her neck until goose bumps tingled and prickled her skin. Skimmed the outer shell of her ear until she shivered and begged for him to stop.

She was going to die. Long before they reached his house.

Finally, he eased her off him. She now sat on the seat, her legs spread. His hungry gaze dropped to her lace-covered pussy, to the center of her pulsing agony.

He bent over her sodden panties. "Thank you. For giving me this little bit of trust. I promise I won't take it for granted."

She believed him. She wanted to tell him as much, but she was too overwhelmed and desperate to speak. Instead, she simply nodded.

He inhaled and the corners of his mouth pulled into a

sexy half-smile. "You smell so damn good. I have to taste you."

Oh God, yes.

His hands skimmed up her thighs, and he caught the sides of her panties, pulled them down. She drew her legs together and lifted her feet, until he had them completely off.

He positioned her on the seat, next to him, facing him. He hooked one of her knees over his shoulder, and the other leg slowly lowered to the floor. The cool air eased the burning in her wet flesh, until he lowered his head to taste her.

Oh God.

He parted her folds with his fingers. His tongue swept up and down along her crest, stopping for a moment to torment her clit and then moving down to thrust into her vagina. Then, adding to the sweet agony, he pressed two fingers into her tight canal, filling her.

When he suckled her sensitive clit, she soared to an instantaneous climax. All the tension that had built in her body from the moment he'd arrived at her house tonight snapped, and pulse after pulse of wet heat pounded through her body.

She was still wobbly when they pulled up in front of Kyler's house. The skirt of her dress fell to the ground when she stood up. The material caressed her bottom as she walked, a naughty, sexy sensation. She leaned against Kyler as they climbed the front stairs and entered his home. She curled her fingers around his hand as they walked up to the dungeon.

He paused just inside the door. "In this room, I am your Dom and you are my submissive." He turned to face her, gently slid a hand up her arm and around to the back of her neck. "My sole focus is you. Your pleasure. Your pain. Are you still scared?"

"A little."

He nodded. "With our history, it's hard to trust. I

understand. But over time, it'll be easier. I'll make it easier, earn your trust." He walked around her back, tugged the zipper of her dress down. The garment skimmed down her body, landing in a puddle of black satin and glittering jewels at her feet. "I need you to kneel now, Elena." He held her hand as she stepped out of the gown and then lowered to her knees. He guided her body into the right position, buttocks up, head down, spine arched.

"Good. Now wait here. Eyes down, bottom up. It'll feel best if you completely turn yourself over. Let go of your fears and reservations."

She lifted her head the second she heard Kyler leave the room. She checked out every piece of furniture she could see from her position. The swing in the corner. The bench she'd sat in when he'd discovered her snooping.

So embarrassing.

Ironic, maybe tonight she'd be on that bench again, this time with Kyler kneeling before her, his thick cock gliding in and out of her pussy.

Her back was to the door but she knew when he'd returned. A whoosh of heat swept up her spine. Her back tightened as he approached.

This was it, she was about to experience her first time—and maybe her last—in a dungeon with a real, honest-to-God Dom.

When he walked around and stopped before her, she couldn't help stealing a quick peek.

Leather. Oh yum. She stared. He narrowed his eyes a smidge, but the sparkle never left them. "Eyes down, Elena."

"Sorry."

He stood before her, his booted feet planted wide, "There are as many varieties of Domination and submission as there are people who participate in them. Whether it's a lifestyle, as full-time Master and slave, or something much more transient, is up to each person to decide. You need to determine what you're looking for. I want to help you." He stooped in front of her. "Have you ever been inside a dungeon?"

"No. Never."

"Come with me." He helped her to her feet, showed her every piece of equipment, explained each one. Then he asked, "Do you have any questions?"

She sure did. One big question. "What if I don't like what you're doing?"

"Then we stop."

"And then what? What if I discover that none of this is for me?"

"We talk."

Could it be so simple? She tells him it isn't for her, and he says that's okay, that he doesn't need it. She doubted it.

Clearly, this bondage stuff had been a part of Kyler's life for a long time, a significant part. He had invested in the furniture, was a member of some kind of group. Gosh, it wasn't just a part of his life. It was a part of him.

He'd already told her he wasn't going to just walk away from it, not for any woman. Not for her. Besides, she couldn't ask him to do that. Any more than she'd expect him to ask her to quit reading or stop loving art.

She'd have to walk away. Call him a good friend, but accept the fact that they weren't meant for each other, regardless of the chemistry they had.

It had been such a short time. What this was between them was still very new, and she completely understood the risks of taking things too fast. Yet just the thought of saying goodbye to Kyler again made her insides ache. In a very bad way.

Maybe it wouldn't be necessary.

She sensed a lot rode on this first time in his dungeon. Perhaps, even, a chance for love.

Kyler had said he'd sensed she was a natural submissive. How he knew that, she had no clue. She could admit her fantasies had always been about powerful men, surrendering to their control. Being stolen away by a time-traveling Viking or hauled from a burning building by a burly firefighter.

But how many fantasies were better left to the imagination?

"We'll start slow and easy. I'll explain everything beforehand. And if you want me to stop, say rose petal."

"Rose petal. Got it."

He took her to the one wall that didn't have a piece of furniture affixed to it. Instead, two long shelves stretched the entire length of the wall. Arranged neatly on the shelves was a wide array of wrapped sex toys. Some she could identify. Some she couldn't. Beneath the bottom shelf hung a variety of whips, leather restraints, feathers, and paddles.

"I want to let you know that your safety is my primary concern. Only new, sterile toys are kept in my dungeon, and my whips, restraints and paddles are sanitized after every use. I am regularly tested for sexually transmitted disease, even though I have not had intercourse with anyone in over two years. During play parties, I act as a Dom or Master only. There is no sex during play. I want you to understand, I only have intercourse when I am in a committed relationship."

Wow, what did that mean? Did he want to have intercourse with her? Did he consider them "in a relationship"? Maybe he was ready to be vulnerable again. Trust her.

She felt genuinely honored.

"You understand now, don't you?" He took her hands in hers. "Regardless of what I said, it's never 'just a fuck'. Not for me."

She thought she might cry, hearing those words.

"Especially with you."

"Why me?"

"I can't say for sure. It's not one thing, I guess. It's lots of things. The chemistry between us is a part of it, for sure. But there's more." He hesitated for a moment. "Maybe it's crazy to say this, to feel it. But the truth is, it hurt when things weren't right between us."

She knew the feeling.

They were both crazy, going this fast. Letting their emotions carry them away like this and indulging in what might be a dangerous game with their hearts.

Once again, she felt like her back was against the wall, although not literally. Kyler was asking her to dive into the deep end, take a chance, let go of all her fears...with him.

She combed her fingers through the leather strands of a whip, letting them slide through her fingers.

"A whip's bite can sting, but its caress is very gentle. This is a cat-o-nine tails." He lifted the whip from its hook on the wall. "I know I have no right to ask this, but trust me."

She nodded.

Kyler walked around to Elena's back, slid a hand around her side, and pressed his entire length against her backside. Little tingles and zingy miniblazes swept up and down her body. "Kneel down, Elena."

Supported from behind, eyes closed, she slowly sank to her knees, settling into the position Kyler had placed her in earlier.

She was so nervous and scared it felt as though her heart was trying to beat its way out of her chest and the air in the room had suddenly been depleted of all oxygen. She gulped in each breath, shaking hands resting on her thighs. She instinctively flinched when the leather strips cascaded over her shoulder. The sensation was sensual, erotic, soft, like fat droplets of water striking her skin. Her body reacted. Her shoulders relaxed. The tightness in her chest eased. But the heat between her legs spiked higher.

It was sexy, this anticipation, not knowing what would happen next. More thrilling than she'd ever imagined.

Then it was gone, the teasing caress. And the next instant the thongs struck her back again, this time higher and a tiny bit harder. It didn't hurt, not really. But it did catch her by surprise. She gasped and her back arched away from the whip's stinging nip. A shudder of heat quaked up her spine.

"How's that feel, Elena?"

How did it feel? Awful? No, not at all. It felt good. The skin of her back was warm, the sensation adding to an already confusing and intoxicating mix of erotic scents and sounds and feelings.

"I-I like it." She could hardly believe she was saying that. "I want more. Not harder. But more."

"This way." Once again, he helped her to her feet, led her to the wall with a big cross-like structure affixed to it. He positioned her so she was facing the wall, arms out to the sides, legs spread wide. He fastened leather cuffs around her wrists and ankles and then hooked chains to each cuff, basically binding her spread-eagled. "You'll enjoy it even more if you're restrained. Remember, rose petal."

She nodded and gulped several times. Her mouth was as dry as sandpaper. Her heart was racing so fast she was dizzy. And she was sure her knees had melted. What was she doing here?

So terrifying. So thrilling.

The whip's thongs cascaded down her back again, tickling her skin, down to her buttocks. The muscles in the small of her back clenched. Her sex clenched. And then every muscle in her body clenched.

She was one tight ball of jangling nerves.

When the teasing touch of the whip vanished, she grimaced and leaned forward, ready for the strike.

Once again, it wasn't as painful as she expected. A million little stinging nips, followed by a million more. She didn't count the number of times he struck her, just closed her eyes and let the anticipation and wicked pleasure swirl through her, carry her away to a quiet place. She nearly wept when he stopped.

"Please, more. Oh God, that feels wonderful." She'd

never felt so alive. Energy was coursing through her body in superheated surges. She felt as if she were ten times stronger than normal, and ten times happier. "I don't want it to end."

"I knew you were a natural." He smoothed his hands down her stinging skin. "Although I had no idea you would take to it so quickly." He unfastened her ankles first, then her wrists. "Come here, my pretty little submissive." She clung to him as he led her to the bench she'd been caught trying on for size the first time she'd entered this room. He helped her get positioned, fastened her wrists and ankles in the restraints and then knelt before her, just as she'd imagined.

"I want you so bad, Elena. My balls are killing me. But I won't take you yet. Not until you're ready."

She was about to spontaneously combust. How could he think she wasn't ready? "Please."

He shook his head and went back to the wall of shelves. When he returned, he held several wrapped toys in his hands and a tube of lubricant. "I want to go slow with you, but dammit it's hard. Especially when I see that pretty little pussy all wet and ready for me. And your tight anus. Have you ever been fucked there?"

"No." Her pussy and ass clenched at the thought. She'd seen Kyler's penis. It wasn't small. She had to guess it would hurt to have him try to put it in her bottom.

"Then I won't try today."

A huge relief.

"But I will teach you how to prepare yourself for me. How to train your muscles to relax so you can take me. Would you like that?"

"I-I don't know."

He looked her directly in the eye as he nodded. "I'm going too fast for you. I'll slow down." He unwrapped one of the toys, a slender, hard vibrator with a bullet-shaped tip, and smoothed some lubricant on the very top. "Today is all about your pleasure. How are you feeling now,

Elena?"

"Really, really good. Hot," she added.

"Excellent." He twisted the base of the vibrator and her pussy once again clenched at the sound of its telltale hum.

This was crazy, how every little sensation affected her body. Never had sex been so exciting for her. Never had every sound, scent and touch been so intense. She flamed at the smoldering hunger in Kyler's eyes, the tension she saw in his rigid muscles as he moved. The scent of leather and man and her own arousal hung heavy in the air. Everything, from the room's semi-sinister appearance to the tingling heat on her back, was like an aphrodisiac. Her natural responsiveness to all the sensations battering her system was amplified. Her body was so hot and tight she trembled.

Release loomed close but just beyond reach. She wanted to close her eyes and throw herself toward the finish line. Or put her hands between her legs and caress away the throbbing ache in her tissues. But Kyler wasn't about to allow either. She could see that.

"Open your eyes, Elena."

She hadn't even realized they were shut.

His expression was dark, feral, so incredibly sexy. "You like being like this, powerless and under my complete control, don't you?"

He was so damn good at the controlling. "Y-yes." Would she have felt safe to allow any of her previous lovers to play with her like this? To actually strike her with something that could no doubt do a lot more harm if he let it?

No.

Kyler clearly knew how to control the whip, and her body. And yet she sensed he wouldn't use the power she so easily surrendered to him against her. Something wonderful was happening between them here and now.

Trust built.

Respect earned.

Love sparked.

He touched her labia, gently, with his fingers. Traced the seam of her nether lips from front to back. It was a deliciously teasing touch. Erotic and tempting, promising so many delightful possibilities. She arched her back, thrusting her breasts forward.

Oh God, wouldn't he touch her harder? Flick that fingertip over her burning clit. Thrust those fingers into her empty pussy.

No. It seemed he meant it when he said he'd go slowly. Even though she was burning for completion, he wasn't going to let her get there, not until he decided she should.

What a fucking blow-your-mind hot way to drive a girl crazy!

"Please, Kyler. I want you inside me."

"Not yet, sweet thing." He slipped just the tip of his finger into her tight sheath and groaned. "When I get inside you, I can't promise anything."

She really liked the sound of that. She tested the restraints holding her arms out to the sides, her ankles tight to the ends of the bench. They were fastened just tight enough to keep her from moving more than an inch or two. Definitely too tight to get a hand down between her legs and stroke her way to bliss.

"You're so fucking beautiful. Your body's absolutely perfect. And your sweet cunt…I want to taste you again." He leaned down and parted her labia with his fingers. His tongue darted out to shyly taste her slick folds. He groaned and she moaned. Her thighs tightened.

"You taste so sweet. Oh fuck, Elena. I want to eat you for hours."

God, no. Please. Not hours.

His tongue danced over her clit and she just about wept in gratitude. Little bolts of pleasure zipped through her body with every wet stroke. It was magic. But it ended much too quickly, long before she could come.

She sagged against the wooden structure behind her, boneless and desperate and burning up. Tears slipped from beneath her closed eyelids. She wasn't sad. In fact, quite the opposite. She was so happy her emotions overwhelmed her, spilling from her body in hot salty tears.

He lifted his head. "Elena. Open your eyes, sweet thing. Look at how hungry I am for you."

It took Herculean effort for Elena to lift her heavy eyelids. Her gaze instantly snapped to Kyler's intense and desperate one. The desire she'd seen in his eyes had become impossibly hotter. There was a wicked inferno simmering in those dark depths, the kind of heat that pulsed through her own body.

He lifted his hand, brandishing the vibrator. "I'm going to put this inside you, but I don't want you to come yet. You understand?"

She didn't want to understand. Nor did she want to obey him. Her entire body, from her scalp to the soles of her feet, was one big pulsating blob of desperation. But she nodded anyway, unable to do anything but obey.

She just knew she'd be disappointed if she failed him.

The vibrator inched into her slick passage, the electric buzz spreading out like ripples on the surface of a pond. With the buzz, came more tight, wet heat. More desperation.

She was going to come.

The vibrator slipped out of her pussy, and her head slumped forward as every muscle in her body sagged. She whimpered, caught up in the twitches that followed.

Only a second more and she would have had release.

"You're ready."

Oh, thank God.

She opened her eyes to watch him shed his black shirt and unzip his snug pants to push them down his narrow hips. His erect cock jutted proudly from a trimmed nest of dark curls. His testicles snugged tight to the base of his rod. A droplet of white pre-come glistened from the ruddy tip.

He rolled on a rubber and slowly eased into her. They groaned in unison as he completely seated himself in her slick heat. "You're so tight, sweet thing. So fucking tight."

He rested his hands on her knees, using them as leverage as he withdrew from her and then pushed back inside. This time, she didn't let herself hide in the darkness, the swirls of colors behind her closed eyelids. She watched his beautiful body work. His shoulders bunch and bulge. The corded muscles of his arms tighten and relax. The planes of his stomach harden when his hips pushed forward.

With every intimate caress of his cock, she soared ever closer to climax. And the erotic sound of skin striking skin as he fucked her harder only made her journey that much swifter.

And then she was there and she couldn't breathe. Her stomach cramped as she gulped in one shallow mouthful of air after another. There was a brilliant explosion, deep inside. Followed by bliss. Like hot honey. Pulsing through her chest, up her neck.

Oh. My. God.

She knew the instant Kyler also found release. He stopped thrusting for a single heartbeat, groaned her name, and then resumed fucking her, his thrusts sharper and harder than ever. Her body welcomed every sweet invasion, until he finally sagged against her, his slick chest sliding over hers.

He kissed her eyelids. Her cheeks. Her mouth. Her neck. "I'm sorry, Elena. So sorry. I wanted to go slower with you."

She was so not complaining.

"I wanted to taste every inch of your body. To play with these beautiful tits. Your soft stomach. Nuzzle your neck and nip your earlobes."

She smiled. Such sweet promises. "There's always next time," she quipped.

"You betcha. And the time after that." He withdrew from her, removed the condom and disposed of it. And then he gently helped her out of the restraints.

She was shaking all over when he carried her to his bedroom down the hall and laid her on the world's softest bed. Warm, safe and adored. It simply didn't get any better than this.

If this was a dream, she never wanted to wake up.

Chapter 6

"Elena, wake up."

It took Elena about ten seconds to remember where she was, and another thirty to gather up the strength to open her eyes. Oh, she was so sleepy, and achy all over. It was a good achy, the kind that came from using muscles that hadn't been tested in a long time.

Kyler lay next to her, his torso uncovered, the crisp white sheets a sharp contrast to his tanned skin and dark features.

"I don't want to wake up." She snapped her eyes shut, wishing they had more time just to be together, another day. Week. Month.

Monday already. She hated Mondays.

"Come on, sleepyhead. I want you to have a good breakfast before heading to work."

"Do I have time to eat? What time is it?" She lifted her heavy head and squinted at the glowing red numbers on the clock.

"Yes. Breakfast's the most important meal of the day. You'll just have to make time."

"Oh my God! Is it really seven-thirty?" Now fully

awake, she rolled onto her side. "I'll never make it to work on time." Nearly in a panic, she flung her legs over the side of the bed. "I have to get home, shower, change my clothes—"

"Whoa, hold up there. You've got plenty of time. The office is five minutes from here. You don't have to clock-in until nine."

"But I can't go to work in yesterday's clothes, and I need a shower." She scrambled around the room, trying to find her discarded garments. She found them draped over a chair back. Her shoes. Where were her shoes?

"Not a problem." Naked, he caught her by the arms, completely halting her progress. "I had a few things delivered for today. I hope you like them."

"What kind of things?"

"Shower first. Then I'll show you." He physically turned her toward the bathroom door and gave her backside a love tap, sending her from the room with a stinging bottom and big smile.

She hesitated just inside the bathroom door, turning to say over her shoulder, "You know, I feel bad that you're the one doing all the giving and I'm the one doing all the receiving."

He caught her hand in his, turned it over and pressed a sweet kiss to her palm. "That's just it. You've been doing the giving for so long you don't know how to receive." They shared a sweet moment of watery glances and understanding half-smiles. "Now get going. I'm going to feel like shit if you're late for work. Then again, making you late could be fun…"

"You're devious." She shooed him away, before swinging the door closed. She cranked on the water and, curious, tiptoed to the door and inched it open. She caught him leaving the room, a glorious sight, nude male perfection.

It was still hard to believe they were doing this—acting like they were a thing, lovers. Just a few days ago, she'd thought he was out of her life forever. What had she done to deserve such a wonderful man?

When she finally left the steamy heat of the bathroom some twenty minutes later, she found the bed had been made. And there was a pyramid of white boxes in its center. A huge red bow perched atop the stack. She unwrapped all the boxes. Beautiful designer clothes, shoes, jewelry. Inside lay a card in a white envelope.

To Elena,
Thank you for being who you are.
Kyler

Oh God. Could a man be any sweeter? Any more generous?

Somehow, she wanted to give back to Kyler, show him how much she appreciated the sacrifice he'd made to let her keep her job.

But how? What could a girl who had nothing give to a man with everything? Christmas was coming. Maybe by then she'd know what that gift should be.

* * * * *

Kyler forced himself to wait until the end of the day before driving over to TK Technologies. He had his reasons for waiting, the main one being if he did find out the driver of what was once his leased Lincoln was Matt Becker, he wanted to follow him, see if he'd head back to Stacy's house.

He couldn't imagine why Becker would pay Stacy a personal visit. She was a Domme. He was a manipulating ass, not a submissive. A blackmailing, manipulating ass.

Maybe he was ready for another promotion, already. Stacy was the CFO's secretary, most definitely in a position to help him if he was after a bigger fish. Shit, that had to be it. Stacy's calls, her nervous act when he'd gone to her house, she was looking for his help but was afraid to ask. She was in over her head.

Becker was at it again. But this time, he'd catch the asshole in the act.

He had his chance a few nights later.

Because Kyler had been in Stacy's home plenty of times, he knew her patio door didn't lock properly. He'd told her to get it fixed more than once, but she'd shrugged him off, joking that he was more worried about her safety than she was. Besides, it locked fine, at least at first glance. Anyone who thought to break in would think so. But if they jiggled the door a certain way, the lock disengaged. How likely was it that a guy would stand around playing with a door, hoping it would magically come unlocked?

This was why he'd known she wouldn't fix it.

Sure enough, a little jiggle and the lock flipped up. He was in, and no one was the wiser. He could hear voices, Stacy's and Becker's, coming from down in her personal bondage dungeon, but he couldn't make out what they were saying. Being careful to avoid making any noise, he slowly descended the stairs to her finished basement, stopping before he reached the bottom.

"You've been such a good slave," Stacy said. "Come here. Serve me. On your knees."

What the hell? It seemed Kyler had been wrong about Becker. He was a submissive.

But he supposed that didn't mean he'd also been wrong about Becker's reason for being in Stacy's house. He could still be trying to manipulate her.

There was only one way to find out.

He raced down the rest of the stairs and stepped around the corner, finding Stacy perched on the bondage chair she called her throne, eyes closed, Becker's head between her spread legs. Her eyelids snapped up a split second after Kyler cleared his throat.

"Kyler," Stacy said, eyes widening for a single heartbeat before narrowing again.

Becker's head swiveled as he twisted at the waist, glancing over his shoulder. "Kyler?"

"Don't stop, slave." She fisted Becker's hair and yanked, turning him back around. "This is quite a surprise.

I didn't even hear you knock."

"That's because I didn't. I…You never fixed the lock."

She smoothed her hands down her torso, sheathed in a red PVC corset, her splayed fingers coming to a rest just above her belly button. "I was hoping it might come in handy someday. And it has."

"Then you want people breaking in your house?"

"Only one."

Kyler shook his head. "What the hell is going on here, Stacy? I came here today, thinking Becker was maybe trying to blackmail you like he did Elena."

"How gallant of you," she said, a sultry smile blossoming over her face. "But you've got it all wrong, in case you didn't realize that by now."

"Why don't you tell me how it really is then?"

Her smile faded. "I can't believe you didn't put it all together. You've really disappointed me. In fact, I've totally lost interest in our game now." She curled the fingers of her right hand into Becker's hair again and pulled, glaring down at him. "What the hell are you doing? You don't eat me like a toddler lapping at a lollipop, you worthless animal. Either do it right or leave."

Was this the same woman he'd known all these years? On the outside, she looked the same. But the Stacy he knew was down to earth, easy to talk to. Outside of bondage play, she didn't play games. "What game?" Kyler asked, completely bewildered.

"This one. The game we've been playing since the day you dumped me."

What the hell? "I never dumped you. We were never…together."

Something flashed across her face, but the expression didn't remain there for long. In less than a blink, her expression was frosty again. "Is that really what you believe? Do I need to remind you of what you said to me?"

Kyler was so confused, he didn't know what to say

next. Obviously, he hadn't just misread Becker, he'd also misread Stacy. In a huge way. Looked like he'd somehow mislead her too.

He couldn't remember having ever said anything to make her think they were lovers. They'd never flirted. Never kissed or fucked. They'd never played in a dungeon together. They'd never shared any really deep intimacies. All they'd ever done was talk.

"It looks like you do need me to remind you." Cruelly, she shoved Becker's head from her then kicked him in the center of his chest with her spike-heeled boot. "You're done. Go, learn how to eat pussy right. And don't come back until you do."

Becker fell backward, catching himself with his hands before scrambling back into his submissive position on his knees. "Yes, Mistress."

Dressed in her PVC corset, and matching red fishnet stockings and knee-high boots, Stacy sauntered over to Kyler, sliding a black-painted fingernail between her lips. "I care about you, Stacy," she said, throwing his own words in his face. "Like I haven't cared about a woman in a long time."

Shit, he had said that, a long time ago. And he'd meant it at the time. But not in the way Stacy had thought. "I meant I care about you as a friend. You're a Domme. I'm a Dom. Neither of us are switches."

"You could be. If you wanted me bad enough. You'd become a switch if you loved me."

"Why would you ask anyone to become something they're not if you love him? That's not what love is all about, making people change."

"Hey, I watched you over the past how many years? How many women have you tried to 'fix'?"

She was right. Now that he thought about it, he had tried to change more than one of his former lovers. He'd fooled himself into thinking it was okay, by telling himself that he was helping them become better. "That was before. I know better now. Love is about…" He hesitated, realizing the real reason why every one of his former relationships had failed. It wasn't because he'd been trying to change the women.

Love is about trusting, becoming vulnerable, giving of yourself, your heart and soul. Whether the one doing the loving is a Dom or sub or neither.

He'd always thought he'd known how to love. But he hadn't. He'd only known how to play the role of lover. He'd always been the kind of guy to throw expensive gifts at his women. But that wasn't truly giving. Those things had only been poor substitutes for the one thing his lovers had all been asking for—his heart. Just maybe, if he'd taken the chance, let himself become vulnerable, rather than focusing on how he could fix the woman or how she was failing him, he would have found true happiness with one of them. Maybe he could have spared himself and them a lot of heartache.

"Oh, are you going to get all philosophical on me now, Kyler? That's so not you." She sighed as she circled him, her eyes assessing. "You've always had the unfailing ability to fool yourself into thinking you see the truth, both in yourself and in everyone around you. Has that changed?"

"If you'd said that a month or so ago, I'd have had no idea what you were talking about." He swore his blood had turned to ice, he felt so cold right now.

She stopped directly in front of him then, her expression turning haughty. "Then you've had a revelation. How nice. Aren't you going to thank me?"

"No. Thank you for what?"

"Blackmailing Becker into getting you fired."

"I quit."

"Yeah, right. You quit." Smiling, she patted his chest. "You had no choice. Although I'll admit, I was surprised to see you give up. I figured you'd put up at least a bit of a fight. After all, you were so proud of where you'd gotten yourself."

"Let me make sure I've got this clear—you were the one who cooked up that scheme with Elena and the money?"

Stacy shrugged again. "Maybe you expect me to be sorry, but I'm not. You didn't deserve to be VP. Becker does. He may be on his knees, but he has a spine...and a heart."

"So that's really it? You did this because your feelings were hurt?"

"No, I did it because you needed me to. You see, I turned it around. I fixed you. Now, thanks to me, your eyes are open and you're not fooling yourself anymore. Someday, you'll see that and thank me."

He'd heard enough. He spun around, hands clenched into tight fists, emotions pounding through his body. He was confused and hurt and sad and furious, all at the same time. He'd been betrayed by a woman he'd once considered a good friend. In one respect, he'd love to bring her down for what she'd done, and Becker for the part he'd played in it too. He'd lost a job he'd worked hard to earn.

But he was done with them, with games, with the shit. He left, not speaking another word.

He realized, after sitting down that night and taking a good, long look at his relationship with Stacy, that the only way to deal with someone like her was to walk away. Fate had a way of taking care of the rest.

At least, in the long run, she'd taught him some things about himself. Maybe she was right. Maybe someday he'd thank her.

Chapter 7

"You don't have to do this if you're not ready. Like I've said before, you don't have to do anything to prove something to me." Kyler stood inside his front door, his fingers curled around the handle. He was wearing his typical Dom gear—leather pants, and leather strap harness that showed off his amazing upper body. "If I officially present you to the group tonight, instead of just having you there as my guest, you're going to be nude, touched by strangers, expected to play the part of perfect submissive. Not to mention, you may see me play with other submissives, both men and women."

Elena couldn't remember ever being so nervous. She didn't even try to hide it. Kyler knew her well enough to recognize the signs, trembling hands, stuttering voice. Over the past year, they'd spent a lot of time together, both in the dungeon and out. Talking. Touching. Sharing. Exploring. In that time, they'd grown, both as a couple and individually. Elena had learned a great deal about herself, thanks to Kyler. Like how hard it was for her to trust. And she'd helped him come to terms with a few issues too. Like how he avoided being vulnerable, stepping out of his Dom shoes and kneeling at the feet of the woman he loved. It had been both the most challenging and wonderful thirteen months of Elena's life. "I know. I understand. But like you said, you don't have intercourse with them. Right? And no one will expect intercourse from me either."

"That's right. It's very different with you, my lover, than it would be with a submissive seeking only a Dom. And no Dom or Domme is going to even touch you without my permission, let alone demand intercourse."

"I think I'm ready."

"Okay." He went back to the dungeon and gathered some toys in a bag. "Just in case you decide you want to play," he explained. "No pressure. If you just want to watch that's okay too. And I want you to tell me if you're ever uncomfortable or want to leave."

"Okay."

"You can't wear that outfit if you're going to be presented. Go change." He gave her jean-clad bottom a playful swat, sending her upstairs giggling. She wiggled into a g-string and fishnet body stocking and clomped downstairs in a pair of outrageously high shoes. On top went the white mink coat Kyler had given her the night of their first official date. "Ready?"

"Yep." She held Kyler's hand as they walked out to the waiting limo. "You said tonight's sort of a Christmas celebration?" The official holiday was still over a week away, their second Christmas Day together. She didn't care if Kyler gave her nothing. She was just grateful to have him in her life. He'd already given her so many things— beautiful clothes, expensive jewelry, himself. She couldn't imagine anything that would be better or more meaningful anyway. He'd totally spoiled her.

"You might call it that. There won't be any Christmas carols or hot chocolate but there's usually a nice buffet and soft drinks. And some of the members exchange gifts."

"Are you giving anyone a present this year?"

"Only one." He didn't say more and she didn't want to pry, although she was seriously curious to find out who had earned a Christmas present from the man she'd fallen in love with. Was it a fellow Dom or maybe one special sub? "The Christmas play party is always at Master Blade's private dungeon. Last year, you weren't quite ready for it."

Master Blade—who she guessed had not been born with that name—was obviously filthy rich, like old-money, rolling-in-it rich. His estate sat on one of Michigan's most well-known roads, Lakeshore Drive, the rear backing Lake St. Clair. A long winding driveway took them through the walled, wooded lot to the house. A uniformed servant opened the limo's door, and Kyler stepped from the car. Elena followed him up the brick home's front steps to the polished wood door. Elena had never seen a house as big and beautiful as this one.

Inside, the building was as grand and breathtaking as its exterior. The foyer's ceiling soared at least three stories up, and the biggest crystal chandelier she'd ever seen hung overhead.

"This way." Kyler led her to a small room to the right. "One last chance. If you want to just watch, you can keep your clothes on. But if you want me to officially present you to the group this time, you'll need to take everything off."

She glanced at a pair of mostly nude women wearing leather collars, g-strings and harnesses, standing nearby. Her heart was drumming against her breastbone, keeping a rapid tempo. And her hands were shaking, mouth so dry she swore her tongue was going to crack. But she still wanted to do this, wanted to become a part of this world. "I'm sure."

The two women in g-strings helped her out of her coat, body stocking and g-string. She felt terribly self-conscious as she left the room. It was amazing how much security a mostly transparent fishnet garment could give her.

Kyler eyed her intensely, his gaze traveling up and

down her body. "This is it. Ready?"

How could she say no when she knew this meant so much to him? She pulled in a deep breath, let it out and clasped her shaking hands together behind her back. "Yes, Master. I'm ready." She held her breath as she took little baby steps behind him, down the hallway to the pair of double doors at the end. She could hear the sounds of the party inside, voices, music.

When the doors opened, it was like a wave of sensation rolled over her. The scents of perfume and pine and sex. The distant sounds of slapping, and closer, voices, music. And the many, many bodies, tall and thin, short and stout, all shapes and sizes and in various forms of undress.

"This way." Kyler led her past dozens of curious onlookers to the room's center, beneath a glittering chandelier where light played out across the room in twinkling mini-starbursts. "Present, Elena." He then moved away from her, walking toward one end of the room, leaving her to present as they'd practiced at home every day.

She'd imagined it would be like this, both scary and thrilling. But she'd had no idea how thrilling it would be. She lifted her chin, pushed her shoulders back and, staring straight ahead while avoiding making eye contact with any Doms or Dommes within eyesight, walked across the empty floor. When she was within about four feet from Kyler, she slowly, as gracefully as she could manage, eased to her knees.

She hadn't fallen over, twisted an ankle or stumbled like an idiot. She was actually able to inhale freely for the first time since arriving at this place.

Now the easy part. On all fours, she crawled toward him, stopping about eighteen inches from his feet. Finally, she took the presentation position he favored when they played at home. Back arched, eyes down, bottom up off her heels, knees spread and hands resting on her thighs.

She stared blindly at the gleaming wood floor and

listened to the room fall silent. Everything seemed to stop, the voices, music. She didn't have to look up to know that everyone was looking at her.

A crazy rush of heat flared through her body on the heels of an equally intense chill. The floor was like ice beneath her knees, the air a fragrant caress around her body, the silence a dark cloud above her head.

More nervous than she had been a few minute earlier, she turned inward, focused on the sensation of air filling her lungs, the pounding of her heart in her chest.

At Kyler's demand, Elena recited the presentation she'd performed for him every day they spent together, "Master Kyler, this submissive presents the Master's body for his examination and inspection. This submissive joyously presents these breasts..." She cupped her breasts. "This vagina..." She lowered her hands to her pussy and parted her labia. "This anus..." She reached around and parted her ass cheeks. "And mouth for examination and inspection." She opened her mouth wide and waited.

What agony. What sweet agony.

Around her she heard voices, commenting on her body, complimenting Kyler on his beautiful new submissive. At his command, she closed her mouth and, avoiding making eye contact with any of her admirers, looked around the room.

How many times had she secretly fantasized about a scene like this, where she was being assessed, objectified? Touched? At Kyler's assent, strangers' hands fell on her shoulders, back, stomach, head. Male and females alike commented on her breasts, her ass, her hair.

Between her legs an aching pounding had begun, and the heat there increased with each throb of the delicate tissues. Even if her mind didn't know it, her body did. This was what she'd been searching for. She'd found her place, among Masters and Mistresses, Doms and Dommes. Slaves and submissives. People she might never have found.

Kyler had gently and patiently led her home.

A beautiful woman, her lush body spilling from a black latex catsuit, bent down and boldly weighed Elena's breasts, her full red lips pursed. "She's just lovely, Kyler. May I?"

"Absolutely, Mistress Jasmine."

Elena gasped, both insanely aroused by the woman's touch and equally shocked. But she didn't flinch or move away. Even when she watched one of the woman's hands move down between her legs.

Her inner thighs tightened and Elena squeezed her eyes closed as the woman's fingers slipped into her slick heat, stretching her. She could swear she was either going to ignite or pass out. She just wasn't sure which.

Reflexively, her vagina tightened around the woman's fingers, intensifying Elena's pleasure.

What was it about becoming an object that thrilled her so much? She was there, on her knees, her pussy full of some woman's fingers. Her entire body open and exposed to so many people.

She couldn't say, but she knew this was what she needed. That instead of making her feel empty and invisible it made her feel powerful and beautiful. She was sad when the woman withdrew her fingers, gave Kyler yet another compliment on his new submissive and left, and the sounds of the party slowly resumed.

Kyler helped her to her feet. "Now we go to the dungeon."

Elena's knees threatened to buckle, she was so aroused and giddy. As she walked, she felt people watching her, admiring her. It was like nothing she'd ever experienced in her life. Past men and women, Masters and slaves, Doms and submissives, down the wallpapered wall lined with expensive looking artwork, to a single door, painted black.

Kyler opened the door, and they stepped into a huge, fascinating bondage dungeon, torn from her wildest imaginings.

Over the past year, Kyler had taught her the proper terms for the equipment—St. Andrew's Cross, sex swing, kneeler, bench, cage. This dungeon had several of each. The room was partitioned into eight areas, each one containing at least a couple of pieces of furniture. At the moment, there was a scene going on in each one. She passed one where a Domme was playing with a submissive man. He was on his knees at the moment, being flogged. And in another scene, a Dom seemed to be instructing onlookers on the art of rope bondage. Kyler continued toward the back of the room, stopping in front of a scene showcasing a man nearly as big as the bouncer outside performing electro play on a bound beautiful blond woman.

That was one line Elena was definitely afraid to cross, but that didn't keep her from watching in silent fascination as the man deftly stimulated the woman with the silver wand. The heat in her pussy inched up even higher, and she ached to have Kyler caress that pounding throb away. Here, in the middle of the crowd. Or there, on that sex swing. Anywhere.

"What do you feel?" Kyler whispered into her ear. He pressed his entire length against her back. His rigid rod was pillowed against her ass.

"I'm...so hot," she admitted, eyes riveted on the handsome Dom who was now removing the restraints from the blonde. "I didn't know how I'd feel about all this. I mean, I've watched before. But it's different, actually being a part of it."

Kyler pulled her tighter against him. "I didn't know either, when I came here the first time to play. I don't think anyone does. But the minute they walk in, they either know it's for them or it's not. I've seen it go both ways."

"It's both scary and exciting at the same time. The scary makes the exciting that much better."

"I've heard other submissives say the same thing. For a Dom, it's a very different thing. You're looking for the thrill you find in relinquishing control to a Dom or Master. You want to feel powerless. We, on the other hand, feel a great sense of responsibility for our submissives. For their safety and pleasure." He reached around with one hand and pinched her nipple between his forefinger and thumb.

She sucked in a sharp gasp and arched her back, resting her head against Kyler's chest. It was strange when she thought about it, shocking, that she was standing in a room full of people with nothing on, letting Kyler tug on her nipple. But strange or not, she wouldn't have wanted to miss this, didn't want it to end.

"I want you," she murmured, rocking her hips forward and back.

He reached between her legs, parted her labia. "Oh, sweet thing. You're so wet. But I won't fuck you here. Fucking is just for us."

She whimpered as he slid his fingers inside, hooking them so that his knuckles rubbed against the ubersensitive front wall of her canal.

"But that doesn't mean I won't let you come." The hand on her chest moved down, his arm now circled around her torso, just under her breasts. "Watch, baby," he murmured in her ear. "Watch the scene."

The big Dom had a new woman now, was tying her bent over a kneeler, her ass high in the air, legs spread wide, her upper body supported by the top cushion. The woman was begging him to fuck her with a dildo. Within seconds, a breathless, inflamed Elena was echoing the woman's pleas.

Kyler scooped up the bag of toys and gently forced her into an empty spot against the wall. He kneed her legs apart, pinned her wrists to the wall and kissed her. His tongue split the seam of her mouth, forced its way in and dominated her own. His rigid thigh rubbed against her throbbing pussy, stirring the heat in her body to obscene levels.

She'd never been so desperate to be fucked.

His sweet Elena was hot. She was ready. And Kyler was in agony. But he refused to take her now. What he could do, however, was give her a little relief. Later, they would take their time, make love.

Supporting her body with his knee and one arm, he bent to rummage through the bag on the floor. His fingers brushed over the gift box he'd hidden in it before closing around her favorite dildo. He scooped it up. With his free hand, he fingered her slick folds.

So fucking hot and wet. A charge of desperate hunger swept through him, nearly knocking him to his knees. And then she whimpered.

Enough of this.

He turned her around, so she was facing the wall. Her spine arched, such a pretty sight. That beautiful, round ass was a delicious temptation.

"Master. Please," she whispered, her arms flattened against the wall, her face turned to the side.

"Okay, baby." He swept her hair over one shoulder and kissed her eyelid, cheek, neck. There wasn't a more beautiful woman in the world. There wasn't a more perfect woman for him. And tonight she would know how much he cared about her.

He forced her feet wide apart and then, giving in to the temptation, he thrust two fingers into her slick heat.

His head fell back. His eyelids dropped over his eyes, shutting him into a world of swirling passion. The other people in the room seemed to fade away, and his entire being centered on the sound of Elena's gasps of pleasure and little moans of wanting as he replaced his fingers with the thick dildo.

"Oh God."

He left the dong in place and dug into the bag again, this time coming up with a butt plug and lube. He spread a large amount of lubricant on the plug's tapered end and then, warning Elena first, slid it inside her anus.

Her knees gave out but he caught her, using his entire body to hold her erect.

"I can't…Master," she murmured.

He kissed the swell of her shoulder again, his gaze focused on the long sweeping eyelashes resting on her high cheekbones. "It won't be long, baby. Just let yourself come. Trust me. I'll hold you."

Wishing his cock was driving in and out of her sweet canal, he fucked her slowly with the dildo. Her juices coated the surface, dripped down the length to moisten his fingers. He could feel her body tightening, the heat of impending climax spreading up her back. She sighed and gasped. Trembled and whimpered. But after several agonizing minutes she didn't come.

He knew what she needed but one hand was busy with the toy and the other was helping support her.

"Touch yourself, baby. Rub your clit."

"Ohhhh…"

He'd never forget that sound or the glorious scent that always filled the air as she came.

He fucked her harder with the dildo, thrusting it quickly to intensify her orgasm. Her moans of pleasure grew louder, louder, until they filled the room.

He read her body, sensing when it was time to remove both the dong and the butt plug. When he turned to drop the used toys in his bag, he wasn't surprised to find they'd caught the attention of a number of club members.

He turned around, his body completely blocking Elena's from their view and whispered in her ear, "It seems you've become an attraction."

He fully expected her to cover her face, blush. Even though she'd been to a few play parties with the club, this was her first time playing. And although she seemed to be taking it all in stride, it was another thing to share such a private moment with a group of virtual strangers. He had personally never come in the club. Not once.

"R-really?" She had a nervous smile on her face as she twisted around to face him. She slid her arms around his waist and pressed her body against him. "That was so hot."

Sweet Jesus, he had found a woman who was not only a natural submissive but also an exhibitionist.

The wanting pounding through his body amplified even more. He kissed her. Not sweetly, but with all the desperation he felt. And then, staring into her heavy-lidded eyes, he reached down and pulled the gift box from the bag.

"This is for you."

"Me? I was the person you were giving a present to tonight?"

"I won't ask who you thought it was going to be." He led her to a nearby chair.

Sitting, she took the box from him and untied the bow with trembling hands. At least three times, she lifted her eyes, giving him a teary smile. She was emotional already and she had no idea yet what was in the box.

When she lifted the lid, he heard her gasp. "K-Kyler?" She jumped to her feet and threw her arms around his neck. She kissed his cheeks, his eyes, his mouth, his chin. Then she stumbled back a step and lifted the delicate collar—really, more of a choker than a typical collar—he'd had his jeweler custom make for her. Almost thirty carats of small diamonds caught the light, flashing like brilliant stars, as she lifted the collar from the box and held it to her throat. "It's...oh my God! I'm speechless."

"With this collar, I claim you as my submissive." He fastened the collar around Elena's neck and then reached in his pants pocket, pulling out a second box, this one much smaller. "And with this..."

His heart had never pounded so heavily in his chest. Afraid it was too soon, that he was pushing Elena too hard, he hesitated for several seconds before flipping the top, revealing a perfect three carat Asscher cut diamond solitaire. "I claim you as my future bride. Will you marry me?"

Elena's jaw flopped open then snapped shut. Silent, she stared at the ring. She didn't reach for it, which set off alarms in his head.

Damn, she was going to refuse the ring.

"Oh, Kyler," she finally said at least an eternity later. She pressed her fingers to her lips and stared, first at the ring and then at his face.

He filled the silence, "I know this is kind of quick. It's only been a little over a year, and because we'd talked about waiting, you probably didn't see it coming. But I have never felt for another woman the way I feel about you. Elena, your secrets don't scare me. I love you. I want you. But more importantly, I need you. Forever. I lay prostrate at your feet." He slowly eased to his knees then dropped his head, resting his forehead on her feet.

"Oh God, Kyler."

He lifted his head, watching as the fingers of one hand traced the diamonds in the collar. The others remained on that lush mouth of hers.

"I—I…"

He'd known he was taking a chance by doing this here, in front of all the club members. But many of these people were like family to him. Master Blade and Mistress Jasmine in particular. He'd wanted to share this special moment with them.

He glanced over his shoulder, knowing they were there, watching. Both of them gave him a reassuring smile.

He plucked the ring out of the velvet box with his left hand, and with his right, he gently lifted her hand. "Please, please tell me you'll be my wife. No pressure, but if you tell me no, there's no telling what I might do."

"No pressure, eh?"

Their gazes met, and there was a tense moment when he was almost certain she wouldn't accept his proposal. But then something sparked in her eyes and her smile broadened. He inhaled for the first time in who knew how long.

"Yes."

The room erupted into loud cheering.

His eyes blurred by tears of joy, he slid the ring on her finger, climbed to his feet and kissed her.

He'd found the woman who understood him, who accepted him, who adored and respected him. And the woman who made his entire world right.

Blade and Jasmine both rushed to him, giving him warm congratulatory hugs. Then they each hugged Elena as well, welcoming her both to the club and to the family.

"Now let's get out of here." He snatched up his bag from the floor and led his fiancée through the clapping, congratulating throng. He didn't wait for her to redress when they reached the coat room, just wrapped her fur coat around her and led her outside to the waiting car. The ride was excruciatingly long, even though it lasted no more than fifteen minutes at most. He spent the entire time thoroughly kissing her, murmuring promises against her full mouth.

He would spend the rest of his life showing her how grateful he was to have her as his wife. And he would start tonight.

* * * * *

Elena just knew she was dreaming now. This couldn't be real. Kyler had not just asked her to be his wife. Her. The office manager. The girl that no one had noticed before, who just a little over a year ago had been struggling to find a way to keep her health insurance. Who years ago had been forced to take another person's identity to keep her brother from being torn from her.

A wonderful, caring, generous and attentive man loved her.

After a year of searching, she'd finally found the one gift she could give him. It was such a simple thing. And yet, she knew it was the one thing Kyler couldn't buy, no

137

matter how much money he had.

Her love. Her trust. Her heart. Her vow, to love him forever.

This time, as they went to his bedroom, they didn't go as Dom and submissive. They entered the room as future groom and bride. Two people who ached to become one. They touched each other tenderly, taking the time to kiss and touch and caress. There was no power play, but only gentle strokes and murmured promises.

Sex didn't always have to be about control and surrender. Hard and hot and intense. Sometimes it could be a quiet, intimate thing. A sharing of emotions so deep they couldn't be exchanged any other way.

The fur coat lay on the floor, just inside the bedroom door. And a trail of Kyler's clothes led from it to the bed. Kyler eased Elena onto the mattress, cradling and supporting her as she slowly sank back. Her gaze never left his face, those dark eyes that now shone with a new light. With love and the kind of trust and commitment that only came once in a lifetime.

She silently thanked Matt Becker. He had no clue what he'd done by trying to blackmail her. He'd not only brought her and Kyler together, but he'd made them both make some changes in their lives.

Ironically, a couple of months after he was named Vice President of Sales and Marketing, the company's books were seized by the government. It seemed a handful of people were fudging the numbers, cheating shareholders out of earnings and padding their personal bank accounts.

A few weeks later, both Becker and Stacy, Kyler's former friend, were collecting severance pay. Shortly after that, they were both arrested. More recently, she'd read in the paper that during their criminal trials, they'd claimed they were both being blackmailed by the company's CFO. It seemed fate had delivered exactly what they'd both deserved.

Kyler flattened his hands on either side of her face.

"What are you thinking about?"

She couldn't help smiling. "Becker."

"While you're in bed with me?" he teased, nipping her lower lip.

"Who would've thought such a terrible thing would lead to such a wonderful one?"

"And who would've thought you'd be making another name change," he quipped as he crawled over top of her.

"I want to fix that. The whole name thing. I want to take my real first name...with your last name, of course."

"Done. But first, I need to finish what we've started." He wedged his hips between her spread thighs and thrust into her.

She moaned, arched her back and lifted her knees higher.

Deeper. Harder. She wanted him. Now. And later. Sweet, gentle and hard, wild. She wanted to explore the exciting world of Domination and submission that he'd introduced her to.

But most importantly, she wanted to simply be one with him. In mind, body, and soul. To face their future together, whatever it might bring.

The End

Pleasing Him

TAWNY TAYLOR

TAWNY TAYLOR

Chapter 1

Britt Olson knew what her fiery best friend's first words would be the minute she was welcomed inside but she opened the front door anyway. There was no getting around it. She'd have to deal with Mary's disappointment—at least until the package they were both anxious to open was located.

Damn postal system. Even armed with full online package tracking capabilities, Britt hadn't been able to figure out what had happened to her gift, lovingly chosen, paid for, and shipped by her mother. Of course, the fact that Britt hadn't bothered to do more than turn on her birthday gift to herself—a new desktop with all the latest bells and whistles—and play a couple of games of Spider Solitaire, probably didn't help any.

But that game was addicting! A lot more fun than trying to figure out IP addresses and work through tedious connection wizards.

"So, where is it?" Mary asked, her freckled face and pale blue eyes full of expectation. "I came prepared." She stepped inside and dropped a large duffel bag on the floor. It landed with a respectably loud thud.

"Sheesh! What's in there? And what are you preparing for?" Curious, Britt glanced at the worn, blue bag before returning to the kitchen to get their drinks.

Mary followed her. "Oh, you'll see. I have a little bit of everything in it. I didn't want to get caught unprepared. So where's your package? I'm dying to see."

"How about you give me a hint first?" Britt struggled with the corkscrew, silently reminding herself of a recent vow to purchase a better one. "I think it was rotten of my mother to tell you what she bought—"

"You want some help?" Mary reached for the bottle.

"No. I'm fine. I'll get it." Britt gritted her teeth and continued pulling on the stubborn cork. "The hint, please."

"I think your mom wanted to make sure you didn't have it already."

"It? What it?"

Britt bit her lip as Mary gave her an I'm-not-telling-smile and shrugged. Prying information out of her best friend was no easier than pulling the cork out of the bottle she held between her knees.

"This isn't fair. You're more excited than I've ever seen you. More excited than the night before you moved into your new house, more excited than the day before you started that nifty new job of yours. Come on! Just one teeny, tiny hint."

"Nope. I'm not talking. Now, where is it? You promised not to open it 'til I got here. So quit with the theatrics."

"Fine. I see how you are. Just wait 'til your birthday." The cork finally slid free of the bottle and Britt smiled in triumph. "As far as where the box is… Well, um…" She poured Mary a glass of wine and handed it to her. "I'm not sure."

Mary didn't bother to hide her disappointment as she glanced at her watch. "It's after seven. You should have gotten it by now. Your mother always has your presents delivered on your birthday. She promised me—"

A resounding knock startled both women, and they simultaneously looked at the front door.

"Are you expecting anyone tonight?" Mary asked.

"Nope."

A second loud knock sent them both scurrying toward the door. Britt peered through the peephole.

It couldn't be. Why would he be here? She blinked then looked again. "It's the guy who bought my house. Andre. Should I open the door? What if he's mad about the bathtub faucet? Or the crappy back door that barely closed. Or the—"

"You sold that dump 'As Is'. You gave him a full disclosure. He has no right to come over here angry. Does he look mad?"

Britt studied his features—slightly contorted by the peephole's curved lens, but still stunningly handsome—for a few seconds. She'd never gotten this close to Andre Manuel Cruz-Romero, better known as Andre Romero, before. Funny the things a person learned about a total stranger during the lengthy process of closing on real estate. She knew practically everything about him but his measurements.

And there were a few of those that she wouldn't mind knowing—specifically the length and girth of one part. She hadn't been able to ignore the sizeable lump in his trousers during the closing meeting.

The slightly magnified effect of the lens gave her a great opportunity to see the olive-skinned hunk up close— well, at least his face. There were the most amazing gold streaks in his deep brown eyes. A sexy mole sat high on one cheek. Dark stubble lined his jaw and covered his chin. And his curly hair frolicked over the top of his head in a flirty wave flopping over one eye. "No, he doesn't look mad. Just a bit impatient." She turned the deadbolt and opened the door. "Hi, Andre. What a surprise."

Perfect, white teeth flashed brightly against his warm,

brown skin. "Hi. You had a package delivered to the house today. I thought it might be important. I hope you don't mind but I signed for it." He thrust a decent-sized cardboard box toward her.

"Oh! Thanks! I don't mind at all. My mother must have forgotten." She glanced at the label then up into his eyes. "That was very sweet." *My God, he's handsome. Look at that mouth! I bet he's an amazing kisser.* She held in a sigh and tried to remember what she'd been saying.

Too late. It was gone.

"It's a birthday gift," Mary said, clearly trying to cover for Britt's major brain fart.

"Really?" he said, those perfect lips pulling into another perfect smile that held just a hint of danger. He leaned closer, and for some reason, Britt felt sure he was going to kiss her. She closed her eyes and held her breath. "Happy birthday, Britt," he whispered.

Nothing touched her lips but a soft puff of air. Damn! No birthday kiss?

Feeling really stupid, she opened her eyes. What had made her think he'd kiss her? While they knew a lot about each other, thanks to the load of paperwork they'd signed a week ago, they were still virtual strangers. After all, it had been a property closing, not a date that had brought them together for a couple of hours.

"Would you like a glass of wine?" Mary offered, giving Britt a nudge.

Coming to, Britt motioned him inside and stammered, "Yes, please. You're welcome to come in. It's a little chilly outside." *You're welcome to do more than that, but sharing a glass of wine's a nice start.*

"Okay, but just one." He stepped inside and took a visual tour of her living room. "Nice place." To his credit, he didn't compare it to the shack she'd sold him.

Still, she had an irresistible urge to explain why she'd sold him a house that was in such rough shape. "Thanks. This place is more my speed. I tried to fix the old place up, but it was too much for me. It belonged to my grandparents, and I loved the old farmhouse, but I'm just not capable—"

He lifted a fingertip and pressed it to her lips. "No need to explain. The house is old and it needs a lot of work. I'd never expect anyone—even a woman who seems as capable as you—to be able to tackle it on her own."

Stunned into silence by the innocent, yet provocative, touch to her mouth, she stared into his eyes and forced herself to resist the urge to tease his finger with her tongue then pull it into her mouth and suck.

His very sexy and dangerous expression made her tingle all over. She felt her panties getting wet.

Only when he pulled his finger away was she able to speak. "I...own a Dewalt, cordless...you know."

He reached for her again, this time seeming to aim for her shoulder. His gaze slipped from her face.

She tensed up with expectation.

But his hand never made contact with her. Instead he smiled at someone or something behind her and said, "Thanks." Then, pulling his arm back, and leaving her to watch the way his biceps thickened as he moved, he brought a glass of wine to his mouth and sipped. His tongue darted out as he lowered the glass. "Mmm. Very good wine."

"Yes." She tried to slow her panting breaths, sure she sounded like a dog.

"So, you were saying you have a Dewalt? That's impressive. I don't know many women who—"

"Would you like to have a seat?" Mary interrupted, standing somewhere behind Britt.

My God, where are my manners? "Yes, please! Sit." Feeling a bit awkward in her own skin and not completely in control of her limbs, she lunged forward to catch his free hand. Naturally, she missed and knocked into the one holding the glass of very red wine. Of course it spilled. All over his white golf shirt. "Oh, my gosh! I'm so sorry!" Not thinking, merely reacting, she reached forward and dabbed at the red stain with her hands. "That was such a nice shirt, too. I'll buy you a new one. I promise," she rambled.

Mary tapped at her shoulder and handed her a damp rag, and Britt started to work trying to clean the large mark from the middle of his chest. The feel of defined pecs and abs were not lost to her, even through the shirt's thick cotton, and even despite her self-conscious panic.

Andre caught her wrists and smiled, instantly stilling her frenzied motion. "It's okay. I have plenty more shirts. This one was old. I wear it when I'm working around the house. Honest."

"If that's what you wear to work around your house, I'd love to see what you wear to go out to dinner," she mumbled, not intending for him to hear.

"I'd like that, too."

She jerked her hands away and cupped them over her mouth, rag and all. "Oh, God! I didn't think you'd hear that." Dropping them and wringing the rag like she wished she could wring her own neck, she stammered, "I've been drinking wine. I can't be held responsible for what comes out of my mouth."

He pulled on his shirt, which had begun to adhere to his chest and stomach like a second skin—which she appreciated—and smiled.

"Come to think of it, I can't control my hands very well after a couple of glasses, either."

"I'm not complaining." He winked. "I don't know many guys who would object to a beautiful woman with out-of-control hands."

Oh my God! He's flirting with me! She shivered as his white-hot gaze slid down her body, then slowly crept back up to her face.

"Okay, you two! You're killing me here." Mary sounded about as flustered as Britt felt but hid it well. She pulled Britt's arm, practically dragging her to the couch. "If you don't get your hands under control soon, I'll be forced to tie them."

When Andre's expression turned wicked-sexy, and sure she was going to melt into a puddle, Britt forced herself to look away. A few naughty comebacks shot to her mind, but she forced herself to remain mute. It was a lot safer that way. She had a feeling Andre played in a whole different league from her—in more ways than one—and although she was more than a little intrigued, she was also a tiny bit intimidated.

Mary eased the tension by shoving the nearly forgotten cardboard box in her hands. "Here. I'm dying."

Me too, but not for the same reason.

"Will you finally open this?"

"Gladly." Britt fought through the packing tape and pulled a smaller box out of the plain brown one. This one was emblazoned with, among other things, the words "Private Games" across the top. "What is this?" She read the top then the sides. "Some kind of board game? Why would my mother buy me this?"

"Haven't you heard of it? It's all the rage. It's a…" Mary cleared her throat. "…well, kind of a dating game. I read about it on the 'net. Your mom and I thought it would be the perfect gift."

"Oh, really?" Britt tried not to sound too insulted. "What do I need a dating game for? I'm doing just fine, thank you." Utterly embarrassed, she refused to look in Andre's direction.

"Oh, quit being such a spoilsport! I know you better than that. Let's have a look." Mary pulled the box out of Britt's hands and lifted the top off. "Let's pull a card."

"How about we don't?" Britt suggested, catching Mary's suddenly busy hands. She motioned with her eyes toward Andre.

"Oh. Yeah. Right." Mary set the game on the coffee table and dropped her hands back in her lap. "It was a silly idea. I confess." She gave an exaggerated sigh. "My love life is in the pits and I wanted the game for myself."

Britt hazarded a look at Andre, not surprised to catch him grinning with disbelief. To his credit, he kept his thoughts to himself.

He drained the rest of his glass and made a good show out of stretching and yawning. "Well, ladies, thanks for the nightcap. I think I'll head home now and hit the hay early. Tomorrow, I'm rebuilding the front porch on the old homestead. Want to get started early, since we're supposed to get some rain later." He stood and smiled down at Britt, staring hungrily at her cleavage. "Thanks again for the wine, and the fun." He leaned lower and his tongue darted out, moistening his lips. "Happy birthday, Britt."

This is it! By God, he is going to kiss me! She wetted her lips, closed her eyes, and waited, breathless.

A chaste kiss warmed her cheek.

What was that? The guy practically ravages me visually, kills me with those eyes, and then gives me a peck on the cheek? "Goodnight, Andre," she forced out, following him to the front door. "Thanks for bringing over my gift."

"No problem. See you later." He left.

Mary and Britt stared at each other for a moment then Britt shrugged as she shut the front door and returned to the living room. "Was he a bundle of confusing signals, or what?"

"No, I think his interest in you was obnoxiously obvious."

"Yeah, but at the same time it wasn't. I got mixed signals. He must be a player, giving me those kinds of crazy signals to string me along," Britt thought aloud.

"He's a sexy one, that's for sure. And there's a little hint of something in his eyes."

"You saw that, too?"

"Yeah. A touch of Bad Boy." Mary sat forward and picked up the game again, sifting through its contents. "For the heck of it, what about pulling one of these cards?"

Britt dropped onto the couch. "Did you really think

this game was a good idea?"

"Naw, but I could tell when she called me that your mother's mind was made up. You know how she is. Although I admit, now that it's here, it does sound intriguing. It might be fun."

Britt considered Mary's suggestion for a moment. Fun—in any form—was one of her favorite things in world. She'd never backed down from a challenge. Skydiving, white water rafting, bungee jumping, she'd eagerly tackled them all, and had a riot. "Okay. Shuffle the deck. I'll draw a card."

Mary grinned and held the cards in her upturned palm. "Already done. I knew you'd say that. Pick a good one."

"You didn't stack the deck, did you?" Britt teased, plucking the top card from the stack.

"Heck, no!"

Britt studied Mary's devious smile—the woman was guilty as hell!—and read the card. "Go to the nearest BDSM-themed dance club and get the name and phone number of a Dom," she read aloud. "What the heck kind of dating game is this?"

"We'll just call it Extreme Dating," Mary said, laughing. She ran to her duffel bag and dropped it on the coffee table.

"What do you have in there? And where do you suggest we'll find a BDSM club? I can't imagine one anywhere near here. We're smack-dab in the middle of the Bible Belt. Heck, the raunchiest billboard we have along the highway is the one with the donkey."

"You'd be surprised." Mary pulled out a fistful of black leather and shoved it at Britt. "Here, this is for you."

"What is it?" Britt unfolded what looked like a miniscule dress made to fit a small child. "You're not suggesting I wear this, are you? And how do you know about these places and I don't?"

"I have my sources." Mary fluttered her eyelashes and held a racy red leather dress, nearly the same shade as her pony-tailed hair, getup to her chest. "How do you think this'll look?" One hand reached up and pulled the ponytail holder out of her hair, and she shook it, letting it fall in shoulder-length waves. "They say redheads can't wear red, but I happen to think this looks fantastic. What do you think?"

"It looks great, I guess," Britt said, admittedly sidetracked. She wanted to hear more about the club. "So, fess up. Have you been there? What's it like?" Britt waited impatiently, watching Mary pull out spiked leather wristbands, fishnet stockings and various other accoutrements and set them on the coffee table.

"I'm not telling. But if you'd hurry up and put that dress on, you could go find out for yourself!"

Britt didn't need to hear another word. She raced to her room to dress.

Chapter 2

"Are you absolutely sure about this?" Not exactly trusting her friend, since Mary had driven them to what looked like an abandoned warehouse out in the middle of nowhere, Britt hesitated before getting out of the car. At this point, she wasn't sure which would be worse, Mary being right, or Mary being wrong and them both being jumped by a group of misguided teenagers out looking for a couple of lost women to mug.

For one thing, the dress—which hardly covered more than a bathing suit would—kept riding up her legs when she moved, the bottom of the skirt seeming to like resting right around her crotch. How in heaven's name would she dance—or even walk—without giving everyone in the place a free show? The rest of the outfit wasn't bad. The heavy silver jewelry was kind of sexy, and the stilt-like shoes made her legs look forever long.

Not good for walking on gravel though. She glanced out the window and grimaced.

"Yes, we're in the right place. Trust me." Mary climbed out of the car and waved for Britt to follow her.

She did. "You've been here before?"

"Yes."

"How did you find out about this place? It's in the middle of nowhere, looks like an abandoned warehouse—"

"I'm not telling. Suffice it to say, you don't know your best friend as well as you thought you did." Mary smiled over her shoulder, the expression clearly meant to jibe Britt.

Britt gritted her teeth against the comeback rearing up in her throat and smiled back as she stumbled across the gravel parking lot. When they approached the heavy steel door, Mary motioned for Britt to keep still then knocked in a short pattern.

The door opened, and a very tall guy in full gothic regalia—including multiple piercings on his face—opened the door, gave them both a once-over and motioned them inside.

"Wow, it's like 'Open Sesame'. Is there a code word too?" Britt murmured as she stepped inside the dark club. "Reminds me of a cave," she added after an initial sweeping glance. Dark, dingy, and echoey. Although this cave was packed full of people—mostly clad in black leather. Strange music played softly in the distance.

"You might want to get a drink before we go inside. It'll help you relax," Mary suggested.

"Why would I need to relax? I'm fine." She rolled her head from side to side. "See? As relaxed as can be."

"Just try to keep an open mind, okay? This is the lounge-slash-bar area. In the next room are the other parts."

"Other parts?" Now, she was curious. "What kind of parts? Body parts? Car parts?"

"Wine first." Mary pulled her to the bar and ordered them both a glass of red wine.

Britt sat on a barstool, swiveling around to check out the crowd. All types of people milled about, mostly young, mostly attractive, mostly dressed in black. Some wore collars and leashes and were led around the room by masked masters. Those—who she assumed were the submissives—were notably silent. The Doms—often men but not always—paused occasionally to speak with someone. "How do we find a Dom who'll talk to us? For some reason, I'm getting the impression this won't be easy."

"It might not be. Can't say I've tried to talk to one before. Sometimes, they'll come to you."

Suddenly nervous, imagining some masked, scary stranger approaching her, she swallowed half her wine. "What do I say if I'm not interested?"

"Thanks, but no thanks?" Mary suggested. "Seriously, it's all a game, and there are rules, but they're still just people inside that leather and latex."

A huge man wearing a leather mask and carrying a horse crop stomped by, his gaze cold and threatening.

"That's hard to remember." Britt looked away, hoping he wouldn't think anything of her staring, and finished off the rest of the wine. Within minutes, she felt braver, thanks no doubt to the alcohol. "Okay. I'm ready. Are you going to give me a rundown of the rules so I don't do something stupid?"

"Sure. I don't know everything, but this is what I've been told. Don't talk to the subs unless they speak to you. Keep quiet, don't interrupt the play. No catcalls or cheering. Keep your distance from the Dom's tools. Don't touch anyone's equipment—"

"As in genitals?"

"As in cat-o'-nine-tails."

"Gotcha. What else?"

"No pictures. And once you leave here, you don't know any of these people. They all have lives, families, jobs. What happens here, stays here. Oh, and since we've drunk alcohol, we cannot play." Mary hesitated at a pair of double doors.

"Really? Why's that? Er, not that I was planning on

playing. At least, not the first time."

"It's not safe."

"Oh." A lump formed in her throat.

"Ready?"

She swallowed hard. "Yeah." For a split second, Britt tried to prepare herself for what she'd see, but having no idea of what to expect, she couldn't.

The doors opened, and a strange world opened with them. A dark world, with people in small fenced-in areas playing out their most secret fantasies in the middle of a small but milling crowd. As they walked past one "stage" after another, she became both more uncomfortable and more intrigued. The good news, the position of her dress was much less of a concern.

Then a familiar voice, male, smooth, sexy, made her turn around. *It can't be...* She scanned the crowd for Andre's face but didn't see it. Strange coincidence. *I could have sworn I heard his voice.* "Mary, did you hear Andre's voice, or am I hearing things?"

"Nope," she whispered, motioning for Britt to lower her voice.

"Wishful thinking, I guess." She turned back around to watch the scene in front of them. A tall, muscular Dom was demanding a woman clean his shoes. With her tongue. "Ewww." The Dom glanced at her, and she clapped her hand over her mouth and whispered, "Sorry."

"Would you please be quiet?" Mary whispered.

"Sorry, but that's gross. Why does she have to lick his shoes?"

"It's a submissive's role to do whatever pleases her Dom," a male's deep voice whispered in her ear, sending shivers down her spine.

"I...see..." She turned her head to see who the speaker was. Andre! It had been him! *I'm not losing my mind! What a relief. My medical coverage doesn't pay squat for mental health care.* "Andre? Fancy bumping into you here, of all places."

"Hi. Yeah, I had a change of plans. The weather

forecast calls for rain all night. I won't be able to work on the porch tomorrow and a friend called me…" Dressed in the same fashion as everyone else, including tight leather pants that hugged a huge bulge front and center and a net shirt that gave her a glimpse of the muscles she'd only caught a touch of earlier—along with a pair of pierced nipples—Andre appeared to fit right in with the rest of the crowd. His gaze dropped to her breasts then climbed steadily lower. "Nice dress."

"Thanks." She tugged the hem back down her thighs. "Leather is tricky to wear." *Does wonders for you though.* Her gaze dropped to his crotch. *Please, tell me that's real.*

"You're doing fine. What do you think of this place? First time, I'm guessing."

"Is it that obvious?" She felt her face heating and wished she hadn't guzzled that glass of wine.

"Yeah, but that's okay. It's hard to hide."

"So, you've come here before?"

"Yeah." A passing woman—a beautiful blonde with long hair and a perfect body sheathed in black latex— tapped him on the shoulder and gave him a coy smile, and he gave her a slight nod in response. "This place is okay."

Who was that? His girlfriend? A sex partner—or whatever they call them here? What were the rules again? *What am I doing? I don't belong here.* For the first time since stepping foot in the bar, Britt felt completely out of place. She wanted to ask who the woman was, but couldn't. It wasn't her right. After all, she couldn't even call Andre a friend, yet. "I've seen a lot of things I've never seen before, that's for sure."

He chuckled, and the sound—plus his playful smile— pushed aside some of her former discomfort. "I bet you have. The first time's a real eye-opener. At least you came dressed. First time I stumbled into this place, I had on a golf shirt and khakis. I stood out like an Eskimo at a nudist colony."

She shared a soft laugh with him, enjoying the way his

eyes sparkled when he smiled and noting the return of the hint of bad boy she'd seen earlier. At least now, she knew where that was coming from. "Are you by any chance a Dom?"

His eyebrows rose at least an inch. "Why do you ask?"

Because I wouldn't mind serving you, you sexy hunk of man. If you aren't already taken. "Well, you remember my birthday gift? The game? Um, we drew a Challenge card. We have to collect the name and phone number of a Dom."

"I'm not your traditional, professional Dom, no. So, I'm afraid you're outta luck. Sorry."

Darn! I mean, yea! I mean...oh, what do I mean? "Traditional? Is there such a thing? And professional? Are you telling me these guys are paid to get their shoes licked clean? What a deal! Where do I sign up to be a dominatrix? I have a few pairs of pumps that could use a good spit-shine." *Although being tied up, maybe teased with a little whippy thingy looks like fun.*

"There's a lot more to being a Dom than what you see. Besides," he leaned closer and whispered, "I think you'd rather do the licking, wouldn't you?"

She felt her eyeballs bugging from her head as the image of her kneeling at his feet, her fist gripping his huge cock and her tongue swirling round and round it like a lollipop shot through her mind. Her pussy tingled.

"Wouldn't you like to serve your master and receive great rewards in return?"

More tingles skittered up her spine. Rewards. *Wonder what kind he has in mind?* She imagined him knocking her flat on her back, parting her legs wide and pushing his cock deep inside her pussy. A lump completely closed off her throat.

"You've always wanted to be tied up, haven't you? Forced by a dark stranger."

How did you know?

"You know," His fingertip traced the line of her throat then continued lower and stopping just above her exposed cleavage, "the beauty of being a sub is in both the giving and in the receiving." His other hand cupped her chin and lifted it, and her gaze snapped to his eyes and froze there for a moment before sliding south to rest on his broad, smooth chest. She swore she could see his heartbeat pounding below the thick muscles. "When you please your master, you receive pleasure beyond your wildest dreams. Let me guess…" When he didn't continue, she glanced up. His smile was more wicked now than she'd ever seen it, yet she was tempted to press in closer to him rather than back away. He licked his lips then continued, "You like to be bent over and fucked from behind, right? That way, you can touch yourself and come over and over."

A sudden case of dizziness left her staggering and wobbly kneed. She gripped his upper arms and stared up into his eyes, eager to see if he was simply teasing her, or making some kind of offer. She couldn't speak. Her tongue was frozen to the roof of her mouth, and her mind had become lost in a hazy fog.

He released her chin and dropped his other hand from her chest. "Have you ever let a lover take complete control? Let him push you to your threshold then pull you back, over and over until you couldn't take it anymore?" While he didn't touch her, he stood so near she could feel the soft puff of air caressing her neck as he spoke. And heat radiated from his body.

"No." *But it sounds damn promising at the moment.* Some of the heat seemed to soak into her pores and shoot down to her pussy.

"Would you like to?"

Are you offering what I think you are? "Maybe." She felt the chill of wetness puddle in her panties.

He pulled a card from his pocket and handed it to her. "Call me tomorrow."

She glanced down and blinked away the blur of confusion and desire.

It was a regular card, from his work. Andre Cruz-

Romero, Engineering Manager. She wasn't sure what she'd expected. Andre Romero, Dom. Specializing in erotic torture. "Okay."

"And wear the dress. I'll supply the rest. See you tomorrow night. I'm looking forward to it."

The tone in his voice as he said the last sentence left her breathless, speechless and both shivering and hot at the same time. Glancing around, she looked for Mary. She'd had enough teasing for one night. She needed to pay a visit with her friendly vibrator. Now.

Chapter 3

"I knew it!" Mary smiled triumphantly. Back at Britt's place, she gathered her things from the coffee table and couch and stuffed them in the duffle bag. "So, your hunky Andre's a Dom?"

"He's not my Andre. And he's not a Dom, at least not in the purest sense of the word, I guess."

"Whatever that means." Mary zipped her bag then slung it over her shoulder.

"My thoughts exactly."

"Sorry about abandoning you, by the way, but I figured you needed a little space. After the first sentence, I was squirming. I had to get outta there. Shit, that man can talk dirty. Is there anything he can't do?"

Not that I can tell. "I'm sure he has his shortcomings. All men do."

"True, but he seems to have a few more…uh…strengths than the average guy." Mary winked. "So, are you going to see him again?"

"Maybe. And it's okay you abandoned me. I found you, eventually," Britt said, stifling both a hint of jealousy over her friend's obvious lust over Andre and the truth about how pissed she'd gotten at the club. It had taken close to an hour to find Mary, huddled in the corner and talking to the scary giant with the whip. By the time she'd found her wandering friend, Britt had been downright seething.

Mary chuckled and winked. "At least I don't have to ask you if you had fun."

"I can't say I had fun—well, not an adrenaline-rush kind of fun—but I saw some interesting things there."

"Like Andre."

"He is the most interesting thing, er person, yes."

"I don't blame you. I'd kill to be tied up and fucked by that man."

And I'd kill you if you did! He's not mine yet, but if I get my way he will be soon. More jealousy wound up her spine. "He gave me his number. So, I guess I'm going on a date with him tomorrow night. Um, that is what it's called, isn't it? A date?"

"Are you playing in his dungeon or going out?"

His dungeon? Not a bedroom? "I'm not sure. I guess I won't know until I call him. He did ask me to wear this dress again, so can I borrow it for a couple more days? I'll have it cleaned before I give it back."

"Sure!" Mary gave her a gentle tap on the shoulder. "Look at you! Getting ready for your first time with a Dom. Are you nervous?"

Hell yes! "A little. Want to give me any pointers? Um, assuming you know about these things."

"To tell you the truth, I'm a watcher, not a doer. But I've learned one thing. Make sure you have a safe word so if he gets too carried away you can make him stop."

"Okay."

"Pick something easy to remember and pronounce, too. You wouldn't want to stumble over the word in the midst of some tense moment." Mary grinned. "That's about it." She shrugged then strolled toward the front door, and Britt followed her. "Good luck tomorrow. Have fun. And call me afterward. I want to hear all about it—

um, some of the juicier parts, at least."

"Okay."

Britt closed the door and headed for bed, sure she wouldn't get a decent minute's sleep. Even after more than an hour since she'd talked to Andre, she was still a tingly, horny mess.

Thankful for the vibrator she had purchased on a whim but hadn't put to use yet, she rummaged through her dresser drawer and pulled it out.

She might be alone in body, but she had one hell of an imagination. She wouldn't be alone in her mind. After pulling off her dress and putting on some soft music, she lay on the bed, parted her legs and turned on the toy.

It hummed softly in her hand as she closed her eyes and imagined Andre's flirty, wicked smile. Her pussy immediately clenched around its own emptiness.

His words echoed in her ears, *Have you ever let a lover take complete control? Let him push you to your threshold then pull you back, over and over until you couldn't take it anymore?* No doubt about it, tomorrow would be an experience she would never forget.

Her body already tense with anticipation, she parted her labia and rested the vibrator on her clit. Immediately with the first touch, heat rocketed through her body and she sighed. It wouldn't take much to make her climax at this rate.

The beauty of being a sub is in both the giving and in the receiving. When you please your master, you receive pleasure beyond your wildest dreams.

She slid the vibrator lower and pushed it inside, gasping at the intense sensations throbbing through her body. Every muscle from head to toe knotting tightly, she pulled it out then plunged it inside over and over, while she stroked her clit with her other hand.

You like to be bent over and fucked from behind, right? That way, you can touch yourself and come over and over.

She imagined herself lying in bed, her legs tied wide,

163

Andre standing over her, watching. Her pussy tightened around the vibrator and her fingers teased her clit then pushed inside her ass. In her head, he smiled, cooing appreciative compliments about her ass and pussy. Encouraging her to come for him.

And she came, calling out his name into the darkness. Her body spasmed, her pussy rhythmically milking the vibrator, her anus pulsing around her finger until she had no energy left. Satiated, she slid the vibrator out, turned it off and set it on the nightstand.

And she slipped into a dream, where she and Andre fucked over and over and over.

* * * * *

Andre made one last attempt to fix his unruly hair. It was humid outside, and he stood little chance of taming the curls. Extra gel did little good, and he didn't like making his hair stiff. Of all days, today he wanted it silky, touchable.

This was it. His dream come true.

Ever since he'd laid eyes on Britt Olson he'd wanted her. She was absolutely stunning, a classic northern-European beauty. Slim, delicately built with smooth ivory skin, brilliant blue eyes, naturally curly hair and feminine features. There was an air of innocence about her, yet boldness, too. Strength, but also vulnerability. Intelligence, but also approachability. He had the feeling she didn't always speak her mind, and he yearned to know what secrets she kept hidden away in the cool depth of her soul. Like a deep pool, the surface seemed calm, but he wondered what currents churned below.

He wondered what a game of bondage and submission might bring to the surface. In fact, he ached to find out.

It hadn't been easy explaining to friends and family members why he'd bought the run-down farmhouse when he could afford a much nicer home. The truth, he knew, would be too ridiculous for anyone to believe.

He had bought it for her. A stranger, yes, but a woman

he'd felt an instant connection with. He sensed she felt the same. If things went well, maybe someday they'd live in the house together, work side-by-side fixing it up. Raise their children.

But one thing at a time. Tonight was an important beginning, and he wouldn't blow it. He'd make sure that by the end of the night, she'd be aching to come back for more.

Years of experience had taught him what most women wanted. They wanted a strong man who could be vulnerable at the right time. They wanted a man who could make demands, take control, but also give back more than he received. They wanted a man who would listen to them when they needed to vent without shoving solutions down their throats.

He could be all those things for her, and more.

After giving up on his hair, he went outside, climbed into his car, and drove to her home. His body was tense with expectation, his cock already at full staff before he'd gotten within a couple miles of her home. Memories alone stirred him to aching arousal. He parked, adjusted his pants to try to hide the telltale bulge. Finally accepting it was futile, he walked to the door. She'd know exactly how thrilled he was to see her. That wouldn't be such a bad thing. Nervous, he knocked and waited.

She smiled as she opened the door, and the sight of her nearly drove him mad with desire. As requested, she wore the skimpy black leather dress she'd had on last night. The dark leather was a striking contrast to her pale skin. And the deep plunging neckline showed off delectable cleavage that he ached to explore with fingers and tongue.

"Hi," she cooed.

"Ready?"

"I'm starving. Dinner first?"

"Absolutely." He motioned for her to walk ahead of him.

The extra-short skirt showed off her long, slim legs to

perfection, and hugged her surprisingly round ass, he noted as she turned to close the front door then brushed past him toward the car.

Licking his lips and wishing he were licking that ass, he followed her, shut her car door, then went around to the driver's side and took his seat. "We can do one of two things, and I'll leave it up to you. I have no preference." He glanced her way, and immediately doubted his ability to concentrate on driving. "I don't want to look like a cheapskate, but I'd like some privacy. So, either we can go get something takeout from a nice restaurant and go back to the house and eat, or we can go inside and eat at the restaurant of your choice. You decide."

She chuckled. "You made that decision easy by asking me to wear this. I might not mind being dressed like this at a BDSM nightclub, but I wouldn't want to wear it at a five-star restaurant."

He nearly slapped himself upside his head. "I should have thought of that. I swear it was an honest oversight. Would you rather go inside and change? You can bring that along for later."

Her cheeks turned a sexy shade of pink and his balls tightened. He couldn't wait to see more of that flush on her neck, chest...lower...

"Oh, that's okay. I vote for carryout. How about steak?"

"Sounds perfect. I'm always game for a nice rare hunk of meat."

"Me, too."

He peered her way and caught a playful smile. His drawers grew instantly snug, and he thanked whatever god was responsible for the blessing sitting next to him. Then he pulled out of her driveway, and chattering about nothing and everything, drove to the steakhouse. After parking, calling in the order from his cell phone, he shifted his body to face her.

It would be so easy to give in to the other hunger. The

one that wasn't housed in his stomach. The one that was scorching him from the inside out. No doubt about it, tonight would be sheer torture—good torture, but extremely uncomfortable nonetheless.

The coy smile had vanished from Britt's face, replaced by a shy, nervous one. "This is so awkward."

"Just be yourself, Britt. No need to be nervous." He reached for her hand and gave it a gentle squeeze. "Tonight I just want to focus on getting to know you."

Relief softened her formerly tense expression and her eyes widened, making her look so painfully innocent and trusting he wanted to wrap his arms around her and pull her to him. "Really?"

"Did you assume we'd skip the beginning part and just go for the other stuff?"

She lifted her free hand and pulled at a lock of hair fluttering across her face on a breeze. She tucked it behind her ear. "Honestly, I didn't know what to expect. We didn't really talk about it last night."

"My fault. I should have been more specific."

"It's not that big of a deal. I know now, so we can go from here and just see what happens."

"Good." *I know what I'd like to happen.* "So, why don't you tell me more about yourself. Thanks to the closing paperwork, I know a few basic facts about you, but I'd like to know more."

"Like what?" Pulling at the hem of her skirt, she crossed her legs. Her thighs were trim and firm. Absolutely perfect. His palm itched to slide over the satiny skin.

"Like do you work out? You look very fit."

"I do, but not as often as I should. Maybe a couple of times a week. In between, I try to watch what I eat. Follow my own version of the low-carb diet."

Whatever you're doing, it's working. "You will eat tonight, won't you?"

"Oh! Absolutely!" She smiled and he suppressed a sigh. Her eyes glittered like diamonds. Her whole face lit up.

She was a glorious sight. "I never let a good steak dinner go to waste. Meat, potatoes, bread. I won't leave a bit of it for the dogs."

"Good. I like to see a woman who's not afraid to eat in front of a man. No need to pretend. I want you to be yourself."

"In that case, how about ordering some dessert, too? I love that brownie-ice cream thingy they make here. It's sinful."

Sinful, like you are in that dress. "Glad to." Sporting a huge hard-on, and not wanting to walk into the restaurant and show everyone what he had on his mind, he called in the dessert order with his cell phone.

Seconds later, a waitress carted a large brown bag out to their car, handed it to Andre through the car window, and returned inside with Andre's cash payment tucked in her apron pocket. Andre, drooling both because of the scent of the food and the sight of the gorgeous woman sitting beside him, drove the few miles to his place. Then he parked, grabbed the bag, opened Britt's car door and ushered her to his front door, his gaze straying to her ass every chance it could. He tripped over a porch step and bumped into her back, and he had to fight the urge to drop the food, grab her body and press her firmly against him.

But he didn't do it.

Proud of himself for maintaining control, he reached around her, slid the key into the lock and opened the door.

She stepped inside and glanced around the living room. "You painted. It looks very nice. And the wood floors. Wow! Did you install new ones?"

"Oh no, these are the original floors. I sanded and refinished them."

"Really? I'd never have thought they could look this great." She smiled up at him and he returned the warm expression with one of his own.

He carried the bag to the dining room and set it on the

table. "I'm glad you approve. I have a lot of plans for this house," he added honestly while not going into detail about what kind of plans he was referring to. It was much too soon to tell her all that he wished for the home—including who might inhabit it.

"You've done so much already. More than I did owning it for six years. My poor grandfather. It was too much for him to handle the last few years he and my grandmother lived here. But I have no excuse really. It sounds silly, but I didn't want to fix it up until after they were gone. I felt guilty. Like I was somehow hurting them by updating."

"It's different for me. You have memories tied to this place. I don't. Plus, I have friends in the trades who owe me favors." He walked into the kitchen for plates, glasses and other necessities.

"My gosh! Look at this kitchen. Is this the same house?" Britt exclaimed from behind him as she halted in the doorway. "It's…wow…like a showroom."

"You aren't upset, are you?" His hands full, he turned to face her, embarrassed by the obvious appreciation—nearing awe—he found on her face. "Well, I didn't do it by myself. Like I said, I have some extremely skilled friends."

"Are you kidding? No, I'm not upset. It's gorgeous. Are those cabinets solid cherry?" She stepped inside and softly stroked a door, and he nearly wilted as he imagined her touching him like that.

"Yep."

"And is this a real granite counter?" Her hand dropped to the cool, smooth stone counter. Her tongue darted out, moistening her lips as her hand ran over the counter's surface in long, slow strokes.

Gimme some ice. I'm in meltdown! "It is. My buddy works at a stone yard. So you like it? Be honest."

She took the glasses and wine from him and returned to the dining room, setting them on the dining table. "Very much. Believe me, I had no emotional attachment to the laminated stock cabinets and cheap plastic counters I put in. Yes, I'm very impressed by what you've done so far. I just wish I could have done as well."

He followed her on wobbly legs. "You did the best you could. Don't beat yourself up over it. This place wouldn't look like this if I didn't have friends to help. If I'd had to pay retail and labor for all this stuff, I'd have never been able to afford it," he lied. The last thing he wanted her to feel was guilt for not being able to afford the latest and greatest just because he could.

"Can I borrow those friends of yours sometime? My new place isn't in a shambles, but there are a few projects I wanted to tackle."

There's no chance I'm letting any of my beer-swilling buddies near you. They're animals. "Sure! What do you need? I'm fairly handy when it comes to small projects. I have my own Dewalt, too."

She giggled, the sound so charming and erotic, he wanted to say something silly just to hear it again. "Oh, yeah. That."

He handed her a plate and silverware and then pulled out the foam packages from the restaurant's paper bag. He put the dessert in the freezer for safekeeping then set one large container next to her plate. "A guy would have to be nuts not to appreciate a woman with her own power tools."

Clearly fighting another blush but losing the battle, she rolled her eyes. "I shouldn't have bragged. I only use it to hang pictures, assemble furniture, stuff like that. I'm sure it's more power than I need."

He paused after flipping the top of his container open. "That depends on what kind of power you're talking about," shot out of his mouth before he could stop it. He loved the game of double entendre, and he suspected Britt would be better than average at keeping up with him. Her mind was razor-sharp.

Eager to see if she'd gotten his message, he glanced at

her.

Yep. She had. Her wide-eyed, shocked semi-smile said it all.

Eager to hear her comeback, he swallowed an apology and went back to unpacking his steak and potato.

"I thought you liked to be the Dom," she said in a low, sexy voice that sent shudders up and down his spine. "I may not know anything about this bondage and submission stuff yet, but I thought the whole idea was for the sub to be powerless."

He cut up his potato and dabbed on some sour cream then added salt. "You see, that's where you're mistaken. The sub actually has plenty of power. Are you intrigued?" He lifted his gaze to her face.

"Yes."

"Later."

Her shoulders dropped. "You're a tease."

"I've been called worse." He took a bite of his steak. "How's your dinner?"

"Delicious. So tell me, how did you get into this bondage stuff?"

He swallowed. "There are different levels, from casual—like lovers who tie each other up on occasion—to serious, people whose lifestyles are fashioned around it. I tend toward the more casual side, although I have a decent collection of equipment for someone who isn't living it twenty-four, seven."

Her fork halted midair. "Really? Will you show me?"

"Later. You're impatient, aren't you?"

"Yes, that's one of my biggest weaknesses. Very impatient."

"Interesting." He imagined the games he could play to take full advantage of her admitted shortfall and his cock swelled even more.

"What about you? I hate to admit a deep, dark, dirty secret and not know one about you."

"That was deep and dark? I think you could do better

than that."

"Well, it's all you're getting for now. Your turn."

"Hmmm... I don't think you're ready to hear about the darkest, dirtiest...yet."

"Chicken," she teased, parting her lips and sliding a piece of meat into her mouth. They closed over the fork, the corners lifting into a flirty smile.

"Oh, no. I'm no chicken. Just don't want to scare you off."

She pulled the fork out and chewed, her gaze fixed to his. He enjoyed the way she looked in his eyes. Confident, attentive. "You haven't scared me off yet. What could be so bad?"

"Nothing. As far as weaknesses go, I'd say I tend to be very stubborn. Once I make my mind up on something, it's practically impossible to change it."

She nodded and took another bite of her steak, chewing and swallowing before saying, "I'm beginning to see that."

"What else do you see?"

"A man who knows what he wants and goes for it. You saw my house once and we closed only a couple weeks later. I've never seen a real estate transaction go that quickly." She paused a moment and her eyebrows dropped. "And I think you're a man with a lot of secrets."

"Me? No. I'm a what-you-see-is-what-you-get kind of guy."

She chuckled. "Liar." Leaning back and setting her fork and knife on her plate, she added, "I've had enough of this steak. It was delicious."

He glanced down at her dish. "You've only eaten a couple of bites."

"Want to save room for dessert."

"Fair enough. Do you want to take this home?" He stood and lifted both their plates.

"Sure. Thanks."

"Be right back." He wrapped their dinners and put

them in the refrigerator then brought out the ice cream along with one spoon. He didn't miss her gaze as it locked on his hands.

"Only one spoon? You aren't going to make me eat that whole thing, are you?"

"No way." He set the dessert in front of her then carried his chair around the table and set it next to hers. "We'll share. I'll feed you." He lifted the spoon, scooped a bit of the white fluffy whipped cream off the side and put it in front of her mouth, breathlessly watching it open and close around the utensil. A tiny bit of white clung to her lip until she licked it away.

"Mmmm…" She closed her eyes, visibly relishing the taste. "So sweet and creamy."

Setting down the spoon, he plucked the cherry off the top, holding it by the stem, and ran it along the seam of her lips. They opened and her tongue slid out and swirled around and around. His heartbeat flew into double time and his cock throbbed.

Then she drew the cherry into her mouth slowly and opened her eyes. "I love cherries."

"So do I." He gave the stem a sharp tug until it pulled from the fruit trapped behind her teeth and dropped it on the table.

"Let me share." She leaned closer and pressed her mouth against his. He slipped his tongue out to taste her closed lips and then she opened them and sucked his tongue into her mouth, welcoming it into the sweet depth.

He found the cherry and drew it into his mouth, biting down to release a flood of sweet juices before opening to welcome her tongue inside. He moaned as her tongue stroked his, slowly swirling. His eyelids grew heavy. His balls grew tight. His heartbeat pounded in his head.

The taste of cherries, the soft scent of perfume, and the sound of her breathing intoxicated him. Quickly, his defenses crumbled, and he reached forward, his hands gripping the soft flesh of her breasts under her snug leather dress. A fingertip slid over the leather, catching the feel of a taut nipple lying below it.

She moaned in his mouth, the sound urging him on. One hand found the deep slitted V of her dress and slid inside. No bra! Still kissing her, he groaned at the feel of soft skin under his palm and eagerly sought her nipple. When he found it, he pinched it between his thumb and forefinger, and her mouth still working over his, she gasped and finally broke the kiss to drop her head back and expose the long column of her neck.

"Oh, God," she whispered.

He traced the line of muscle and tendon down her neck with his tongue, then nibbled where the collarbone met the neck, and she shrugged her shoulders and giggled.

"That tickles. I'm getting goose bumps."

"Good." He pinched her nipple harder and she gasped. "Oh!"

"Do you like that?" He rolled it again between his finger and thumb. "A little bit of pain, a lot of pleasure."

"Yes," she said breathlessly, pushing her chest toward him. "More."

His tongue trailed lower between the crest of her breasts before he pulled the leather aside to expose the nipple he'd been teasing. Deep pink, erect, it beckoned him, but he resisted the urge to taste it. Instead he blew a soft stream of air on it and fought for control of his raging urge to fuck. "Your breasts are absolutely perfect." Then he felt her hand massaging his cock through his clothes, and his self-control snapped. Blind with need, he pulled her arms until she was sitting on his lap, her legs on either side of his hips. Her pussy ground into his cock, through layers of clothes, and he gritted his teeth, anxious for release.

He slid his hands around her back and dropped them to her ass, which had become conveniently exposed as her dress bunched up around her waist. She wore a thong. His fingers eagerly followed the line of velvet from her hips down between two firm, luscious ass cheeks.

Tense and frustrated because he couldn't allow himself the relief his entire body sought, he squeezed the flesh under his hands as his tongue drew circles round her pebbled nipple.

She moaned, the sound a sweet melody in his ears, as he pulled her nipple into his mouth and suckled. "Oh, yes!" she whispered, rocking her pelvis and grinding her pussy. "Oh, Andre. Yes. Fuck me."

Lifting one hand from her ass, he pushed her dress aside to expose her other breast, and took great care to give it as much attention as the first one received.

Her pleas continued, her voice rising until he knew he had to stop. He knew his limits, and he sensed she was nearing hers as well.

When he ceased, instead of drawing her to him in a warm hug, she pulled back, and looked at him, clearly confused.

"What's wrong?"

He sighed. It was never easy to explain these things to a woman. He hoped she'd understand.

Chapter 4

She was so close to orgasm she could practically taste it. He had to know what he was doing to her. What man stops things midway and then makes excuses? It made no sense. She was perfectly willing to go all the way.

She studied his flushed face for a clue but found none. So she waited.

"This probably sounds weird, but I think we should wait."

Was Andre a male? She'd never known one who turned down sex. "Why?" Suddenly uncomfortable, she scrambled to her feet, adjusted the top of her dress to hide her breasts and pulled down her skirt.

He watched her with a pained expression, convincing her he was as ready for sex as she was. So why stop? "Because it's too soon."

"Too soon for what? We both want to. Don't we?"

"Oh, yes." He nodded boyishly.

"You are certainly no virgin."

"No." He pulled her chair closer and motioned for her to sit.

She sat. "Neither am I."

"Glad to hear it."

He combed his fingers through his hair and she stifled a sigh. The man had amazing arms. An amazing body. She was dying to see what hid behind his snug short-sleeved shirt and trousers. But would he ever let her?

"I want to be honest about this. Forthright. We don't need to play games, do we?"

"Actually, dating and sex are both games, aren't they? Games of seduction. The chase is half the fun." She gazed into his eyes, hoping to find the truth. A notion struck her swiftly and without mercy. She glanced down. *I'm making this too easy for him!* "Ah. I see. So, are you one of those guys who get bored if it's too easy to get the girl?"

"No. But I'm a guy who likes to savor every moment, from the first time you look in each other's eyes..." He leaned forward and his heated gaze captured hers, making her breathless and squirmy. "...to climax. Why rush things? We have all the time in the world."

She fought to speak. Her tongue felt thick and clumsy. "Um...I guess it's that impatience thing again."

He smiled and her pussy tingled. "Oh, yes. We'll be exercising that little limitation of yours. I enjoy taking advantage of a woman's weaknesses, am not above using them for my own benefit."

"You jerk!" She reached out to give him a playful slap, but he caught her wrist and held it firmly, mid-strike.

He squeezed slightly and his expression grew intense, hot, pussy-melting. "You'll be grateful. I guarantee it." With a slow nod, he released her hand. "Domination and submission are about more than spreaders and cat-o'-nine-tails. At its best, it's a powerful tool that can help a relationship strengthen on all levels."

She reflexively rubbed her wrist to return blood flow to her hand. "I don't follow."

"What are the most important elements of a relationship to you?"

Beautiful eyes. *Look at that face! He's so hot. So intense. Oh, what did he say?* Unable to concentrate when staring at his face, she dropped her gaze to her hands.

"What is important in a relationship," he repeated as if he'd read her mind.

"Um...trust, for one."

"Yes. And blindly putting your body in a man's hands, and allowing him to serve your every need, to push you to explore aspects of yourself you've never dared delve into. To open yourself up to another human being like you've never done before. Those all build a very intense relationship where trust is absolute. Wouldn't you like to know without a doubt how your man feels? How he thinks? What he needs? Wouldn't you enjoy being in a relationship where you're free to tell him your deepest desires and fears? Where you're free to explore and experiment however you like?"

"Yes." She looked up into his eyes. "I would."

"This is new to you. Trust me. We'll take it one step at a time."

She nodded, not sure exactly how she felt. "Okay. What's next? Can I see your equipment? Your dungeon?"

"Are you sure you're ready?"

"I'm, uh, curious. And nervous. Maybe if I saw it, I'd feel better. At least, then I'd know whether my imagination had run wild."

"Okay. We can save the dessert for later." Taking her hand in his, he stood and picked up the dish of ice cream. After covering the uneaten dessert and stowing it in the freezer, he led her across the kitchen to the basement stairs. "It's down here. Just remember. We will only do what you're ready for. One step at a time."

She felt her palm sweating as it pressed against his, and her heart hammered against her ribs as she descended the stairs she'd trotted down zillions of times in the past. Now, they didn't lead to her workout room and laundry facilities. Instead, they led to a strange new world, and she wasn't sure if she was ready to enter or not.

Trust. That was what it would test. How could she trust

a man she'd spent such a short time with?

He paused at the foot of the stairs, at the door that had once led to her workout room. "Ready?"

"Yes. It's just stuff. Nothing to be scared of."

He smiled warmly and pushed open the door, and she pulled her gaze away from his handsome face to scan the room beyond.

The doorframe offered welcome support as she slowly took in the details of the room. "Wow. Those aren't weight benches and stair climbers in there, that's for sure."

All but one wall were painted black. The fourth was mirrored as it had been when she'd lived in the house. And strange contraptions filled much of the space. One looked like some kind of swing, another, a large box resembled a dog crate, and still others that looked like various racks for medieval torture. The room wasn't romantic—not in any sense—yet it stirred something deep inside. A slightly uncomfortable feeling that made her tingly and energized. Her pussy was dripping wet, both from Andre's earlier kisses and her curiosity of what was to come next. She'd never felt so much anticipation mixed with reluctance. It was a crazy brew that made her all jittery inside. "When do we start?"

"We already have. It's a process, Britt. Not an event."

Her gaze fixed on the swing, she nodded. "That one looks interesting. How do you get into that contraption?"

Her hand in his, he led her closer, then reached for one of two bands overhead, secured at opposite ends of a metal bar suspended from the ceiling. He fastened it around her wrist. "First we secure your arms like this." He buckled the second one around her other wrist, and she shuddered. The simple loss of control was already making her hot.

Andre stood in front of her, his hands sliding down her arms then skimming her sides. His thumbs tickled the sensitive flesh of her breasts. "Then you sit back." He dropped one hand, reaching behind her as he eased her back with the other one. Something bumped her spine. "This part rests at the small of your back and the other slides under your ass." He helped her into position then smiled. "Your thighs go into the stirrups."

Stirrups? White heat shot through her body as he first lifted one leg and secured it and then did the same to the other. His gaze dropped to her pussy, which was barely covered by the slim strap of her thong. Her breathing came in short gasps as her heart raced.

"Comfortable?" he asked. One hand gripped her ankle and the other traced a line from foot to knee.

She gasped. Her pussy flamed. *Not at all! Hot, bothered, and miserably horny is more like it.* Her blood heated to boiling and goose bumps followed in the wake of his touch. "Yes…"

His exploring fingers wandered higher, over the band of leather holding her thigh until it tickled the sensitive skin of her inner thigh. "How do you feel?"

So hot I could melt! She drew in a deep breath, catching a hint of an unfamiliar musky odor. "Uh, really good."

"Oh, you can do better than that." His fingers drew lazy circles on her inner thigh, each time venturing closer to her pussy. "How do you feel? What are you thinking?"

"Think? I can't think. Not when you're doing that." She tipped her head and motioned toward his hand.

He chuckled. "Do you want me to stop?"

Don't you dare! "Hell, no!"

He chuckled, his grin wicked. "What if I do this?" His fingertip traced the line of her thong.

I wouldn't complain. Her eyelids dropped closed and her whole body stiffened. "Oh, God."

He continued to stroke her pussy through the thin material. "How do you feel now?"

Was he a closet shrink? What was with all the questions about feelings? *I don't want to talk. I don't want to think. I just want to fuck.* "I…oh…" She couldn't speak. Her thigh muscles became rigid, pulling her legs further apart as she opened herself to his touch. "More."

"Hmm... Seems to me you're in no position to make demands," he teased. "I asked you a question. I expect an answer. How do you feel?"

Like stuffing a gag in your mouth, ripping your clothes off, and fucking you until you're as brain-dead as I am. "I can't."

"I can stop." He pulled his hand away.

"No!" She struggled with the bindings at her wrists. "Oh, please, don't stop."

"Answer my question, Britt," he demanded returning to caressing her pussy with long, slow strokes. "How do you feel?"

"Like I'm going to combust."

"What about up here?" He tapped her chest. "What do you feel in here?"

"A little tight. Could be cardiac arrhythmia, maybe."

He chuckled. "That's not what I meant. What do you feel in your heart and soul?"

So deep! It's impossible to meditate with my legs spread wide and his hand on my pussy. "Er...elation?"

"Is that a question or an answer?" One finger slipped inside her thong and teased her slick lips.

"Oh, God! How do you expect me to carry on a conversation like this?" She struggled to tip her hips up and take his finger deeper inside but she couldn't. The scent of her own arousal filled the air and her lips dried. She licked them.

"You must try. I want to know everything. What you're thinking, feeling, seeing, hearing, smelling."

"That I can handle. I see a sexy man driving me to the brink of insanity."

He chuckled again. "Well, that's a start. Tell me more."

Glad to see I'm amusing you. "I smell my own pussy's wetness."

"Heavenly, isn't it? I'm getting hot from your scent alone."

Then fuck me. She shuddered and her insides clenched

tight.

"What else? What do you hear?"

"Your finger sliding in my juices and your sexy voice."

"This sound?" He moved his finger more vigorously, producing more of the erotic, soft sounds. "It's so sexy, makes me so hard I want to drive my cock deep inside you."

"Please do so. I wouldn't object."

"Nope. Not yet. Remember, I'm the one in control here. I demand. You do."

She groaned as he hooked his finger to stroke the sensitized walls of her vagina. "You're killing me here."

"You'll live. I promise." He pushed his finger deeper inside and she screamed in delight.

"Oh, yes!" Her hands gripped the cool steel bar above her head as she tried to leverage herself and push her pussy against his hand. It didn't work. She had no control over the depth of his penetration. She nearly wept in frustration, then consciously tightened her vaginal walls around his finger.

"That's it, love. Oh, yes, so tight." Andre pulled his finger out, then pushed two inside. "This is all you'll get today. But you will come for me to show your gratitude."

She was so close. Every muscle inside pulled into a cramped ball. Wave after wave of heat rushed through her body, but she couldn't release. Something was stopping her.

"Come for me, Britt."

"Believe me, I want to."

"Come." He plunged his fingers in and out in a slow, seductive rhythm.

The threshold seemed just beyond reach. She pulled deeper inside herself and tried, imagining his cock driving into her. But her imagination wasn't enough to push her over the edge. "I can't."

"You will." With his second hand he stroked her clit, drawing slow circles, round and round in time with the fingers thrusting in and out.

She felt herself losing control, felt her breathing speed up, her legs quivering, her stomach tightening. "Yes! Oh, yes."

"Are you coming?"

"Almost."

"Tell me." The pace of his plunges sped up and he increased the speed of his strokes over her clit as well. Each touch drew her closer. Each time his fingers filled her pussy, she flamed hotter. Each time she drew in a breath, she grew dizzier with need.

And then she felt the flush of impending climax, and she sighed, relieved, giddy, as the climax took over and her body spasmed, sweeping her away into a cloud of energy and light and pleasure. Each heartbeat pounded in her ear as she came, counting out the beat of time for what seemed like an eternity. And then she sagged, every part of her body relaxing. "Oh." Her eyelids lifted and she focused on Andre's face.

He gave her a warm smile, lifted his hands to his nose, inhaled and drew each finger into his mouth, sucking them like a lollipop. "Delicious."

Her face flamed.

"That's enough for one day." He unstrapped her thighs and helped her find her footing before releasing her wrists. "Did you enjoy?"

She stumbled slightly, catching her balance by gripping his upper arms. "Wasn't it obvious?"

"Anyone can come. An orgasm is rarely disappointing, but I want to know if you enjoyed it all—the swing, the shackles."

"It was very erotic. Yes, I liked it. A lot."

"Good! Just wait 'til you see what I have in store for you next time." He drew her into an embrace and touched his mouth to hers, and she tasted herself on his lips. "Next time, you'll show me exactly how much you appreciated it. Understand?"

She licked her lips and clung to him, relishing the feel of his hard planes as they pressed against her soft curves. His erection was a rigid bulge under his pants, pressing seductively against her lower stomach. "I will. I promise."

"Good. I can't wait. Tomorrow, then." He kissed her softly, his moist lips sliding over hers. And then he released her and she staggered, unsteady, dizzy and exhausted. He gripped her waist and held her until she was firmly on both feet and her wobbly legs were able to support her weight.

"Tomorrow?"

"Yep. I want to give you some time to prepare."

Prepare for what? "Okay."

"I'll take you home now. Did you bring a purse or anything?" He followed behind her as she slowly ascended the stairs.

"Yes. I nearly forgot." She went to the dining room for her purse.

He stopped in the kitchen and pulled a container out of the refrigerator. "And I want to make sure you take this. You might get hungry later." He winked.

Her stomach growled in response, and she salivated. "Oh, yes. I'm starving now."

Holding his hand, she walked out to the car, settled into her seat then, a smiling, giddy goof, she rode in silence, determined to be fully prepared for tomorrow—whatever that meant.

Maybe it was all a silly game, but she was hooked. Andre had already proven to be an attentive, masterful lover. And he hadn't even actually made love to her yet—in the purest sense of the word. She wanted to learn more, to overcome what reservations remained. To explore and grow and experiment.

And Andre was the perfect man to do that with. Perfectly handsome, gentle, sexy…and patient. The man had the self-control of a saint. But she was determined to find a way to shake that a bit. Next time, she wanted to see him as desperate for release as she was.

Chapter 5

A lengthy Internet field trip revealed some interesting pictures, but little else. She found lots of photographs of bondage gear. Spreaders and special toilets—yuck!—and ball gags, and leather straightjackets. All kinds of stuff. But nothing about the actual use of the items, or the dom-submissive lifestyle. How would she be prepared if she didn't know what she was preparing for?

Finally, frustrated after hours of scouring the 'net, she called Mary. Since her friend lived only a few blocks away, she was at Britt's door within minutes.

"It's about time you called me!" Mary burst into the room with her usual bluster. "What happened last night? Give me all the juicy details."

"I'm not telling you anything. Come over here and help me."

"You promised." Mary plopped into the kitchen chair Britt had pulled up to the computer. "I can't believe you're holding out on me."

"There isn't much to tell."

"Much. Ha! You expect me to believe that? You went on a date with an incredibly sexy man, wearing a leather dress—my leather dress, may I remind you?—not to mention he's a confessed dom. Either you think I'm completely ignorant, or you're hiding something."

"I'm not hiding anything. I just like to keep things private."

"Since when? You told me when you lost your virginity. I taught you how to perform oral sex on a guy. Remember that?"

"How could I forget?" Britt giggled, remembering the scene in Mary's parents' kitchen, Mary being caught by her obnoxious baby brother, Adam, as she was sucking and slurping on a carrot.

"Up until now, we've talked about everything." Mary's voice echoed the hurt and disappointment in her eyes. "We've been friends since kindergarten."

"And we're still friends. I love you like a sister." Britt gripped Mary's hand and gave it a squeeze. "I just don't know how to talk about this stuff. It's all so strange and new to me. I honestly don't know how I feel about any of it yet."

"Then why did you call me?"

"I wanted to do some research on the Internet, but I can't find anything. I was hoping you could help me."

That seemed to boost Mary's suddenly glum mood. "Okay. What are you looking for?"

"Stuff on the bondage lifestyle. I found lots of sites that sell bondage equipment, but nothing else."

"You're looking under the wrong key words. Scoot over." Mary settled her chair in front of the keyboard and punched in a command. A black page with dozens of links appeared. "See? Lots of stuff. You can find anything on the 'net if you know where to look."

Britt skimmed the headings. "Oh, this is great! Thanks!" She clicked on a link for slave training, and immediately felt a flush spread over her face.

"What is it?"

"This...this sounds like Andre. He kept talking about my thoughts and feelings. I didn't know what he was doing."

Mary's eyebrows lowered as she read the glaring white print on the black page. "Master and slave are a little different from sub and dom, although the difference between them is subtle. A slave eventually grants her choices to her Master where a submissive doesn't. It sounds like Andre has big plans for you.""Yeah, it does." She squirmed as she read the slave rules, all one hundred and twenty-eight of them. In one way, the idea of serving someone, of turning over her will and freedom to a Master was exciting. In another it was absolutely terrifying. "Do you think he'll expect me to follow all of these?"

"It says you can choose how to interpret these rules for yourself."

"It also says that eventually I'd have to make a choice to let him do all the decision-making for me. I can't imagine doing that."

"It's new. You have to go slow. He's not asking you to do them now, is he?"

"No. We just played around with a swing in his basement. It was an amazing experience."

Mary grinned. "I bet it was. But what do you think about all of this?"

"I'm not sure. But at least now I'm not going into it blindly. I wonder if that's what he meant." Britt skimmed further down the list of rules. "These rules include undressing in public, and licking his ass clean? Oh, God! Do I have to get my labia pierced?" She shuddered at the imagined pain.

"Sounds like you need to talk to Andre. Find out what he's thinking. Maybe he doesn't want to take it this far."

"I guess you're right."

"When are you seeing him again?"

"Tonight. And he said to come prepared." Britt clicked the print icon at the top of the screen. "At least I'll have this."

"Sounds like a good start." Mary stood and rested her

hands on Britt's shoulders.

Her eyes drifting from one shocking rule to another, Britt muttered, "After reading it, though, I wonder if I'm really cut out for this. Look here. It says he will decide what my sexual orientation is. How can he do that? My undergrad psychology professor said we can't even make that choice for ourselves. I'm not a lesbian."

"Don't worry. I'm sure he'll take things slow for you. I've got to go. Call me if you need me."

Britt's gaze refused to stray from the screen. "Okay. Thanks for coming over so quickly. Really."

"No problem." Mary pulled open the front door and exited, leaving Britt with a horde of doubts and fears running through her mind. And a heaviness in her pussy.

She couldn't deny it. For some reason, although the idea of being Andre's slave was scary, it also made her hot and bothered—in a good sense.

What would tonight bring?

* * * * *

That night, after a full day's work, she sat in her living room waiting for Andre to arrive, barely able to contain her jitters. She squirmed. She paced. She chewed her lip. She played with her purse strap.

How would she ever get through the evening? She was a walking bundle of nerves. At one point, she even picked up the phone and dialed his cell phone number, intending to cancel. But before it rang, she hung up.

This was silly! Not once had he ever made an unreasonable demand—unless she counted his unusual request to chitchat while in the middle of heavy petting. He'd never told her she couldn't look him in the eye, or had to kneel on the floor with her head down, or had to have sex with another woman.

That website was for people who lived the extreme. Outside of the fact that Andre had a basement full of bondage gear, he didn't appear to be one of those kind.

Yes, everything would be fine. He was a sexy, kind

man. They would have a great time together.

Her doorbell made her jump nearly out of her skin, highlighting the fact that her feeble attempts at calming her fears hadn't helped much. Determined to find out exactly what Andre's intentions were, she scooped up her purse and walked to the door.

When she opened it, she found Andre standing on the porch, a huge bouquet of red roses in his hand.

"Hi, beautiful." His gaze wandered over her face, and his wide smile faded as he handed her the flowers. "Are you okay?"

"Oh, yes. I'm fine." She took the bouquet and turned toward the kitchen to put it in water. "The flowers are beautiful. Thanks."

Andre followed her. "You look gorgeous." He slipped an arm around her waist and pulled her closer then placed a chaste kiss on her cheek.

She felt herself flinching slightly.

"What's wrong?" he repeated, this time more sternly. He took her hands in his and coaxed her to face him. "Why won't you look me in the eye? What happened?"

"Nothing happened. I'm just nervous." She lifted her eyes, meeting his penetrating gaze.

"Why?"

"I read some things on the 'net."

"I see." He nodded. "Let's go talk." He took her hand and they walked outside, down the sidewalk and past his car.

"Where are we going?"

"On my way over I passed a nice park. It's a beautiful day."

"Okay." She strolled beside him, enjoying the feel of his warm hand wrapped around hers.

"I see you took my request to heart. I'm very pleased."

"I'm glad you're happy. Although I have to admit, reading that stuff has made me a little unsure about things," she confessed, knowing she had to be honest.

There was no way she'd be able to pretend to enjoy some of those things on that list. Heck, some of them sounded downright excruciating and humiliating. She was an independent, intelligent woman. Allowing another human being to treat her—or any woman for that matter—like trash went against everything she believed in. This was one instance where complete honesty was vital. He had to understand where she was coming from.

"But it has made you aware of what being submissive can mean. And it's opened you up. You're talking about things now instead of hiding."

"Sure, out of shock and fear."

He sighed. "If you feel that strongly about this, then maybe it isn't for you. That's okay. I was just hoping we'd be able to talk about it. No rules are set in stone. I...haven't done anything wrong, have I?"

She glanced at him, catching his forlorn expression. He looked genuinely disappointed, and that left her feeling worse. "No, you haven't. I'm just being goofy. Maybe a little defensive. I'm sorry. I do want to talk about it."

They rounded the corner and followed the path into the park. She pulled her snug skirt down over her bottom and sat on a swing, heating slightly at the memory of the last swing she'd sat on. He stood in front of her, his legs straddling her knees. His hands gripped the chains suspending the swing and his gaze fixed to hers. "Tell me. Please. What did you read?"

"I found this site about Masters and slaves. It had over one hundred rules. All sorts of things about piercing body parts, stripping naked in public, kneeling nude with eyes lowered, the Master choosing the slave's sexual orientation. Enemas and whipping and humiliation. Some of the milder stuff I could handle—as a bedroom game, maybe. I'm too independent, too stubborn, to live like a slave all the time. And I know for a fact I couldn't handle torture. Pain does nothing for me sexually. Some of those punishments were—do I need to explain further?"

"No. I understand. Really."

She hesitated and tried to read his expression. It hadn't changed. Was still encouraging and gentle and kind. Her heart felt heavy even though she was relieved. "Are you disappointed?"

"No way! I'm glad you told me. I'm glad you've opened up to me. That's all I ever wanted."

She felt a giggle wiggling up her throat. "Really?"

"Later, if or when you decide we should, we can go over those rules and talk about each one. Until then, we'll talk about other things. We can explore and learn about each other. I'm not just looking for a slave, Britt. I'm...looking for more. A partner. I want to settle down soon. In the next few years. Get married. Have children."

"You do? You are? I would never have—"

"Yeah, you figured I was out for a good time. Miss Right-for-Now. I'll ask you the same question. Are you disappointed?"

"No," she answered honestly. "I've been feeling the itch to settle down soon, too. It's time. My life is good. I'm not needy or desperate, so I know I'll make the right decision for the right reasons."

"I'm glad."

She didn't know what to say. It was mighty soon to be talking about long term relationships, marriage. In the past, if a guy mentioned marriage on the second date, she'd bolt. Rushing into a serious relationship was plain stupid.

But with Andre, in this situation, it felt right. She needed to know where he was headed, what he expected. Knowing he wanted more than a woman to chain to the wall eased her fears considerably. Knowing he understood her reservations, and supported her decisions, made her feel even better...cherished.

If Andre Cruz-Romero was everything he seemed to be, she could see herself falling fast and hard for him. Like a block of cement from a third-floor window. Thunk.

Then the image of the basement popped into her head.

"I wonder, what will you tell your future kids about the toys in the basement?"

He grinned, stepped around her and gave her back a push, sending her swinging into the air. "That's Mommy and Daddy's playroom. My kids will be so spoiled they won't care what's down there."

She closed her eyes, enjoying the feeling of the fresh, cool air blowing in her face as she ascended and the funny feeling in her belly as she descended. "That's where you're wrong. Kids are like all humanity. They want what they can't have."

"Hmm. You probably have a point. Do you have any suggestions?"

"Keep the door locked?"

"Sounds like the perfect solution, at least until they're teenagers and learn how to pick a lock." He plopped into the swing next to hers and watched as she skidded her swing to a stop, sending a cloud of dust up from the ground. "Are you ready for some dinner? It's a work night. I don't want to keep you out too late."

She stood and took his hand in hers, giving it a playful squeeze. Her shoulder brushed against his arm and she felt her face warming with a blush. "Yes, I'm starving. Let's go eat." As they walked back to her place, she added— surprising herself, "Then, maybe we can go back to your place for a little while? I'm in the mood for a visit to the playroom. I've rediscovered a fondness for swings."

Chapter 6

After eating more than her share of jambalaya at an upscale seafood restaurant nearby, Britt eased into the passenger seat of Andre's racy red Mustang and smiled. "That was delicious. Thank you."

"You're welcome." He started the car and she watched him, intent to study his features as he drove.

She could look at his face forever, the hollows under his high cheekbones. The curve of his lips. The long eyelashes that fringed his eyes.

Sure, she'd had her moments of doubt about whether to purse this thing with him. But deep down, she'd known he would be the sweet, gentle, sexy man she'd thought all along. Attentive, patient to a fault…and a genuine pro at seduction and flirting. By the end of dinner, Britt was not only laughing at his wit, but squirming, for an altogether different reason than she had been earlier.

And the silence that fell over them as he drove the short distance to his house did nothing to ease the burning between her legs, yet she didn't feel compelled to fill it with incessant, meaningless small talk to distract herself. Instead, she watched familiar neighborhoods pass by and imagined what game they might play that evening. Would he tie her up? Would he spank her? Would they make love?

Her instincts told her they would, and she was glad she'd made special preparations just in case. Every inch of her body was shaved smooth, including down there. Being completely shaved made her feel sexy. So did the lace thong and bra she wore under her skirt and top. She hoped Andre would appreciate the special preparations she'd made.

She knew it wouldn't be long before she found out. As they turned down his street, he reached across and slid his right hand up her thigh. Her pussy started throbbing instantly, and she shifted her posture slightly, parting her knees and tipping her hips up, giving him access to the more delicate regions under her clothing.

Unfortunately his straying hand couldn't stay where it was long enough. There were real drawbacks to manual transmissions.

She groaned when, just before his fingertips dipped under the hem of her skirt, he had to shift the car into second gear.

"What's wrong?" He slid her a playful smile.

"Oh, nothing," she said on a sigh.

"Put your hand on my stick."

"Your what?" She reached for his lap, figuring there was only one stick he had to be thinking of.

"That's not the one I had in mind, but I like the way you think." He winked then turned his attention back to driving as she rubbed the rigid swelling at the front of his khaki pants.

"Well, if you didn't mean this one, what stick were you talking about?"

"Here." He patted the gearshift, and she lifted her hand, raising it to her face to hide her heating cheeks.

"Oh! I can't believe I thought—sheesh! My mind's in the gutter."

"I'm not complaining."

"No, what guy would?" Encouraged by his smile, she dropped her hand to his lap again and began caressing his cock through his clothes, for which she received a gratifying groan of pleasure.

"You, my dear, are wicked." He sighed. "I like wicked."

She playfully patted the bump in his lap. "I can tell. I can't wait to get my hands on this."

He chuckled. "I can't wait either."

"And my mouth, and tongue." Feeling naughty, she licked her lips and continued stroking.

"Just wait until I get you inside, you little tease."

"Who's teasing?"

He pulled the car into his driveway and cut the engine then got out and opened her door for her before leading her up to the porch. "We'll find out in a moment who's teasing, won't we?"

"Now it's my turn to say I can't wait." She intentionally lowered her voice, erasing the playful tone. "But before we go in, I want to tell you something."

He turned the key in the front door's lock then faced her. "What is it?"

"I want to tell you again how much I've enjoyed today. The walk in the park, the dinner. But most importantly, the time you took to talk about my feelings. I don't think many men have the patience to do that. I...half expected you to say 'fine' and leave."

He shook his head, furrowed his eyebrows and rested his hands on her shoulders. "I'm more than a Dom. I'm a man first."

"I know."

"I was serious when I said I'm looking to settle down. It's too early to talk about this, I know. But I want to be honest with you. I won't pursue a relationship that I believe is bound to fail eventually." He paused, licked his lips and tipped his head a little closer. "And I won't ruin something that has the potential to be wonderful by pushing too hard."

"You think this could be wonderful?" she managed to squeak out. It wasn't easy speaking with her breath jammed up somewhere below her breastbone.

"Don't you?" He pressed his mouth against hers, and she nearly crumbled to the ground.

Her knees went limp, and she wrapped her arms around his neck to hold on as he slowly, deliciously explored her mouth with his tongue. His kiss was as patient and seductive as he was. Warm tingles washed down her neck and pooled between her legs, and she pressed her pelvis forward and ground her pussy into his leg. A soft moan sounded in her head.

He broke the kiss.

Dizzy, and having forgotten where she was, she opened her eyes.

"We better take this inside before it goes any further," he half-said, half-growled.

Unable to speak or think...or do much of anything requiring the coordination of multiple neuron pathways, she merely nodded.

He smiled, took her hand, and led her inside. "Do you need something to drink?"

Drink? Oh, yes! A big glass of wine would go a long way toward getting rid of the last nervous jitters, but probably not a good idea. She coughed into a cupped hand to clear her clogged throat. "Some water would be perfect."

"Coming up." He patted the couch as he passed it. "Make yourself comfortable. I'll be right back."

She glanced at the soft chenille fabric on the couch and carefully considered the many meanings of the words make yourself comfortable. So many possibilities. One could take them literally, change into sweats and recline on it like a couch potato. Or...one could take them another way...

Oh, what the hell?

She pulled her skirt off and stepped out of it, taking

care to leave on her high-heeled pumps. Then she pulled off her top and positioned herself in a sexy reclining pose and watched the doorway to the kitchen for Andre.

She wasn't disappointed by his reaction.

His jaw nearly dropped to his chest. But his shocked expression was quickly replaced by one that made her pussy wet with anticipation.

He smiled, licked his lips like a hungry lion, and took long, purposeful strides toward her. When he reached her side, she half expected him to pounce on top, but thankfully...or not so thankfully...he didn't.

Instead, he handed her the glass of cool iced water. "Your water." He visibly swallowed.

Feigning nonchalance, not easy when facing the heat of a raging inferno in his eyes, she took the glass from him and smiled. "Thank you." She sipped daintily before handing it back to him. "Very...er, refreshing."

He barely had the glass on the coffee table before he swept her into his arms and carried her down the hallway.

"Where are you taking me?" She giggled, feeling small and weightless in his strong arms. He carried her with such ease.

"To my bedroom." He pushed open the door, revealing a tidy, stylish room. He dropped her on the bed then leaned over her, his hands pressed into the mattress on either side of her shoulders. "Dressed the way you are, I'd say you'd be more comfortable in a bed. Wouldn't you?"

"I thought we'd—"

Bending his elbows, he lowered his chest and face closer and whispered, "I want you here. In my bed. Now. We can play later."

Her breath caught in her throat. "Okay. Later."

He kissed her ear, pulling her earlobe into his mouth. His teeth nipped at the sensitive flesh. "I didn't think you'd complain."

A blanket of goose bumps covered her upper body and

she shivered. "What's there to complain about, as long as you make yourself comfortable as well?" Her pussy throbbing, wet and achy, she lifted her feet and wrapped her legs around his waist. Her hands explored the rigid planes of his chest and stomach through his shirt before sliding down to pull the soft cotton knit up over his head. She gasped at the sight of his upper body uncovered. Thick arms with bulging biceps and triceps. Defined shoulders, a broad chest with chiseled pecs and a stomach most men would only dream of having. Absolutely awe inspiring. "My God! How many hours a day do you spend in the gym?"

"Probably too many." He ground his pelvis into hers and teased her nipples through the lace of her bra with his fingertips. "I'm glad you like what you see."

Her back arched as she strained to push her breasts up into his hands. "Oh, I like what I feel, too."

"This?" He pinched then released.

"And this." She reached down and slipped her hand between their bodies to caress his erection through his clothes. "Don't you want to take those pants off yet?"

"In a bit. I'm more content to tease you first."

"Well, that's no fair!" She started to lever herself up, but he pushed her flat on her back then held her there by the shoulders.

"Let's play a game."

She struggled a little to test how firmly he intended on holding her. He didn't let her budge. "I thought you said we would play later."

He grinned and shrugged his shoulders. "I changed my mind."

She returned his grin with one of her own then reached up. "Changing one's mind is a woman's prerogative, not a man's."

"I never said I played by the rules." He leaned lower and nibbled on her neck, producing more goose bumps.

"And you expect me to play a game with you? A

199

confessed cheater?" Hot and breathless, and anxious for more, she tipped her head to give him better access to her neck.

His kisses and licks and love bites traveled lower, to the cleft between her neck and collarbone then lower still to the valley between her breasts. He hooked the lace demi-cup with a fingertip and pulled, uncovering the full globe of her breast and her erect nipple. He blew a cool stream of air on it and she sighed. "Why not? I think you'll find out that losing a game with me is as much fun—if not more—than winning. So, what do you say?" One hand pressed firmly against her lace-covered pussy.

A moan rose up her throat. "How do you expect me to say anything when you're torturing me like this?"

"It isn't difficult to say 'yes'." One fingertip slipped into her panties and teased her lips.

"Yes," she gasped. "Oh. Yes. What game do you want to play?"

The same finger that had rimmed her pussy touched her mouth and she licked it, tasting her own musky-sweet flavor.

"I like to call this game 'Master, May I?'." He pulled her nipple into his mouth and bit gently then twirled his tongue round and round, licking away the sting. "Ready?"

For anything! "I...oh...I..."

"Sounds like a yes to me. You ask the question, and I'll tell you the answer."

"Question? What question?"

He chuckled and she opened her eyes to see his expression. His wicked-hot smile did nothing to help her regain her mental facilities. "Master, May I?"

"Master, May I what?"

"You have to supply the what."

"Oh!" A glimmer of comprehension lit up her brain. "Okay. Master, may I fuck you?"

He cupped her breast in his hand and caressed. "Oh, no. You're not nearly ready for that yet."

"Speak for yourself, buddy."

One hand still working over her breast, he slid the other one down her stomach and slipped it into the waist of her panties. His fingers stroked her clit, and she involuntarily pressed her pelvis up and spread her legs wider. "See? Not even close." He pulled his hand out of her panties and held it up as illustration.

"What are you talking about? I'm soaking wet down there."

"You're still able to speak."

"Ha! Barely."

"Try another one." He pulled the lace away from her other breast and nuzzled it, cupping it in his palm.

"Another what?"

"Another question."

"Oh, okay. Master, may I...oh..." She pushed her chest up as he pulled her nipple into his mouth and suckled. His hand returned to her pussy, his fingers stroking her outer lips through her panties until she was ready to beg him to remove them. "Master, may I take off my panties?" she finally whispered.

"No, you may not." His kisses ventured lower, over her stomach and down to the low-riding waistband of her lace underwear. He pushed her knees further apart and rubbed her pussy.

Chapter 7

He didn't say what I think he did, did he? The air seeped from Britt's lungs, and dizzy and blind with the need to be filled, she tangled her fingers in his hair. She pulled. "What do you mean, no?"

"I mean I will take them off for you."

"Oh." She eased the tension on his hair but didn't release him completely. It was so soft, the curls so silky between her fingers they tickled her palms. She shifted her hips as she felt him pulling her panties down over her mound. And she gasped and moaned as he kissed the flesh exposed as he slowly, torturously slid them lower still until her thighs were drawn together by the material, trapping her throbbing pussy between them.

Gently removing her hands from his hair, he pulled on her ankles until her legs straightened. Then he pushed them up until her feet were high in the air. "Now there's a sight. So sexy. So sweet."

Her legs trembled as his tongue glided up and down her slit. "Oh, God." The muscles running along the backs of her legs stretched tight as rubber bands, she fisted the bed coverlet.

He slipped the panties up her legs and pulled them

over her shoes. Finally, he pushed her legs apart and pushed two fingers deep inside her pussy.

She screamed at the welcome invasion, grateful for his slow but rhythmic strokes to her inner walls. Her knees bent and lifted toward her shoulders, she welcomed each thrust of his fingers with a slight tip of her pelvis.

His tongue danced over her clit, and waves of heat pulsed out from her center. And the flush of an impending climax warmed her face and chest. Then, he stopped. "Oh, no you don't. You didn't ask."

She drew in a ragged breath and dropped her hand to her pussy. If he wouldn't finish the job, she'd do it for him.

He caught her wrist and pulled it aside, trapping it in a tight fist. "Although I'd love to watch you do that, I can't let you. Remember the game."

"Shit!" she cursed, so frustrated and lost in her need she could barely think. "I'm so close. And I know this one's going to be powerful."

"Ask."

She inhaled against the urge to growl. Why was he making things so difficult? Didn't men love to watch a woman? Didn't they get off seeing a woman lose control? "Master, may I come?"

"No, you may not."

She slapped the mattress with her one free hand. "You never say yes!"

"I would if you asked the right question."

"Right. Wrong. Who the hell knows what's what at this point? All I know is that you've been teasing me and I'm hot, horny and ready to come. Isn't that a guy's wet dream? What are you waiting for?"

"I'm waiting for the right time."

"When will that be? I don't see it being any more right than now."

"What makes you think that?"

"I'm dying here. That's what. My heart is thumping so

hard in my ears that I can barely hear you. My pussy's so hot that if you touch it again, it might combust. My breasts are so achy that I fear they'll never be the same."

"And what about your mind? Your spirit?"

"What about them? My mind's gone, lost in a fog. And spirit?"

"You see? You're so lost in the sensations of lovemaking that you've lost the connection."

"What connection? I'm confused." She dropped her feet to the bed and drew her knees together.

"Nope. Don't you dare close up. Not now." He caught her ankles and pushed them back and apart.

"I'm not. It's just hard to think when I'm hanging open like this."

"Try. I want you to understand. To me, sex isn't just about body parts, smells and sounds and touches. It's about souls and spirits and minds."

"Well, I can appreciate that. I don't do empty, meaningless sex, either. But in the midst of a climax, I'm afraid my spirit is the last thing I'm thinking about. Everything kind of closes in on me at that moment. And sensations take over."

He nodded and reached down to stroke her pussy, for which she was mighty grateful. "I understand. That's why at this point I've been concentrating on giving and not receiving."

"When will you receive?"

"Not today. I want today to be for you."

"No! What if I want you inside?"

"There are other things that are more important right now." He pushed two fingers inside her pussy and turning his hand, stroked the sensitive upper wall.

She groaned with the need to be filled completely.

"Do you trust me?"

"No," she teased, half meaning it. "You've done nothing but torture me since our first date. How could I?"

"Is that honestly how you feel?" His fingers slipped

out, leaving her pussy achingly empty.

"No. I don't. I'm teasing you."

"So, you do trust me then?"

"Yes. Outside of teasing me to death, you've done nothing to make me distrust you."

"Good. I want to do something." He slid off the bed and walked to the closet. "Don't move."

Curious, but feeling a little strange lying flat on her back, her legs spread wide as if she were about to give birth, she watched him pull some metal rods from the bottom of the closet.

He returned to her side. "These are spreaders. They fasten on your thighs and wrists and hold them apart. Would you like to try them?"

Heat rose to her face. The idea of being tied up left her breathless and nearly ready to climax. Then he produced a large dildo and she squirmed with anticipation.

"And I think you know what this is."

"Yes. But can I see you first? Will you undress for me?"

"Maybe, after I secure you. I wouldn't want you taking advantage." He winked then reached for her wrist, his chest and upper body lowering until it hovered a fraction of an inch above her erect nipples. He secured both wrists in the leather straps then trailed a line of kisses and light bites down her torso.

Her eyes closed as she waited anxiously for him to strap her thighs.

"Uh-uh. I want you to watch me. Open your eyes. You cannot do anything without asking. Remember the game?"

"Master, may I close my eyes?"

"Nope. Watch." He kissed her inner thigh and her pelvis rocked rhythmically to the pounding of her heart. With a smile, he buckled the leather strap and pulled the second leg into place. Before strapping that one, he lowered his head and tongued her clit with quick jutting movements until her breath came in short, shallow gasps.

"Oh, God!"

"Don't come. You didn't ask. And I said to keep those eyes open."

She swallowed a scream of frustration and forced her eyelids to lift, not even aware they'd closed. "I hate this game!"

At least she was rewarded for the effort it took to focus her vision. On his knees, Andre slid down the zipper on his pants and pushed them down before flipping onto his back to remove them completely. His snug athletic boxers housed a huge bulge that she couldn't wait to see.

He returned to a kneeling position and pulled down the tight black cotton, releasing a very impressive, very large erect cock. Her hands wriggled against their bindings, itching to caress it, to grip it, to glide up and down its length. She licked her dry lips.

He shook his head, gripped his cock in his hand and gave it several smooth pumps. "This isn't for you yet." Then he picked up the dildo. "But this will be almost as good. Are you ready?"

"Hell, yes! Though I wish I was getting the real thing. My God!"

"Patience, love."

"I told you. I'm impatient."

He grinned. "I know." Then without warning, he parted her labia and pushed the dildo deep into her pussy.

Her fingernails dug into her palms as her entire body stiffened. "Oh!"

"Look at me." His expression intense, he pulled the dildo out then plunged it inside again. "Do you see how much I want you? Your pussy is so tight. So hot and wet. I'm going to come just watching you."

"Oh, God!" Her thigh muscles bunched into tight spasms and pulses of heat radiated up and out from her pussy. The sound of her juices as the dildo slid in and out echoed in her ears. The smell of her own arousal filled her nostrils. The sight of his hungry gaze on her pussy burned into her memory. "Master, may I…?"

"What, love?"

Her blood pulsed through her body in hot bursts, up through her chest, to her face. Her breathing ceased. "Come?"

"Yes, love. Come for me," he said, sounding as breathless as she felt. "Come for me now." He pushed a finger into her ass just as the first spasm of her climax blazed through her pussy. He groaned.

Heart-stopping spasms racked her body as it clenched and unclenched in time with her pussy. She felt her heart take flight, her soul and spirit. They rocketed through space and time, whirling, dancing, twining around a vivid blue light until the light opened and let her in.

And then, awash in a warm glow, she descended, back into her body. Onto Andre's bed, by his side. Little twitches skittered through her and a goofy sense of giddiness made her giggle.

A shiver reminded her she was cold but she didn't want to move yet. It was as if she was still in the middle of a wonderful dream, and she feared if she opened her eyes it would end.

"How do you feel?"

"Wonderful." She listened to the rattle of metal as he unfastened her wrists and thighs. Soft kisses took the place of the leather straps.

"Thank you," he said. "Thank you for giving so much of yourself. For trusting me." Dropping to his side, he pulled her to him until her entire body was crushed up against his. She sighed at the warmth and at the wonder of how great it felt in his embrace. Something slick and wet made her skin cling to his.

Never had a climax touched her the way that one had. And he still hadn't actually been inside her yet.

"Oh, and sorry about the mess," he murmured as he stroked her hair.

"What mess?"

"On your stomach. It's pretty wet. Let me get a

washcloth."

"No!" She wrapped her arms around his chest and clung to him. "Just stay here a minute more. Please?"

"Okay." He chuckled. "If you insist. I thought you might be uncomfortable."

"Nope. I'm great. Just being with you like this. It's wonderful."

"Does that mean you'll stay the night? It's almost eleven. If you're going home, we need to get moving."

"If you're inviting me to stay, I'm game." She nuzzled his chest, enjoying the distinct scent of sex and man she found there. "Just make sure to set the alarm for early. I'll want a nice long shower in the morning before I head out to work."

"No problem. I have to be out early, too. We can conserve water." He winked.

A fresh wave of tingles washed over her body. Closing her eyes, she fell asleep, dreaming about sharing a shower with a sexy man with a hot body and the most beautiful eyes she'd ever seen.

* * * * *

Unfortunately, thanks to the fact that Britt couldn't sleep soundly, she woke late. That meant there was no time for the leisurely shower with Andre she'd hoped for. Instead, she dashed home to change and arrived at work with no more than a second to spare.

Work was boring, as usual. The office was empty. All the salesmen were out making calls on clients. The phones didn't ring. But her memories of the previous night, Spider Solitaire, and a half dozen caffeine-loaded diet sodas were enough to keep her awake. By lunchtime, she was jittery, thanks to all the caffeine she'd consumed. But she wasn't in the best of moods, especially when she met up with Mary at the restaurant, and Mary had the look on her face the minute she sat down.

What disaster would it be this time?

"Are you going to tell me, or are you going to torture

me?" Britt asked when Mary didn't say a word after at least five minutes. Mary was never quiet for that long. Not even in a movie theater.

Mary peered over the menu and blinked. "I'm not sure how to tell you this."

"Quit hiding." Britt pulled the menu away from Mary's face. "You look like a lost kitten. What are you scared of?"

"Nothing. Well, that's not true either. I'm worried. I've never seen you go so crazy over a guy before. You spent the night with him last night, didn't you?"

"Maybe." Britt tried to look nonchalant as she stirred her iced tea, but she knew she was failing. Mary knew her better than she knew herself. And even Britt knew she never spent a work night with a man.

"You're serious about him, aren't you?" Mary pulled the menu back over her face, leaving only her eyes and forehead exposed again.

"Would you quit doing that? And no, I'm not serious about him, yet. It's too soon."

"I don't believe you. And I'm afraid you'll go a little berserk when you hear this."

"Oh, for God's sake, just spit it out. I'm not married to the man. If it's something important, I need to know."

"Okay." Mary lowered the menu and leaned forward. "There's another woman," she whispered.

"Really?" Britt wasn't convinced. Surely Andre—Mr. Let's-be-honest and I'm-looking-to-settle-down—wouldn't have kept something that important from her. Heck, when did he have the time to see the other woman? "What makes you say that?"

"I talked to her at the club."

The club? A little twinge of suspicion slid up Britt's spine. "Maybe she's lying."

"Maybe. Then again, maybe she isn't. I had to tell you. I figured you have the right to know some woman—and let me tell you, she's gorgeous, not that you aren't—is running around saying she's involved with Andre."

For the most part, Britt didn't believe what Mary said, but a very small part of her had some doubts. She recalled that first night at the BDSM club, the buxom blonde in latex who'd tapped Andre on the shoulder. He'd known that woman, hadn't tried to hide it. What if all that talk about settling down and commitment...and my soul...and trust...was just talk? *I haven't known him for long. Am I being a fool for trusting him?*

"I appreciate your telling me. But we're not engaged or anything. I don't have any right to stake a claim on him. I have no right to be jealous."

"You don't expect me to believe you're okay with this."

Britt shrugged again. "What am I supposed to do? We've only seen each other a couple of times. I can't demand to know his every move."

"Find out the truth, so you know."

"Fine. I'll ask him if he's dating anyone else. Will that make you feel better?"

"You know, I told you only because I care. I like Andre...er, at least what I've seen so far. I want you to be happy."

"I know."

"When are you going to see him next?"

"Friday." Britt slid lower into her seat and guzzled her iced tea, knowing she wouldn't get a decent night's sleep until then. Friday couldn't come soon enough. And until then she couldn't get enough caffeine if it was pumped into her veins through an IV.

Chapter 8

By the time Andre's car had pulled in Britt's driveway Friday night, Britt was again a miserable bundle of nerves. There was definitely a pattern developing.

Although now she wasn't afraid Andre would lock her in a cage or mercilessly torture her. This time, her fears surrounded a more delicate matter—one that involved her heart. She knew, in her current state, it was far easier for her heart to be crushed than for her body to be.

Regardless of what she thought she wanted, it was too late. She had developed feelings for Andre. Strong feelings she could no longer deny. Not only was he a giving lover, warm and tender and sexy, but also seemed to be a genuinely nice guy. He talked to her. He listened. He wanted to know how she felt, what she thought. It was impossible to have a casual relationship with him. He encouraged more, pulling her in.

She could see what he was doing, dropping bits of bait to lure her closer, to gain her trust, but she couldn't stop herself. The bait was so...compelling.

He smiled as she opened the front door, his gaze wandering up and down her form. "You look incredible. I have a surprise for you." His expression eager, full of childlike excitement, he reached for her hand.

Curious, she pulled the door closed behind her, stepped onto the porch, and took his hand. "What kind of surprise?"

Taking long, quick strides, he pulled her toward the car. "If I told you, it wouldn't be a surprise. You'll just have to wait."

"Are you testing my patience again?" She sat in the passenger seat and looked up at him, catching his gaze as it dropped to her chest. Without looking down, she knew what he was staring at. The V-neck top she wore provided a nice view of her cleavage. A warm blush settled over her face.

He licked his lips. "Maybe. But you won't have to wait long." Before she could respond, he shut her door, walked around the front of the car, slipped into the driver's seat and closed the door. The car's engine roared to life as he turned the key.

Shifting into reverse, he glanced over his shoulder. "You're a little quiet tonight. Is everything okay?"

This was it, her opportunity to bring up the topic of dating other people. If she could just put aside that one worry, she could genuinely enjoy the process of getting to know Andre better. She could maybe even let herself fall in love with him. "To tell you the truth, I'm a little nervous."

"Again?" He shifted the car into first and hit the gas. "What's wrong?"

She pulled a deep breath into her lungs, knowing it was likely to be the last deep breath she'd take in a while. Past experience suggested when she was involved in a tense discussion, she tended to hyperventilate. "I...uh..." She glanced down at her hands, noting a slight tremble. She tried to remind herself that she couldn't avoid asking the question that was weighing so heavily on her heart. It was impossible. She'd go downright insane if she didn't. Things were moving too quickly not to know which direction they were headed. "I just need to get something straight."

He glanced at her then returned his gaze to the road. "Okay. What do you need to know?"

"You said you're looking to eventually settle down, but—" She stopped herself. *This is stupid! We've only gone on two, er, three dates. What man would make a serious commitment after such a short time? Why would I want that, either? I hardly know the man. He's a free agent, and so am I. We can date anyone we well want to, including beautiful blondes with perfect bodies…that I'd love to hate.* "Oh, forget it. Let's just go have some fun. That's what we're supposed to be doing. Right? Just have fun and get to know each other. No strings. No pressure."

He stopped the car at a red traffic light and studied her with narrowed eyes. "No strings? Am I going too fast for you?" The light turned green, and he pulled away, smoothly shifting gears. First, second, third.

"No. You're not going too fast."

"Are you sure?"

"Yes."

"Then why did you bring up the no-strings thing? That's not something I expected to hear from you."

"Why's that?"

"Because we've been pretty intense—at least I thought we have been. If you're looking for something casual…hmmm…" He let his sentence trail off unfinished and silently drove for a mile or two, and she remained silent, too.

What should she say? How could she explain what was going on inside of her? His words suggested he wasn't looking for a casual relationship. Did he genuinely mean them? Had her doubts been unfounded? Was she just buying a lie fed to her indirectly through a friend? Was the woman from the club just trying to scare her off? Andre's actions spoke volumes. He never spoke of other women. He never looked at other women when they were out. He never talked about being free or wanting space.

Quite the opposite. He seemed to be focused on one

woman. Her.

The heaviness in her heart lifted slightly.

Moments later, he drove the car into a parking lot in front of a small dance studio. As he exited the car and opened her door, his expression remained friendly but lacked its former obvious glee. "I hope you enjoy my surprise."

"Are we taking dance lessons?"

"A close friend of mine owns this place. She offered to teach us a few moves. I thought you might enjoy it." He took her hand and together they walked across the empty parking lot.

"That's very romantic," she said, impressed by his sentiment. But as he pulled the door open for her, the rest of the compliment she'd meant to say lodged in the middle of her throat.

There, behind the front desk, stood the blonde from the club, decked out in a black leotard with a low scooping neckline that emphasized the size of her ample chest.

Taken off guard, Britt stepped backward but was stopped by Andre's bulk behind her.

"Britt," Andre said, "this is Stacy. Stacy and I have been friends since college. Stacy, this is Britt."

A genuinely warm smile on her face, Stacy stepped from behind the counter and offered Britt her hand. "It's very nice to meet you finally. Andre has told me so many great things about you."

"He has?" Studying Stacy's face for some sign of deception, Britt hesitantly took Stacy's hand and gave it a quick shake. But as she tried to pull her hand free, Stacy's grip didn't release. And then she realized something very shocking.

Stacy was checking her out! And she seemed to appreciate what she saw.

Britt didn't know how she felt about that. Relief—knowing Stacy wouldn't be interested in Andre if she was gay—and discomfort. Maybe even a little bit aroused.

"Are you ready to begin your lesson?" Stacy released Britt's hand and motioned toward a room to the right. "Follow me." She walked in front of Britt, flipping her long hair over her shoulder and swaying hips sparsely covered by leotard, opaque tights, and translucent skirt. Only a few steps behind, Britt had to admit that the woman did have a to-die-for body—not that she was attracted or anything. In the center of the room, Stacy spun around unexpectedly, and Britt nearly walked straight into her. "Andre suggested ballroom lessons. Would you like that or something else? He said it's entirely up to you."

Feeling very clumsy, Britt halted suddenly then staggered, trying to catch her balance. "What other kinds of lessons do you offer?"

"All the usual. Tap, jazz, ballet. We also offer ballroom, belly dancing—"

"Belly dancing? I've always wanted to learn to belly dance."

Stacy gave her an appreciative smile. "Belly dancing it is, then. Andre? Do you want to watch?"

"Hell, no," he answered from behind Britt.

Assuming he was leaving, Britt turned toward him to thank him for the thoughtful gift. But, as she faced him, she realized by the way he was swinging his hips he had no intention of leaving.

And then his words reaffirmed that assumption. "I'm staying. I want to learn, too. Sounds like fun."

Stacy laughed. "Why does that not surprise me?" She walked across the room to a small closet and opened the door, pulling out some fabric. She shook out one piece then handed it to Britt then found a second one—a lovely shade of bubblegum pink—for Andre. "Tie these low around your hips, like a sarong skirt."

Britt secured hers over her jeans then watched Andre struggle to tie his over his khaki pants. Unable to stop herself, she giggled. "Do you need some help?"

Andre lifted his hands in defeat, and in a mockingly

feminine voice he said, "They say these things are one-size-fits-all, but they never are."

That was it. Britt burst out in laughter, and Stacy joined her. Between the two of them, they managed, between fits of body-quaking hilarity, to tie the skirt around Andre's hips. Then Stacy turned on the stereo and the room filled with the sound of Turkish music.

Not surprising to Britt, the lesson went very quickly. Stacy occasionally stepped up to Britt and laid her hands on her hips or stomach to help her learn a movement. But the touches, which normally would bother her because they were from a strange woman, had a very different effect. By the end of the lesson, thanks to Stacy's gentle strokes and Andre's flirty escapades, including a few maneuvers that reminded her of lovemaking, Britt was warm and tingly all over.

And the heaviness in her heart had nearly completely lifted.

Even while in a room with a woman who looked like she belonged on the cover of a swimsuit magazine, Andre's eyes were on Britt only. His playful smile was directed toward her only. His flirty innuendos were whispered in her ear only.

More than that, Britt could see the depth of his feelings in his eyes as he watched her dance. There was no hiding it. He didn't even seem to try. He was developing feelings for her.

When Stacy announced the lesson was officially over, a flush-faced Andre thanked Stacy for the lesson, then turned toward Britt and drew her into a hug. One hand dropped to her bottom. "Did you have fun?"

Fighting a shudder as he squeezed her ass, she forced out, "Yes, I really did. I've always wanted to learn belly dancing."

"You're a natural. And you're always welcome to come back for more lessons—on the house," Stacy offered.

"Really? Wow, thanks!" Moving carefully, hoping to

avoid making Andre release her, Britt pulled the knot at her hip loose and handed the scarf-like material back to Stacy. "But I feel like I should pay something." Andre began trailing tiny kisses down her neck. Carrying a conversation with Stacy while Andre produced goose bumps on top of goose bumps was no simple task. "I...uh..."

"No way." Stacy shook her head, her expression stern. "I would never charge a...friend...of Andre's. You'll just have to come after hours. Here's my card. Call me and we'll set up a time."

"Okay." Without reading it, Britt slid the card into her back pocket.

Andre gave Britt's shoulder a final bite then said, "Better get going. Dinner's ready at home. Hope you don't mind a home-cooked meal." He removed his skirt then took Britt's hand. "Do you mind if Stacy comes over, too? I kind of offered it as payment for the lesson."

"Oh, no! Not at all. That's the least we should pay. Heck, seeing you in a skirt was worth a hundred dinners." She chuckled at the memory of his comical attempts at a belly roll.

Andre kissed her nose, then whispered, "Just don't tell anyone. I'd never live it down." He gave her cheek a final caress with his thumb, then steered her toward the door by the shoulders.

"Who would I tell?" Britt called over her shoulder as she headed out the front door first, followed by Andre, then Stacy.

She rode in Andre's car while Stacy drove her own.

Warm all over, thanks to Andre, and energized from the exertion of dancing, she turned to him as he drove. "Stacy seems very nice."

"She's been a very good friend for a long time. But I want you to know, she's gay."

"I figured that out already."

"Does that bother you?"

"No, actually, I'm a little relieved," she admitted, watching his face for a reaction.

His eyebrows rose in a classic illustration of surprise. "Why's that?"

"I thought you were dating her."

He smiled and glanced at Britt. "A lot of people have made that assumption. She's a beautiful woman. And I admit we spend a lot of time together. But I'm not her type and she's not mine." He turned his head forward again. "I don't date more than one woman at a time, anyway. I'm a terrible juggler and an even worse liar."

"That's good to know."

"Yeah. When I try to lie, I break out in hives. My throat swells up." He closed his hand around his throat to illustrate. "It's not a pretty sight. I've learned to avoid lying at all costs."

"I can appreciate that. I'm a terrible liar, too."

"Um, there is one thing I want to tell you about Stacy, though."

Unsure whether she wanted to hear what was coming next, she reluctantly said, "Oh? What would that be?"

"Like I said, I'm a one-woman man, but Stacy would like to play with us a little."

One-woman man? A terrible juggler? *Yet you're asking to invite another woman into the bedroom with us?* Images of Andre and Stacy fucking in front of her passed through her mind, and she immediately hated the idea. "Oh. I don't know."

"I won't touch her and she won't touch me."

"I guess I'm not sure what she'd do then. Oh!" A few pieces of the puzzle dropped into place, and her face heated. *She's gay.* "Wait a minute. You mean she'd do stuff to me?" A warm wave rocketed through her body.

"Only what you're willing to let her do. She's a slave. She does as she's told."

Confused, but also intrigued, Britt turned and stared blindly out the window. *Oh my God! Another woman? Me?* "I've never... I don't know." She tried to imagine what it would be like to have Stacy touching her breasts, her pussy.

Her body's instant reaction was impossible to ignore. Her heartbeat raced, her body tingled, her pussy throbbed. Uncomfortable, thanks to the heat radiating from between her legs, she shifted in her seat and opened the car window a crack. *I'm not a lesbian. Why does the idea of this turn me on so much?* "

"It's your decision. I won't force you to do anything you don't want to."

"Okay. I'll think about it," she agreed, knowing already what the answer would be.

There was something about having another woman touching her, watching as Andre made love to her. Her panties were becoming more soaked by the second.

Much to her surprise, Britt wanted to try it.

* * * * *

Dinner—a luscious slow-cooked roast and potatoes— was accompanied with friendly, animated chatter. Andre seduced Britt with heated glances and flirty winks. His hand rested possessively on her knee throughout most of the meal, occasionally wandering higher to caress between her legs. The teasing touches drove her crazy with desire.

Stacy gave her one or two heated glances, seeming to try not to be too forceful or intimidating.

After they'd laughed, and eaten, and exhausted all casual conversation, Andre cleared the dishes and announced, "How about we go downstairs for a while?"

Stacy, who sat to Britt's left, turned to glance at her, an unspoken question on her face. Britt knew this was it, her final opportunity to back out. A momentary panic gripped her right around the throat, leaving her speechless.

Stacy looked at Andre. "I should probably go. Maybe another time?"

"No," Britt forced the word past the mountain blocking her trachea. "I want you to stay."

Stacy answered her request with a beaming smile. She

stood and reached for Britt's hand. "It'll be okay. Better than okay. I promise."

"I promise, too. Trust me," Andre said, motioning her toward the kitchen.

Andre's hand clasped around her right hand, Stacy's around her left, she descended the stairs at the rear of the kitchen slowly, unsure of what to expect.

The minute they reached the playroom, Stacy excused herself to change her clothes, leaving Andre and Britt alone.

Andre pulled Britt into an embrace, resting one palm on her cheek while pressing the side of her face against his chest. She let his heart's slow, steady beat soothe her quickly frazzling nerves. "I know this is your first time. I want it to be memorable, not scary."

She nodded.

He palmed both her cheeks and turned her face to his. Two brown eyes with flecks of gold stared straight into hers. "Listen to me closely. If either of us do anything you don't like, I want you to tell me. Okay? Pick a safe word. Something you will remember. Something you wouldn't normally say during lovemaking."

"Tomato?"

He chuckled and nodded. "When I hear the word tomato, I'll stop whatever I am doing, and so will Stacy. I want this to be a very intense experience for you, but also pleasant, special."

"I have a feeling it will be."

Stacy returned to the room wearing the same black latex catsuit she'd worn at the club. The center zipper was unfastened down to her navel, exposing a V of tanned skin and the inner curves of her breasts. "Is everything okay?" Her gaze hopped back and forth between Britt and Andre.

Andre nodded. "The word is tomato."

"Got it." Stacy stepped closer, approaching Britt almost as if she were approaching a scared child. But instead of touching Britt, Stacy dropped to her knees before Andre, bent her head forward, and remained still, one hand resting on each thigh. "Master."

Here I go! No turning back, now.

Chapter 9

Not sure what she should do, but having an inkling, she glanced at Andre for a cue.

He smiled then nodded slowly, and she dropped to her knees beside Stacy and repeated, "Master." It felt a little unnatural, like she was putting on a show, but she took the role of slave and waited for Andre's next move.

He rested his hands on the top of her head. "It pleases me to see you submitting at last, Britt. However, when you come to me, I expect you to be completely unclothed. You may hide nothing from me."

"Oh. Sorry. I didn't know. We didn't go over the rules yet." She started to pull her top over her head.

"No. Stop."

Britt released her shirt, the bottom hem around her shoulders.

"Stacy will undress you."

"Oh." Her heart beating in her ears, she dropped her arms and turned toward Stacy. She closed her eyes.

"No, Britt. Open your eyes. Look at Stacy."

She stared at Stacy's face, surprised to see an almost complete lack of emotion. The woman looked more like a nurse than a lover. Her unaffected expression slowed

Britt's racing heart a bit. *It's just like being at the doctor's office.*

Stacy pulled Britt's top over her head, then reached around to unhook her bra, pulling each shoulder strap down until the garment fell on the floor. Then she unzipped Britt's jeans and pulled them over her hips.

"Lie down, Britt," Andre commanded.

She lay on her back and lifted her hips to allow Stacy to pull her shoes and jeans off. Then Stacy hooked her fingers under Britt's underwear and pulled.

Britt glanced at Andre, not sure if he expected her to remain lying down or return to kneeling. Meanwhile, Stacy resumed her obedient pose, head down, hands resting on thighs.

"Much better, Britt. Now, to assure you won't forget, you will pay the consequences for coming before me fully clothed."

Uh, boy! Here it comes. Her pussy tingled as Andre's hot gaze raked over her flesh. She felt her skin warming.

"Stand up," he demanded.

Both Britt and Stacy stood.

"Stacy, place Britt on the spanking bench."

"Yes, Master." Stacy took Britt's hand and led her to a piece of furniture that slightly resembled a weight bench. With hands on Britt's shoulders, she coaxed her to kneel on the floor then rest her upper body on the leather seat part. Then she pulled Britt's knees apart and secured Britt's wrists in leather cuffs.

By the time Britt was in position, her pussy was throbbing with expectation. Stacy pushed lightly on Britt's back, encouraging her to arch it and tip her ass up in the air.

She'd never felt so exposed, so out of control. It was a wonderful, erotic feeling. Her entire body was energized, her blood pumping hot as acid through her body. Her breaths failed to fill her hungry lungs.

And then she felt the slap, and in a heartbeat a sharp stinging pain warmed her backside. She squirmed, breathless, and tried to look over her shoulder to prepare for the next one.

"No. Look forward."

She obediently stared straight ahead.

"Arch that back."

She arched her back, lifting her smarting ass as high as she could.

"And relax the muscles."

She forced herself to slacken her ass muscles.

A second swat sounded in her ears, and another rush of biting pain razored up her spine. She gasped at both the pain and the pleasure ripping through her body, gripped the chains holding her wrists to the underside of the bench, and forced herself to hold her position.

"Very nice, Britt. What have you learned?"

"To come before you undressed."

"Very good."

A soft touch smoothed over her bottom, cooling the heat. "You have a perfect ass. So full and round." Fingers dipped between her ass cheeks, teasing her anus, and she reflexively tipped her hips higher giving him better access. "Oh, yes. Just like that. Your hole is so tight. I want to fuck it."

Recalling the size of his cock, she shuddered. "I've never...you're so big."

"Trust me. I won't hurt you."

She dropped her head to the bench, tipping it to the side and relishing the cool touch to her flaming face. "Yes, Master."

"Good! I want to reward your trust. Stacy, the beads."

"Yes, Master," Stacy responded.

The hands that had been soothing Britt's ass lifted and Britt wondered whose they had been.

A moment later, Britt felt a touch to her ass again, fingers pulling her cheeks apart.

"Your ass is perfect. So tight and smooth. Have you ever had anal beads before, Britt?"

"No," she whispered, completely aroused at the soft exploring touches. Fingers probed her pussy, slipping up to circle over her clit before dipping down into her vagina. More touches wandered up and down her crack.

"Your pussy is so smooth."

Hands messaged her thighs with strong pressure, working out knots she hadn't known were there. More hands worked over her ass and pussy, stroking, teasing, fingers dipping inside.

She moaned at the sensation overload. The feel of hands all over her pussy and ass and legs. The sound of her own shallow breaths in her ears. The scent of oils. "Yes, thank you."

"For that you'll be rewarded as well."

"Thank you."

Fingers pulled her ass cheeks apart, exposing her anus, and then something pushed at the barrier.

"Open to me, Britt," Andre demanded.

She tried to force her muscles to relax against the pressure, to allow whatever was pushing inside. It was nearly impossible. Her entire body was tensing as waves of heat pulsed up and out. The pace of each wave increased with each heartbeat.

And then she felt a pop as the first bead slid inside, filling her anus. She gasped, her pussy throbbing, juices dripping down the front and cooling her skin. "Oh!"

"I want to reward you some more," Andre said.

"Yes! More."

Another bead slipped inside, giving a slightly increased feeling of fullness. It was a very pleasant, erotic feeling. "More?"

"Yes!"

A third bead popped inside and her fingernails dug into her palms as she fought to control the rush of tingling heat radiating through her body. Climax was just on the horizon. She could feel it.

"Release her hands."

Stacy kneeled beside her, releasing first one hand, then the other.

"Turn over, Britt. With your ass on the opposite end. You have been very, very good. You deserve another reward."

Dizzy from the rewards she'd already received, and not sure how many more rewards she could take, she turned around and lay on her back. Stacy lifted her ankles and strapped them high in cuffs suspended from the ceiling.

Legs spread in a wide V, Britt watched and waited as Andre pulled down his pants and unwrapped a rubber. He pulled it over his erection, then kneeled. The bench was the perfect height.

She arched her back, silently pleading for him to fill her.

Stacy kneeled to one side.

"Another bead." He pulled his cock away slightly and Stacy lifted her hands to Britt's anus, pushing a final bead inside.

Breathless with the urgent need to be filled, out of her mind with arousal, she watched Stacy touch her. Stacy's hand wandered higher, her fingers dipping into Britt's pussy before circling over her clit.

It was too erotic to watch. Britt dropped her head back and closed her eyes, intent to concentrate on the touches to her pussy and the fullness in her ass.

"Is she ready for me yet?" Andre asked.

"No, Master."

"Slacken the chain. I want her knees bent, her legs wider."

"Yes, Master," Stacy answered.

The tension on Britt's legs eased, allowing her to lower her ankles. A gentle push on her knees forced them apart and high up on either side of her body.

Oh, so wide. So hot. *Fuck me!*

Britt felt she would go insane if he didn't give her release. Her entire body was pulling into tight knots. She couldn't breathe or think. Sensations were blurring into colors and sounds. She tasted the musk of her own arousal as it filled the air.

Then, fingers pulled her labia apart and a warm tongue flickered over her clit, sending white-hot bolts of desire up to her belly.

Andre's cock pushed inside, stopping just inside before filling her completely and stretching her vagina.

She thrashed her head back and forth, her eyelids clamped tight. Her stomach muscles spasmed and her feet curled. "More!"

His cock pushed another fraction of an inch inside and she consciously tightened her vaginal walls around it, savoring the increased sensation. She was so close, so very close! Cold and hot zipped up and down her body as the throb of her impending climax took hold of her.

"Now," Andre shouted.

And as the first spasm of orgasm gripped Britt's body, he thrust his cock deep inside. That, with the added sensation as the first bead slid out of her ass, magnified her climax until she lost all control. Andre's cock thrust in and out, in and out as her pussy spasmed around it. And with each thrust, a bead was pulled out of her ass.

She screamed with release, so overcome by the sensations pummeling her body to sort one out from the other. Then she felt the swelling of Andre's climax, and he growled before thrusting inside her one final time.

And then breathless, dizzy and disoriented, she opened her eyes.

Stacy smiled at her and unable to speak, she smiled back.

Andre pulled out, removed the condom and unbuckled the straps holding Britt's legs, then pulled her to him in a tight embrace. "How do you feel, Britt?"

She took stock of the various sensations and emotions still rushing through her body. "Overwhelmed." She watched as Stacy stood and silently left the room.

Andre stood and led her upstairs. "In a good way?"

"Oh, yes. Where's Stacy going?"

He led her into his bedroom and lying down, pulled her into the bed with him. "Home. She only came here to serve you. Her task is done now."

She rested her head on his chest and curled up against his warmth. "I've never had an experience like that before, with another woman."

"Did you like it?"

"Honestly, I wasn't sure what she was doing and what you were doing. But the whole thing was incredible."

"Good. I'm glad you enjoyed it."

"Very much."

"I'm not your average Master. You see, we're bending the rules to meet our needs. Do you like our game? Would you like to play again with me?"

"Oh, yes! Couldn't you tell?"

"Then I have to ask you for a promise." His fingertip pulled at her chin until she tipped her face toward his.

"What promise?"

"I know it hasn't been long, but I want you."

Not sure if she understood him correctly, she asked, "What are you saying?"

"I want to make a commitment to you. Right here. Right now. Britt, our game is just beginning. But already, I 'm developing feelings for you. Real feelings. I may play your Master in the bedroom, but you are the one capturing my heart. I won't let you go. I can't let you go. I want you to be mine."

Tears burned Britt's eyes as she read the truth in his.

"Thank you for being so willing to open up to me, to share your thoughts and fears and joys with me. I hope you want to do that for a long, long time."

She swiped at a hot tear as it slid down her cheek. "Thank you for helping me learn how to open up. You've shown me how to be a better person. How to explore and share. How to let go." She chuckled. "I had no idea that paddles and spreaders and swings could do that, teach such deep lessons. You were right. It's more than dominating another human's body. It's about learning about yourself and each other. Encouraging each other to grow and learn. Andre, I'm yours. Your slave. Happy to do as you ask."

That night, they stayed up all night, making love, pleasing each other…and planning their future, together.

The End

Ties That Bind

TAWNY TAYLOR

TAWNY TAYLOR

Chapter 1

Damon Butler dropped his head and closed his eyes, letting the decadent pleasure of his lover's cock stretching and filling him, carry him away.

Oh yeah, so good. One slow inward thrust, followed by an equally slow and torturous withdrawal. *Damn.*

He'd been fucking Trey for years, and it was this magical every time. The guy knew exactly what Damon needed, how to bring him to the cusp of orgasm and then stop, slowly building the need inside until he came so hard the heat swirling in his belly blazed through every cell in his body.

Every single time he was sure he'd die from the pleasure.

"When I see Blair," Trey murmured, digging his fingers into Damon's shoulders, "I'm going to fuck her pussy just like this. Slow and deep at first, and then hard and fast like this…" Trey slowly amped up the pace of his thrusts, driving his thick rod deep into Damon's hungry ass.

Damon's legs, shoulders and back tightened as another jolt of erotic hunger licked up his spine. "Yeah. Fuck yes." He could see her now in his mind's eye. Blair's pouty lips pursed, eyes closed, sweet face flushed as Trey's cock pounded into her slick, tight passage.

His body rigid from the waves of heat simmering through his veins, Damon felt his mind being tugged out of the moment, into the past. But he fought the urge to sink into those memories, focusing on the sounds of skin striking skin, the delicious flavor of Trey's kisses lingering on his tongue. The scent of Trey's skin teasing his nostrils.

So close already.

Damon wrapped his fist around his cock and squeezed. "We're both going to fuck her, at the same time. You'll fill her sweet pussy. I'll cram her ass full of my cock. She'll be begging us for more."

"Shit yeah. God, the thought of having her again makes me want to come." Trey gripped Damon's hips and drove into him harder, rougher, with a desperation Damon had never felt in him before.

Sensing Trey was on the verge of losing the self-control he always exercised so flawlessly, Damon pumped his cock faster, matching Trey's almost frenzied pace.

This was good, better than good. They hadn't seen Blair in years, yet she was already bringing something new and exciting to their relationship. They'd finally found her, after years of searching. He could hardly wait until she was there with them, lying beneath him, submitting.

Trey's blistering hot, hard body bent over Damon's, skin gliding over skin, short, panting breaths teasing Damon's ear and making him hot and cold at the same time. Goose bumps sprung up all over his back, and he growled, tipping his hips, taking Trey's dick as deep as he could. "We're going to make it good for her. So good she'll beg us to do it over and over again," Damon vowed, meaning every word he uttered.

"Yeahhhh. Oh fuck." Trey's body stiffened. He groaned. "Too fast. Gotta stop." Trey eased from Damon's ass, leaving him achingly empty, charged up with sensual need and frustrated to the point of desperation.

Now that was a first. Trey'd been so close to losing

control, he'd had to pull out. Damn, that was hot.

"No, dammit." Damon sagged against the back of the couch. "I was so close."

"Tell me how it's going to be with Blair," Trey whispered against Damon's neck. "And fuck me while you tell me."

His body like an overtightened spring ready to snap, Damon lubed up his cock then spread some lubricant over Trey's anus. "She's been looking for us too. Waiting. Hoping. It's going to be even better than it was before. We're all older now. We understand each other's needs. We know how to give, not just take." Damon eased into Trey's ass, mesmerized by the sight of Trey's back and shoulder muscles rippling and bulging as he moved into position.

"Yeahhhhh."

"The magic we shared years ago with Blair, that wasn't an illusion. It was real. And real magic never goes away. She still loves us as much as we love her." Damon fell into a steady rhythm, his hips rocking back and forth, driving his rod up Trey's tight ass. His mind filled with images from the past, memories of the many sweet moments the three of them had shared as teens. The first time he'd fucked Blair. The first time he'd watched Trey fuck her.

Their bond had been like nothing he'd experienced since. Three people who shared the same soul, same heart, same mind. When Blair had been ripped away from them, he and Trey had been left with a huge gaping wound that had never healed.

And then there was the physical part, the way their bodies had been made for each other. He loved fucking a man and being fucked. But he also craved the feeling of Blair's soft, lush body beneath his. And Trey shared the same needs as he did, along with a deep-seated need to dominate. Both bisexual. Both active Doms in the BDSM scene. Both looking for the one submissive who would make their lives complete. And both still very much in love with one woman, their Blair.

His body reacted to Trey's soft moans and the sensual memories. More simmering pleasure gathered in his gut. He pounded into Trey harder, faster, taking him the way he liked, needed.

"Yes, more. Don't stop."

Trey was just about there again. So was Damon.

"We're going to give her everything we couldn't then," Trey vowed, sending more sparks flashing and flaring in Damon's body. "She won't say no. Right?"

"Not a chance."

Three months. They'd been planning for tomorrow for three months. And that was after fifteen years of searching for her. She'd changed her last name, moved a few times, obviously running away from something. She wouldn't run anymore. She wouldn't need to. They'd take care of her, love her, protect her and cherish her, like they'd promised to do all those years ago.

Finally, they'd have their chance to make up for their failures.

Damon's heart soared to the stars as his body was swept up in a vortex of carnal pleasure. "We don't have to wait much longer. We'll be together, complete. Happy."

"Yes, happy," Trey echoed on a moan.

* * * * *

"Oh gawd, tell me they won't be sawing people into pieces," Blair Groves joked as she thumbed through the program her friend had just handed her. "Because you know how I am about blood."

"Puh-leez!" Her best friend, Sandy Schubert, rolled her eyes and shoved a ticket into Blair's hand. "You know there won't be any blood. It's all illusion. Fake." Dressed in full magician-wannabe regalia, Sandy looked like she could be part of the show rather than a member of audience. "Oh cool! They're selling DVDs." Impatiently, she hustled Blair toward a booth selling overpriced videos and t-shirts. "Oh, this is perfect. Here. Put this on over your tank top." She tossed Blair a t-shirt emblazoned with a couple of men's faces with glowing eyes—printed in real glow-in-the-dark ink!—and the words, *I've been mesmerized by the Masters of Illusion.*

Groan.

It was official. Blair's social life had hit an all-time low. "This shirt is so cheesy it smells like limburger." Blair grimaced. "I can't wear this. Just look at it." Even as an eight-year-old, she wouldn't have been caught dead going to a magic show, let alone wearing a t-shirt advertising one. Everyone knew magicians were creepy.

Case in point, Wally the Amazing, the magician who'd kidnapped a little girl from a nearby junior high last week. The child had been twelve years old.

It didn't help that Blair was in a crappy mood today, after being passed by *yet again* for a promotion. She'd watched not one, or even two, but three people hired after her get promoted ahead of her because she didn't possess one silly piece of paper.

Some mistakes in life came back to bite her over and over.

Sandy donned her best pout. "Come on, Blair, be a sport. You promised to have fun…or at least fake it. You know how much this means to me. It's my *birthday.* Remember what I did for yours…"

"I knew you'd get back at me for that someday." Blair gave her friend a weak smile. Like Sandy had so kindly pointed out, last August Blair had dragged her to the *Dancing With The Stars* live show. Ballroom dancing made Sandy's teeth ache. The poor girl had been in agony the entire show, and because she'd gritted her teeth for over two hours, her TMJ had acted up for weeks afterward. She was definitely due a nice birthday night.

Time to buck up and be the best friend Sandy deserved. Blair took a few deep breaths. After all, it wasn't Sandy's fault she was stuck in an entry-level job and barely made enough money to keep her in ramen soup.

"Fine. I'll wear the tacky t-shirt with the glowing eyes. Just for you. But that's it. I've gone above and beyond to make your birthday special. So…happy birthday."

Blair yanked the garment over her head and poked her arms through the sleeves. "Great, now I've got two sets of eyes on my boobs. Literally." She swallowed a sigh and whispered, "Of all the millions of radio show call-in contests to win, why'd it have to be this one?" She followed a jubilant Sandy as she wound her way through the milling throng in the theater's lobby.

Sandy glared over her shoulder. "What is your problem today? You're not your usual cheery, sunshiny self tonight."

"Nothing I want to talk about now. Sorry I'm such a grump."

"Don't worry about it. You *will* tell me later," Sandy stated.

"Yes. Later."

Turning again to face forward, Sandy continued through the lobby. "Anyway, I was totally geeked to win these tickets. This show's been sold out for weeks and you don't want to know what the scalpers were asking. It's a small fortune."

Blair smiled at her friend's back. "I'm sorry your boyfriend couldn't make it instead. On your *birthday*."

Sandy went silent and stiff, and Blair was immediately sorry she'd said such a stupid thing. When Sandy had called to invite her yesterday, Sandy had claimed it didn't bother her that her boyfriend hadn't been able to come. Obviously, it bugged her more than she was letting on.

"Eddy couldn't find anyone to take his shift," Sandy grumbled, wiggling through a group of teens. "He was very disappointed he couldn't come with me. I could tell."

"Yes, of course he was disappointed. I'm sorry for bringing it up, sweetie. I'm in a kind of crappy mood tonight, but I'll try not to let it ruin your special night." Blair gave Sandy's shoulders a squeeze, and at her friend's forgiving smile, released her so they could continue toward the theater's entrance. "Magicians are sadists, you know," Blair teased, echoing the threat Sandy always used whenever Blair tried to interrupt her when she was practicing. "They like to think they're gods, and they get off playing with sharp stuff." She slid a glance at her friend, who sent her back a faux-angry glare. They both burst into hysterical laughter at the inside joke. The people nearby gave them bewildered stares, which made them laugh even harder.

They entered the semi-dark theater, showed their tickets to the usher then headed down the narrow aisle to the very front. Of course they had first-row seats.

The lights dimmed, signaling the beginning of the show. Blair settled in for a long, tedious program, which she expected would be filled with predictable illusions presented with the usual theatrical flourish. A pair of men—gorgeous men—dressed in the standard magician uniform, black suits and gloves, stepped out onstage, and the audience erupted into applause.

Wow, they hadn't even pulled a rabbit out of a hat yet.

She glanced over at her friend, who was also clapping like mad. Then she turned her attention back to the stage, watching, growing increasingly absorbed as the two men performed trick after trick, involving scarves and birds, panthers, big boxes with uber-skinny assistants and lots of sharp stuff—knives, swords, arrows.

Oddly, these two kept the theatrics to a minimum, no plumes of smoke or flares of flame. No blinking lights or distracting music. The show's tone was dark and mysterious, intimate. Seductive and, even though they didn't show a bit of skin, surprisingly erotic.

It was the stories they told as they performed their tricks. They were about faraway lands and obscure legends. Fascinating. Sensual. Mysterious.

The Masters of Illusion, as they called themselves, had striking faces, their features cut in masculine angles. And they both wore their dark hair long. She'd always had a weakness for men with long hair. Maybe that was why she was practically enthralled an hour later.

And then they stepped forward. One of them, the taller of the two, announced, "We need a volunteer from the audience."

As expected, Blair's friend started waving her hand like a maniac. The magician glanced at Sandy but then his gaze inched to the left. The corners of his mouth quirked into a wicked smile.

Oh no, he's not going to...

He pointed. At Blair. "We have our volunteer."

"No, no." She shook her head, but the usher in the aisle didn't accept her refusal. Neither did her friend, who was squealing like a stuck pig.

"You're so freaking lucky!" Sandy exclaimed, shoving her out of her seat.

Blair stood and followed the usher down to a side exit, around to the backstage door and through a maze of magic stuff. And then she was onstage, under all those hot, blinding lights. Standing between the magicians, who looked a whole lot bigger—and better!—from this vantage.

"What's your name?" the magician on her left asked, thrusting a microphone at her.

"Blair," she said, staring at him.

"Please, join me in giving our lovely volunteer Blair a warm welcome," he said, blessing her with a big smile that revealed a pair of adorable dimples and the world's most perfect, blindingly white teeth.

The room filled with lukewarm applause.

Suddenly feeling woozy, she glanced at the man on her right, meeting his gaze. Something flashed in his eyes, capturing her attention, and for a heartbeat she swore she knew him from somewhere.

He reached for her, and she awkwardly accepted his hand. An odd sensation rushed through her system. It was like an electric charge. "Blair, can you give me a personal item? Like a picture or piece of jewelry?"

Personal item? Her purse was sitting down there, next to her seat. As he released her hand, her bracelet skimmed down her wrist, one of her diamond charms catching the light and flaring brightly.

Aha!

"Sure. Is this okay?" She unclasped the bracelet and held it in her flattened palm.

"It's perfect." He reached into his pocket, pulling out a red scarf. He flattened the scarf in his upturned hand. "Place it in the center of the scarf."

She dropped the silver bracelet in his hand and watched him fold the scarf's corners over. Meanwhile, his partner stepped up with a small wooden box decorated with glittering red stones.

He gently placed the little bundle inside, covered the box with a scarlet piece of cloth and then turned to the audience, the covered box in his hands. "There are many legends about the ruby. The ruby has long been associated with love and passion. But it's also been said a ruby's wearer will be blessed with health, wisdom and success in affairs of the heart. And ancient peoples of the orient believed the ruby was a drop of Mother Earth's blood."

He pulled the scarlet cover off the box and lifted the lid, tipping it so the audience could see first. Then he turned it toward Blair.

It was empty.

Blair wasn't particularly surprised. She knew those boxes had special compartments. Her friend had one, although it wasn't even close to as gorgeous as this one.

The magician closed the box again and replaced the red cover. "Hindus believe the red color of the ruby comes from an inextinguishable flame." Once again, he pulled the cover off the box and opened it.

The audience applauded.

His partner lifted a red scarf from the box and held it

in front of Blair. "Please, open the scarf."

She hesitated, wondering if some animal was going to jump out at her or something. If not, this trick was nothing short of predictable. But at the magician's encouraging nod, she peeled away the corners of the scarf.

What the hell?

Confused, she lifted her bracelet, realizing it had been threaded through a small, delicate ring. A tiny ruby stone cut in the shape of a heart caught the light, flashing like a flame.

"Oh. My. God." Her gaze lurched from the ring that had once been her most prized possession to the men standing before her, and she knew in that instant why she'd felt as if she knew them.

She had, many years ago.

"Damon? Trey? I should've recognized you," she whispered as she studied their features. Their eyes were the same. And she could still see a hint of the gangly teenage boys she'd known so long ago. But with age their faces had become harder, more mature. And the bodies that had once been so thin and lanky were now filled out with heavy, rippling muscle.

"Let's give Blair a round of applause," Trey said before ushering her off the stage.

"But…" She had a million questions she wanted to ask, like if they'd known she'd be here ahead of time. And where they'd been for the past fifteen years. There hadn't been a day she hadn't thought of the two guys she'd once called her best friends. Her first crushes. Her first loves.

The day her family had moved from the sad and dirty neighborhood on the outskirts of Detroit to the pretty house in the 'burbs had been one of the saddest in her life.

An usher stepped out of the shadows and immediately rushed her toward the exit. She stopped outside, in the corridor, her back pressed against the wall, a million wonderful and sad memories playing through her mind. One day in particular got stuck in her head, repeating over and over until tears streamed from her eyes.

Her first time having sex, which of course had been with Damon and Trey. A week before she'd moved across town.

It had been Damon who'd actually performed the deed that first time, but Trey was right there too, holding her hand, stroking her face, making her feel cherished and special.

That day, she'd given those two teen boys her ring—and her heart. A week later, she'd had her insides ripped from her chest and shredded. Even today a scar remained, the product of that awful pain. Who would've guessed it would still be there, after so much time had passed?

Inside, she heard thundering applause but she couldn't care less about the show. She just wanted to talk to them, to spend time with them, to see if those little zaps on the stage were all that remained of the magical connection they'd once shared. Or whether the love and passion was still there, just waiting for a spark to reignite it.

She had to know, had to at least have an hour with them.

The doors to the theater flew open, and a river of people flowed out into the hallway, filling it with wall-to-wall jabbering audience members. She made her way down to the door where she expected her friend would exit and waited, intending to ask her if she'd wait for a while so she could hunt down Damon and Trey.

As the seconds ticked by, while Blair watched hordes of people file past her, she became jittery and nervous. Would the guys leave without trying to find her? They had to tear down and pack up, right? They had to stick around for a while.

God, she hoped so.

Finally, she saw Sandy, who was scanning the crowd, no doubt looking for her. Sandy's features brightened as their gazes met, and her friend rushed toward her. "What was that trick all about? Ohmygod! Where were you? Did you see the last illusion? It was amazing! The best I've ever seen!"

"Listen," Blair said, grabbing her ecstatic friend's hands. "Those magicians are old friends of mine. I wanted to find you first. Let's go see if we can talk to them."

"Friends of yours? You're joking, right? Because if you're not, I swear I'm going to scream or something."

"Not joking, but please don't scream."

Her friend let out a little "Eep!" as Blair caught her hand and tugged her back to the backstage exit.

"I'm hoping they'll come out this way, or we can get someone's attention and they'll let us go backstage."

"This reminds me of the time we went to the Duran Duran concert. You remember?"

"How could I forget? So tell me the truth. Did you or did you not fake the contest win so that I'd come here with you?" The door swung open and a huge man hurried past them. "Excuse me!" Blair said, trailing him for several steps before giving up. "Damn." She headed back to the door and tried it. "Locked."

"We can catch it when someone else comes out," her friend suggested.

"You're brilliant. Now the answer."

"No way. I won the tickets."

"Then how did they know I'd be here tonight?"

Sandy shrugged, looking as bewildered as Blair felt. "You got me. I'd say it was real magic but I know you don't believe in that."

"No, I don't."

They waited.

Waited some more.

Waited even longer, until the entire building was silent and Blair knew in her gut she'd somehow missed them.

She felt sick.

"I think they left," Sandy said.

"Yeah."

"Sorry. Maybe if you hadn't come to find me—"

"It's not your fault. I guess it was just rotten luck."

They both sighed.

Blair knew it had been too long, that the guys were probably already in their hotel room, relaxing. But she couldn't bring herself to give up, to leave. Why hadn't they come to find her?

"How about a beer?" Sandy asked a long time later.

"That sounds good. Really good." Blair blinked away a tear of disappointment.

* * * * *

Five beers and several hours later, Blair was still completely and utterly bummed about missing Trey and Damon. No doubt her earlier disappointment at work only made things ten times worse.

Sandy, bless her heart, tried everything to drag her out of the dumps, but nothing was working. Not even a really bad rendition of Madonna's "Like a Virgin" at their favorite karaoke bar. Not even a hot fudge brownie sundae from her favorite restaurant. Finally, she decided to quit torturing her friend on her birthday and called it a night. No doubt she'd feel better tomorrow after she'd had some sleep. Maybe she'd even brainstorm how to track the guys down. Her brain definitely worked better when it wasn't floating in a bucket of beer.

Sandy drove her home and crashed on her couch. She slept like a baby.

Blair did not.

By the next morning, Blair was more frustrated and irritated with herself than sad. But she had a game plan. While Sandy took a shower and emptied half of Blair's box of cereal, Blair called every hotel in the area to see if a Damon Butler or Trey Foster were registered.

After an hour, she gave up and joined her friend in the kitchen, drowning her disappointment in soy milk and corn flakes. She fingered the little ruby ring as she ate, tracing the shape of the stone with her index finger. "Please, please tell me you were lying last night. That somehow Damon and Trey tracked me down and asked you to get me to the show?"

"Sorry, I wish I could say I was lying but I wasn't. I had no idea you knew those guys. I'm sorry, sweetie."

"We were best friends for years. Even more than that. Damon was my first...you know. We had sex, Damon, Trey and I. We loved each other. But my family moved and I was too young to drive. My stepfather restricted the long-distance service on our phone so I couldn't call them. I always wondered what happened to them, where they were, what they were doing. I gave them this ring on the day I moved, and we swore that no matter what, we'd be together someday. The three of us."

Sandy's smile was dreamy, wistful. "I wish my first time had been that wonderful. That's such a sweet story."

"Yeah." Blair plunked her elbows on the table and dropped her chin on her fists. "It's too bad it didn't have the ending we all hoped for."

"Well, I said I was going to be a doctor when I was younger," Sandy said, chuckling. "I quit pre-med after my first semester of college. I think most people kiss their teen dreams goodbye when they grow up."

"But they gave me this back. Why?" She slipped the ring off her pinky and looked inside. Yep, it was the ring she'd given them, not a copy. Her initials were there, where they'd always been, engraved on the inside of the band. And the nick in the stone was still there. "They remembered me. But why didn't they try to talk to me later? After the show?"

"Maybe they couldn't find you, or they got tied up with packing up their stuff. Or they had wives to go home to. Who knows?"

"It's just so frustrating, to have them so close, only to have them slip away without getting at least a few minutes to catch up."

Sandy thought for a few minutes and then said gently, "Maybe it's for the best. If you're this upset after just seeing them, maybe you shouldn't spend more time with them than that. Think about it. What are you expecting here? The Masters of Illusion are performers. They travel around the world. It's not like they can settle down and spend any real time with you, no matter what your history is."

Those words stung big time. But Sandy did have a point. She'd reacted so strongly after just a few minutes onstage. If Trey and Damon were around for a few days, if she got the chance to spend some real quality time with them and all those old feelings were stirred up, how would she deal with them leaving? She was just a little over-emotional right now, thanks to her frustration at work. "You're probably right. But darn it, I'm having a hell of a time with this."

"I'm sorry, sweetie." Sandy gave her a hug, patting her upper back. Releasing her, Sandy stepped back to study her face for several seconds. "Are you going to be okay? Do you want to tell me what else was bothering you last night?"

"No, it's not that big a deal anymore. I'm fine. A little bummed, that's all. I'm tired, and that's probably making things ten times worse. But there's a reason why I reacted so strongly to them. I don't think anyone could possibly understand."

Sandy nodded and stooped over to grab her purse. Standing, she dug inside, her car keys rattled.

"Those two men, they were more than friends," continued Blair. "More than first boyfriends or lovers. They were my lifeline. And I was theirs. We knew each others' secrets, had met each others' demons. Like Trey. His mom was an alcoholic, and his dad sold their food stamps to fund his gambling habit. And Damon's dad blew his head off in front of Damon when he was just eight years old. After that, Damon slept in my doghouse for three nights, and his mother didn't even notice, she was so out of it. She tried to hold it together for him, but she just

wasn't strong enough. And then there were my parents..."
she laughed bitterly. "So you see? We weren't just friends
from the time we were able to talk. We were each others'
stability. We held each other up. I don't think any of us
could have survived those early years if we hadn't had each
other. Those two boys were the only ones I knew I could
count on."

Sandy didn't say anything for a long time, and once
again, Blair regretted opening her mouth. They headed
toward the front door, Blair following Sandy.

"I had no idea," Sandy said, stopping in the middle of
the living room, nervously fiddling with her purse strap.

"That's why this is so hard. We'd always said we'd be
together when we grew up. I guess a part of me was still
hoping that might happen, despite the years that have
passed."

Sandy's eyes filled with pity, which only made Blair
regret trying to explain more. "Oh sweetie."

Blair shook her head, "Like I said, it's impossible for
anyone else to understand."

"Maybe I understand better than you think." Sandy
flipped her key ring over in her hand. "I'm going to head
home, let you get some more sleep. I'll see ya tomorrow."

"Okay." Blair turned a one-eighty, heading back toward
the kitchen.

"Hey, what's this?" Sandy called.

"What?" Blair glanced over her shoulder, halting
midstride when she saw her friend stoop over. "Did the
neighbor's cat throw up on my welcome mat again?"

"Uh. No. You've got a package." Grimacing down at
the brown cardboard box in her arms, Sandy stepped back
into the house.

"A package? It's Sunday. Nobody delivers on Sunday."

"I don't think this was delivered by a courier. There's
no address label or anything."

"Weird."

Sandy set it on Blair's coffee table and stepped back,

almost as if she was scared. "Are you going to open it?"

"I don't know. Should I?"

"I don't know either."

Blair walked a wide circle around the table. "I saw a television show once where a woman received a box without a label and it was a bomb from her pissed-off ex-husband."

"You don't have a pissed-off ex-husband," Sandy pointed out.

"I know."

"You don't have any enemies either."

"Maybe it's a random thing?"

Sandy chuckled. "I'd say it's highly unlikely. But maybe we can take it outside into the garage and carefully open it out there?"

"Sounds like a plan...I guess." Blair cautiously carried the box back out through the front door and around the side of the house to her detached garage. Meanwhile Sandy opened the garage door.

It was already hot outside. The heavy air promised yet another day of record temperatures, which meant the garage's interior was like a gasoline-scented oven. Blair set the box on the ground and went for the garden tool with the longest handle—a hoe. Feeling like an idiot, she poked and prodded the box with the hoe, while Sandy stood outside laughing her ass off.

She gave up some ten minutes later, plunked the tool down and glared at her friend, who was finding this whole thing hysterical. "It's not working."

"No kidding."

"So what do I do now?"

"Well, either you call the bomb squad or you take your chances and open it."

"I'm not crazy about either option, but oh well. I guess I'll open it. The chances of the stupid thing being a bomb are slim to none, right?"

"Right." Sandy shuffled back another few feet.

"You're not making me feel any better about my decision here."

"I'm sure it's safe. I'm just being extra cautious. One of us has to be safe, just in case we need to call 9-1-1."

"Sure." Blair knelt on the floor beside the box and slowly ripped the tape off. Nothing blew up. She lifted the top flaps. Nothing blew up. She glanced inside. Nothing blew up.

She gasped. "Ohmygod!"

It was the box from the magic show. The beautiful one with all the glittering red stones. She gently lifted it out of the cardboard box and hurried to Sandy. "Look! It's from Trey and Damon. They know where I live."

"Wow, it's so beautiful." Sandy ran an index finger down the side.

"Yes, it is." Hot tears burning her eyes, Blair cradled the gift to her chest and headed back inside. She sat at the kitchen table and set the magic prop in front of her. "I wonder why they sent me this?"

"Look inside."

She flipped the lid up but there was nothing inside. "There's a magic compartment in this thing. How's it work?"

"Let me see." Frowning, Sandy inspected the box from every angle. "Hmmm, this one's tricky. My box has a little hinge thingy on the side that flips up. The one I want to buy has a button. But I can't find either on this box."

Blair sighed and took the box from her perplexed friend. "Of course they're not going to make this easy for me." She opened the lid again, just to make sure she hadn't missed something, like a special button or loop to unlock a hidden compartment in the bottom.

But this time the inside wasn't empty. An even smaller box had appeared somehow. Red, velvet, it looked like a jewelry box. "There's something in here now."

Sandy leaned closer. "This is so cool! What is it?"

Blair lifted the little red box. "This." She turned it and

flipped the lid, revealing an absolutely breathtaking garland brooch with a large ruby in its center. The pin was piercing a small folded piece of paper that had only an address, date and time printed on it.

"June twenty-third? That's today." Sandy plucked up the paper as Blair took a good, long look at the beautiful piece of jewelry. "They want you to meet them tonight. At this address."

Blair was so thrilled she could hardly speak. She gave her friend a watery smile. "They want to see me."

Sandy hopped out of her chair and threw herself at Blair, giving her an exuberant hug. "I'm so happy for you! But I've got to know how that box works. Can I see?"

Blair's head was not on any box. It was flying ahead about six hours, to tonight. She'd been nearly heartbroken when she thought she wouldn't see her guys again. But now that she knew she'd see them, she was nervous as hell. "Sure."

Why had they tracked her down? Did they feel the same way about her as she felt about them, even after all these years?

Six hours was such a freaking long time to wait for answers.

Chapter 2

Blair sat in her car, alternately staring at the address on the creepy old warehouse and rechecking the one on the piece of paper. Yes, the address was right. So why did this place seem so wrong? Why would Trey and Damon ask her to meet them here? In some old industrial complex?

Granted, they'd never been what she'd call traditionally romantic guys. Instead of giving her flowers or candy when they were teens, they'd given her practical things, stuff she could really use, like warm socks…and cans of Spam. But having a date meet them at a warehouse? Bizarre was the only word that came to mind.

She checked the clock again. It was now five after six, and the paper said six. There weren't any other cars in front of the building. Were they running late? She was so wired and jittery a minute felt like an hour. The thought of sitting inside the car for even a few seconds made her want to scream.

Check the door.

What the hell? For all she knew, the guys could have parked their cars around back. The neighborhood was safe. It wasn't like she was taking her life in her hands by walking across the parking lot.

The door was all glass. She peered inside. Looked empty, quiet. She pulled.

Unlocked.

"Hello? Damon? Trey?" She stepped into a silent reception area. To the left stood one of those reception counters. No one was posted there. The overhead fluorescent lights were off, and the deeper she walked inside, the darker it grew, the heavier the shadows became, and the edgier she felt.

She smoothed her hands down her legs, flattening her skirt against her thighs. Her pumps made little tap-tapping noises on the tile as she ventured to the back of the reception area. There were three wooden doors spaced evenly along one wall. One was marked with a sign, a bathroom. The second opened to a small office. Empty. The third opened to the cavernous warehouse. "Trey? Damon? Hello? It's me."

Creepy.

She almost turned around, called it a total wash and headed home, but then she heard her name, whispered, and she instantly recognized the voice.

She stopped, held her breath, searching the deep shadows. Where were they hiding? "Damon, you dork. Are you two trying to scare me? Quit playing."

There. She heard something moving. She rushed forward, eager to touch her old friends, to give them a hug and thank them for the wonderful gift. But she stopped midstride, a scream shooting up her throat, when one of the enormous black cats from their show, wearing a sparkling red collar, stalked from the shadows, its glittering eyes fixed on her.

Absolutely terrified, she froze in place. "D-Damon, I think one of your pets is loose," she whispered, afraid to speak louder. Oh God, that animal was huge. Those paws. Those teeth!

And then the cat stood up on its hind legs and the scream she'd been swallowing flew from her mouth. She whirled around and slammed into one hard male body. "Trey! Ohthankgod! Help me!"

Trey smiled as he eased her around.

The panther was gone. Damon stood in its place, dressed head to toe in black. The top two buttons of his crisp shirt were unfastened, revealing a vee of suntanned skin and a silver charm hanging from a thick chain. The panther's glittering red collar lay in his outstretched hand.

Blair let loose with a huge sigh. She accepted the proffered jewelry, which up close looked more like a choker and less like an animal collar. "Thank you. But you just about scared me to death."

"May I?" Damon asked, pointing at the jewelry.

"Sure." She dropped it in his hand.

Damon's eyes glittered with smoldering heat as he stepped closer to fasten the choker around Blair's neck. It felt cold and heavy against her skin, even with the little flares of heat erupting beneath the surface. "Welcome, Blair."

"I'm so glad to see you two. I have so many questions, like how you—"

Damon pressed his index finger against her lips, silencing her. "Later." His gaze meandered down her body then slowly climbed back up. The corners of his mouth lifted into a naughty, predatory smile. "You look beautiful. You've always been beautiful, but you've changed. In a very good way."

Her cheeks had to be as red as the fiery stones in her new choker. She nervously fingered the jewels as she met his gaze. "Thanks. But I think most of the changes haven't been for the better. You, on the other hand, both look amazing. You really...er, filled out." That was an understatement.

Damon looked very pleased by her compliment. "Thank you." He motioned toward the far corner of the warehouse, which was completely cloaked in thick black shadows. "This way."

"I'm not sure if I'm liking the magic thing or not. Gotta admit, it's a little strange. Scary, even."

"There's nothing to be afraid of," Trey said behind her, gently coaxing her forward with a hand pressed to the small of her back.

Little prickles danced up her spine. She would have shivered but she stopped herself. Somehow.

A small part of her felt like bait being coaxed into a trap for a big, hungry feline. But a bigger part knew better. These two guys had been her soul mates. And even though it had been years since they'd last seen each other, she knew they wouldn't hurt her.

Damon flicked his hand and poof, a dozen candles or so lit instantaneously, illuminating a table draped in white and set for three. She had to give it to them, these guys had the magic thing down pat. Another flick of the hand and the warehouse was filled with the low, sultry sounds of jazz.

And it looked as if they'd learned a thing or two about romance since she'd last seen them too.

"This is so nice. Do I need to ask though, where the big, scary black cat is?"

"He's safely put away," Trey reassured her, giving her a not-so reassuring smile. As Trey pulled out her chair, she noticed he was wearing an identical necklace to Damon's. The silver disk flashed when he moved, catching the flickering light of a candle.

They both held her chair as she sat and then Trey took the seat on her left, Damon the right. Damon poured her a glass of wine. Trey lifted the covers off her plates, revealing a full dinner, complete with salad, vegetables, loaded baked potato and some kind of beef. It looked and smelled delicious, which was too bad, because with her jangly nerves and twitchy insides, she knew she wouldn't eat much.

"Tell us," Damon said, looking over the rim of his wineglass, "where have you been since you moved away?

What have you been doing?"

"I'm not saying a word until you tell me first," she challenged, giving both of them a devious grin. "How'd you two end up with this gig? Magicians?"

"Illusionists," Trey corrected. "We decided the priesthood wasn't for us."

"You were going to become priests?" Blair asked, her gaze shifting back and forth between her two charming, handsome hosts.

They both nodded.

"It sounded like a good idea at first," Damon said as he lifted a forkful of potato to his mouth. "Free meals. Peace and quiet. Stability."

Now she could understand where they were coming from. None of those things had come easily to any of them, Blair included, as they'd been growing up. Instead, their lives had been full of screaming voices, chaos, instability and the kind of gut-burning hunger that few people in the United States could relate to.

"But there was one big problem," Trey added, his eyes sparkling with humor. "Neither of us believes in God."

She couldn't help chuckling. "Yeah, I guess that would be a problem."

"So instead we decided we'd be illusionists," Damon said.

"A logical choice," she said, laughing. "There's gotta be lots of stability and peace with this career."

The guys joined her, and the sound of their laughter echoed through the huge warehouse.

Sobering, she sipped some wine. "It's so great to see you. I can't tell you how many times I wondered where you were, what you were doing."

Damon reached for her hand, resting his on top of hers. "Same here. It took us a long time to find you."

"But you did. You looked for me. You found me."

"We couldn't stop until we did."

Their gazes tangled, and the same sizzling chemistry

they'd shared when they were younger zinged through the air and buzzed through Blair's body. It was as if the years had rolled back and they'd just said goodbye yesterday.

A hot tear slipped from the corner of Blair's eye and dribbled down the side of her nose. Damon thumbed it away and Trey leaned closer, wrapping a protective arm around her shoulders.

Damon's index finger traced her upper lip. "Tell me you've been okay all this time, because it was killing me that we weren't there to take care of you."

"Once I left home it was okay. I'm doing okay. Renting a house in a pretty good neighborhood from a friend's brother—got a great deal since he's out of the country for a few years with the military—and I have a job that doesn't involve taking off my clothes or schlepping food to customers. Considering everything, that's pretty impressive. Right?" She lifted her right arm, threading her fingers through Trey's, and leaned into his bulk, grateful for his strength and warmth. It had been a long time since she'd been held by a man. And even longer since she'd been held by a man she cared this much about.

It was magical. She just hoped this magic wouldn't prove to be all an illusion, fleeting and phony.

Damon nodded. "It's very impressive, what you've accomplished." His expression changed. "Are you happy, Blair?"

"Happy?" She considered her current situation, the okay-but-not-great job, and the okay car that ran more days than not, and the okay house she rented in the okay part of town. Considering the start she'd had, her life was damn good, even if she hadn't been in a relationship with a man in years. Hadn't had sex for even more because of a very severe and persistent case of guilt she couldn't shake, no matter how hard she tried. She'd long known there was something missing but hadn't known what to do to change it. "I'm content most days. Some days, though, I want more."

"More what?" Damon asked, leaning closer.

"More...living. More special, memorable moments." She traced each of the three curved lines on his pendant, briefly wondering if the design had any special meaning. "Most of my minutes, hours, days, weeks, are the kind I don't want to remember. They're just blah, nothing special. But at least they aren't the kind I have to force myself to forget either."

Damon's gaze shot to the side, to Trey.

"Why?" she asked. "What are you thinking? Why did you bring me here?"

"We want to give you some special, memorable moments," Trey answered, tightening his hold on her hand. The oddest sensation, a bizarre blend of hot and cold, swept through her body. His thumb stroked across her palm, sending the slightest quiver of heat up her arm. "Will you let us?"

"I guess that depends. How long can you stay?"

"Only a couple of weeks," Damon answered.

Her heart dropped to her toes.

A couple of weeks. A couple meant two. That was only fourteen days at the most. How would she say goodbye after spending two weeks with her guys?

How would she say goodbye after spending an hour?

She couldn't.

"I understand," she said, nodding. "I want to make the most of the time then. I'll spend every moment I'm not at work with you."

Damon's smile was more a pained expression than a gleeful one. "We were hoping you'd say that. Every minute is precious, which is why I can't wait another second to do this..." He leaned closer, brushed his mouth over hers, and she swore the world stopped spinning for a split second. The universe stopped whirling and all the galaxies crashed together, creating a mighty explosion in her head.

Oh God, how long had she been waiting for this moment?

Eager to deepen the kiss, she released Trey's hand and looped her arms around Damon's neck. Turning in her chair to face Damon, she pulled until her chest was flattened against his. She parted her lips, inviting him inside with a moan. But he didn't accept her invitation. Instead, he sprinkled torturously soft kisses over her mouth.

She could see some things had not changed. "You tease," she murmured against his mouth.

"You love me anyway," he whispered between kisses.

Did he have that right!

Trey decided right then was a grand time to skim his hands around her sides and lean into her back. She was now wedged snugly between the two sexiest, most amazing men in the universe, and she never wanted to leave. She gave a little mewl against Damon's mouth, wishing her skirt wasn't so snug around her thighs. For the first time in fifteen years a pounding heat was slowly gathering strength between her legs and she was in the perfect position to grind away that ache against Damon's legs. If only she could part her legs.

She knew it was just a matter of time before they were naked, their slick bodies gliding over one another. In a way, she'd known it since she'd taken her first look at them. She felt the heat in their gazes. Saw the desperate wanting they were trying so hard to hide.

She wasn't afraid or struggling too much with that awful, nagging guilt.

"Damon," she murmured, tightening her hold on his neck. "Please."

"Soon, sweetheart." Leaning back, he gently unclasped her hands and lowered her arms. "Forgive me," he whispered, looking as dazed and breathless as she felt.

"Forgive you for what? For kissing me? Or stopping?" She shifted her weight back, once again letting Trey's bulk support her as she sat sideways in her chair, facing Damon. They all knew where this was heading. Why fight it? If she wasn't, after so much time had passed since she'd had sex, why should they?

"There's one more thing we want you to know before you decide whether you want to spend the next couple of weeks with us."

"What's that?"

"It's easier to just show you." Standing, Damon offered her a hand. She kicked off her shoes, knowing she was too shaken and wobbly to walk in them, and followed Damon around a towering stack of crates. Trey fell into step beside her, taking her free hand.

They stopped in front of a collection of bondage furniture, set up in a corner of the warehouse that had been obviously set up as a bondage dungeon.

Bondage? This couldn't be a joke. She had no idea how to react, what to say. Taken totally by surprise, and nearly numb from the shock, she just stood there, her gaze wandering from one end of the room to the other.

Most of the furniture was freakish. Ugly. Scary. But the room itself wasn't ugly at all. On long lengths of wire strung along the walls hung swathes of red crimson fabric, from the ceiling to the floor. And the concrete floor had been covered in a plush red carpet. It was like fluffy cotton balls under her feet. So soft, impossibly soft. In one corner of the makeshift dungeon stood an enormous bed with an unusual canopy frame draped in even more translucent fabric. The lightweight draperies fluttered on a fragrant breeze.

The room was exploding with sensual textures and scents and colors, drawing her in, beckoning her like a siren's song, despite the scary bondage stuff. The ubersoft carpet under her feet. The scent of her favorite flowers in the air—lilacs. The soft music playing from hidden speakers.

This would be the place where a lifetime of special moments could be experienced, even if she wasn't exactly sure what all that bondage stuff was. All that mattered were Trey and Damon, she reminded herself.

How long had she wondered where they were?

How long had she dreamed that someday she'd find them? Now that time had come, and it was like a gift from heaven.

Any place Trey and Damon had been with her had always been heaven. Even the shitty dark corner under the freeway overpass years ago. This warehouse was a thousand times nicer than that.

"Have you ever been in a dungeon like this?" Trey asked.

"No, never."

"Do you know what this is?" Damon rested a hand on a piece of furniture she couldn't name.

"I have some general idea, but I don't know the proper names for anything," she said, nodding. She pointed at the piece he was touching. "I was at Sandy's house once. She has a computer with internet, does lots of research online. She showed me pictures of stuff like that, a bondage dungeon."

"Then you know what these items are used for," Damon said, sounding relieved. "Does it scare you that we have set up a dungeon?"

"No." She paused. That wasn't true. "Maybe." She sighed and tried to get a handle on the flurry of emotions pummeling her system. "Okay, scared might be the wrong word for it. I think I'm feeling more shock. Surprise. Disbelief. Confusion, even? I never in a million years would've guessed you'd be into this kind of thing... I don't really know what it involves." Unsure what to think, how to act, what to say, she met his gaze. "Should I be scared? You wouldn't hurt me."

He shook his head. "Never. We love you."

"Then I'm not scared," she said, trying to convince herself. "I'm just uncomfortable." She stepped up to the thing he was touching and ran a finger down the side. It was wood, polished and smooth, coated with a slick, glossy finish.

"We'll go very slow," Trey promised, his expression sincere.

"Is this really that important to you both?"

They nodded. Damon reached around the back of his neck, removed the chain she'd noticed earlier and handed it to her. "See the charm? That symbol is more than just a pretty design. See? It's like a three-part version of the ying and yang." He traced the three lines curving out from the center with his index finger." This emblem means something to the people who wear it. It means we live a certain *lifestyle*. This isn't a game to us. It isn't a hobby. It's a way of relating to each other, of communicating our feelings." He closed her fingers around the necklace, cupping her fist in his. "It's been a long time since we've seen each other. I understand if you're having a hard time trusting us."

"Oh, I trust you. That's not the issue. I believe you don't want to hurt me." Turning, she faced them both. "It's just a lot to understand." She opened her hand and stared down at the pretty silver charm. "This is a lifestyle? Really?" At their nod, she sucked in a deep breath. "Show me what this is then, what you do here. What you want from me." Her hands trembled as she reached around her back and unzipped her skirt. It slid down, slowly at first as it slipped over her round hips and full thighs. And then it fell faster, landing in a heap at her feet. She stepped out of it, shivering at the nuclear-hot blazes she saw in Trey and Damon's eyes.

Something inside her had changed. Already. She felt kind of free, as if she'd just been cut loose from some kind of invisible bindings.

A part of her wanted to shock them a little. Or maybe tell them that she could handle this, whatever it was. Let them know she wasn't too delicate or innocent.

It seemed they were getting the message. Both of them stripped nude and fell upon her like men who hadn't touched a woman in decades. They yanked and pulled, stripping the rest of her clothes off within seconds. They tormented her sizzling skin with soft touches and not-so-soft ones. Kisses and licks and nibbles.

She stood in the center of a vortex of male caresses and luscious scents and whirling sensations, her eyes closed, her body igniting one cell at a time.

So right. So good. So…not enough.

Her knees began to tremble, threatening to give out. She pulled Trey closer, dug her nails into the velvety skin of his upper back, and flattened herself against the rigid planes of his chest and stomach. More heat pounded through her body.

Her head fell back, resting against Damon. His thick rod singed the soft skin of her buttocks, branding her. Succumbing to instinct, she rocked her hips back and forth, rubbing at the scorching touch of his cock, taking the heat inside. Trey's mouth closed over hers, and he swallowed the sigh that slipped from her lips.

His tongue teased the seam of her mouth before slipping inside, filling her with his delicious flavor. She suckled his tongue, eagerly drinking in his essence. The heat inside cranked up another notch to nearly blinding. A sharp need, a hunger she'd never known, speared her insides, making her cry out.

"She's so fucking hot, Trey," Damon murmured against her nape.

Hot and cold, burning up with fever, she shivered and whimpered. Oh God, it was sexy hearing Damon talk about her like that. His voice was gritty and raw with erotic hunger.

"I love the way she tastes, smells, feels," Trey said after breaking the kiss. He fisted her hair, tugging it to the side, and her head went with it. He dragged his tongue up the column of her neck and a thick coat of goose bumps sprang up all over her body.

Damon groaned. "I need to taste her pussy. I'm going

to die if I don't."

"The bench." Trey led her forward by gripping her upper arms and pulling, taunting her to take one step then another by teasing her mouth with his. Blindly, obediently, she followed him, stealing kiss after kiss, until he stopped and shuffled around, taking her with him. "Sit."

She settled on a padded bench that looked a lot like a weight bench, her legs extended straight in front of her on the bench. But instead of supports fastened to either side to hold barbells loaded with heavy weight plates, there was a single wooden center post fastened to the end of the bench. A horizontal beam was bolted to the center post and she quickly realized there were two chains ending in leather cuffs hooked to each end of the beam.

She quivered and burned as Trey enclosed her right wrist in a cuff. Damon buckled a matching cuff around her left. And then Damon straddled the bench and her legs, his ruddy, fully erect cock at her eye level. If she'd been able to reach with her hands, she would have gladly closed her fists around it and stroked him. Hard and fast. Slow and easy. Any way he wanted.

He stepped back and slipped his hands between her knees, forcing them apart, and oh God, did it feel sexy having him take command of her body like this. He wasn't exactly rough but he wasn't gentle either. He was firm and decisive and commanding and totally, overwhelmingly sexy.

She never would have guessed that she would like this kind of thing. Outside of that brief glimpse of a website, she'd had no idea this kind of sex existed. That she could let a man tie her up and take charge of her body, and it would be good. Wonderful. Mind-blowing.

"What do you think of this, Blair? How do you like being tied and helpless, while I stand over you, free to do whatever I want to you?"

"It's sexy. Exciting. With you."

He looked pleased with her response. "I've been

waiting so long for this day. I want to tie your legs too. Like this." He caught her ankles in his fists and lifted them up and out, until her legs formed a wide vee in the air. "I want your pussy open to me, so I can eat you. I'm going to suck that sweet little clit of yours and fuck you with a dildo."

She was going to die.

"And Trey here's going to have his turn too. But not until after I've made you come so hard you scream. How's that sound, sweet thing? Are you ready?"

She couldn't speak but she managed a nod.

And then they shackled her ankles and she was open and vulnerable and struggling to take each breath. Sex with her guys had always been fun, special, wonderful. Memorable. But never like this—a thrilling, intoxicating adventure.

Yes, the living had begun, and the special moments were piling up by the hundreds. And it had only been a short time. Such a short time.

But she knew, even if there were millions of special moments between now and the time her guys said goodbye, she'd remember every single one of them. Every detail, right down to the wicked gleam in Damon's eye.

Surely these moments would hold her over for a lifetime.

Chapter 3

"You taste so fucking good, I don't want to stop," Damon murmured between licks. Damn, he'd known this first time would be good. But this good? Holy fuck! His balls were heavier than concrete and his dick so hard he had to grit his teeth. He could see that Trey was in the same condition, hurting all over with desperate need.

All he wanted to do was cram that sweet, wet pussy full of dick and pound away the ache, but he couldn't. Not yet.

Soon.

He had to step aside and let Trey have a taste.

Their beautiful, perfect Blair was almost ready. The dildo he was fucking her tight cunt with was coated with her sweet honey now, and she was quivering all over, the heady scent of her arousal filling the air.

Standing, he motioned to Trey, letting him take his place. As they brushed past each other, Trey grabbed his face and kissed him, hard and hot, his tongue spearing in his mouth. It was a kiss Damon wouldn't forget, not for a long time, but he broke it, anxious to get back to Blair.

Trey brushed his mouth over his once more then settled down to devour Blair's clit with sexy slurps and licks. The sight of Trey feasting on Blair was almost enough to make Damon double over with erotic need. His balls were so tight, it almost felt as if he'd been kicked there. And the blood pounding through his body was like acid, it burned so hot.

Watching Trey's perfect mouth work over Blair's clit, Damon attacked her tits, kneading the soft flesh, suckling her hard little nipples. He wrapped a hand around his cock and gave it slow, soft swipes.

Damon groaned.

In the years since he'd seen her, Blair had matured from a cute, thin and fragile teenager into a lush and beautiful woman. Her body, with all its feminine curves, was pure perfection. Round hips and ass. Full tits. Smooth stomach. And her legs...damn.

He wouldn't last long. It was going to be hell holding back.

What felt like eons later, Trey stood, licking lips gleaming from Blair's juices. One hand was fisted around his cock, gliding up to the tip and then back to the base. In the other, he held the dildo.

"I want her," Trey murmured, dropping the toy on the floor. "I want her bad."

Damon nodded. "Soon."

Blair moaned. "Please, I can't take any more. Let me come."

Damon rolled on a rubber and positioned his hips, driving into her tight channel. She took him hard and fast, whimpering and moaning and begging for more. Her legs tightened as she trembled and writhed her way to a hard, fast climax. Her fingers curled around the chains securing her arms. "Damon!"

Goddamn, she was going to make him come too early.

He moistened a fingertip and stroked her hard little clit while simultaneously slowing his thrusts, deepening them.

Her pussy clamped hard around his cock, and a heartbeat later she shouted, "Oh yes!" Her channel milked his dick with smooth, swift contractions.

Trey came up behind him, slid his flattened hands around his sides and pinched his nipples. The pleasure-pain sent him over the edge. His cum seared up his cock and then burst from the tip, hard and fast. He quickened his pace, driven by the urgent need to pound every drop from his body. He bent over and kissed his sweet Blair, letting his lips and tongue tell her what words could not. And then, before his cock softened, he pulled out and removed the rubber.

It was an awesome sight, watching Trey bring their sweet Blair to the quivering cusp of orgasm again. Trey's body moved with the sleek grace of a panther, muscles rippling and bulging. Skin smooth and suntanned and beautiful. And Blair's body was the perfect complement, soft and warm and feminine.

He straddled the end of the bench and leaned into Trey's back, absorbing the blistering heat coming off his body. He let his hands explore every hard-muscled inch of flesh he could reach—shoulders, arms, chest, stomach, buttocks. He moistened a finger with some lube and teased Trey's ass, running his slickened fingertip 'round and 'round his anus.

Close, Trey was close. And little Blair was trembling, her swollen labia slick with her juices, nipples pointed. Damn, did they look hot. Hot but also as lost in their desperate need as he had been.

He pushed his finger into Trey's ass, working past the slight resistance. Then he added a second finger and Trey let out a low growl as he found his release. His anus tightened around Damon's fingers, locking them inside. Damon flattened himself against Trey, stroking him intimately, caressing him through the full length of his climax, refusing to stop until Trey withdrew from Blair's body. He kissed Trey's neck, nipped his earlobe and then stood.

"Our sweet Blair," Damon murmured as he walked around to the front of the bench. He kissed her tenderly, released her arms and legs and sat, pulling her onto his lap.

She wept, her tears burning his skin.

"Oh sweetheart. We're here, and we love you, baby. We're yours. We didn't hurt you, did we?"

She shook her head. "No, I'm just...overwhelmed. There's so much I don't know. About you. About this..."

Once Trey was done disposing of his condom, he sat opposite Damon, spreading his legs to inch as close as possible to them both and wrapping his arms around them.

Damon met Trey's gaze. They shared a look that said more than he could ever hope to utter. He palmed Blair's lovely face and kissed her eyelids, the tip of her nose, her cheeks and forehead. "Come back again tomorrow. And the next day, and the next. We need you."

She nodded, her eyes teary and red. "I need you too. Both of you. Nothing could keep me away."

* * * * *

Blair hadn't thought it was possible, but she was more nervous before the second night than she had been the first.

Last night had been so much more than she ever would have dreamed. It had been exciting, a little scary, thrilling, erotic and both incredibly wonderful and sad at the same time. After they'd had sex, she'd cried. Literally. Those salty droplets had been tears of both joy and sadness. Confusion and understanding. Relief and restoration, as well as deep sorrow.

In a way, she felt like Damon and Trey were still a part of her, as if no time at all had passed. But in another, they were strangers.

Like seeing them touch each other last night. While she'd be the first to admit their sexual behavior might not have been typical for kids their age, they hadn't gone that far years ago. But now, it seemed, the guys were lovers. They were gay. Or rather, bisexual. And into bondage.

Who were Damon and Trey? How had those years

changed them? She ached to know what other secrets they would reveal.

Two weeks wasn't enough time.

In her car, parked outside the warehouse, she checked her makeup in the mirror one last time before cutting off the engine. Her hands shook as she dug for her lipstick in her purse. Lost somewhere. She gave up, deciding she'd make a big mess if she tried adding a little more anyway. Her hands were shaking too much. Her stomach churned as she pushed open her car door. It had been a bad idea eating but she didn't want to be starving tonight. Since they were meeting later, to accommodate her work schedule, she assumed there'd be no dinner tonight.

Squinting at the low-lying sun sinking into the western horizon, she hurried across the parking lot. Like yesterday, the reception area was dark and quiet. She went straight to the back and through the rear door, into the warehouse.

She stopped dead in her tracks.

Before her, dressed in an absolutely stunning red gown, stood herself. Or rather, a spooky, semi-translucent version of herself.

The other self met her gaze squarely, smiled softly and silently motioned for her to follow her—it—whatever.

How freaking bizarre.

Would she ever get used to the idea of her guys being illusionists?

This time a black curtain cut the warehouse into two sections. The spooky faux her stopped in front of the curtain, pressed a fingertip to her lips and mouthed, "Wait." And then with a flare of red light, she vanished, leaving a red box about half the size of a shoebox sitting on the floor.

Sure it was yet another gift from her thoughtful, if not over-generous, duo of magicians, she scooped up the box and lifted the lid.

Inside she found an ornate picture frame made out of heavy metal and red crystals. It was breathtaking, like no picture frame she'd ever seen. A narrow band of black metal rimmed a picture of her guys in the center. And then outside, dozens of red crystals formed an intricate pattern of leaves and flowers. She smiled as she traced the line of Damon's jaw in the photograph.

"Do you like your gift?" Trey asked, appearing out of nowhere.

"I love it. Although I was a little freaked out by the delivery girl." Smiling, she lifted up on tiptoes to give him a thank-you kiss. He swept an arm around her waist and crushed her against him. "Oh God," she murmured into his mouth as he slanted his mouth over hers, deepening the kiss.

Someone gently tugged the frame from her hand and in the next moment, she found herself staggering and shaky, smooshed between two hulking male bodies. Hot. Burning up. A spicy male tongue exploring her mouth. Strong hands exploring her body.

"Do you know who that delivery girl is?" Damon whispered in her ear. A soft puff of breath tickled her neck, making her shiver.

Her eyelids fluttered then closed, shutting her into her secret world of warmth and wanting and sensation. "Sure, it was me."

"Yes and no," Trey said against her mouth.

"I don't understand." She felt air brushing over her bare arms, as if she was moving, but the ground beneath her feet was solid and still.

"You will. Soon."

She was drifting backward, falling. She opened her eyes, stiffening.

Trey smiled. "Trust us."

She glanced around. They were in the dungeon again. How had they done that?

"Play with us. Let us possess you like we did last night." Holding a set of leather cuffs, Damon looked at her with fire in his eyes. The heat in his gaze ignited a

271

smoldering blaze in her blood.

"Yes." She eagerly offered him her wrists, watching breathless and giddy as he fastened the cuffs around them. Then she followed him to a table the size of a large formal dining table, at least eight feet long and four feet wide, and looked up. There, hanging a few feet above the table's top, was a bar suspended from the ceiling. And attached to that bar were four chains, two shorter ones and two longer ones.

Just the thought of these guys tying her up again, fucking her until she thought she'd pass out, made her shudder. Her heart slammed against her breastbone, and her lungs refused to draw in air.

Trey lifted her onto the table. "Lie down, Blair. Let us take command of your body. Play our games of domination and submission with us. Discover the secret pleasure in submitting to us."

"I want to know," she whispered, slowly lying back. "Show me."

At her feet, Damon caressed her calf. "Did you know you were submissive before last night, Blair?"

"No."

He nodded then leapt up onto the table, straddling her waist. "You never fantasized about being tied up?"

"Not exactly."

"What does that mean?" Trey asked as he too levered himself up onto the table. His feet were planted on either side of her head, so when she looked straight up, she had a nice view of the thick bulge in his pants. "Tell us."

"Do you remember those games we used to play when we were kids, you know, where I was the princess, and you were the pirates or Native Americans or dark, dangerous renegade princes? You captured me and held me captive."

"Then we will be your dark, dangerous renegade princes again." Trey moved back, squatting over her abdomen. His dark eyes glittered with sensual hunger, desperate wanting. "And you are our captive. We will not stop tormenting you until we've conquered you, until you're breathless and begging for mercy."

A game? She'd never thought to try playing games during sex. Maybe if she had, she would have been able to let go of the guilt from her past and allow herself to have sex before last night.

Fifteen years was a long time to be abstinent.

"Strip," Damon demanded, giving her a yummy glare.

"Oh God," she whispered. It wouldn't take much to convince these two that she was a petrified princess. She was already a ball of jumpy nerves, despite the simmering heat coursing through her veins.

Clumsy from the excitement, she fiddled with the buttons on her dress. What had made her think it was a good idea wearing a garment with a bazillion buttons tonight?

Standing, Trey snatched up one of her wrists and pulled until she was sitting upright. He didn't hurt her but he wasn't exactly gentle either. "What's taking so long?"

Whew, Trey played one convincing dark and dangerous prince.

"I-I'm trying."

Trey glowered. "Try harder. Or you'll be punished."

A chill burned up her spine. Not sure whether she wanted to be "punished" or not, she started working the buttons faster, concentrating on the first few, knowing if she got those, she could simply yank the dress over her head.

Trey's glower grew darker.

She whimpered, gave up and just grabbed the bottom of the dress and pulled, hoping the two buttons she'd managed to unfasten would be enough. It was a struggle, but the dress came off, and the expression she found on Trey's face once her vision was unblocked by yards of black material was much friendlier. In fact, it was beyond friendly.

It took little effort to get rid of her bra. Her panties,

however, were another matter, thanks to Damon standing straddled over her legs. She had to kind of wriggle her way out of them.

Naked.

She felt their gazes scorching her skin like branding irons being passed slowly over her breasts, stomach, legs. Oddly, the heat made the nervous chill feel all the more frosty. Hot and cold. Aroused and nervous. Unsure and thrilled. If the point of these games was to bring her head into the act of sex, then it was working. She didn't want to just lie back and wait for them to poke her. She was trembling with suspense, eager to see what would happen next. Waiting, breathless, her heart racing.

"Give me your arms," Trey growled.

She lifted her arms over her head.

Not surprisingly, he fastened the cuffs to the short chains hanging from the bar. Now she could not lie back. Nor could she cover her tingling nipples, hide herself from his hungry gaze.

Damon stepped back a little until he was straddling her calves. "Bend your knees."

Knees together, she bent her legs, sliding her feet up toward her bottom.

"Now open your legs."

A flare of heat flashed in her pussy.

This game wasn't just fun, it was wicked. Naughty. Thrilling.

She wrapped her fingers around the chains at her wrists and slowly dragged her feet apart. Oh God, she felt so exposed and vulnerable, sitting like this, naked, her legs spread, her two guys practically devouring her with their eyes.

In the past, she would have felt dirty and objectified. But not now, not with Damon and Trey.

Damon's expression took on a decidedly nasty gleam, the kind that only made the hot-cold shivers quaking through her body that much worse. He stooped down, his sharp gaze snagging hers and holding it hostage. "Such a sweet and obedient little princess, aren't you?"

Obedient wasn't an adjective she'd normally apply to herself. But in this case it sure did seem to fit. "Um, yes."

"Very good," Damon said, his voice so low it almost sounded like a purr. He pushed on her right knee, forcing it out farther. "So if I told you to cream for me, you would."

Just him saying those words made hot juices gather in her pussy. "Yes," she said, her voice shaky.

"And I could check you, like this." An evil grin quirking his lips, he teased her labia with his fingers. "Mmmmm. You feel warm, but not wet enough."

She would get plenty wet if he filled her with those naughty fingers. If he pushed them deep inside and stroked that special place where it felt so good, so wonderful.

"Cream for me, princess." Damon's fingers stroked her labia, up and down, just missing the hood of her clit.

He was one teasing bastard. And yet, despite the fact that he wasn't touching as intimately as she wanted, the heat inside her womb inched up higher. The pounding, throbbing need inside amplified. She let her head fall back and closed her eyes, let the pleasant waves of wet heat overtake her.

In her mind's eye, she replayed the first time she'd had sex with Damon. They'd been in her bedroom—she'd sneaked both him and Trey in. And he'd been so sweet. He'd held her, kissed her, slowly and patiently gotten her ready...

A brush across her tight nipple yanked her back to the present. This wasn't the same slow and gentle Damon she'd known then, but she wasn't complaining. He was still attentive and giving, getting her ready, teasing and tormenting, building the fire inside her.

She was going to melt. Or die. Or burn to cinders.

She glanced down, first seeing Trey's fingers pinching

her nipples. Somehow, he knew exactly how tight to pinch, how much pain she could endure. Down the slope of her stomach her gaze traveled, to the juncture of her spread thighs. The sight of him reaching to her pussy was enough to spike her body temperature another dozen degrees or so.

Dipping two fingers into her slit, Damon lifted his dark gaze to hers. "I love the smell of your cream, the taste, the way it feels on my fingers." He lifted his fingers to his mouth, swirled his tongue around them and then dragged that naughty tongue across his bottom lip.

She sighed. A tongue could be such a sexy thing, especially when it was doing stuff like that to the world's most perfect lips…and belonged to the world's sexiest man.

"She's not begging for mercy yet," Trey grumbled as he rolled her nipples between his fingers and thumbs.

"No, she's not." The corners of Damon's mouth lifted again, forming that devious smile she'd come to appreciate so much. "I think we need to torture her more, show her how devious her renegade princes can be."

They both leapt off the table, leaving her panting and hot and wondering what sort of delicious agony they would inflict on her next.

They headed for a large wooden trunk in the back of the room, returning a short time later with hands full of sex toys. A rubber dildo, a smaller toy with a flared end, a tube of lubricating jelly, a slender vibrator.

Like she wasn't about to die before!

Every muscle in her body stiffened. That dildo was bigger than your average guy. At least, in her extremely limited experience.

Now the little vibrator didn't look scary and that other thing, whatever it was, was small and innocuous enough.

Again, her gaze flew back to the dildo. That thing was intimidating. Instinctively, she jerked her legs together.

Both Damon and Trey gave her a mean-eyed glare.

Her teeth chattered. "That thing is...yikes!"

"Trust us." Damon squeezed some lube out of the tube and slathered it over the tip of the dildo, stroking it like it was his cock. He curled his fingers over the flared head, and something inside her snapped. The need Damon and Trey had been cruelly building inside her morphed into agonizing desperation. Not only did she want him to fuck her with that toy, but she needed him to do it. Now.

"Yes. Oh yes," she whispered, pulling her legs wider apart. The inner walls of her pussy clamped closed, and her body stiffened the second the toy teased her opening. But she couldn't help rocking her hips forward in a silent plea for sweet invasion.

There was no doubt they were going to top last night. They were going to blow her mind with all these wonderfully wicked games and toys. And she was so overwhelmed, tears were once again threatening to gather in her eyes.

As she'd dressed for the first night with Damon and Trey, she'd never dreamed what these nights would turn out to be—dark, sexual experimentation. But she'd never complain. Now that she'd had a taste of their kind of decadence, she would never look back.

This was what sex was supposed to be about—the unleashing of her inhibitions, the exploration of her darkest fantasies. Not the empty, dirty act of her last experience, so many years ago. That night, something had snapped, cutting off a part of her, forcing it deep into the shadows.

Damon and Trey had so easily coaxed that part of her out of the shadows. It was...magic.

She watched in awe as Damon inched that thick dildo into her hungry pussy, filling her fully before withdrawing. And then smiling, she met his gaze and sighed.

Chapter 4

Trey watched, transfixed, as Damon crammed that dong into Blair's sweet little pussy. The room's air was thin and blistering hot, heated by the inferno burning in Damon's eyes.

Damn.

Trey had shared a woman with Damon before. Plenty of times. But never had he seen Damon react to one like he was now.

It shouldn't have surprised him as much as it did. Nor should it bother him. Blair wasn't like the others. She was the one. Their first.

But all those things that he knew in his head didn't make the pain in his gut any less agonizing.

First, there was the way Damon was reacting to Blair. Like now. Damon should have let Trey fuck her with the dong, let him fuck her with his dick first tonight too. Damon had taken her first last night.

Jealousy was a bad thing in a threesome.

Second, there was the way Blair was reacting to Damon—because Damon had been the first one to take her. Hell, she'd looked at Damon like he was a god, just because he'd fucked her with that stupid toy, and it had been his idea. His plan. His turn!

Jealousy was a very bad thing in a threesome.

Trey adjusted the chains holding her wrists, lengthening them so she could lie on her back. Then he left his post at her head, walked around the table and nudged Damon, but the bastard didn't move aside. Furious, he stepped back, knowing if he didn't, he was bound to do or say something he'd regret. Through a haze of rage, he watched Damon fuck that tight little pussy with the dong. And then Damon left the dong in, slathered the butt plug with a thick coating of lube and slowly pushed it into Blair's anus.

Her throaty moan vibrated through his body, shoving aside the anger that had wound itself around his gut. She was so lovely, her nipples hard and tight peaks, her legs spread wide, her pussy and ass full, her face flushed and eyes glassy. Her head rocked to the side, and her gaze found his, locked onto it like radar. The air blasted from his lungs.

"Trey," she mouthed. "I need you. Please," she murmured.

She wasn't going to let him withdraw. Wasn't going to let him feel as if he was invisible.

He nodded and turned his attention back to Damon, whose beautiful body was visibly tight with need. Shoulders, neck, arms. The muscles rippled as he moved, clenching into sinewy lines and bulging ropes as he dragged his hands down her torso.

Trey could only see his face in profile, but he could tell Damon's desperate need was etched into his perfect features, making them that much more striking. There were days when Trey thought it was too good to be true, that he was with Damon, that they were still together after all this time and even more deeply in love than they'd been years ago.

This was one of those times.

"Oh my fucking God," Damon said, sounding awestruck. "Do you see how she responds to me—I mean us. Responds to us?" Damon glanced at Trey. His expression darkened. "Oh fuck, Trey."

An apology.

Trey nodded. He just had to be patient, give Damon the chance to face the emotions he'd been struggling with over the years. Deal with the guilt he'd felt for supposedly failing Blair so long ago. In the long run, they'd be much happier, their relationship stronger.

This time when Trey stepped up beside Damon, Trey resisted the urge to take over, to stake a claim to Blair like he ached to do. Instead, he pressed his body against Damon's back, reached around his sides, unzipped his pants and shoved his hands into them. His gaze locked on Blair's eyes, catching them widening with surprise. But that deer-caught-in-the-headlights look quickly changed. The expression in her eyes turned dark and hot. Her cheeks flushed. Her mouth pursed into a sexy little pout. They exchanged erotically charged smiles.

Damon's cock was hard, his balls snug against his body, the heat of building need radiating from his skin. Trey closed a fist around Damon's dick and gave it a few slow caresses, knowing what that would do to him.

It nearly brought Damon to his knees.

Damon let go of the toys he'd been tormenting Blair with, dropped his head back, and let loose with a guttural roar, which satisfied Trey. Then, taking Trey by surprise, Damon whirled around, slanted his lips over his and speared his tongue in and out of Trey's mouth until he too was on the verge of dropping to his knees.

The sound of Blair's breathy whimper made Trey tear his mouth from Damon's. Damon forced Trey around, practically tore his pants down. "Take her. Take her now, or I can't be responsible for what I'll do next."

"Please," Blair begged, blinking open teary eyes. The skin of her chest and neck were stained pink, the effect of the carnal need they had so skillfully built up. "I can't wait another second."

Quickly, Trey rolled on a rubber, gently pulled the dildo out of Blair's pussy and jumped up on the table. He wedged his knees between her thighs and angled over her, kissing her mouth, her eyelids her cheeks. "Our sweet baby. You've been so good. So damn good." After dropping a trail of kisses along her jaw, he sat back on his knees and gripped the satiny skin of her hips in his hands. "I'm going to fuck you now, with the anal plug in place. It'll make you feel even fuller than normal. Tell me if anything hurts."

Blair nodded but didn't speak.

Damon ran around to the head of the table, hopped up on the table and sat behind her, lifting her upper body up at a shallow angle and gently cradling her head and shoulders in his lap. He nodded and Trey, still sitting back on his knees, lifted her hips and drove his dick into her tight cunt.

Ohhhh fuck.

How could he have already forgotten how tight she was? How fucking delicious it felt to have her pussy clamp around his dick? He was in heaven and hell both. Shaking his head, he met Damon's gaze. "Goddamn it, Damon. She's so tight."

"Yeah," Damon grumbled, jerking his head to the side to bite on the soft swell of her shoulder.

Trey closed his eyes and settled into a steady rhythm of deep thrusts. With each inward stroke his need for release swelled, and with each withdrawal his fever climbed, higher, higher, until he couldn't think, could barely sort out the glorious sensations battering his body.

The scent of woman, so sweet. The simmering heat burning the skin he touched. The sound of Damon's kisses and licks, Blair's throaty moans. The lingering flavor of her skin on his dry lips.

Hot. Tight. His body charged forward. Closer. Yes, so close now.

And he sensed she was there too, with him at the cusp.

He moistened a fingertip and teased her clit, and her sweet pussy quivered around his cock. His balls tightened. His cum burned at the base of his cock. Pressure building. It wouldn't be much longer.

"Come for me, Blair. Come now." His lust-roughened voice sounded foreign to his ears, like it belonged to someone else.

Closer. Hotter. Oh fuck, so good.

He increased the pressure on Blair's clit only slightly, stroking the hard pearl in a desperate attempt to send her over the edge. He wouldn't come before her, couldn't.

There. The scent. Exquisite pleasure complemented the exquisite pain he was enduring.

Blair's cry of release started low and built to a keen wail.

"Yesssss!" He pulled back, leaving just the flared head of his cock inside her spasming pussy and then, losing all control, drove into her like a feral beast. His cum blazed down the length of his cock and shot from the tip, each spurt a split second of absolute paradise.

It ended way too soon.

Sated, he pulled out, and removed the anal plug, disposed of the condom and helped Damon free Blair from the restraints. To his surprise, Damon carried her cradled in his arms to the bed, lowered her gently onto the mattress. He didn't try to fuck her. Instead, he lay next to her, arms and legs thrown over her body in a show of masculine possession.

Trey walked around the end of the bed and lay curled up against her other side.

She smiled at him. "I can't believe this is really happening. That it's really you, and you're here with me. I was so sure I'd never see either one of you again. Will you tell me now? Tell me where you were? How you found me?"

Damon bent an arm, lifting up to rest his head on his fist. "You tell us first. Did that asshole stepfather of yours treat you any better after you moved?"

She stared at the ceiling for at least a handful of heartbeats before answering, "Maybe a little. I'd rather not talk about him. I don't think about him. I don't talk about him. I refuse to waste my time and energy."

Damon caught her chin and tugged, forcing her to look at him. The icy fury in Damon's eyes made Trey's heart skip a beat or two, or ten. "Blair—"

"No, Damon. Please. Don't ruin this."

A tense silence fell over the room. Damon's gaze met Trey's again. Trey felt Damon's frustration in his gut, sharp, hot, burning.

"Damon," Trey said, nodding. "We were too young—"

"I should've killed him when I had the chance."

"No, nonono." This time, Blair rose up on her knees and caught Damon's face in her hands. She leaned forward until her mouth hovered over Damon's. Trey's lungs emptied of air as yet another unwelcome dose of jealousy rippled through his body, making him ache all over. "I'm glad you didn't. You would've ruined your entire life, given it up for that bastard—"

"No, for you. I would have given up everything for you."

"I'm okay." She brushed her mouth over Damon's and then straightened up, glancing over her shoulder at Trey and giving him a soft, sweet smile. "I'm fine. I swear. You know that, don't you, Trey?"

"Sure."

She reached for him, threaded her fingers through his. "The past doesn't haunt me anymore. I'm free now. I'm strong. I'm independent. You understand what I mean, don't you?"

Trey nodded. "Yes. I do."

She turned and flopped down on the bed, landing between them once again. She took Trey's hand in her right and Damon's in her left, pulled them onto her soft stomach. "I'll never forget this place. It's so wonderful.

Thank you for doing all of this for me."

"I just want you to be happy," Damon said, sounding anything but.

"That's just it. I am. I'm happier right now than I've ever been. And I can't wait for the next twelve days. After tonight, I can't imagine how you'll make them any better."

"We're going to try our damnedest," Trey promised.

She rocked her head to the side. "Has anyone ever told you you're too good to be true?"

His face warmed. "No."

"Well, you are." She gave him yet another gentle kiss, the kind that he guessed wasn't meant to stir his lust, but did. He grappled for her, but she rolled over, did the same to Damon. "Now, tell me all about the past fifteen years."

Trey chuckled, throwing an arm around her waist and tugging her back, until she was spooned tightly against him. He kissed her temple. "We've got a lot of ground to cover."

She smiled. "That's okay. I've got lots of time. I'm not leaving until I absolutely have to. I want to hear everything. About your exciting lives, traveling the world as illusionists. Where have you gone? What have you seen? But more importantly…" She hesitated. "I want to know how long have you two been lovers, and have either of you taken other lovers? Gotten married? Had children? What do you want for the future?"

Trey nuzzled the crook of her neck. "And we want to hear all about your life, what you've been doing."

"What you hope for your future," Damon added.

They spent the next several hours talking and laughing. Sharing and deepening the bond with Blair that had been there all along, making it stronger. But Trey could tell Blair was still holding back for some reason. She did a lot more listening than talking, and when there was a lull in the conversation, she'd ask Damon another question about their act or traveling. Clever girl. She knew exactly what she was doing.

She left them just after sunrise, promising to come back later that night.

Then it was just the two of them again. And the huge pink elephant that neither wanted to talk about. If they didn't find the words, Trey was terrified that these two weeks might do the one thing nobody had ever been able to do before—destroy their love.

* * * * *

Twelve nights gone. Somehow. Too fast. Much too fast. The day her guys would leave was creeping closer, closer. No, it wasn't creeping, it was charging at her like a pissed-off bull. She'd never dreaded a day more, not even the day her family had moved.

They were closer now, the three of them. Much of it had to do with time spent just talking about things. Jobs. Hobbies. Dreams. Hopes. As well as disappointments.

But the sex had also played a huge part, especially the bondage. Over the nights, Damon and Trey had pushed her a little farther, helped her work past her doubts and fears, her guilt and regrets. And in the process, they'd gained her trust, her unflagging faith. And, most of all, her love.

With Trey and Damon, sex was all about giving, sharing, trust and love.

Tonight, she wanted to ask them to do something special for her. She could see the emotions in their eyes when they looked at each other, and she sensed something was building between them, something that was threatening to tear them apart. She'd hate herself forever if she caused them pain, even if it wasn't anything she'd done intentionally.

She did a final makeup check in her car before heading into the building for her thirteenth night. Only one more night to go. Oh God.

Tonight, she wasn't greeted by a semi-translucent image of herself, or a black panther or any other bizarre illusion like she had the last twelve. Nor was there a gift like there had been every night. No earrings, necklaces, picture frames, jewel-encrusted boxes. Nothing.

Instead, she headed empty-handed straight back through the reception area, through the warehouse, past some stacks of crates and boxes, to the dungeon. The empty dungeon.

What the hell?

Something squeaked behind her, and she swiveled around.

"Where did that come from?" she asked, breathing a sigh of relief. Standing before her was a super-sized replica of the box Damon and Trey had sent to her house that very first day. She just knew her guys were in that box.

Too bad she'd never figured out how the smaller version worked. Neither had Sandy.

The box stood roughly five feet tall, not quite as high as her refrigerator. The lid was freaking heavy. The hinges stiff. She struggled to get it open.

The box was empty, as she expected.

"Well, hell." She fought the lid back down then gave the big, stupid, infuriating thing a long glare. "I don't want to spend the night trying to guess how to get my guys out of this silly contraption. I want to spend it with them!"

She walked around the box's perimeter then pushed open the lid again, hoping it was just a matter of closing and reopening the box, like it had been the smaller version.

No Damon. No Trey.

"Haven't I had enough of the magic stuff, guys?" she called out. "Come on, let's play another game, something more fun, like 'tie up the girl'."

Nothing.

She shut the lid, took another trip around the box, using her fingers to search every inch of all four sides. She found no secret button or lever.

Growing more frustrated by the second, she walked back into the reception area and dragged a chair back to the box. Again, she pushed the lid up. This time, however, she climbed up on the chair to get a good look at both the lining of the lid and the padded interior of the box.

A little scared, she climbed over the side and dropped inside. The floor was hard, solid. She walked back and forth, stomping her feet, searching for the trap door she just knew had to be there.

She found it!

The floor gave way beneath her feet and the world around her became a blur of colors for less than two racing heartbeats. She landed on a huge padded cushion. The trap door above her closed with a dull thud, closing her in pitch black so thick she could practically taste it. There was no sound but the resonant pounding of her heart and the whistle of her gasping breaths. A soft, scented waft of air caressed her cheek, and out of pure instinct, she turned toward it. "Damon? Trey?" The shadows swallowed up her voice.

Shivers quaked up her spine, despite the fact that the darkness had always been an escape, the most reliable source of protection. She'd learned at an early age that the monsters didn't hide in the shadows. They walked in broad daylight.

She fingered the velvet-covered walls around her, stood on her toes and reached as high as she could, trying to find the latch for the trap door. Still, she remained trapped.

This had to be part of the plan. But why? Why'd Damon and Trey want her in this stupid dark pit? This illusion was nothing like the rest.

"Is the dark still your refuge, Blair?" one of them whispered. Damon, it was Damon.

"Not as much as it used to be."

"Why are you still hiding in the shadows?" This time it was Trey's voice. "What are you hiding from?"

"Nothing. I'm not hiding from anything. I fell when I was looking for you two. In the box. Can you guys get me out of here?"

"No, we can't help you," Damon whispered from

somewhere close by. "It's your choice, to step into the light or not."

What kind of game was this? It wasn't like the others. It wasn't sexy or mysterious or exciting. No. More annoying and frustrating, confusing. "There's no light down here. I'm in a pit or something. Underneath the floor."

"Tell us your secret and we will tell you ours."

"I don't have a secret." That was a lie. She did have a secret, one she'd never told anyone, not even her mother. But it was about something that had happened a long time ago, and really it didn't matter anymore because she'd finally put everything behind her. There was never a good reason to stir up old crap. It would just kick the stench into the air again. Better to leave it alone, cover it up with layer after layer of defenses—denial and justification being a couple of her favorites.

"It's your choice," Trey said a little louder.

Silence.

Oh, this sucked in so many ways. Sure, she wasn't claustrophobic, so at least she didn't mind sitting in dark so thick she couldn't see her hand in front of her nose. But she only had one more night with Damon and Trey. They should be teasing and tormenting her like they did so well, not leaving her to sit here by herself.

They were losing out too. Didn't they realize that?

"We're wasting a lot of time," she said on a sigh.

"We don't think this is a waste," Damon countered.

"What are you hoping to accomplish?" she shot back, her voice reflecting the rising level of her frustration.

"Something more important and meaningful than an orgasm," Damon said.

He didn't say the words, but she heard *we're not going to back down* loud and clear in his tone.

She was totally clueless why things that happened over a decade ago would be so important now, with only one day before they left. She'd already overcome them. Why ask her to open up to them, become more vulnerable?

They had to know what that would mean, how agonizing it would make their leaving.

Shouldn't they be withdrawing from her? Preparing her for their departure? Distancing themselves?

Hot tears gathered in her eyes and her nose started to burn. She didn't want them to leave her. It was going to feel like her heart was being ripped out of her chest. Maybe to some people the games they played in the dungeon were just about the sex, fantasy, exploration, orgasm. But for her they ended up being so much more.

Trust. Vulnerability. Self-discovery. Healing.

It was easy to think in the box, the dark, to let her mind wander. Kind of like it did when she was in the shower, or lying in bed at night, semi-awake but with her eyes closed and the soft sounds of the nighttime drifting through her window.

If this was the culmination of all the games they'd played thus far, it might actually make sense. It wasn't as erotic, maybe. But it was still centered on the theme of trust and secrets. The box was just another way of restraining her, she supposed. The only thing missing was the erotic element. But maybe that would come after she answered their question.

She could tell them just a little bit, hold back the worst. Maybe it would be enough and they'd reward her like they had every night before.

She just wanted them to hold her. Touch her. Kiss her.

Reluctantly, she searched for the right words. It wasn't easy, putting into words the kind of pain she'd endured back then.

"Okay. I'll tell you. Are you still there?"

"We're here, sweetheart," Trey said, his voice encouraging.

"I wish I could see you."

"I think it'll be easier this way," Damon suggested.

Maybe he was right.

"I think you know what I'm about to say. It's probably

just a matter of me actually speaking the truth, so I'll do it." She took a few deep breaths. "After we moved, things got worse with my stepdad. You knew it would, didn't you?"

"We hoped we'd be wrong." Damon's voice was tense, his words clipped. "Tell us."

"He went from verbally abusing me—calling me names, humiliating me, that kind of thing—to physical abuse. And finally, when I was sixteen, he—" Shit, this was hard. "He tried to sexually abuse me too. He didn't actually...he made me take him in my mouth. So there you have it. My dark secret. You've heard it. Now please. Just hold me."

That was it. That was all she was going to say. All she could say. Her throat had collapsed like a rubber hose under an elephant's foot. Her chest felt like tight bands were squeezing, tighter, tighter. Hot tears streamed down her cheeks.

"Turn toward my voice," Damon whispered.

Blair turned.

"Reach straight in front of you."

When she did, a blade of red light illuminated her hand. Something small, kind of long and sparkly dropped into her palm. A chain? Necklace maybe? She closed her hand around the thing and looked up, shocked to find a black tube with a red glowing light inside, directing a stream of crimson light down. She reached up, touched the tube and realized it was rubber. A soft tug and the entire side of the pit fell open.

Blinded by the soft light outside, she staggered out, accepting Trey and Damon's gentle help.

Damon yanked her against him, holding her tightly, one hand cupping the back of her head, the other splayed across her lower back. "I'm sorry we weren't there for you. Didn't protect you."

"How could you? We were too young. You weren't ready to take care of me. Hell, you had your own problems to deal with."

"My problems were nothing. You were all that mattered."

Trey moved up behind her, wrapped his arms around her waist and rested his chin on the top of her head. "We did try to find you. We were caught, taken home. But when we left again, they didn't take us home the second time. We were locked up for two years after being caught breaking into what we thought was an abandoned trailer home."

"See? You tried. It's not your fault."

"It will always be my fault," Damon muttered, sounding tortured. "Because if we hadn't been caught, we would've gotten to you."

Her fist still closed around the small thing from the box, Blair tried to back away a little, just enough to be able to look up into Damon's dark eyes. But he wouldn't loosen his hold on her.

Trey was being much quieter than usual through all this, she noticed. She wondered why.

"I'm okay now. Honest. I'm not an emotional train wreck like you seem to think. I live with the past the way most normal people do—by putting it behind me and moving on. That's what everybody does. Either that, or they let the past eat them alive. I wasn't going to let that happen. Walking through hell just means you grow a thick skin. Right?"

Damon didn't answer.

"Sure," Trey agreed.

Time to change the subject. This was too intense. Too everything. She turned her head and pressed her ear against Damon's chest. Not surprisingly, his heart was pounding hard and fast. He was angry. But it wouldn't do any good, being furious about something that couldn't be changed.

"So what's your secret?" she asked, remembering Damon's earlier promise.

"Well, actually, I kind of made that up to get you to talk. Both Trey and I sense you're holding back."

"Yeah, I...was. I didn't know if I wanted to tell you. Or how to tell you. I wanted this time together to be a good thing, about the present, not the past." Once again, things were turning to her again. She didn't want them to realize there was still more she hadn't found the courage to tell them yet. She peered up at Damon's face. He was getting angry again. She knew how to turn things around. "I wanted to ask you two if you'd do something special for me tonight."

"What's that?" Damon asked.

"You two have been lovers for a long time."

"Yes, we have." Trey kissed the top of her head. "What do you want to ask us?"

"If you'll make love to each other this time. I want to see you share that intimacy with each other."

"Why?" Damon asked, finally letting her go. He caught her face between his hands and lifted it, forcing her to look up into his eyes. "Why ask such a thing?"

"I don't know." She thought about it for a minute. "I guess because a part of me knows you two have been together as a couple for a long time. But right now you're so focused on me it's hard to see that. I want to know you as you were before this. And know what you'll go back to being...after."

"We won't go back to being the same after," Damon said, shooting a glance over her head. "There's no way we'll be the same."

What did that mean?

"I don't know about this," Damon said finally after a long and awkward silence. "Our time together is coming to an end, and I'd rather spend it with you—"

"I'd like to do what Blair asked," Trey interrupted.

More silence. The air felt heavy, the room charged with electricity. She watched the guys exchange looks, Damon's tight and unrelenting, Trey's equally demanding.

"It could bring her closer to us," Trey suggested.

"Or it could make her feel uncomfortable, like she doesn't belong with us," Damon volleyed back.

Blair felt herself frowning, uncomfortable with the tension she saw pulling her two guys apart. "I'm not going to be uncomfortable, Damon. Maybe you should talk about this privately, just the two of you."

"Good idea," Trey agreed.

"No," Damon snapped. "We're not going to talk about anything. We had a plan for today, and that's what we're going to stick to."

Trey dragged his fingers through his hair. "But Damon—"

"No!"

Wow, she felt like this huge wedge, pushing the two of them apart. She pulled away from Damon, turned an apologetic glance to Trey. The frustration and hurt she saw on his face nearly made her weep.

That was it. Somehow, she had to convince Damon to do this. From what she could see, his relationship with Trey wasn't just on shaky ground, it was sitting on top of a huge fault line. And the big earthquake was about to start.

She unfurled her fingers, finally taking a second to see what she'd caught inside the box.

A beautiful bracelet, alternating diamonds and, of course, flashing red rubies.

Chapter 5

Trey could see the center of his world, the relationship that had been the cornerstone of his life, crumbling like a sandcastle being battered by a tsunami.

Yet he felt absolutely powerless to do anything about it.

Right here, just now, a huge chunk had broken off and shattered into a million pieces. And what made it a thousand fucking times worse was that Damon wasn't just clueless or blind to what was going on, he was the one who was busting it apart.

Fuck. Damn.

He felt sick, as if someone had kicked him in the balls, run over him with a Hummer and then disemboweled his quivering, crushed body. The guy holding the fucking knife was Damon.

He couldn't breathe.

Trey caught Blair's wide eyes, so full of shock and worry. Normally he'd be right there, looking for the words to comfort *her*. Not this time. The words were gone. He simply lacked the ability or strength to utter them. Everything was slipping from his grasp, like sand sliding through his fingers. Going, going, gone.

He needed some air. He needed to get out of that

fucking warehouse, away from Damon. For just a few minutes. To find his head. To suck in a few breaths. To get his feet back under himself.

He did a one-eighty, made it only a couple of steps away before Blair grabbed his arm, slowing his progress. "Please," he said, prying her fingers away. "Just give me a minute."

"No. I'll go."

"No you won't," Damon said, dragging her back to him again.

So that was really the way Damon wanted it? Had Damon decided he was done with them, that he wanted Blair now, only Blair?

The man could have put a knife in his gut and it would've hurt less.

"It's fine. I'll go." More desperate than ever to get out of there, Trey hurried toward the exit.

This time it was Damon who stopped him. Not with his hands but with one word, "Please."

"Please what?" Trey asked, not turning around. He couldn't look Damon in the eye right now, couldn't stomach seeing the flatness in his gaze as he looked at him. The glimmer that used to be there was gone.

"Don't leave."

The tiniest spark of hope ignited inside Trey's cold heart. "Why?" he asked, still staring straight ahead, at the door. He knew if he stepped through that door that would be the end for them. He was not ready to face that possibility.

"Because I love you."

Oh God. If ever there'd been a time when he'd needed to hear those words, it was now. Finally, he found the strength to turn around. Immediately, he saw the dark desperation carved into Damon's features, and the tension pulling at his body, making the ropey sinew of his shoulders and arms that much more noticeable.

Trey swallowed, attempting to clear away whatever

hard substance had coalesced in his throat. Didn't work. "What's happening to us, Damon?" He shook his head. "Things are going to hell between us. I'd rather talk about this in private, not in front of Blair."

"No, she stays. I won't have her feeling like she's not a part of this, of us."

Dammit, Damon was going to force him to do this with her there, hearing things she didn't deserve to hear. She wasn't going to walk away from today without some hurt and regret. Didn't Damon realize that?

"I think you're making a mistake," Trey said.

"I'd be happy to go." Once again, Blair started toward the door. "In fact, I need to run an errand…"

Again Damon stopped her. "Stay here."

Blair stole a glance at Trey before turning pleading eyes at Damon. "But this is between the two of you, and it's important."

Damon smoothed a hand down the side of her face. "It's between the three of us."

What the hell did that mean? Did Damon want to make this threesome more permanent than they'd talked about?

Blair gaped but didn't say another word.

"What are you thinking?" Trey asked, bracing himself for what he knew in his gut would be bad news. Or at least a huge surprise.

"I'm thinking you need to stop being so fucking jealous. You knew what these two weeks were all about. So why are you being like this?"

Great, so now this was all his fault. He was the one who was acting like an ass.

It was always that way. Every problem they had was because of something he'd said, done, didn't do, whatever. Not this fucking time. Hell no!

These two weeks hadn't gone the way they'd talked about. Something was off. Way off.

His heart banged hard against his breastbone, sending

liquid fire through his veins. "Fuck you, Damon. If you can't see what a prick you're being, then there's nothing to talk about." This time he made it to the door, had his fingers curled around the knob, before Damon tried to stop him again.

"Trey, dammit!"

Trey jerked the knob and pushed open the door.

This time, Damon literally broke into a run, slammed into him from behind and sent him hurling into the carpeted reception area. Somehow, Trey managed to stay on his feet. He shoved Damon back. Damon grabbed Trey's arm. "Dammit, listen."

"If you're just going to give me more of that 'it's all your fault' shit, I don't need to listen. I've heard enough for a lifetime."

They stood staring at each other for a handful of agonizing seconds, nostrils flaring, faces flushed, bodies tight. Trey refused to say another word. He'd be wasting his breath.

Damon stared at the floor, crossed his arms over his chest, nervously rocked his weight from one leg to another, the way he always did when he was struggling with something. "I don't know how to explain."

"Try. Or you know what's going to happen."

"Yeah," Damon said on a heavy sigh. "I know."

"So?"

"So..." Damon's brows knit together. The guy was your typical male, didn't know how to talk about things that mattered. Ask him about last night's game, and he wouldn't shut up. Ask him what he was feeling, and he shut down.

Trey wasn't going to let him get away with that anymore. He couldn't. It was too one-sided now.

This thing with Blair hadn't started their troubles. He could be objective enough to see now that they'd been having problems for a long time. He shared the fault for one very important reason—he'd been the one to let it go on this way for so long. Too long.

"I didn't know it would be like this," Damon admitted, lifting his gaze but still avoiding Trey's face. He glanced over his shoulder, back into the warehouse where Blair was waiting, quietly, patiently for them to sort this shit out. "I mean, I knew I still loved her. But I had no idea I'd feel so…" He dragged his fingers through his hair, finally making eye contact. "So fucking desperate to be with her, to touch her, fuck her, to have her all to myself. We've shared so many women. It's never been like this."

"Yeah, I noticed. I might as well not be here."

"Shit, Trey. I still love you. That hasn't changed."

"Are you sure?"

"Positive. I can't lose you."

"Then you better start showing me. Today. Now. Because otherwise…" Trey couldn't say the words. Didn't want to hear them spoken, because then he knew it could really happen. They might say goodbye, and he'd lose the one human being on the planet whom he'd ever trusted completely.

Damon hesitantly stepped forward, reaching for him, but Trey didn't step into his embrace. He wasn't ready to pretend it was all better. Damon's arms dropped to his sides. "What more do you need?"

"We haven't fucked since the first night with Blair. What do I need? I need you. I need to feel like I'm not just another accessory in your bondage arsenal. Or your competition for Blair. I'm your best friend. Soul mate. Lover. Or I'm nothing. Only you know what I am to you."

"You are everything to me. The air I breathe. Don't ever doubt that." Damon didn't wait for him to accept his embrace. Damon just yanked him against his body, tangled his fingers in Trey's hair, tugged back and kissed him. Hard.

Trey's body, of course, responded to every stab of Damon's tongue. His already racing heart did its damnedest to kick its way out of his chest. With mouth and hands, Damon said all the things he'd struggled to say with words. With kisses, he said, *I love you more than anything.* And with his grappling hands, he said, *I need you more than I can ever say.*

It had been a long time since they'd had this kind of erotic tension between them. Damon's touches weren't sensual, or even erotic like usual. They were possessive, demanding, urgent. Damon moaned into their joined mouths, the sound vibrating in Trey's head, buzzing through his body. He pulled Damon's tongue into his mouth, suckling, drinking Damon's spicy flavor.

Trey gathered Damon's hair into his fist and pulled sharply, forcing his head back. Against the salty-sweet skin at the base of Damon's throat, Trey muttered, "Let's go give Blair what she asked for. Let's let her be a witness to our hunger, our love." Reaching down, Trey caressed the hard bulge between Damon's legs.

"Yessss," Damon murmured.

They walked into the warehouse, finding Blair sitting on the bed in the dungeon, her eyes teary and face blotchy. "I'm so sorry," she mumbled, sounding as miserable as she looked. She sniffled, dabbed her nose with a tissue. "I hate that you two were fighting because of me."

"It's okay." Damon sat beside her on the bed but didn't release Trey's hand. He rested the free one on Blair's knee. "We talked. Things are better now."

She turned those misery-filled eyes to Trey. "Are they?"

"I didn't leave," Trey answered. He couldn't tell her a lie, that everything was perfect and they'd solved their problems with just a short, albeit heated, argument. But things were on the right track.

"We want to give you what you asked for," Damon said, dragging his hand up her thigh. "We're going to fuck, Trey and I. And then we're going to fuck you, both of us, like we talked about."

Her smile was shaky but sweet and sexy too. "Thank you."

"No, we should thank you. You're the one who helped us see we had—have—problems." Damon gave Trey a guilty smile. "Or rather, you helped *me* see we have problems. I think Trey here's pretty in touch with things. I have a harder time. But if it means making sure this man is in my life for another fifteen years, then I'll do whatever it takes. I'll talk about my fucking feelings until he screams enough." He chuckled.

Trey sat beside him, laughing. "If that day ever comes, I'll eat an entire pan of squid, just for you."

"Hah!"

Blair giggled nervously. "What's that all about?"

"This guy has never tasted seafood of any kind. Not even tuna," Damon explained.

"Really?"

Scowling, Trey nodded. "It's a thing from when I was a kid. And it's just something I never bothered to try to overcome."

"Looks like we're all dodging the skeletons from our past," Blair commented, looking guilty.

"Does that mean you're still hiding a few?" Trey said, turning some dark eyes on her.

Blair smiled, shook her head. "We're talking about you, not me."

"Nice dodge," Damon said, sliding Blair a grin. "We'll get back to that later."

"Yes, we will." Trey was all too happy to divert their collective attention from him back to Blair.

Unfortunately, it seemed Blair had her own gift for diversions.

Standing on the mattress, she clapped her hands and scrubbed them together. "So about this sex thing, do I have to just sit here and watch, or can I participate in some way?"

"What way would you like to participate?" Damon looked surprised, shocked.

"Well, one thing that drives me absolutely crazy when

we're together is the way you talk to each other, tell each other how I taste, smell, what you want to do. I want to be in charge this time."

"Oh no, we're not switches." Damon shook his head. "Sex between us is strictly sex. No power play, no submission."

"Okay, maybe I misspoke. I like how you dominate me. I don't want to lose that. I'm thinking more like, 'Damon, will you please stroke Trey's balls?' That kind of thing."

Trey liked the sound of that. Both Blair's suggestion itself and the idea of her being something of an active participant and asking them to perform for her.

A blade of heat speared his insides. His balls tightened. Yes, that sounded like fun.

Damon and Trey exchanged a heated glance and then both barked, "Sure!"

This was bound to be a new, thrilling experience for both of them. Maybe, just maybe, they'd found a way to bring Blair into their lives in a more balanced way. That made Trey feel tons better and made the still uncertain future look a little less dim.

"But before we start, our sweet girl needs to agree to a few terms," Damon announced.

"What kind of terms," she asked, knowing they were going to be naughty and delicious and oh-so wicked.

"First, we want you naked. Everything comes off," Damon began, looking at her like she was a scrumptious treat.

Yes, naughty.

Damon crossed his arms over his chest. "But you're not permitted to touch yourself. Not your nipples and definitely not your pussy."

And yes, delicious.

"And you have to sit right here, next to us, close enough to touch us, to hear every gasp and sigh."

And oh yeah, very wicked.

"Okay," she agreed, hoping she'd have the strength to

keep up her end of the bargain. Sit next to two beautiful men, as they fucked, and not masturbate? Was that possible?

They both looked at her expectantly, and she realized they were waiting for her to strip.

She promptly, gladly, peeled off every scrap of clothing she had on, even the cute lace thong. Then she fluffed some pillows, stacked them at the head of the bed and leaned back, ready to watch the show of a lifetime. "Damon, will you undress Trey for me? Slowly."

Damon gave her an evil smile, let his gaze wander over her body for a super-heated moment and then licked his lips. "You bet I will." He positioned Trey so they were both kneeling profile to her and she could see them both. Trey lifted his arms, and Damon dragged Trey's shirt up, revealing his gloriously sculpted upper body one tasty inch at a time. Damon tossed the shirt and then unzipped Trey's snug jeans, uncovering a wedge of tanned temptation.

A huge knot formed in Blair's throat. She gulped. Gulped again. Lifted a hand to her forehead to sweep aside a piece of hair that was falling over her face.

Trey glanced at her for a moment, and a buzzing, zapping connection charged through the air between them. She could almost feel the need gathering in his body, swirling and churning like storm clouds.

Down the pants went. No underwear. Trey's thick rod sprang free, his tight balls snug against the base. The sight took Blair's breath away for a split second. She gasped to reinflate her lungs.

In the next instant, Trey was naked, his glorious body there for her to admire. So perfect. Tanned skin smooth and velvety over hard, rippling muscles and sinew. Strong. Powerful, sleek.

"Now, Trey, will you please undress Damon."

Trey gave her a look of raw hunger then turned to Damon. His hands deftly worked as he removed Damon's shirt, his pants. His fingertips skimmed over Damon's skin as he worked, teasing him and Blair.

And Damon reacted so visibly, it increased Blair's thrill a hundred times. His eyelids fell closed and his head dropped back. His mouth pursed in a semi-pout, and the muscles of his neck and shoulder tightened until she could see the lines separating each one. Until he looked like a hard, sweaty warrior, preparing for battle.

Perfect. They were both so perfect.

Her hands skimmed up her stomach, stopping before they reached her tingling nipples. A twitchy tightness was pulling between her legs. She wanted to rub it away.

Can't. Oh this is torture.

"Now kiss, please. I'm burning up. I need to see you touch each other the way you do without me, when I'm not here."

They tipped their heads and their mouths met in an open-mouthed, mind-blowing kiss. She could see their tongues stroking and stabbing, almost like a battle for possession. Very masculine. And very sexy. They stroked each others' chests, shoulders, stomachs. Their touches weren't soft and gentle but strong, hard, possessive. Damon curled his fingers slightly, raking them down Trey's tight chest, leaving red stripes. Trey groaned, the sound somewhat swallowed up in their kiss, and did the same to Damon.

Someone moaned. It was her. Her hands crept higher until her fingers rested just below her hard nipples.

This was impossible. Cruel. Her legs fell open a little and she glanced down, not surprised to see her folds shimmering with her juices.

"Don't touch," Damon growled, his voice gritty and raw.

Her eyes snapped up to meet his, and she licked her dry lips, nodding. She might be telling her two guys what to do, but they were still very much in charge. And oh yes, that was the way she wanted it. Needed it. Had to have it.

"I'm so hot," she said, her voice reflecting the bone-deep desperation she felt. "This is so good, it's torture."

They both smiled at her.

"Good," Trey said, reaching out and closing a hand around Damon's cock to give it a slow, yummy pump.

Blair watched his hand inch up to the base then glide back down to the flared head. Her mouth watered at the sight, and she could imagine dropping her head, licking away the pearl of pre-cum gathering on the center slit, tasting, devouring, begging for more.

"Who do you want to see fucked?" Damon asked, his eyes still closed. "Whose ass do you want to see get crammed full of hard cock?"

Once again, the air slammed from her lungs, like she'd been socked in the chest. Those words? Holy smokes! So sexy.

She gulped in a shallow breath. Did it matter who was fucked and who did the fucking? Yes. And no.

She wanted to see Damon give the pleasure, Trey receive, to witness that dynamic and discover what vulnerability he'd reveal when he was giving pleasure to Trey.

"Damon, will you fuck Trey? Will you fuck him with all the love you have for him?"

"Yes, I will." He went to the cabinet, returning less than a minute later with some lube. No rubber. He smoothed some on his cock, working it around the head, over the tip and down his full length. It felt so right watching him, watching them together. She held her breath as he applied more over Trey's anus then tested his puckered opening with two fingers.

Blair's heart started pounding so hard and fast she could hear it.

Then he turned Trey around, so he was on his knees, facing Blair, his head close enough to rest on Blair's bent knees if she drew them together. Close enough to smell the scent of her pleasure, which hung heavy in the air.

Trey's nostrils flared slightly as he inhaled, his lips curling into a half-smile, his eyes gleaming with raw male wanting.

"I love the way you smell," he murmured, sending a quake racing down her spine.

As much as she'd wanted this, to witness the intimacy between these two men, to understand their relationship better, she was in agony. There was no more erotic a sight than a pair of perfect men touching each other this way. Both strong and powerful. Damon held Trey's hips as he drove his cock in and out of Trey's anus. And Trey tipped his head back and rocked on his hands and knees, taking each thrust hard. The depth of their pleasure was plain on both their faces and in the taut muscles of their shoulders and chests.

Within minutes the room was filled with the scent and sounds of sex. The sensations whirled around in the air, seeped into her body and charged through her veins until she was lost in them. Her hands slid down her torso, skimmed over her pubic bone and out to her thighs.

Don't touch myself. Can't touch myself.

How much longer would they make her wait?

She could hear Trey's breathing speed up, grow shallow. A deep rosy flush was spreading up his chest, his neck. She checked Damon. His gaze tangled with hers, dark eyes full of raw sexual power. His lips parted, as if he was about to speak, but no sound came out. His jaw tight, he surged his hips forward harder, faster.

"Trey's cock," he murmured.

Yes, Trey had one, and uh-huh, it looked good. But what was he trying to get at?

"Take it in your hand," he added, sounding as breathless as a marathon runner. "Your mouth. Whichever."

Oh, thank God, she wasn't going to have to sit and just watch anymore. Happy to be putting her hands to good use, she grabbed the tube of K-Y, slicked up her fingers and scooted forward, wrapping them around Trey's thick rod.

Trey growled.

It was a very nice sound, the kind that made her insides get all tingly. Smiling into his semi-glazed eyes, she gave his cock a few slow caresses. "How's this?"

"Uhhhhh," he groaned.

She'd take that as a "Just fine". Encouraged, she tightened her grip on his penis and fell into a steady pace, not quite as fast as Damon's. As she stroked him, the heat radiating off his body seemed to seep into her pores. It swirled inside her stomach and spread through her body in ripples.

Damon released Trey's hips, dragged his fingers down Trey's back as he looked down at Trey with eyes full of love and wanting and desperate desire.

Instinctively, Blair tightened her fist a little more, and Trey moaned again.

"Gonna come, Trey," Damon said. "Can't stop."

"'S'okay. Me too."

The room filled with the sound of two men's sighs of relief. Trey's eyes opened. "Blair," he whispered. He licked his lips. "Kiss me, baby."

Still pumping his cock, Blair leaned forward, tipping at the waist and settling her mouth over his. She opened to accept his tongue, welcoming the invasion, trembling with the intensity of his kiss.

Hot cum spurted from the tip of his cock. Droplets sprinkled over her hands, breasts. She smiled, whispered over and over, "Thank you." When he broke the kiss, stealing his delicious mouth from her, she released his still-hard cock and smoothed her hands down over her breasts.

A husky growl from Damon's direction caught her attention and she looked up.

He stood, his plump, fully erect cock gripped in one fist. "Now, beautiful, it's your turn."

Chapter 6

"I want you both to take me," Blair said as she let Trey ease her onto her back. "Please, at the same time."

"No." Trey stared down at her with tender eyes, full of emotion. His hand gently cupped her breast, his palm heating the hard tip of her nipple, rasping it gently, too gently.

She arched her back, pressing her breast firmer into his hand. "I've been preparing. Please."

Damon, returning from a visit to the bathroom, knelt beside her, opposite Trey, hooked a hand around the back of Trey's neck and pulled. They kissed overtop of her. In between slow, sensual licks and nips, they murmured words of love with lust-roughened voices.

She could have cried, seeing such a show of emotion this close after having witnessed their fight earlier. She'd been so sure she was going to see the end of something beautiful and rare. Just as she had when she was a child. It had been her parents' love she'd watched being destroyed then. And now it had nearly been Trey's and Damon's.

Instead, to her relief, she'd seen its rebirth. If only the same thing had happened with her parents.

Someday, she might have a love like this, the kind that

was worth giving up everything for.

The love she had for these two men was as close as she'd ever come to that kind of miracle. These past nights had definitely deepened her feelings for Trey and Damon, especially tonight. Her heart felt so light she thought it might float out of her chest.

Tears gathered in her eyes. They saw them, Damon and Trey, when they broke the kiss and together turned their attention back to her.

Damon cupped her face, thumbing away one of the salty drops as it seeped from the outer corner of her eye. "Why are you crying?"

"They're good tears." She gave him a watery smile, sniffled. "I've never seen the kind of love you two share. If I hadn't seen it with my own eyes, I'd never have believed it was possible."

"Oh baby." Damon smoothed her hair off her forehead. His gentle touch made her feel so cherished, adored. "We love you too. I hope you know that."

She did. "Of course. Nobody's ever done anything like what you two have for me. And I'm not just talking about all the beautiful presents, which I hope are all fake because if they're not, I'm not even sure what to do or say." She waited for him to either acknowledge or deny whether the stones adorning all the pieces of jewelry, the picture frame and the wooden box were real. He didn't.

Being a practical person, she took his non-response as an admission that they were fake. After all, it was unreasonable to even consider that all those gems were genuine—with the exception of that first one, which she knew was real since it had been hers.

"Do you like the gifts?" Trey asked.

"Yes. Very much."

Damon smiled and ran his flattened hand over her hair again. "Then that's all that matters."

"But like I said, it isn't just the presents. Or the magic tricks. It's this…" She motioned to the two of them. "The way you planned everything and make me feel so special, like I'm the last woman on earth and you're both going to make sure I never experience a moment of longing or uncertainty or loneliness again. I'd swear..." She swallowed the words that sat on the tip of her tongue, unwilling to utter them, afraid if she did the magic of the moment would be lost.

There was nothing that could change reality, as much as she wanted, or even as much as it seemed Trey and Damon might want to. They were going to leave. Tomorrow night. Their time together was almost over.

Oh shoot, her mind was heading into a dark place again. "Please, no more talking. We're running out of time."

Damon pressed his index finger to her lips. "Yes, no more talking." He lifted that finger to his mouth, swirled his tongue around the tip and then teased her nipple with it.

Trey bent over, lapped at the other one. They licked and stroked and teased and tormented until she had to squeeze her eyes closed and her world narrowed to a pinpoint of light. Hands. Mouths. Touches, nips and kisses. Pinches and strokes. They mapped every inch of her quivering body, from her earlobes to the soles of her feet.

Burning up. So tight.

The air was too thin. The room too hot, not cold. The passion that had banked to a low simmer reignited again, flaring hotter than ever.

And still her pussy was empty. They didn't offer any relief, not from a finger, a dildo, nothing.

"Please, Damon. Both of you," she begged, over and over. She didn't know how many times she'd said it.

One of them sat behind her, lifted her shoulders off the mattress and slipped their body beneath hers. Damon. "Okay, beautiful. We can try if you want."

Her legs draped over Damon's legs, her feet resting on

the mattress on either side of his ankles. His hard body supported her, cradled her, as he slowly pushed up into an incline with her sitting on his lap, reclined against his upper body.

Trey knelt at Damon's legs, caressed her feet, her calves, her thighs. He pressed against her inner thighs, pushing them apart. Wider, wider.

Yes, oh yes, he was finally going to touch her pussy. Her womb spasmed as anticipation whipped through her body.

"You've never taken a man in the ass," Damon murmured against her cheek.

"No, I haven't, but I've been practicing. With a dildo. I wanted this last time to be special and this is something I've always wanted to try with you two. Not with anyone but you."

Trey took up the lube and applied some to his fingers. "Let's see how ready you are." He traced those moistened fingertips from her pussy down to her anus. He pushed, gently.

Her first instinct was to tighten up, but the nights of practicing had taught her how to overcome instinct and relax, allowing the tip of his finger to slip inside. Then it was a matter of remaining relaxed as he gently massaged and stretched, testing her to see how much girth she could take.

He was big, slightly larger than the dildo she'd been using the past couple of weeks. There was a small chance she wouldn't be able to handle it. But her need to be possessed by both these men at the same time, to have them come to her together, as two equals, two parts of a whole, was somehow absolutely necessary right now. She couldn't explain it, not even to herself.

"She's a little tight," Trey said, inserting a second finger.

"You've been practicing? For us?" Damon murmured into her ear. "Why? What made you think we wanted this?"

She answered, "I didn't know. I hoped you would. I…need you both. "

Trey scissored his fingers, stretching her more, almost to the point of sharp pain. The torment was almost too much to bear. The way his fingers glided in and out of her bottom, filling her for a moment, only to cruelly withdraw. The swirling, rippling need inside her gathered in her center, gaining strength like a summer storm. Jolts of electricity arced from the axis out, like spokes on a wheel.

Her pussy.

She shuddered, her muscles alternately tightening and relaxing as more throbbing need shot to her center. "Please," she whispered.

Trey's fingers withdrew, and she gave a little mewl of protest. And then strong hands gripped her hips.

"Brace your feet on the bed," Damon said. "Spread your legs."

Oh God, yes! He was going to do it, or at least try. She gleefully spread her legs as wide as she could, relaxing back against his bulk again when Trey bent low and started teasing her burning pussy with his hand and mouth. Slow, long drags of his tongue, followed by short, hard flicks over her clit. He added two fingers to the mix, and she felt like she was about to come apart, just explode into a million pieces of glittering, sparkling light.

"Now, baby," Damon said, lifting up on her hips.

Her legs were soft as molten marshmallows, as wobbly as they'd ever been. But Trey helped her from the front, Damon from behind. Supported by her shaking legs and Trey's not-shaking arms, she waited as Damon rolled on a rubber and smoothed some lube over his cock and around her anus. And then she eased down on him, taking him inside.

Stretching. Burning. It was almost too much. But oh, the delicious fullness. It was so much better than the toy.

With the support of both guys, she managed to lie back

again with Damon's cock still buried deep in her ass. Now all she needed was Trey. She prayed it wouldn't take him long, because she was at the cusp, the glorious sensation of Damon's cock sliding a little in and out, stirring up those storm clouds to huge heights.

This wasn't going to be just another climax. This was going to be the climax of a lifetime, the one she'd never forget.

Trey finished up his preparations, a condom and a little lube, and he applied some jelly to her clit as well, lifted her legs and positioned himself at her entry.

She cried when he entered her. Not because it hurt. But because she finally had what she'd been searching for. What her body had been screaming for.

Possessed by two men. By the only two men in the world she might ever love. Talk about magic.

They coordinated their movements as one, gliding in and out of her body, bringing her closer, closer to that pinnacle with every thrust. They lavished attention over her breasts, plucked at her nipples until they ached, blew tickly streams of air in her ear until she shivered, stroked her clit until she was trembling.

She soared toward completion too swiftly, and yet her body pushed to go faster.

Harder they thrust. Yes, so much better. She was getting tight all over, hot. Desperate. Couldn't breathe. Couldn't think. Just. Needed. Release.

Oh yes. It was...there.

Her climax felt like an enormous wave of hot water rolling over her body. She tingled everywhere. Her scalp, chest, stomach, feet. Her pussy and ass spasmed around two thick, hard cocks.

The guys groaned, thrust harder, faster, making more and more waves splash over her body, up from her stomach to her head, down to her toes. They came too. Both of them. Growling, groaning, their breaths bursting from their bodies in short puffs. Damon's skin was slick beneath her, her body gliding and sliding over his as he rocked his hips up and down. Driving his cock inside, faster, harder, until his orgasm ended.

There was a collective sigh.

Twitching all over, she whimpered when both guys withdrew from her. They peeled off the rubbers, discarded them, then lay on either side of her.

She didn't want to leave. Couldn't leave yet. This was heaven. This was where she belonged, and there wasn't much time left. She wanted to say to hell with her job, with everything. If they asked her, she'd do it. For them.

She wanted them to ask her. Desperately.

* * * * *

Later that night, as she lay in her bed, at home, alone, she made a decision. She'd tell Damon and Trey everything. That was what they wanted. All her secrets laid bare. She knew it. Even if it might pile more guilt on Damon. He'd rather know everything than learn she'd lied to protect him.

After all they'd done for her, giving him this last gift was the least she owed them.

* * * * *

Tonight was the last night, and Blair couldn't pretend to be okay with this any longer. Couldn't lie to herself or comfort herself with the knowledge that she still had time to come to terms with Damon and Trey saying goodbye.

Oh God, she felt sick.

Just like she did every night, she shaved and plucked and primped for them. Made herself look as beautiful as she could. Sadly, no matter how hard she tried, there was nothing she could do about the red eyes or hideous blotches marring her complexion. Crying made her ugly.

Finally, she gave up, headed to her car and drove to the warehouse in silence. Her heart weighed a ton, dragging her down, stealing all her energy. Slowly, she walked up to the door. As always, the reception area was dark and quiet. Picking up speed, she rushed to the back, opened the door.

Total silence. Complete darkness.

Her heart stopped. The air flew from her lungs in a hard huff.

Oh God, had she misunderstood? Was last night the final night? They'd never actually talked about tonight. She hadn't thought to double-check.

"Trey? Damon?"

In the next blink, there was a scarlet circle of light on the floor, illuminating two beautiful—absolutely terrifying—black panthers. One of them opened its mouth, giving a snarl, white teeth flashing.

Blair stood transfixed, both scared and intrigued. She remembered the first night, the black panther. She'd run and missed the illusion. Tonight, she'd watch.

The snarling one pawed at the air. The other started licking its shoulder. They reminded her of Damon and Trey. Damon, the aggressor, the predator. Trey the quiet and content one. She smiled.

And then in a flash of white light they were gone, and Damon stood where the aggressive cat had been. Trey in the place of the quiet one. She rushed to them, threw herself into their outstretched arms and didn't even try to pretend she was happy.

How could she go on with life without these two? In such a short time they'd become everything to her all over again. The reason she woke up every morning. The last thing she thought about as she fell asleep.

They sandwiched her between them, whispered sweet words to her. Trey cupped her chin in his hand and lifted. "What's wrong? Why are you crying?"

"Isn't it obvious?" she asked, sniffling. "Tonight's the last night. Did you expect me to be jumping for joy?"

"Not really. But maybe I didn't expect this either." He glanced at Damon then took her hand and led her toward the front of the warehouse, out to the reception area.

Why was he ushering her out?

"Where are we going?" She dragged her feet.

"We just want to talk," Damon said, his voice smooth and reassuring.

They pulled up a chair for her.

"Okay." She sat and concentrated on breathing and swallowing because neither function was coming naturally at the moment.

Trey and Damon both pulled up chairs and sat in front of her.

"Blair, what have these past two weeks meant to you?" Trey asked.

"Gosh, I don't know how to put that in words." Blair struggled to think of what to say and then gave up. "These past two weeks have been magical."

Damon shook his head. "No, we need to know more, Blair. Be specific. We're not sure what to think."

"Think about what?" Her gaze hopped back and forth between the guys. They were being vague, cryptic, and she had no clue what they were getting at. What did these nights mean to her? "When I saw you that first night onstage, so many things went through my mind, so many emotions, memories of how things had been with us."

Trey nodded, encouraging her to continue with his eyes, a hint of a smile.

"And then I found out you had not only seen me but you'd sought me out, and I was over-the-moon thrilled. These two weeks have been more than I'd ever imagined. More exciting. More sweet. More sensual. More intense. I learned about bondage and about myself. I learned I've been hiding from something for a long time, and finally last night I accepted the fact that the secret I've been hiding has been poisoning me."

Damon tipped his head slightly, his lips thinning almost imperceptibly. "What's that mean, Blair? What secret?"

She couldn't look at Damon. Instead, she stared down, at her hands, clasped in her lap. "I haven't been totally honest with you. But I want to be. After we moved, things got worse with my mother and stepfather. Much worse.

My mom got stoned on pills every single day, to the point where she had no clue where I was, what was going on, whether we had food in our house. My stepfather, the bastard, took advantage of her being so out of it."

She couldn't believe she was about to tell Damon and Trey this, to actually reveal something she was so ashamed of, she'd punished herself for it for over fifteen years.

"I felt like I was invisible, like I didn't exist anymore. Nobody cared whether I was alive or not. There was no hope I'd ever find you two. My mother...she was lost. I dropped out of school shortly after we moved. I had no friends. I was totally isolated."

"What happened?" Damon leaned forward and took her hands in his. "Did the bastard rape you?"

"No, it's much worse than that." She studied his hands. Neatly trimmed fingernails, skin slightly roughened. Strong hands. Masculine.

"Worse how?" Trey asked.

"He had a party one night, and his friends noticed me. They talked to me, made me think I was special. But it was all a game, a bunch of lies. I found that out, but not until after it was...too late. He might have forced me to...do things to him, but they didn't have to. I did it. Willingly."

Damon squeezed her hands. "You were young, Blair. Lonely. Desperate for attention. You wanted to believe they felt something for you because you had no one else. They manipulated you."

"I was their whore," she confessed coolly. "But only that one time. I left that night and never went back. I tried to get back to you but couldn't. Eventually, I ended up in a home for runaways and it was okay. I met Sandy there. Made friends. Got my life together. But I wouldn't have sex again after that. Because I didn't want any other man playing me, taking advantage of my weaknesses to get what they wanted. Sex was about power. Not love. It was empty. Dirty."

"You had sex with us. You played our games."

"It's different with you two. You don't take. You give. Don't manipulate and lie. You see? You taught me that sex could be about giving, about loving, rather than just about taking. And so when you ask what these past two weeks mean to me, I have to say they meant freedom and truth. Through submission, I gained liberty from both the guilt of believing those assholes' lies and from the chains that had bound me, not allowing me to accept my own sexuality. And through your games and illusions, you helped me face the truth, about myself and the past I'd been punishing myself for."

"Thank you for sharing that with us," Damon said.

There was this awful, agonizing silence that Blair wasn't sure she could endure. It lasted at least a half an eternity too long. Finally, Trey asked, "Do you know why all our gifts had rubies in or on them?"

Why were they talking about rubies now? After what she'd just told them. "No, other than maybe you remembered that rubies were my birthstone."

"No, there's more to it than that." Damon pulled on her hands, tugging her to him. She shuffled around and settled on his lap, leaned back into his warmth. She felt so safe. So cherished. Loved.

"Do you know anything at all about rubies?" Damon asked.

"Not really."

"Let me explain." He laced the fingers of one hand through hers. "The ruby is a very rare and precious gem, a symbol of the relationship we shared when we were young."

Still confused why they seemed to be skirting around what she'd just told them, she nodded. "That's very sweet. And romantic."

"The stones are refined with heat, their brilliance and color amplified," Trey added.

She glanced at him. What were they trying to tell her? "Heat?"

"With heat—trial, pain, conflict—our relationship has been refined too, just like a ruby, to become what it is now. Fiery passion, abiding trust and...lifelong devotion." He pulled a small red box from his pocket and lifted the lid, revealing a sparkling ruby ring.

Finally, something she understood. Lifelong devotion. Ring. Marriage. Oh God! The breath caught in her throat.

"After what you've just confessed, I have no doubt that we've made the right decision. We said we had to leave in two weeks," Damon explained. "But we hoped we wouldn't have to leave without you."

"We had to make sure it was what you really wanted," Trey added. "Not every woman would be happy in a relationship as complicated as ours."

Happy? What she felt went beyond joy. But this was too wonderful to be true. She wanted to believe and yet she was afraid to. She needed to hear one of them say the words, to tell her exactly what that ring and what all this talk about rubies meant. "You want me to go with you?"

Damon nodded, his eyes sparkling with love and hope. "We want you to be our wife, to share our lives. We don't want to live another day without you."

Wife. He'd said it.

The world was spinning. Or she was spinning. Or maybe it was both. She squeezed her eyes closed and clung to Damon, half expecting to wake up and realize she was still sleeping, that the whole night had been a dream and she was still hours away from seeing Damon and Trey for the last time.

One of them stroked the back of her head. "Baby, are you okay?"

"I think so."

"Do you need some time to think about this?"

What was there to think about? Sandy would be sad but she would understand. Sandy was a true friend, wanted Blair to be happy. "I-I don't. No." She forced her eyes open and stared into Damon's dark gaze, seeing for the first time a spark of fear. He was afraid of what? Of losing her? She flattened her hand against the side of his face. "Where are we heading?"

"California."

"That sounds good. I can pack light. But how much time do I have to wrap things up? There's my friend Sandy, the rental house and my job. I need to give notice."

"Take as long as you need," Trey said.

"To hell with that," Damon snapped, the fear evaporating from his eyes. "We'll pay a moving company to get her stuff and move it to our place, and the job..."

"The job's nothing," she said, laughing through the sobs gathering in her throat. "I don't know what I was thinking. I can quit tomorrow. After all, if I'm not important enough to promote, then I can be replaced in a day or two. Right?"

"Exactly," Damon said, kissing her cheeks, her nose, her chin. "Not important enough to them, but you are to us. You can't ever be replaced."

Blair leaned back. "Was this your plan all along? To see if I might fall in love with you and agree to go on the road with you?"

"Not exactly." Damon and Trey exchanged smiles. "After spending years searching for you, months working out our schedule, and weeks devising a way to get you to our show...we were thinking much, much bigger. Our plan was to make you fall in love with us and convince you to marry us," Damon corrected. "That was our hope. Our dream."

"I can't marry both of you. It's against the law."

"You'll be legally married to Damon but married to both of us in all other ways." Trey plucked the ring from the box and slipped it on her finger. Smiling, he said, "It fits perfectly."

"Yes, it does. But I want to know one more thing. About the woman in red. You'd asked me if I knew who she was, and I said 'me'. Damon, you said that was sort of true. What did you mean by that?"

"I meant she was you, but the red dress represented your acceptance of our protective love, a love that will never let you down again."

"Okay, I understand now. But you need to forgive yourself too, Damon. You did all you could at your age. And you never gave up. It's because of you that we have a lot of wonderful years to look forward to."

For the first time in her life, Blair did look forward to the next five, ten, more years. Because she wasn't living in the shadows of a secret. She had Trey and Damon, their love and their magic. Freedom.

"By the way, you call yourselves Masters of Illusion, but the magic you perform is real. I think I'll call you Masters of Magic from now on."

"You can call us anything you like." Damon kissed her, showing her yet again how very real and very powerful his magic could be. And then Trey did the same, and she knew she would never again doubt the fact that magic was real. Or look at another ruby without thinking of her two wonderful men and the many gifts they'd given her. The most precious one being their hearts.

The End

Enslaved by Sin

TAWNY TAYLOR

A monster.

A man.

I didn't know for certain what he was. I only knew one thing--the legendary Master of Sin called to me. Not just intellectually, as a grad student seeking facts about a man who had lived hundreds of years ago. But also psychically, spiritually, emotionally. As a woman chasing mysteries, secrets.

As a woman searching for myself.

My quest had sent me into many dark corners and discreet places before I'd found my way to this castle in Eastern Europe. I'd haunted singles' bars, swingers' parties, dating services, and bondage dungeons. But I hadn't found what I was seeking anywhere. Something was always wrong. Missing.

But here, I felt different, like I could breathe. Like some part of me that had been suppressed was alive and free. His presence--his energy--was with me from the moment I'd stepped inside the old stone building. He was here. No doubt about it.

For instance, now, here, in what had once been the library, his presence was so strong I could imagine his hot breath fanning over my cheek. And as I stroked the worn cover of a book, a low, throaty rumble vibrated in my ear.

I shivered. My skin puckered with goose bumps.

There was a picture of him in the book I was holding, a photograph of an old painting. I traced the line of his jaw.

He was mine. My monster. My fantasy lover. My Master of Sin.

This was the way I always imagined him, the way he looked in my dreams. His black hair was a riot of sexy, playful waves, curling at his collar. His eyes were fierce, dark and piercing, his nose a straight blade, cheekbones hard slashes angling up to his temples, and his jaw strong and masculine. It was a fascinating face, mesmerizing. Not beautiful, but extraordinary.

Sitting on the floor, before a towering wall of bookcases, I read further, my index finger skimming across the yellowed page.

Count Konrad von Vidmar was known widely as the Master of Sin. He held gatherings of dubious nature within the walls of Castle Greh, welcoming attendees to taste the decadent pleasures that were otherwise denied them, forbidden in polite society. Some claimed he was not human, but the son of a demon or possibly a vampire. Mere mortal or not, he disappeared without a trace at the age of forty...

A man's passionate moan echoed in the distance, and my nipples hardened, the fine hairs at my nape standing on end. What were those sounds? The voices of ghosts or merely the wind whistling between loose boards? As much as my romantic nature wanted to believe the former, I knew it had to be the latter.

I went back to reading. ...welcoming attendees to taste the decadent pleasures... What exactly did that mean? What kind of carnal diversions did visitors enjoy within these walls?

Instantly, as if a switch had been thrown, images from my dreams flashed through my mind, like scenes extracted from erotic movies. Nude women writhed on beds piled with vibrant hued silk, their arms and legs bound, their stomachs, backs, and buttocks marred with red welts, their faces flushed with erotic heat. Lips parted as they sighed in ecstasy.

I sighed too.

Yanking myself from my daydream, I shook my head to clear it and focused on the fragile book cradled in my hands. Something large crossed between my back and the gas lamp sitting on the desk behind me, throwing a cold shadow over me for a moment. Startled, and shivering with an uneasy chill, I twisted to look over my shoulder.

Nothing.

"Is someone here?" I called out, my voice ruining the heavy silence. "Gospod Skoda?" I called in Slovenian, hoping the elderly caretaker had returned and was simply checking on me before going home for the night.

No response.

The place gave me the creeps. Yet, at the same time, its dubious past and countless secrets beckoned me.

I glanced at my watch, realizing a lot more time had passed than I'd realized. It was very late. Too late to get a cab to take me back to the hotel.

Mr. Skoda had offered to let me stay on the premises tonight, but I hadn't planned on accepting his offer. Castle Greh was solid. Safe. But more or less abandoned. The owner was in the process of turning it into a resort of some kind, but the work had just begun--thus the lack of electricity in most of the rooms. I wasn't big on staying in places without modern conveniences--shower. Phone. Central heat.

Feeling invisible eyes watching me, I snatched up the gas lamp and hurried through the dusty building. The main entry was closed, and I found no cars parked outside. I checked my cell. Dead battery.

Shit.

No phone. No ride.

Looked like I would have no choice, now. I'd have to stay.

Luckily, I'd come prepared, just in case. I had the basics in my bag--blanket, food, water. And fortunately the kitchen, ballroom, and one or two bedrooms and bathrooms had been restored. I wouldn't be sleeping on the floor or using an outhouse.

I headed back to one of the renovated bedrooms, changed into a pair of sweats and a t-shirt, ate a quick snack and climbed into bed, waiting until I was so exhausted I couldn't keep my eyes closed before I cut off the electric lamp on the nightstand. Instantly, the shadows closed in on me.

Warm fingers stroked my arm, and I sucked in a gasp. A rat?

"The Master is waiting," a female whispered.

That was no rat.

"We cannot make him wait," this time, a male.

"The Master will have what he wants, or he will punish us all," another female's whisper.

Was I dreaming?

I jerked upright, blinking. Chills as sharp as claws raked down my arms and legs. Shivering, I frantically searched the inky blackness, blinking at the thick darkness as if it would clear away. "Who's there?" I scooted back until my spine ground against the headboard, dragging my blanket with me.

"He has been waiting," the female whispered.

"Waiting for what?" I asked.

"His slave," the male said.

I jerked my head to the left and held my breath. "Slave?" *The lamp. Light. Now.* I snapped the blankets off my legs and scrambled across the bed sightlessly grappling for the light.

"The Master waits." This time the female's voice was behind me. Too close.

I whipped my head around, and lunged forward, both arms stretched in front of me. "Who?" I touched nothing but air. But as I flailed, ice-cold fingers dragged down my arm, nails gently grazing my skin. Something clamped around one of my wrists.

Eyes wide, heartbeat racing, I fingered it with my free

hand. "What's this?"

No answer.

A second cuff snapped around my other wrist, and seconds later, I was yanked across the room, stumbling and blind. Terrified.

"Oh God, please stop," I begged.

"He has waited long enough," the female whispered, in front of me.

"Don't hurt me, please." Powerless to do anything else, I followed the lead of whoever was dragging me down the dark corridor. But I didn't do so silently. I plead. I begged. I made promises I could never keep. My words fell on deaf ears.

We turned left, right. Left again. Down stairs and around several more corners. I tried to keep track, but after even more turns, I was completely lost.

Finally, we stopped.

A door slammed shut behind me. I tried to whirl around, toward the sound, but the tension on the cuffs securing my wrists wouldn't let me. My right arm lifted then my left. Metal chains clanked. Something hard and cold snagged the neckline of my t-shirt and before I knew what was happening, a bone chilling riiiiip filled the darkness. I swallowed a scream, teeth chattering, heart in my throat. A cool breeze whisked over my stomach and chest as the torn material flapped open.

I couldn't see a thing. It was so dark I was completely blind. My arms were secured over my head, and I was vulnerable, nearly powerless, and at the mercy of my captor.

I've never felt this kind of stark terror. Tears burned my eyes, seeped from the corners and trailed down my cheeks.

Who were these people and what did they want from me?

With the absence of sight, my other senses grew more acute. A soft shuffling signaled the movement of someone next to me. The clatter of metal told me more chains were being handled.

Another wave of icy panic charged through me. If they secured my ankles, I'd be even more defenseless.

I felt the knife again, and I froze, too frightened to move. This time, it slid between my body and the waist of my pajama pants.

"He comes," a female whispered.

Once more, the sound of rending fabric echoed through the darkness. And again, flesh that had been covered was bared to the cool, crisp air. My skin tingled as goose bumps covered every inch of my body, from my scalp to my feet.

I took a chance, kicking forward, hoping to catch someone. Surely, if it was too dark for me to see them, it was too dark for them to see me too. But I made contact with nobody, nothing. I didn't stop. I thrashed and kicked and fought. Minutes later, breathless, legs burning and lungs starving for air, I finally accepted the truth. It was useless. I ceased struggling.

Seconds passed.

Silence.

Thick darkness.

Had I scared them off?

The answer came when that blade returned a third time, this time piercing the skin between my breasts. "The Master will not tolerate this behavior, slave," a male voice warned.

Furious, I spit.

"Prepare her," the male voice demanded.

"Prepare me for what?" I squeaked, my throat squeezing tight.

"For pleasure," the woman whispered in my ear. "Close your eyes. Relax."

The blade twisted, the tip biting into my skin, and even though I would normally writhe with delight, I bit back a yelp. Then it jerked, and my bra snapped open, the shoulder straps sliding over my shoulders.

More hot tears streamed down my face. "Please stop," I begged.

"This is what you've been seeking," the woman soothed. "You'll have everything you've always wanted. You'll see."

How could she know what I wanted?

"What did you say? Who are you?" I asked.

"There's nothing to fear. The Master knows why you've come to him."

"Really? How?" Defying all logic, my terror faded. I had told no one the real reason why I'd come here. And even if I had, I couldn't think of anyone who'd pull a prank this devious. I had no idea who the mysterious woman was. I certainly had no reason to trust her. And yet...I believed her. I wasn't in danger. "Is this a game?"

The woman giggled. "The Master's games are wicked. They make me wet." After a beat, she added, her tone more subdued, "It's time now, for our slave to submit."

"Who, me? Submit?"

Unseen fingers explored my body. My stomach. My back. My face and legs.

A jolt of longing blazed through me followed by an icy sting of fear. Oh God, this was exactly what I'd been searching for all this time--a taste of danger blended with carnal heat, the kind of submission no one had ever demanded from me before. Unlike what I'd found at the bondage dungeon, this was real. Not role playing. Not an act. Honest-to-God fear chilled my insides while intense lust licked through my blood.

"He knows your every desire," the male voice said smoothly, his low, rich voice making even more erotic promises. Cool metal skimmed over my hard nipples, and a moan drifted up my throat. Bone-quaking shudders slammed through my body. Before I could suck in a deep breath, the knife left my breasts to slip beneath the waist of my panties, the tip grazing the skin of my shaved mound.

A whimper of pure desperation slipped from between my clenched lips, and every bit of air inflating my lungs seeped out. Seconds ticked by, measured by the hammering of my heart.

The knife jerked, and my panties fell from my body.

Nude.

The wicked ecstasy.

"Master," the female voice said with awe.

A soft light ignited in a far corner of the room, a single yellow flame. Dancing on a soft breeze. The weak light punched a ragged hole in the darkness, outlining the shapes of nearby objects. And then the candelabra overhead flared to life, dozens of flames flickering, dancing.

Finally, I recognized where I was. I was in the ballroom. But unlike earlier today, half of it was now furnished with modern day bondage furniture. Kneelers, a couple of benches and tables, a pair of swings and a wooden cross were positioned in the end of the room where I was tied. The other side was still completely empty.

"What's happening?" I asked.

No answer.

I glanced around but saw no one.

Seconds later, one cloaked figure, face obscured, entered the room through the double doors on the far wall. More people entered behind him, dressed in historical garb. The women were bedecked in glorious silk gowns dripping with lace, their faces covered by ornate masks. The men wore dark suits and masks.

None of them looked at me. It was as if I was invisible.

Music filled the room, and the costumed people started prancing around to the music, an elegant display of beautiful women and mysterious men.

Then the one in the cloak came closer. Closer still. He was male. Large. He stopped directly in front of me, lifted his head. A black mask hid his face. His gaze caught mine.

I gasped.

He had cool blue eyes, the shade of deep ocean waters. Eyes like his.

This was...like a dream.

Without saying a single word, he stepped to my side.

"What's happening?" I asked.

"Silence," he warned.

I bit my lip. I knew most people in my position would scream. Or plead. Demand. Negotiate. Do whatever it took to gain their freedom. But I didn't want to escape. I was spellbound. Enthralled.

I watched the dancers.

The music's pace sped up, the tone changing, and with the shift in the music, the dance transformed from smooth, controlled elegance to something more carnal and wild. The men shed their jackets and shirts and the women gathered their skirts in their gloved hands, dragging them up to expose bare legs and pussies. The couples kissed, they stroked, they grabbed and pulled, licked and bit, took and gave. And by the end of the song, the dance floor was covered with puddles of silk, satin and velvet, and I was caught up in the dancers' fever, my body trembling and tight.

I had no idea who these people were or why I was chained to the wall. I didn't feel threatened anymore, only aroused and curious. A part of me longed to be a part of their magical, erotic dance. But more than anything, I desperately wanted to know who the man was at my side.

In my imagination, he was the Master of Sin. My fantasy lover.

Once again, the music changed, the tempo slowing, a heavy bass beat pounding through the room like a heartbeat. It was very sensual music, and what was already an erotic scene took a dark turn. Some of the dancers fell to their knees right there, on the dance floor, placing mouths to pussies or cocks.

Others came closer to me, positioning partners on the benches, tables, and swings. Arms and legs were shackled. And while I stood there, riding the currents of desire churning through my body, Masters and slaves, Doms and submissives played out their fantasies--and mine.

Breathless and trembling, my insides coiling like a spring, and a fever sizzling in my blood, I watched. No one touched me as I watched their games of domination and control, and yet I felt every bite of the whip, every thump of the flogger, and every slap of the paddle. My skin tingled and burned. My pussy ached.

I wanted my Master of Sin.

Touch me. Please. Stop the torture.

Next to me, a raven-haired Domme was fucking a beautiful blonde girl in the ass with a dildo. The girl's pretty, heart-shaped face was flushed, her gaze fevered. Our eyes met, and I sucked in a gasp when a single tear seeped from the corner of her eye. It was an intense moment, one I knew I'd never forget. Her lips curled into a smile, and she shuddered.

Somehow, impossibly, I felt her orgasm. At the precise moment she came, a current of electricity charged through my body. My knees buckled and I jerked them straight again, whimpering at the cruel man who had yet to touch me. It was no longer a matter of wanting, but of needing now.

The voices of the dancers, their sighs and shouts and cries, grew louder, louder still, until they almost drowned out the music. And with each scream, the heat blistering within my body amped up another dozen degrees.

Yes, oh yes, this was what I'd searched for, what I hadn't been able to find anywhere. I could hardly breathe, and my legs were about to give out. Slick heat pulsed from my core and coated my inner thighs.

The music stopped. Silence swallowed the room, broken only by the heavy pounding of my heart in my ears.

They all turned to me, eyes glittering with carnal

hunger. The man next to me lifted a hand and pulled his mask off.

That face! A gasp swept up my throat and past my lips. It was him. The Master of Sin.

How?

His eyes met mine again, and a jolt of energy charged through my body. "Who are you?" I asked, unable to believe what I saw, unwilling to accept the impossible. Men didn't live for hundreds of years.

"I will be your Master. But only if you pass the tests." He moved closer, and my body instantly reacted to his nearness. Goose bumps dimpled my skin. My nipples hardened. My pussy throbbed. Every cell in my body ached for his touch and rejoiced in the feral glimmer I saw in his eyes. "Now, it's time."

Tests?

He lifted a gloved hand. Black leather stroked my cheek, trailed a gentle touch down the side of my neck. Eyes bore into mine. "I have waited so long for this day, my sweet."

I realized in that instant that I'd been waiting for this day too, without expecting it would ever come. "Master. I'm yours."

"Not yet." Smiling, he trailed a fingertip over my lower lip. "You are so pretty." That finger traveled lower, along my neck, between my breasts, to a nipple. "Perfect." He pinched, and a blade of pleasure-pain stabbed through my body.

So wicked. So right.

I felt my lips curling into a smile of sincere joy. My Master knew me. Somehow. Understood my dark desires.

He leaned closer still, until his nose nearly touched mine. "Ask me, pretty slave." His sweet breath warmed my face.

"More please, Master."

"Like this?" Seemingly satisfied with my words, he pinched again, injecting another dose of wanton pleasure into my system. His gaze raked down my body then back up. He walked around me, ducked under the chains holding my wrists to stand between my back and the wall, leaving me to look straight ahead at the crowd of onlookers I had almost forgotten. His gloved hands glided over my skin, skimming along my sides, chafing my nipples then traveling down my torso to my mound.

I arched my back, desperate to feel his hot length pressed against my body. Seeming to answer my silent plea, he roughly jerked me against him.

Ahhh, a moment of delicious bliss. But it ended too soon. He slipped around me again.

Thanks to his cruel torment, my body was pulled taut, the heat almost unbearable. Now that he'd given me a taste of forbidden pleasure, I couldn't live without another.

"More, Master--"

"Silence." He unfastened my wrists and turned me around so I faced the wall. Then he pushed me roughly to my knees and bound my arms over my head.

How I loved the feeling of utter vulnerability, of knowing that my Master and all those people were feasting on the sight of my body and sharing in this magical moment. I shuddered when that eerie music began again, and the pulse of the drumbeat vibrated through my body. I didn't know what my Master was about to do. A dozen different emotions were playing through me.

"My slave must hunger for pain, must crave it like nothing else. Do you?"

"Yessss." I heard the snap of the whip. A second later, its kiss speared my back, just below my right shoulder blade. Glorious pain.

That whip kissed me again and again, the stinging bites of pleasure-pain sending me hurtling to a magical place where I was lost in sensations, where tastes and touches and sounds were as much a part of me as my fingers and toes. Colors swirled and danced behind my shut eyelids. Tastes danced on my tongue and the thrum of the music hummed through my body.

When the lashes stopped, I cried again as I was ripped out of that magnificent place. I opened my eyes to find my Master standing before me, looking pleased and proud.

"Thank you, Master," I whispered.

His lips curled up into the smile that had haunted my dreams for years, and yet a dark shadow passed across his eyes.

My breath caught in my throat.

I whimpered. "Take me, please."

His fingers uncurled from around the whip, one at a time. It dropped to the floor, striking the polished surface with a dull thud. "If only I could." He stooped down, leaning close enough to kiss me. His gaze swept over my face, and for the briefest of moments, I regretted being restrained. I burned with the need to capture his face between my hands and kiss away the dark shadows I glimpsed in his eyes. "But I cannot take my pleasure. Not with you. Not with anyone."

"Why?"

He shook his head, standing. "No questions." Once more looking as fierce and wicked as his picture, he unhooked the chain securing my arms over my head and instead attached it to a metal loop bolted to the floor. He pressed on my back, between my shoulder blades, forcing me onto my hands and knees. "It's time for your second test." He mapped my curves with his gloved hands, his hot breath and strokes singeing my flesh. Back. Buttocks, legs, breasts, stomach.

I trembled and quaked, sighed and moaned. Whimpered and groaned. Still, my pussy remained empty, my clit untouched. It was agony. Wickedly sweet torture.

He walked around me, stopping directly in front of me just as a pair of rough hands grabbed my hips from behind. The head of someone's cock prodded at my slick passage. Startled, I lurched forward, throwing a glance over my shoulder. But before I got a look at who was about to

335

drive his cock into me, my Master caught my head in his hands. "No. Look at me. Only at me. If I take you, you will be mine. Always mine and only mine."

I nodded, settling my eyes on his.

"That's my cock," he said, his face pulling taut. "My hands stroking your ass."

"Yes, Master." As a wave of blistering heat overtook me, I let my heavy eyelids fall shut, burning the image of my Master's face into my brain. His jaw, so strong. His mouth, lips that tasted like sweet wine and hot man. His eyes, which drilled through my defenses and saw into my soul.

I trembled as his rod drove deep inside, a hard possession. Fingertips dug into the soft flesh of my hips as my lover pulled, using my body with his to amplify his pleasure.

My Master's quickened breathing echoed in my head, its pace matching my own. Again and again he drove into me, harder, faster, until our bodies pounded together, the sharp slap of skin striking skin filling the room. My back became slick with sweat. My arms trembled as my legs, spine, and stomach tightened. Closer he pushed me, to the edge of bliss...only to stop and leave me panting and aching for completion.

"No." I whimpered and crumbled to the floor.

"This is what you've been searching for, is it not?" He scooped my chin in his hand and pulled, forcing me over onto my back so that my arms were bent at the elbows, lifted up, wrists still secured to the floor. "You want to be mine."

I nodded.

"You've been dreaming of becoming my possession. Of knowing my touch and tasting my kiss." He knelt over my chest, his legs straddling me. I could smell him now, the uniquely sensual scent stoking the desire in my body to even greater heights. His warmth swept over my chest and stomach like a soft tropical breeze. "Why do you want me as your Master, slave?" He dropped onto all fours and levered his shoulders lower, until his lips hovered mere inches from mine. "When you could have any Master, why did you come to me?"

"Because..." Why had I become so obsessed over a man who by all rights shouldn't be standing here right now? I recalled my dreams, all of them so memorable, so lifelike. And then images of the many nights I'd spent exploring the dark side of my passion played through my head. Moments spent with other Masters, men who were just as powerful, attractive and dominant as this one.

What made him so special?

I couldn't find the words. I didn't want to. I wanted to taste his kiss, to tremble beneath him as he drove his cock into my body again.

"You realize this is all we can have?" He tipped his head, tilting it to the side so that his breath tickled my ear, my neck. Once more, goose bumps prickled over my arm, my chest.

"Whatever you can give me will be enough."

His gaze captured mine again. "It will never be enough." He pushed himself upright again, swung one leg over so he was kneeling beside me. "But tonight you will have everything you've been waiting for."

Again, fingernails dragged over my flesh, the burning, scratching sensation driving ripples of ecstasy up my arms and down my legs. I knew those weren't really his fingers clawing at my body, but it didn't matter. I let myself believe they were, closing my eyes once again and losing myself in the sensations he stirred within me.

Hands hooked under my knees, forcing them up and out until they were spread wide. Straps were fastened around my thighs and a spreader attached so I couldn't draw them closed. Again, that feeling of utter vulnerability swept over me, stealing my breath and making me dizzy.

The head of a cock pressed between my thrumming tissues, inching slowly into my slick passage. I tightened around it, heightening his pleasure, giving as well as taking. He pulled out and crammed that hard cock into me again. Once, twice, three times. Something slick teased my anus, pressing, invading. My tissues burned and stretched. My body trembled and quaked. I opened my tight hole, accepting a probing finger then a second while his prick pounded into my burning pussy.

Hot. Burning. Ready to melt.

I had to fight for every inhalation. My body was so tight cramps seared my limbs. Arms. Legs. Hands. Feet.

"Take me," my Master demanded as his cock possessed me, his fingers drilling into my anus.

"Yes, Master." The tingles of a powerful climax erupted deep in my belly, exploding outward, and I arched my back, rocking my hips up to meet his every thrust. "Coming..."

"No. You may not have release until your Master tells you," he warned, his voice sharp.

"Oh, God." I fought to subdue the inferno engulfing me. Flames licked my arms and legs but I couldn't douse them. I rocked my head from side to side, desperate to throw myself into the blaze, let it burn through me, consume me. "Please...I cannot..."

For the second time, he withdrew, and I was left breathless, on the verge of tears and twitching all over. It took every ounce of my strength to force my eyelids up. "Why?"

He didn't answer.

I glanced around me. The dancers had all gathered and were standing in a circle around us. Most of them had redressed in their beautiful historical gowns and suits. They all were looking down at me with longing. Men and women, both.

One, the young woman who had been fucked by the Domme earlier smiled and stepped forward. "I warned you, the Master's games are wicked." I recognized her voice. It was the woman who'd brought me here. "They make me wet." Stripping away her clothes as she walked, she circled me. "Your obedience and self control pleases the Master. After one more test, he will reward you."

A flare of joy bloomed deep inside me. I arched my back, stretching my neck to find my Master. He stood at my head, far enough back that it was difficult for me to see him. He smiled, and that expression brought joy to my heart.

The young woman squatted over my face, her pussy hovering over my mouth, her musty-sweet scent filling my nose. She parted her smoothly-shaved labia with her fingers.

"Eat my pussy," my Master commanded.

I'd never so much as kissed a woman, never touched a woman sexually, never fantasized about one. But between her glorious scent and the sharp edge in my Master's voice, I was trembling with anticipation.

Still completely powerless, tied up and unable to move, I took my first taste, letting my tongue explore her slit.

Delicious.

Above me, the young woman sighed, and a wave of desire crashed through me. Hungry now, I flicked my tongue over her hard pearl, her juices coating my lips. I stabbed my tongue into her canal then went back to her clit, licking and nipping and suckling. Her soft sighs turned to low moans and groans. Her tiny trembles turned to sharper quakes and her skin warmed, heat simmering all around me and enveloping me in a cloud of female desire.

I knew the moment she came. My mouth filled with her essence, my nose with the scent of her musk. I drank deeply, sucking and pulling, each taste a powerful aphrodisiac. By the time she crumbled at my side, I was burning with fever.

Oh God, I would never have guessed how absolutely intoxicating it would be to give another woman pleasure. The sight of those delicate tissues. The flavor of honey on my lips. The silky skin of thighs wrapped around my head.

How many other dark pleasures would my Master of Sin show me?

He knelt beside me again. "Our time is almost over."

Sickening dread hit me like a punch in the gut. "No. So soon?" I didn't know this man. I didn't know if he was a ghost, a man pretending to be someone else, or the actual Master of Sin somehow magically come to life. And I had no idea if I'd ever know the truth.

But one thing was certain--I belonged with him. To him.

"We'll have many nights together." He cupped my face, his thumb grazing my lower lip. Then he removed the cuffs from my thighs and wrists. He turned away from me, and a young man handed him a small box. Facing me once more, he flipped it open. "Tell me now, before it's too late. Why do you belong to me?"

Again, memories--both good and bad--played through my mind. The dates. The meetings. The visits to counselors, churches, bondage clubs. The lonely nights and days spent staring into the mirror, questioning myself. "I belong to you now because...somehow I always have, and I always will. You are my one true Master. The Master of my heart. My soul. And my sin."

His smile was more brilliant and spectacular than anything I'd ever seen. He lifted his hands, pulling them apart to reveal the collar he held between them. Without a word, he locked it around my neck. Then he cradled my chin in his hand, forcing me to tip my head to the side, and bit me.

Finally, after years of struggling, searching and doubting, I had my answer. He was no monster. He was no man.

He was both.

And neither.

And I belonged to him.

The End

Please turn the page for a special sneak preview of
DARKEST DESIRE, the second book in my Black Gryffon
series.

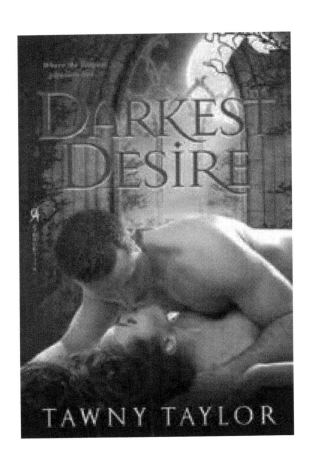

An Excerpt From: DARKEST DESIRE

Copyright © TAWNY TAYLOR, 2012

All Rights Reserved, Kensington Publishing Corp.

Beautiful.

Exquisite.

Thoroughly, utterly, intoxicatingly sexy.

And as deadly as a cottonmouth.

That was Malek Alexandre, summed up in twelve concise words.

A spectator at the private bondage club, standing in the shadows at the back of an open dungeon, Lei Mitchell moved aside to let a slave wearing a black thong and dog collar pass. Her gaze never left Malek. Not for a second.

This was an opportunity she couldn't deny herself.

For once she was free to just . . . enjoy. Without fearing she'd be caught by Malek, one of his brothers, or her sister, Rin.

Lei's hungry gaze wandered up and down his body at leisure now, taking in the full glory of his heavily muscled form. He was wearing a simple outfit—black, snug-fitting knitted shirt and tailored trousers, no leather for this man—but still Lei could make out the rippling bulges and clean lines defining each muscle as he lifted his arm and flicked his wrist. The leather tails of his flogger sailed through the air toward their target, and Lei's breath caught in her throat.

Malek was not just any dom. He was *the dom.* The one who made her blood pound hard and hot through her veins. If only submitting to him wouldn't mean her destruction.

Warm and tingly all over, even though her insides ached a little at knowing she would never—could never—know the pleasure of submitting to her master, Lei stood in that dark corner, just out of his sight, and watched as Malek trained a submissive. The sub, a male, clearly enjoyed every stroke of the lash, as evidenced by the look of utter rapture on his face . . . and the large bulge pressing against the only garment he was wearing, the snug black

G-string. Like Malek, the sub was lean, firmly muscled, bronzed, attractive. He was also delightfully responsive. She wouldn't mind taking him back to her private suite sometime.

Since being rescued from a nightmarish life as a sex slave, Lei had come to this private bondage club to exorcise her demons. One of her previous owners had trained her to dominate him. As it turned out, his kink had become her salvation. Now she was the one in control. She was the one holding the whip, tying the knots, instead of receiving the blows or being bound and forced to fuck.

Free now from that horrendous life, she couldn't seem to stop herself from seeking out opportunities to dominate men. She wasn't sure why. She received no sexual fulfillment from it. She received no emotional fulfillment either. She was still the empty shell of a girl she'd been the day her sister had bought her out of hell.

But now she was an empty shell with a compulsion.

And a fascination with a certain dom.

As Malek released his submissive from his restraints, in preparation for a change in position, Lei tried to walk away.

But she couldn't. Her feet simply wouldn't move.

Her body was tight. Hot. Her heart was pounding. It was as if she were lowering to her knees before Malek, waiting breathlessly for his next command.

Malek ran his fingertip down the sub's spine.

A tiny shudder of pleasure quaked through Lei's body. Her pussy clamped tight against an aching emptiness. She licked her dry lips and curled her fingers into fists.

What would he do next?

The submissive settled on his knees on the floor, butt lifted high, rather than resting on his heels. He tipped his head down. Waiting. Patiently.

Lei had been forced into that position too many times to count. She'd never voluntarily kneeled before a man. She couldn't now. But that didn't stop her from imagining herself in the submissive's place at this moment. If she closed her eyes, she could feel Malek's gaze sweeping up and down her body. Her skin burning. Her nerves prickling.

It was anxiety and anticipation both. A touch of fear coupled with the expectation of good things, wonderful things. Of unimaginable pleasure. And glorious pain.

If only . . . if only . . .

"Is that a smile I see?" Malek's voice was unexpectedly light, playful. His tone both put her at ease and made her that much tighter.

"No," the submissive answered.

"No, *Master*," Lei whispered to herself as she opened her eyes. Such a show of defiance surely deserved a punishment. She didn't want to miss this.

What would Malek do?

A chill skittered up her spine.

Malek's brow lifted, but he said nothing.

Ah, he was going to let his submissive wait, wonder.

She unclenched her hands and dragged her sweaty palms down the sides of her legs. A huge lump congealed in her throat. She swallowed hard and squeezed her thighs together. The burning in her pussy was becoming intolerable.

Malek used the tip of his whip to lift his submissive's chin. "I asked you a question, and I expect a proper answer. So I'll ask again, is that a smile I see?"

The submissive's lips twitched. "Maybe."

This was a submissive who liked to push his luck. Lei had scened with more than enough to know the type. They craved the punishment and weren't by nature submissive. They merely took on the role so they would be in a position to get what they wanted. Depending upon the submissive, and the dom, that could be a few lashes, being humiliated in public, or perhaps being paddled to within an inch of their limits.

But what he probably wasn't expecting was what Malek

did, even if they had discussed the possibility ahead of time.

Malek walked away.

The submissive's eyes widened. His mouth formed an "O" of shock; then his lips clamped shut.

Damn. Lei couldn't help but smile at the submissive's reaction. She'd put money on him thinking twice about playing Malek like that again. Or maybe he'd make a different choice in a dom, if that was his game. Either way, it was something to watch.

While Lei continued to study Malek's behavior as he prowled around the open dungeon, he turned. His gaze swept the crowd of onlookers gathered around the perimeter of the room. It snapped to her.

Their eyes met.

The air seeped from her lungs.

Her face burned.

He smiled, and she swore her heart skipped a beat. Maybe two.

Dangerous. That's what that man was.

Her body had never reacted this way to any man before, especially since . . . being rescued. She met his smile with a tiny nod, then forced herself to walk through the throng toward the back hall, toward her private suite, her haven. Her sanctuary.

ALSO BY TAWNY TAYLOR

Wild Knights
Wicked Knights
Wanton Knights
Wild, Wicked & Wanton
Dark Master
Decadent Master
Dangerous Master
Darkest Fire
Darkest Desire
Claim Me
Wicked Beast
Prince of Fire
Girl Enslaved
Dirty Little Lies
Triple Stud
Enslaved by Sin
Double Take
Behind the Mask
Plays Well with Others
Lust's Temptation
Wrath's Embrace
Burning Hunger
Torrid Hunger
Everlasting Hunger
Slave of Duty
Flesh to Flesh
Compromising Positions
Breathless
Pleasing Him
At His Mercy
Ties That Bind
Heart Throb
Burn For You
Her Lesson in Sin
Touch of Fire
His Dark Kiss
Playing for Keeps
Your Wicked Game
Make Me Burn
Make Me Shiver
What He Wants (My Alpha Billionaire, 1)
What He Demands (My Alpha Billionaire, 2)
What He Craves (My Alpha Billionaire, 3)
Yes, Master

ABOUT TAWNY TAYLOR

Tawny Taylor has been writing erotica for women for ten years. Her first erotic romance, Tempting Fate, was published in 2004 and was an RT Reviewer's Choice nominee and highly reviewed book. To date, Tawny has over 50 published books by 5 publishers, including Pocket, Kensington, Ellora's Cave, Samhain and Changeling Press. They include several subgenres of erotica and erotic romance including paranormal, menage, contemporary, and romantic/erotic suspense. Many of her books contain D/s, bondage, and domination and submission. Among her best selling books are Dark Master (Vampire, BDSM), Decadent Master (Vampire, BDSM), and Wrath's Embrace (Menage, BDSM).

Tawny is grateful to her readers for allowing her dream of writing and publishing to come true. Her hope is to continue to write hot, sassy, sexy erotica for women for many years to come.

Tawny loves hearing from readers! Drop her a note anytime:tawny@tawnytaylor.com.
website: http://www.tawnytaylor.com
Twitter: @tawnytauthor
Blog: http://tawnytaylor.net

Printed in Great Britain
by Amazon